SOUND OF LIGHT

MARTI WIBBELS

Copyright © 2017 Marti Wibbels

All rights reserved.

ISBN: 0-9746124-5-6
ISBN: 978-0-9746124-5-4

DEDICATION

To my beloved husband, Alan, who continually encouraged me to write *Sound of Light*—and happily traveled with me to five countries to help make it real.

CHAPTER ONE

Molly Montgomery didn't look like a runaway. Her blonde hair pulled under a white ball cap, she looked more like someone trying to escape recognition. Her clothes were expensive but understated. Her eyes were another story. Unblinking, brilliant blue, unreadable. If anyone could have seen beneath her façade of simple elegance, it would have been obvious she was running—from everyone and everything she knew.

Barely noticing the last passenger seated, the motley assortment of people riding the shuttle to LAX was already engaged in multiple conversations. A man near the back bragged about getting away from LA for a few months to invest in property in Costa Rica. "Last summer, I went to Bermuda. I'm working my way through the alphabet. Costa Rica this summer, Denmark next summer." His voice was brash, grating.

Two women on the bench seat in front of Molly spoke loudly, nervously—strangers united by a mutual fear of flying. "That one was a heart-stopper," the brunette told the blonde beside her, her irritating voice increasing in volume with each word. "I'm telling you, the stewardess was crawling on her hands and knees in the aisle. Later we figured out that when she looked up with a fake smile and said, 'Don't worry, everything's fine,' she was *really* listening to hear if the landing gear came down. Then the captain said we'd have a normal landing—and the runway at Logan was full of emergency vehicles—you know? The ones that spray foam on fire." Her laugh ricocheted throughout the van.

A flight attendant seated next to Molly spoke, directing her comments to the brunette. "That had to have happened a long time ago. Today, the landing gear on our planes are loud enough that we never have to wonder. If there were any doubt, though, the pilot would have someone on the ground check. He would never have one of us crawl along the floor." She smiled. "Planes today are much more sophisticated than they were years ago."

"Did we ask you?" The brunette cut her off, then resumed talking about other flights, her strident voice representing the only authority she recognized.

Molly was glad they were talking at full volume. It helped her forget.

To the brunette's nervous laugh, the blonde replied, "I hear you. I can't sleep before I fly. Maybe I should try religion. Someone told me it helps to pray while you're up in the air."

Molly pretended to look for something in her purse, forcing herself not to think of what Peter would say to the woman. At the stop for American Airlines, she hurried off the shuttle and rushed to check in. *Maybe I can crash and join my dad.*

Was it only this morning when she still had a fiancé who was more wonderful than anyone she could imagine? She could be with Peter right now, talking, laughing. She could be preparing for the summer semester of grad school. Instead, she was lost in the crowd at LAX.

En route to her gate, she stepped into a store, glancing at overpriced lures for the traveler. Greeting cards. Books. Stuffed animals. Children's gifts. Her breathing tensed; she didn't notice. She had to get away from this store, fast. Part of a future she had to escape. A quick pull and her hastily-packed bag rolled behind her, its sophisticated exterior like her own, enveloping chaos.

She'd packed in fifteen minutes—and, though she tried, at the moment she couldn't remember what she brought with her on this strange exodus from life. "Think of it as money," she told herself, checking her bulging purse to be sure she had her debit card, her mother's one tangible acknowledgment she even existed. *You shouldn't feel like that.* She reminded herself she would have missed this handy escape maneuver if she hadn't answered her mother's call after the wedding.

Babs Montgomery had called her daughter only once during the past semester. Not that Molly cared. Their relationship had been distant for years. So, it was surprising that she picked this day—of all days—to call.

By the tone of her voice, crisp, all-business, Molly knew the call wasn't motivated by a renaissance of motherly concern.

"Molly, I know you're planning on summer school. Really, I do. But, I have a little problem here. There have been robberies in my neighborhood lately, and I need someone to housesit while Harry and I travel Europe this summer. I thought I had someone, but she reneged today. And we leave tomorrow."

"Mom, you live in a gated community. Don't you have guards to make sure your house is safe?"

"If that were working, I wouldn't be asking you for help, would I?" Molly could hear her mother's long, manicured nails tapping impatiently on her steering wheel.

"Is your steering wheel chipped where you keep tapping on it, Mom?" Molly didn't really want to know. She wanted to change the subject.

"I have a gorgeous new car, my dear. A Maserati Quattroporte." Babs exhaled, proud she knew how to keep herself from losing her temper. This had to work. She smiled, something she learned long ago to help convince potential clients to buy houses. Pause. Smile. Ask the closing question. "So are you coming?"

"I was in a wedding this morning, Mom. Remember my roommate Kate, my fiancé's sister? I'm exhausted. Anyway, Peter just dropped me off at my apartment—if I weren't so tired, I'd be helping with all the post-wedding activities."

"But you're not. Is something wrong between you and Peter?"

"Come on, Mom. Why the sudden surge of concern?"

"Touché, Molly. I deserve that. I'm sorry I haven't called," she said, smiling again, not meaning it. Brightly, she continued, "Maybe it would be good for you to have the house to yourself this summer. I'd cover all your expenses. You can leave everything in your apartment there."

"I don't know."

Her volume rising, her tone agitated, Babs continued, "Look, I pay your rent, this is the least you can do for me." Molly heard the familiar sound of her mom's garage door opening.

"You're home?"

"Just getting out of the car." Suddenly Babs knew exactly how to sweeten the deal. "If you need anything while you're here, you'll have an expense account...and I'll let you drive the Maserati all summer."

Molly had a weakness for fine cars. She took the bait. Surprisingly, the idea of a summer away from school, from complicated relationships, from everything—sounded like just what she needed.

"OK, I'll come."

Molly heard the click of computer keys and pictured her mom in the study.

"I'm checking flights," Babs explained. "I can book you out of LAX at 10:45 tonight—you'd have to be there by 9:00 to check-in. Can you make it?"

Molly looked at her clock—4:30 PM. "Email me the itinerary."

"I appreciate this, and you're going to be happy with your decision." Her voice was the voice of a realtor happily closing a deal. "I've booked you nonstop, on first class. I'm also reserving your seat on the airport shuttle in Santa Barbara. All you'll need to do is cab there, and it will take you to LAX. Your flight is four hours, but you lose two, you know. I've emailed you the flight and shuttle confirmations. You should arrive in Chicago tomorrow morning at about 4:50, and our flight doesn't leave for Europe until seven tomorrow evening, so Harry and I can pick you up at O'Hare and still have time for coffee before we leave..."

Molly didn't wait for her to finish. "OK. See you then." As soon as Molly hung up the phone, she felt a surge of energy. Her mind in overdrive, she reviewed her courses' catalogue descriptions—and, before she could think about what she was doing, a few rapid-fire keystrokes deleted the entire summer semester of a music grad program that had been her sole focus only the week before.

Central American Ethnomusicology: explore the rich cultural diversity and expressions of music of the Caribbean and Latin America.

Music Perception and Cognition: determine how one's thinking impacts music appreciation.

Systematic Musicology Specialization: understand the fundamental nature and properties of all forms of music.

Her next step was to let Peter know she was leaving for the summer. *He knows something's wrong. I'm going to set him free.* Molly wasn't impulsive. She made decisions only after careful deliberation. Except today. *I need time to think,* Molly rationalized, tugging her suitcase out of the storage closet.

Her actions were as random as her thoughts were chaotic. She wrote a brief note to Peter to enclose with the ring, sealing both in a padded envelope. "There's somebody better for you, somebody without all of my emotional baggage." Molly changed to jeans and rode her bike the two blocks to the cottage that her brother temporarily shared with Peter; she sighed, relieved Peter couldn't possibly be there. He was where she should have been, enjoying visiting with his family after Kate and Carlos left for their honeymoon flight to Hawaii.

Molly planned to leave her envelope under the welcome mat—but Jeremy was sitting on the front porch, a beer in his hand, a nearly empty six pack beside him.

"I thought you weren't drinking," she said, glaring.

"My very own private wedding celebration," he said, raising his bottle with a hollow laugh. "Here's hoping the happy couple does better than I did."

Surprising herself, Molly felt a surge of compassion, aware his memories were at least as difficult as her own. She reached to pat his shoulder. He squirmed away.

"Be sure Peter gets this," she said, her tone formal, all feelings of good will vanished.

"No problem," he set the padded envelope on the step.

"Could you please take it into the house so you don't lose it?"

"You don't have to be uptight, Sis. Think I can't deliver a simple—what is this, anyway?"

She didn't respond.

"Let me show you how it's done," he bowed with a flourish, holding his sister's envelope upright, like a scepter.

She waited until he reached the door. "I have to go," she turned away, afraid she might change her mind.

Jeremy set the packet in Peter's room, on the edge of his desktop. His head hurt. He felt too tired to make it back to the porch, so he collapsed on the living room sofa.

* * *

Molly pedaled back to her apartment, worrying that her note hadn't said enough. She wrote an email to Peter promising, "We can talk soon, because I want to explain more about why I left my engagement ring at your apartment. Please don't worry about me—or about us. It won't be long before you see that this is the right thing—really the only thing—for us to do. I hope to be back in time for classes in the fall. But I want you to be free in case you meet someone this summer." She exhaled, relieved she took time to help Peter understand. But in her rush, she forgot to press "send."

CHAPTER TWO

Waiting for her plane, Molly couldn't stop thinking about Peter.

He astonished Molly the day he'd asked her to be his wife. That day began with a drive to Newport Beach to fly kites—a simple tradition initiated the summer before. That day, as soon as he opened her car door, Peter surprised her with a new kite. His hand on her shoulder, gently steering her toward their cherished beach, he fumbled for words. "I ordered this for you because it's a biplane—double wings help it sail higher...better. Molly, you know? Like you and me," he said, kneeling in the sand. "Will you fly, um, I mean, sail the winds of life with me?" Her face must have looked as confused as she felt, because he added, "Will you marry me?"

The universe went into slow motion as she stared into his eyes, transfixed by the sheer joy of his unconditional love. Amazed, she watched Peter untie a tiny blue satin bag from the kite. Gently he tugged its silk cord open. His fingers tenderly pressed against hers.

"Because you are worth more than rubies...more than diamonds...more than any words I can find," Peter told her, his tears speaking for him.

Time and rational thought evaporated. Molly felt his touch, saw his heart, and let herself believe. "Yes," she responded. Kite flying was forgotten as they dreamed of life together.

The engagement ring—perfectly sized, its gold band displaying an exquisite emerald-cut diamond sparkling between two rubies—stayed on her finger for over a year. Until Kate's wedding day.

* * *

Molly's thoughts continued their downward spiral.

Rubbing her finger, suddenly horrified at what she'd done, Molly stood to find an airline agent to ask why the flight was delayed.

The pert young woman barely glanced up. "A severe thunderstorm has delayed all flights in and out of Chicago. We'll change the board as soon as we know anything," she said, her eyes fixed on the computer screen.

Molly wanted to cab back to Peter. She sat down in the gate waiting area, then stood, pacing. *I can't sit here. I have to keep moving. I can't let myself think. What's done is done.*

After pacing the terminal for ten minutes, she sat down at an empty table in the first airport café in her path. *Why did I leave without talking with Peter?* Forcing her mind to stay focused on the menu, she looked up to see an annoyed waitress, waiting, tapping her foot. "Caesar salad—no dressing," she said, ordering her usual choice. She tried to study fingerprints and dirty streaks on the plate-glass window beside her, but racing thoughts crushed her mind to numb oblivion.

Not wanting food, wanting Peter, she pressed her head

against the window, staring at planes as they rolled into their ordered positions. *Why is my life falling apart? I thought I was happy.* She looked at her watch. *How can both my friendship with Kate and my engagement end like this? But Kate is so blind; she doesn't even know there's a problem. What is Peter going to think of me when he reads my note? Why has everyone forgotten me? It has been impossible to talk with Kate for months—and I've tried to connect.*

Her mind like a computer, scanning multiple programs in rapid succession, Molly remembered the day she called Kate between classes to invite her out for dinner. That day, she'd swallowed her pride, attempting to bridge the growing gap between them. Though roommates, they hardly saw each other any more. Her heart surged with hope when Kate answered in her brightest voice, and fell—just as quickly— when her best friend's voice changed. "Oh, hi, Mol," Kate sounded disappointed. "How's it going?" Before Molly could respond, Kate dismissed her. "Hey, thanks for checking in. I didn't look at caller ID because I thought it was Carlos. Sorry about that. I'm on my way to talk with Aunt Zoë. I'll tell her 'hi' for you. Gotta go—like I said, I'm waiting for a call from Carlos."

That explained Kate's cheery voice. Carlos. Kate couldn't talk about anything but Carlos. Carlos this. Carlos that. Ad nauseum.

Kate's aunt Zoë let her down, too. Molly felt close to Zoë throughout her undergraduate years—but not anymore. For the past two months, all Zoë could talk about was "Kate and Carlos," or their wedding plans. Zoë even offered to make Kate's wedding cake. If she and Kate weren't poring over bride's magazines for ideas, they were baking and sampling different recipes. "Italian Cream Cake will be a perfect complement to a wedding brunch," Kate and Zoë agreed.

Remembering Kate's happy laughter, Molly flinched, as she did when she recalled Zoë's offer. "I'd love to host a brunch for you—and bake your wedding cake, too," Zoë said, turning to Molly, sensing her disappointment—and widely missing its source.

Molly didn't want to think about cakes, showers or weddings. She wanted Kate. And she wanted life to be like it was before everyone fell in love.

Molly didn't want to dwell on the months before Kate's wedding. In her opinion, Kate and Carlos' entire relationship was a big mistake. But no one seemed to care about her opinion. She only meant to help Kate avoid being hurt when she told her six months wasn't long enough to know someone before getting engaged.

"Molly, you don't know what you're saying," Kate had replied, her eyes flashing. "Besides, I think you're jealous of my relationship with Carlos."

"Jealous? What on earth are you talking about?"

"I see you sulking whenever I mention him. I would think you would be the one person in the world who would understand my joy," Kate said, her voice increasing in volume. She'd waved her arms for emphasis. "I'm happy that you and my brother are engaged. Why won't you be happy with me?"

* * *

Her best friend since kindergarten, Kate had been Molly's sounding board throughout their undergraduate years. Everything changed when Kate fell in love with Carlos. Molly remembered every detail of the day she first heard his name.

Kate rushed into their apartment in graduate student

housing, "Molly, I've met the man I'm going to marry!"

"How can you be so sure?" Molly said, eyebrows arching.

"I'm sure. I've never felt so sure about anything in my life," Kate beamed, twirling, dancing, arms splayed. "I love him. He loves me."

"How long have you known him?" Molly frowned.

"Why does that matter?" Kate's eyes flashed.

"Believe me, it matters. People aren't always what they seem."

"I've known him long enough," Kate sighed, smiling contentedly.

Molly glared at her. "What is 'long enough,' in your opinion?"

Kate hugged a pillow. "Long enough to know he's the most wonderful man in the world!"

"There is no such creature."

"How can you say that? You're engaged to my brother! Don't you think he's the most wonderful man in the world for you?"

Molly didn't want to argue, especially about that. She wouldn't admit to anyone, especially Kate, her doubts about getting married. Engaged to Peter since their first year of grad school, she still didn't have an answer when he asked why they couldn't set a wedding date.

"I give up, Kate," Molly said, with a forced laugh. "I'll make coffee. Tell me about your most wonderful man in the world." The intense aroma of freshly ground coffee beans helped distract Molly from her galloping emotions. Pouring water with a shaky hand, Molly kept her back to Kate until she was sure she wouldn't cry.

Missing Molly's heart, Kate sat at their tiny kitchen table, launching into a nauseating hour-long description. "He's from Guatemala, but his family moved to California when he was only five. Not only did they all become citizens; they all have gone to college. The entire Cordoba family is incredible—especially Carlos. He has the kindest dark brown eyes—and the biggest smile of anyone I've ever known. And he's the graduate assistant in one of my classes, and…"

"You're falling for a Latino. I can't believe it. And he hasn't even finished school! Don't you know better than to trust him? Latinos are known womanizers. He's probably just trying to get you into bed!"

Kate's face flushed to match her red hair. "Molly Montgomery, do not insult me—or my friend with ridiculous racist stereotypes! Carlos is not a womanizer! He's never even tried to touch me."

"You still haven't answered my question. How long have you known him?"

"Five months."

"You're kidding."

"No, it has to be at least six months. We're in a lot of the same grad classes."

"Kate, this is the most ridiculous thing I've ever heard you say. You've known this guy five or six months, and you think you're in love? You think you can actually know someone in less than a year?" Molly rolled her eyes, and then shrugged.

Kate looked away. "Normally, I wouldn't think so," she said, pausing, trying not to lose her temper. "But, that was before I got to know Carlos."

"Kate, you're making a huge mistake. The cultural differences between you two will be like a noose around your neck. Have you met his family? Do you know his friends? Do you have the same interests?" Pouring steaming coffee into mugs, Molly continued bombarding Kate. "Why haven't you introduced him to anyone before?" She set Kate's mug down so hard that coffee splashed on the table. She didn't notice. "If you marry and have kids, it would be a disaster...they would have a perpetual identity crisis. I'm right, Kate."

"No, you're not," said Kate, wiping up spilled coffee and forcing herself to speak softly. "I don't want to argue with you. I want you to meet him. You'll see what I mean."

Molly still couldn't agree with her. Because of Carlos, she was losing her best friend. Ever since her engagement to Carlos, Kate was never there for her. The second her cell phone rang, Kate jumped to answer it. And when she wasn't with Carlos, she was thinking about Carlos, talking about him, wishing she were with Carlos. Molly no longer registered on Kate's radar.

Kate's aunt and uncle weren't any better. Zoë and Dan planned a fiesta when Kate and Carlos announced their engagement. They invited dozens of friends, family and acquaintances, and what seemed like most of the university faculty. Molly tried to comfort herself. *I guess that makes sense, since Dan teaches there and Kate and Carlos are grad students.*

During the party, Molly slipped into the kitchen to get away from the crowd, quietly loading the dishwasher, remembering quiet evenings spent with Kate there during their undergrad years. She jumped, startled when Zoë came up behind her, gently touching her shoulder. "I'd love to do something like this for you and Peter, too. Peter's open to the idea."

Molly felt like she was hyperventilating.

Thankfully, Zoë turned to stack sandwiches on a tray and didn't seem to notice Molly's lack of enthusiasm.

"Oh, thanks, I'll think about it," Molly stalled.

After the party, Peter urged her to accept his aunt's offer. "I've been telling you Zoë hasn't forgotten you, Mol."

Molly hated it when Peter remembered her complaints and attacked her with them. "I know. But she has her hands full helping Kate and Carlos plan their wedding. With your parents two hours away, Zoë is doing a lot of the work." She couldn't tell Peter she wasn't ready to celebrate either his sister's or her own engagement. She could not admit to herself how terrified she was about getting married. *Why did I ever say I'd marry him?*

CHAPTER THREE

"Your salad, Miss."

Molly had to stop thinking and remember where she was. The airport. Running away.

She looked up. "Thank you." She couldn't eat. Her stomach felt like concrete.

Molly noticed the familiar, aromatic smell of coffee drifting from a nearby table but knew her stomach couldn't handle it. She picked at her salad as her mind continued unraveling. Memories from the past six months continued to tumble into the present.

Even the smell of coffee brought painful memories, like the night Carlos came to their apartment unexpectedly. Molly answered the door. "I'll get Kate," she said, without welcoming him.

"I brought you something," he said shyly, handing her a colorful, red-striped cloth bag.

"Me?" Molly took it, surprised, especially since she was usually rude to Carlos.

"Kate told me how much you like coffee, so I asked my aunt to send some from Guatemala for you."

Kate walked into the kitchen. "Carlos!" She beamed at him, then noticed Molly holding his gift. "You brought her the coffee you told me about! Yum. Molly, it's from Antigua, where some of his aunts and uncles live. You'll get to meet them at our wedding!" Without taking a breath, Kate continued, "Antigua is in a valley between three volcanoes; the volcanic soil provides perfect conditions for producing one of the world's best coffees. Let's make some now!"

Involuntarily, Molly grimaced, reminded of how thoroughly Kate was being indoctrinated in Guatemalan life. Even so, she couldn't help noticing the coffee's spicy aroma. The three of them sat together at the kitchen table, discussing the coffee's chocolate undertones, savoring first its smell, then its piquant flavor. Molly thanked Carlos with as much enthusiasm as she could, sensing his kindness, realizing he didn't want a barrier between him and the best friend of the love of his life. But none of his efforts was enough to break the wall Molly continued to erect in her mind.

* * *

The one truly bright spot in Kate's marathon wedding plans was seeing Kate's parents and two youngest sisters more often than usual. Brandon and Kelly Johnson and their daughters Mary and Grace made the two-hour drive from Burbank at least once a month. Molly still missed Kate's sister Sarah, who was four years younger than Kate and Molly.

Was it only a month ago that Molly felt like she was more excited about seeing Kate's parents than Kate was? She woke at ten on Saturday, feeling happy, blanketed in the comforting aroma of chocolate. Her happiness evaporated when she heard Kate's cheery voice at her bedroom door.

"Hey, Mol, I have a group project for my marketing class, so I'll be at the library when my family arrives. There's fruit and cold cuts in the fridge for lunch; croissants for the sandwiches are on the counter. Brownies just came out of the oven—and mom is bringing homemade cinnamon rolls! Can you help them set everything out? You guys can go ahead and eat whenever you're hungry. And I should be back by two—

or three at the latest."

"On Saturday?" Molly took off her headphones, annoyed. "I have homework, too, but I can be hostess for you." Seeing Kate's eyes register the hurt she'd delivered, Molly almost felt sorry for being snarky. She softened her tone. "Sorry, I forgot they were coming. Sure, I'll be glad to help." Kate didn't seem to care either way.

Molly looked out the window. Carlos was out front, waiting to walk Kate to the library. *Sure you have a group project.*

One hour later the Johnson van parked in front of their apartment. Watching Mary and Grace bound out of the vehicle took Molly back to a time when people and relationships were uncomplicated by wedding plans.

"Kate gone again?" Grace asked, peering into her sister's room.

"As usual," Molly said, an edge in her voice. No one seemed to notice her attitude.

"We dropped Brandon off at Peter's. My husband and son are going to spend the day doing guy stuff," Kate's mom announced brightly. "So it's just us girls today!"

Molly shifted mental gears, choosing to give herself permission to enjoy being with the Johnson family. "Hey, how is Sarah doing at school?" A sophomore in college in Illinois, Sarah wouldn't be back in California until her sister Kate's wedding.

Mrs. Johnson looked at Molly, her eyes lit with a gentle smile. "Thanks for asking about Sarah, Molly. She is having a tough semester. Roommate problems. I'm thankful you and Kate don't struggle with that."

"Thank you, Mrs. Johnson," Molly smiled, hoping her expression looked more sincere than she felt. Turning to Grace and Mary, she asked, "What projects are we doing today?" Work was much easier to discuss than relationships.

Grace set a large box on the kitchen table. "This is what we're doing today—making favors for all the wedding reception guests." She lifted a large bag of sand from the heavy box. "Each guest will get a little glass globe with a tea light perched above sand and shells, see?" Grace held up a sample favor, festooned with a ribbon and a miniature card proclaiming 'thank you for sharing our joy.'"

"Let's have lunch before we start, OK?" Molly laughed, trying to get into the spirit of the day. She helped Grace move the heavy box to the floor.

Mrs. Johnson helped Molly set out croissants, cold cuts, and everything else they needed for a quick lunch before beginning the day's projects. Still oblivious to Molly's apprehension, she said, "I hope you know how much Brandon and I are looking forward to the day you and Peter are married, Molly."

Her stomach tensing, Molly turned away, unconsciously covering her face with her hand. "Thank you, Mrs. Johnson."

Assuming Molly's body language indicated overwhelming joy, Kelly touched her hand affectionately, adding, "You know you can call me Kelly, honey. And someday soon, I hope you'll be calling me 'Mom.'"

Molly's phone rang. Perfect timing. "I'll be right back. Go ahead and start lunch without me. I need to take this call," she said, grateful for any excuse to walk into her bedroom. For ten minutes, she listened to a salesman tout the benefits of solar panels, something she would never want or need. Her stomach hurt too much to eat, anyway.

She returned to a kitchen bustling with activity and happy conversation, all focused on Kate, Carlos and weddings.

That was the last time Molly looked forward to the Johnsons' visits.

CHAPTER FOUR

"Miss, are you finished with your salad?"

Molly didn't hear her, her thoughts continuing their spiral into the abyss of recent months.

"There are people waiting to be seated, Miss. Are you finished? Or do you want to order something else?"

Molly felt frozen to the chair. She stared at the waitress, trying to orient herself. She noticed her suitcase. *I can't face the throng of people out in the terminal.*

"Miss? Do you want to order something?" The waitress pushed a tawny curl back from her face, tapping a staccato rhythm on her order pad with a pen.

"No. I mean, yes. I want a hamburger, grilled, um, with cheese. No, make it a double cheeseburger. With French fries. And a Coke." *I never eat this much food. I'm not even hungry.* But she had to fill the void in her soul with something.

Waiting bought time for her, time to be alone, time for her mind to continue tumbling backwards. For the past two months, Molly hadn't been able to stay busy enough to numb her emotions. She couldn't define what she felt. Frustrated? Angry? Sad? She only knew she hated the strident emotions brashly struggling to surface from wherever it was she'd suppressed them.

* * *

The last time she'd tried to run away from confusion was at Christmas, breaking her habit of avoiding her mother, stepmother, and everything that went with them. She'd convinced Peter then that she had to visit her family because her mother was complaining she never came home. She'd convinced herself that a change in scenery would help.

Almost as soon as she arrived at O'Hare, Molly became acutely aware it was a mistake to substitute one set of complicated relationships for another. During the interminable drive from the airport to her home in suburban Chicago, it was clear that Babs Montgomery was still focused on three things: herself, making money, and what she cryptically called her "Man-of-the-Month Club." Serial monogamy was her forte. "Molly, you are going to have lots of time to catch up on sleep. I have elite clients here looking for a seven-figure home, and they have to be my priority. I know you get that," she laughed. "It keeps the caviar and filet mignon on the table." Though Babs was a novice vegetarian, she still used her favorite old joke.

Three days after arriving at her mom's house, Molly was ready for a change—even one that included her former stepmother. "Please come spend a few days of your vacation with me, Mol," Mercedes called, begging, within seconds after Molly texted that she was in town. "You have no idea how cavernous and lonely this apartment can be. Besides, I want to catch up on everything—and tell you my news!"

Molly took the bait and cabbed to her stepmother's apartment, leaving her mother a terse note.

Thanks for sharing the holiday. Since your schedule is full, I'm sure you won't mind me visiting Mercedes for a few days. Happy New Year.

After her father's suicide, Molly avoided phone calls, visits, and even emails from her stepmother. Mercedes' callous response after Jameson's death had made Molly suspicious of anything she said. Their time together at Christmas changed

Molly's opinion. From the second she saw Mercedes at the apartment door, Molly thought her stepmother looked different—nicer, softer somehow, than before.

Maybe it was her hair. Instead of bleached blonde, it was a honeyed brown, with curls dancing softly around her face. The wrinkles around her eyes made Mercedes seem—*what is it?*—Molly wondered. *She seems caring—like Zoë used to be.* Although Molly didn't want her mind to go there, it went, anyway. Not only was she losing her roommate to marriage, she'd already lost her roommate's aunt and uncle. *What an idiot I was to think they were like adopted parents,* Molly thought with disgust. Everything about the way they were around Kate and Carlos felt like betrayal. During her Christmas visit, it was Mercedes who helped her see the light.

"Molly, you seem a little down," Mercedes said, touching her arm. "Care to share?"

In the past, that question from Mercedes would have sent Molly to her room to call Kate. But there was no Kate to call. She was with her family—and Carlos—in Colorado, skiing. They'd begged her to come, but she couldn't endure a week listening to Kate and Carlos gush about how "in love" they were. She didn't want to face Peter's interminable questions, either. "What's wrong, Molly? Don't you want to talk about it?" Slowly, steadily, subtly, a cataclysmic change was taking shape in Molly's mind. Instead of remembering she was in love with Peter, she felt like he was a stranger. She forgot uncomplicated things, like how much fun she always had skiing with him and his family. Everything felt different. And she trusted her new feelings, implicitly.

She looked at Mercedes as her new best friend. For the first time in months, she let herself relax. "My roommate got engaged to a Latino, and I think it's a big mistake." At her stepmother's sympathetic nod, Molly exhaled, giving vent to thoughts that had been stealthily growing for months. "Kate barely knows Carlos—he's from Central America—they're both still in grad school—and everyone just ignores the obvious problems. What I keep wondering is how can her uncle—he's actually a psychologist—I don't know how can even he be so blind to how wrong this is. Instead her entire family says, 'Oh isn't this marvelous? Aren't they perfect for each other?' I'm fed up with all of them."

Mercedes was in her element. "Oh, Molly, I get it. I hear you. What a pity she can't see the obvious." She paused, framing years of covert cynicism for a perfect delivery. "Now, let me be sure I have this straight. I know Kate has been your friend since you were in grade school. Is her uncle the one who helped you—when you were going through—ah...," she let her eyes linger benevolently on her stepdaughter, "...so many difficult memories?"

Molly was astonished that her stepmother remembered anything about her childhood, especially since Mercedes married her dad when Molly was in high school. "Yes," she said, feeling understood. "Dr. Johnson is the head of the psych department at Pacific Harbor. I guess I should say 'Dan,' since he always wanted me to use his first name." She shrugged. "I actually became good friends with Dan and his wife Zoë."

"I'm surprised," Mercedes said, growing silent, her eyes compassionate, her mouth a worried frown.

"What?"

"Oh, I shouldn't tell you what a huge concern that is." Mercedes ground coffee beans and poured purified water into her espresso machine, forcing herself to wait.

"I don't understand," Molly responded, twisting a napkin into a knot.

"It's not that you shouldn't use your therapist's first name. What worries me, actually, is that he encouraged a friendship with you when you were his client..." She paused, frowning thoughtfully. "That's how a therapist can lose the ability to be objective. It's inappropriate," she added solemnly.

"Oh," Molly said, forgetting she wasn't really Dan's *friend*. She remembered meeting Dr. Johnson and his wife Zoë when she and her best friend Kate began attending college at Pacific Harbor in California. Kate invited her to go with her for dinner at her aunt and uncle's nearby home.

Mirroring Mercedes' indignation, Molly forgot Dan initially suggested she meet for counseling with one of his colleagues. She forgot she was the one who insisted she wouldn't feel safe with someone else when troubling memories from childhood tumbled out of the storage vault of her mind. Her mind blurring reality, she forgot that Dan carefully maintained what felt like a safe boundary between them, especially when she became close to his wife Zoë. Sighing, she looked at Mercedes. "I feel betrayed."

Mercedes exhaled and looked down. "I totally agree with you, Love."

Molly flinched. She hated it when Mercedes called her "Love." But she saw the tenderness in her stepmother's eyes and decided to suspend judgment.

"I've been seeing a therapist, too," Mercedes continued, looking down, taking time to create a look of humility on her face while waiting for Molly's response.

"Really?"

"Ever since your dad's suicide, I've been so depressed I could barely function. I haven't been able to work; I haven't been able to sleep." Mercedes loved weaving lies. "That's when I realized I needed to get into therapy. I've even started going to church."

"You're kidding!"

Mercedes pretended not to notice Molly's shock. "That's my big news! It's the first time I've gone to church since junior high. At my stage of life, it's hard to meet people, and a woman at my fitness center invited me to come to their singles' group." Placing a monogrammed napkin under Molly's espresso cup, her words were clipped and distant. "The man who facilitates the group, Dr. Jacobs, is actually my psychotherapist." Forcing her face to express renewed indignation, she added softly, "The first time Dr. Jacobs saw me at church, he didn't even speak to me."

"He didn't speak to you?"

Mercedes wiped a single tear from her eye. From her years

as a model, she knew how to create the exact look needed for the moment. "No, he did not. I'd been seeing him for therapy for a couple of months before I decided to try the class. Since he is so incredibly kind and caring at my sessions in his office, I felt hurt when he ignored me at the singles' group." Mercedes stood, opening a pale pink box on the counter. "I almost forgot these yummy cookies. Want one?" she set two buttery Christmas cookies on a china plate, recalling how annoyed her stepdaughter became in high school when she'd insisted Molly avoid sweets. "It's Christmas! Let's celebrate!"

Molly took a tiny bite. She smiled. "Delicious!"

"So glad you like it. I picked them up at the new bakery across the street when you said you'd come. Anyway, at my next session, he noticed something was bothering me, so I said it was because he acted like he didn't even know me at the group. He said it wasn't personal," she sighed, clenching her fist. "He said therapists can't have social relationships with clients because they lose objectivity." She twisted her napkin into a knot, smiling. "But therapy is helping. I'm really learning how to process the grief and move on."

Mercedes skillfully avoided sharing why she *really* decided to begin therapy. Lonely and bored, she joined a fitness center near her suburban Chicago apartment for one purpose only: to meet a man. Constantly on the lookout, she was sure she found him when she spotted Benjamin Jacobs stepping out of his silver BMW convertible in the fitness center parking lot. Black hair peppered with flecks of gray, his face wore a perpetual look of concern. Mercedes focused on his body, rippling with virility. *He's the kind of man meat who could satisfy my appetite,* she decided. *And a Z4 Roadster belongs next to my SLK.*

The next week, he was at the gym again, lifting weights, a perfect viewing distance from where Mercedes worked on an elliptical machine. She pretended not to notice him, introducing herself to the woman next to her instead.

"Hi, I'm Mercedes," she smiled. "And you are...?"

"Stephanie," the woman paused, coughing. "The one who

is so out of shape I can barely talk and work out at the same time." The petite brunette laughed, adding, "Have you been coming here long?"

"This is actually my second month," Mercedes said, forcing a smile. "And I'm still terribly out of shape."

"You look fabulous to me," Stephanie said, glancing at Mercedes' tall, svelte frame. "You look like you could be a model," she gushed.

"Actually, that has been my vocation most of my life," Mercedes said, changing the subject, avoiding being asked what her current modeling jobs were, since there had been none—not even demeaning catalogue work— for over a year. "Do you know many people here?" Mercedes asked instead.

"Oh, I know a few—the man across the room—Dr. Benjamin Jacobs. Ben leads the singles' group at my church, and he's a fabulous therapist, or so I've heard," Stephanie added, a little too quickly.

"Really? What's his specialty?"

"I'm not sure. I think he's a psychologist. I've talked to people at church who go to him for help with a variety of issues. Depression, grief, anxiety, things like that."

Mercedes quit talking, pretending to concentrate on her workout. Her mind was moving much, much faster than the elliptical machine. She decided she had to get home immediately, find Dr. Jacobs' number on the Internet and sign up for the therapy for which she felt a sudden, urgent need.

Stephanie was oblivious. "Every woman in our class says he would be a fabulous catch—OK, every woman I know, anyway," she said, laughing. "It's so sad his wife died last year. Horrible cancer. She was a natural beauty. One of the nicest people I've ever known. They were in practice together."

By that afternoon, Mercedes discovered his web site, took his first available appointment, and called her stylist for an appointment to change her hair color. *I've wanted to have a softer look for a long time.*

* * *

At first, their sessions had been spectacular. Dr. Jacobs intently listened to every word she said. He helped Mercedes process what she described as unresolved grief. She found that term on a website devoted to helping people deal with grief. At her appointment, Mercedes skillfully mirrored what Dr. Jacobs said, pretending it was exactly what she needed to hear. She even cried when he gently asked about her husband's suicide. "I felt abandoned when Jameson died—his suicide note didn't even tell where he was. They finally found him in a rented storage unit. He actually drove in there and killed himself—carbon monoxide." She punched the pillow next to her on the sofa. "I, I still feel lonely all the time. I fall asleep crying," she said, twisting the fringe on the pillow, impatiently craving his sympathy.

Waiting, he said nothing.

She took the opportunity to wax eloquent. "This morning, I stood at my window watching the falling snow, weeping, wondering if my heart will always be in winter and never again experience spring." It was fiction, and she marveled at her creativity. She produced soft, elegant tears, letting them trickle slowly down her cheeks.

He didn't take the bait. "You feel lonely?"

Her pace picked up. "I have no family, no one to be with for Christmas," she said, fishing.

Analyzing that session later, Mercedes concluded she either said too much or did not cry enough. She was blind to what really happened.

"What about your husband's family?" he asked. "You said he had three children. Will they visit for Christmas?"

"We aren't close," she told him, brushing away a tear and reaching for his arm. "But you and I could be, Ben." Without pausing, she launched into her plan. "Why don't you spend Christmas with me—I have reservations at a wonderful little resort in Wisconsin—near Lake Geneva." She would make online reservations the minute she got home.

The tension in the room was palpable. Dr. Jacobs sat up straight, pulling from her grasp, speaking slowly, firmly. "Ms. Mauritz, I am your therapist, which means I cannot at the same time be your close friend. Objectivity is an important part of the therapeutic process. If you've been seeing me in hope of developing any kind of relationship other than a therapeutic one, then I must refer you to another therapist."

"Please, Benjamin—or shall I call you 'Dr. Jacobs'?" Mercedes said, her tone stiff, formal, her hands shaking. "I am afraid you misunderstand my intentions. I was only trying to be nice."

"Let me be perfectly clear," he told her, his brown eyes intense, noticing her pain. "I do care about you. I want to help you. If you're willing to continue the process as it is designed, I can help. If you've come in here expecting something else, you've come to the wrong place."

Mercedes felt humiliated by her faux pas. She wanted to stand, walk away and never come back. But her body wouldn't move. He was leaning forward, every line of his body emanating compassion. She knew she would come back, because she couldn't imagine life without anyone to care.

How and why her therapist corrected her was information Mercedes carefully withheld from her stepdaughter. Instead, she quietly infiltrated Molly's mind with ideas designed to steadily deteriorate all relationships in her life except the one Mercedes ravenously desired—with herself. An emotional vampire, Mercedes did not know how to share.

Molly thought it was her best Christmas vacation in years. Sipping wine with Mercedes at elegant restaurants, she felt far too sophisticated for the college crowd. It was hard to return to California.

CHAPTER FIVE

Kate and Molly were still roommates, but only in the sense that they each had a private bedroom suite and a shared kitchen in the same apartment. Kate's classes took her one direction; Molly went to another part of campus every day. That was nothing new. The change was that Kate and Molly no longer shared any part of their hearts with each other.

Kate tried. "Molly, why don't we have dinner together tonight? Neither of us has class on Wednesday night…"

Molly cut in, "Actually, I have to be on campus late for a group project." The lie came out of her mouth so easily that she tried another. "But I'd love to try another time."

"Oh, great," Kate enthused. "I miss our times together."

"Me, too," the third lie spilled out without any effort at all. Molly's mind reeled with a new emotion—bitterness. All she could think of were the many ways Kate and her family failed her.

Peter tried, too. "Hey, Mol, let's do something fun this weekend. We haven't had much time together since Christmas break."

"I know. This semester is a tough one for me. I'll definitely carve out some time."

The weekend came and went. Molly texted Peter to say

she had to help Kate with her wedding all weekend. And she did, smiling, laughing, pretending it was fun to shop for bridesmaid dresses. When Peter showed up, unannounced, at their apartment Sunday night, she pretended she was glad to see him, too. Pretending was getting easy. But pretending was exhausting.

Since Christmas, Molly morphed her usually-busy schedule into a staggering pace—balancing a full load of graduate classes, teaching flute to private students, volunteering as a campus tour guide for undergraduate students, practicing flute, composing music. Anything to keep her away from all members of the Johnson family, especially Peter and Kate.

Since grad school is typically a demanding, busy time, no one but Peter noticed her avoidance tactics.

Peter couldn't push through the invisible walls she steadily erected. "Let's go to the beach tonight, Mol—or we can do anything you want."

"Just a few more weeks, then I promise we'll have time to talk."

"I miss you, Molly. What's bothering you?"

"Nothing. I'm just so busy with classes…"

"I wish we were married now," he said, too often.

Molly couldn't allow herself to imagine why she wouldn't spend time with her fiancé. She didn't know why she wouldn't discuss setting a wedding date. She couldn't think at all. And by not thinking, her mind was tricked into believing one lie, two lies, then a series of lies.

* * *

Mercedes, lonely, loved having Molly as her long distance pet project. During their time together at Christmas, she was the cunning stimulus for Molly's deteriorating opinions of the Johnson family. She said only enough for Molly to think the ideas were her own.

They talked on the phone several times a week. Three

weeks before spring break, Molly called Mercedes. "I can't
wait for this break—especially since I got out of going home
with Kate and Peter. Their family is planning a big 'farewell'
for Kate since she is finishing her master's and getting
married—and they actually expected me to be there. I told
them I have to stay and work on a group project for a class."

Mercedes chuckled. Molly had already told her she had the
project finished. "Good job. So what will you do with all of
your free time?"

"Sleep. Sleep. And more sleep."

"I have a stellar idea. There is this great resort just outside
of LA; I used to stay there during modeling gigs. I would love
to treat you to a few days of spa treatments. What do you
think?"

"I don't have to think about it. Yes!"

Mercedes booked her flight from Chicago and a villa at the
spa, her plan working even better than she anticipated it
would. Molly could easily drive from college and meet her
there.

Molly began to feel guilty about lying to Peter and Kate,
especially when she found the flowers Peter left on her
kitchen table. His note said, "I miss you. Praying your project
goes great—and that you can get some rest. It won't be the
same visiting my family without you. Love always, Peter."

Kate left a sticky note on top of a plate of chocolate chip
cookies she baked for Molly. "Your favorites. Miss you!"
They were seldom home at the same time any more.

Molly took the cookies with her to the resort. Driving to
the spa, she forgot everything but spending time with
Mercedes. When they met in the main lobby Friday, as
scheduled, Mercedes gushed, "Let's get settled in our villa!"

It was stunning. Each woman had her own elegant suite,
positioned on opposite sides of the living room, each
overlooking the private lanai. They stepped outside to admire
the tropical flowers and lush greenery encircling their private
hot tub, then sat in the chaise lounges to admire the elegant
fountain cascading into it. Back inside, a basket of organic

fruits, bottled waters and assorted crackers welcomed them. "Don't you love it here, Mol?" Mercedes enthused.

"It is beautiful," Molly absently twisted her hair.

"I've booked massages for both of us this afternoon, then tomorrow it's mani-pedis, facials, the works!" Mercedes beamed, waiting for a compliment.

"Great!" Molly pretended to be happy, wondering why she couldn't mirror Mercedes' enthusiasm.

"My treat! Aren't you thrilled?" Mercedes looked ready to pout.

"Oh, of course I am. Wow! Thanks!" Molly played the game.

"We can have wine on the lanai after dinner."

Mercedes intensified her web spinning Friday evening at dinner. She looked tenderly at Molly, then, pretending to be surprised, stared at her ring. "You're still engaged? I thought you were having doubts."

Molly didn't recall telling Mercedes about her doubts. She hadn't even been able to articulate them in her own mind.

Mercedes did it for her. "When you're not sure about marrying someone, you need to end the engagement. It's a kindness to you. And a kindness to him. And you're too exquisite to waste your life on something you don't really want."

The seeds were planted.

At breakfast the next morning, they relaxed together in a garden café where tropical birds sang from an aviary that looked like a miniature Taj Mahal.

"Isn't this magical?" Mercedes gushed.

"Yes," Molly responded, realizing she felt relaxed enough to eat for the first time in weeks. She ordered an omelette, and chose fresh fruit from an elegant tiered tray their waiter brought to the table. Sipping perfectly brewed coffee, she felt soothed by the sound of a waterfall splashing into the nearby rippling stream. It *was* magical.

The magic ended for Molly at the nail spa that afternoon.

"I couldn't get appointments for both of us to get

pedicures at the same time," Mercedes said. "They told me they're booked months in advance. But at least we have appointments. You'll have your pedi while I have my mani, then we'll switch places."

Molly appreciated being alone. Kendra, her nail technician, gave her a card describing the state-of-the-art chair, with optical body scanning and custom-tailored massage. Sitting in it was so relaxing that Molly fell asleep until Kendra gently tapped her shoulder.

Molly, startled, jerked to attention, wondering where she was.

Kendra smiled. "Your pedicure is all finished. How do you like it?"

Molly looked blankly at her French pedicure. "Um, nice. Thanks."

"My pleasure. Please go to table two and choose a color for your manicure. Would you like a cappuccino?"

"Uh, sure." Still disoriented from her twenty-minute nap, Molly sluggishly moved across the room.

Kendra directed Molly to soak her hands in a bowl of lemon-scented sudsy water, then left for what seemed like a second. The aroma of fresh cappuccino helped Molly's mind begin, slowly, to move from what felt like the La Brea Tar Pits toward something more like a desert spring.

"Did you choose a color?"

Molly smiled sheepishly. "Uh, no. I forgot."

"No worries. What color do you like?" Kendra nodded toward the shelf on the wall at Molly's left. "These are some of this season's top color picks. See anything you like?"

To Molly's exhausted mind, it felt like she was looking at the entire Pantone color spectrum.

Kendra sensed her tension and held up one bottle, a pale pink polish. "A lot of people like this for their fingernails. What do you think?"

Relieved, Molly nodded her assent, then let herself unwind again, as Kendra gently massaged her arms and hands. Her mind drifting into peaceful oblivion, Molly came back to reality when she heard a familiar voice that triggered something repulsive in her mind. She opened her eyes, shocked when she noticed the man seated at the manicure table on her right.

In his peripheral vision, he saw her notice him. He felt more than a little annoyed at how long it took her to realize he was there, so he remained focused on his manicure. It would be good to keep her waiting, he decided. Intensely studying his nails, he spoke to his nail technician. "Excellent work. You remind me of Mina in Chicago. She keeps these marvelous hands in mint condition. In my line of work, it's essential to have my nails buffed twice a week."

He turned to Molly, magnanimously wreathing his face in a smile, lifting one hand in mock salute. "Don't look so shocked, Mol-Doll. Didn't Mercedes tell you I'm here every year at this time? A hard-working man has to take care of himself." He smiled again, amused at her discomfort.

Molly's stomach churned. Mercedes knew he was going to be here and didn't tell her? She had to know Anson Greeb was the last person in the world she wanted to see. Ever. Again.

Anson owned one of Chicago's most successful modeling agencies, inherited from his father. Mercedes worked there for years, first with Anson's father, then with Anson. Unable to accept the end of her own modeling career, Mercedes found new purpose when Molly was a high school sophomore and she coerced her stepdaughter to be part of the one world she loved.

Molly's lungs felt so tight that she couldn't breathe. Her heart was pounding. Her hands were clammy. *I have to get out of here.*

Anson's grating voice imposed on her mind. "Hey, Miss, easy on those cuticles, I'm a tender guy," he chortled. Turning to Molly, he resumed his one-sided conversation. "Isn't this spa the best? I never relax as much as I do here. Well, almost never," he stared at Molly, slowly studying her body, callously tearing open old wounds in her soul.

Molly looked down, pretending not to hear him.

Molly's technician slowly removed the lid, then gently pried open Molly's fisted hand so she could begin applying polish on her fingernails.

"Um, Kendra, I, um…I'll skip the manicure. I have to go. Thanks for everything, though." Without acknowledging Anson, Molly rushed out of the salon and back to her suite.

She was throwing everything into her suitcase when Mercedes returned.

"What are you doing? I saw you leave the nail salon without even saying goodbye. You can't leave yet. We still have another day of treatments booked."

"How could you, Mercedes? You knew Anson was here! Was this some kind of set-up to get us back together?"

"Now, Love, you know me better than that."

"No, Mercedes, I don't. But I think I'm getting to know you now."

"I am doing you a favor. You and Anson are perfect together…"

"Perfect? He destroyed my senior year of high school…I'm still recovering," Molly stifled a sob.

She couldn't remember anything about the drive from the resort back to college. Her apartment was blissfully quiet when she arrived there. Molly went to her room and curled up on her bed, in the fetal position. She was too numb to cry.

The next day, she noticed her hands, wondering why only two nails were polished.

The day after that, she woke at noon to Peter's voice in the kitchen just down the hall from her bedroom. Listening to him talk to Kate, she heard his kind voice and wondered why she kept pushing him away. But she didn't get up to tell him hello.

CHAPTER SIX

All semester, Molly rigorously trained herself not to think about Peter or their relationship. And now, during this interminable wait for her flight, Molly couldn't stop the whirlwind of regrets.

She thought of him standing next to Carlos, smiling as best man. Was it only this morning he walked next to her—best man and maid of honor? Both were smiling; his smile was genuine, hers fake.

She thought of Peter trying to hug her at Kate's wedding reception—and saw the pain in his eyes when she squirmed away. She thought of how sad he looked when she told him she didn't feel well and would have to have him drop her off at home before everyone cleaned up at the reception site. She thought of the deafening silence flooding the car when he drove her back to her apartment. She heard his voice, hopeful. "Can't we talk for ten minutes before I go back?" And she heard her own voice, cold. "No. Later. I told you I'm not feeling well, remember?" In her mind, she watched him drive away, not turning back. He should have made me talk! But she knew how to stonewall; and he knew it was an exercise in futility to break through her barriers.

How could one day—today—already feel like years ago?

* * *

"Miss, here is your check. Shall I remove your dishes?" the waitress looked at Molly, then pointedly turned toward the line of people waiting for seats.

"Sure." Molly had eaten four small bites of the burger, one French fry—and gulped the entire Coke, something she never did. Ever since her brief stint as a model, even the thought of extra calories fueled anxiety.

She looked at the departure board. Her shoulders slumped when she saw the flight to Chicago was still delayed. Her head hurt. Near her gate, she found a seat, away from people, and tried to fall asleep. But memories continued to pummel her mind.

She stood up, walking the concourse, quickening her steps in a futile attempt to quiet her mind. Stopping at an ATM, Molly refilled her wallet, then turned in to a candy shop adjacent to her gate. *Chocolate. I need chocolate.* Handing the clerk two crisp bills, she bought a box of chocolate truffles. Paying with cash instead of a credit card felt like it safely hid her choice. Hurrying, she towed her suitcase into a large restroom stall. Her back to the door, afraid someone would walk in on her, she quickly jammed one piece of chocolate after another into her mouth, barely chewing or noticing the taste.

Carefully checking her face in the restroom mirror, Molly felt relief when there were no stains. *I don't remember the last time I ate chocolate…I think I was in high school.* Suddenly she was overwhelmed with guilt. *It was spring break. The chocolate chip cookies Kate made when she thought I had to study. I ate them all at the spa, hiding them from Mercedes. She would have told me to throw them away. Too many calories. Too much fat.*

She walked back into the corridor. At her gate, every chair was full, so she sat on the floor, closing her eyes, leaning her head against the wall. *I'm doing the right thing. Peter will understand. My email explained it clearly enough.* But when she tried to picture him reading her message, she thought of her brother Jeremy instead. Thinking of him brought back all of the reasons she had to leave. *Why did Peter think he could help Jeremy? And why did Kate get married?*

Her older brother Jeremy, her nemesis. Even though he was invited, Jeremy chose not to attend Kate's wedding. Two weeks prior, he told Peter and Molly why. "I've gone to both of my own weddings—and all I got from those was two divorces," he said, his face desolate. "I don't do weddings anymore. I'm bad luck."

"We don't believe in luck—and we want you there," Peter said, looking at Molly for confirmation. "Yes," she responded, forcing a weak smile. Later, Peter asked her why she didn't try to encourage her brother. "Couldn't you at least say you believe in him? He needs to hear that from you. He hasn't had a drink in months, and he's working hard in rehab," Peter said, pressing her hand. His voice softened, "Besides, Molly, he has asked you to forgive him…"

She pulled away. "Peter, you know I forgave him…but you don't understand how hard it still is for me to be around him. You don't understand…," she finished, her eyes flashing, her heart hardening.

He tried to hold her hand, but she pulled it away. "You're my number one priority, Mol," he said, his voice tender. "Jeremy's going to move out soon, just as soon as he finishes this treatment. Remember, the only way they would let him into the program was if I agreed to sponsor him? You know he had nowhere else to go. Your mom won't help; his friends have bailed on him. He needs to see real love. And he's really looking forward to getting a new job and moving back to Illinois. He wants to go back and apply what he's learning so he can spend time with his kids."

Molly thought of the nieces and nephews she barely knew. "Yes," she said, trying hard to empathize. "They need a father. Maybe he can make a new start," she finished, not sounding convinced.

Molly's stomach hurt. *Why did I eat so much? I've never eaten that much chocolate,* she lamented. *I feel sick.* She rushed down the corridor again, hurrying to the bathroom stall furthest from people. Bending down, she forced herself to vomit. As she left, she looked around her, hoping no one noticed. Everyone seemed focused on their own luggage, their hair, their plans. She splashed water on her face and went back to her spot on the floor.

* * *

When the plane finally lifted off, Molly felt an unexpected surge of relief. Gazing out the window, she studied highways crisscrossing the landscape below, gray ribbons dotted with shimmering cars on their way to countless destinations. *This is the right thing to do. I know it will work out for the best,* she assured herself. The sound of two dull thuds brought Molly's thoughts back to the plane. *The landing gear retracted.* A voice came over the loud speaker. "This is your captain, John Marquardt. We'll be climbing to an altitude of 31,000 feet today. Keep your seat belts fastened in case we climb into choppy air. We apologize for the departure delay. It looks like the Windy City has calm skies now. Our current scheduled arrival time in Chicago is 7:00 AM, Central Standard Time."

* * *

The man seated next to her liked what he saw, but Molly didn't notice his surreptitious stares. She sat stone-faced, her thoughts alternating between panic at her abrupt decision to bail out of life and trying to convince herself that she had no alternative. *When Peter reads my email, he'll understand.*

When the roads below her disappeared under a thick bed of clouds, Molly's left thumb absently reached to twirl her engagement ring. She gasped. It wasn't there. What had she done?

CHAPTER SEVEN

It was dark when Peter returned to the four rooms he and
Jeremy shared. Behind his aunt and uncle's house, a large
evergreen dwarfed the tiny cottage. He tripped on something
on the darkened porch, but didn't take time to see what it
was. He was too tired to care. Talking with family friends and
getting acquainted with Carlos' Guatemalan aunts, uncles, and
cousins had taken far longer than he'd planned. He pressed
Molly's number on his cell phone, trying for the umpteenth
time to reach her. He wondered why she was in such a hurry
to leave her best friend's wedding, then remembered how
pale she looked when she said, "I'm not feeling well." *At least
she hung around until Kate and Carlos left for Hawaii.*

She let him drive her home but wouldn't take time to talk
with him. *She's not well. That must be why she isn't answering her
cell.* Thinking of Molly, he remembered how she cringed after
the wedding when he told her he wished they were the ones
getting married instead of Carlos and Kate. Forcing himself
not to worry about why she didn't answer, he collapsed in his
bed, exhausted.

He wasn't tired enough. He lay tossing and turning,
remembering the night before. For the rehearsal dinner,
Carlos' family had asked him to "think of something fun and

unusual to help everyone get to know the happy couple." He planned a game, one he thought was creative and fun. After taping paper footprints in a winding path encircling the restaurant floor, he asked Kate and Carlos to stand back-to-back where the path began. "I know most people hate wedding games, so this is something different. You two are going to walk around the room in opposite directions, and you can only take a step forward when you make a compliment about your fiancé," he said looking at his sister. "And your fiancée, Carlos. Since that term is from the Latin and literally means 'to trust,' think about compliments that demonstrate how much you trust the one you're marrying tomorrow. You'll meet each other after you've given enough positive comments to take you around the room. And your comments can't be about anything external," he added.

Looking backwards over his shoulder as he lunged forward, Carlos began, "Kate, you're the kindest woman I've ever met. I trust you with my life—and with our future children."

Her eyes misting, Kate stepped the other direction. "Carlos, you always encourage me with your words—and your actions. I feel safe with you." She laughed and took another step. "That's three!"

"You're a great cook—with a tender heart," Carlos said, taking two steps closer to his bride. "I don't think I'll ever get food poisoning from you." Everyone laughed.

"And you are a fabulous leader," Kate beamed.

A half-hour later, after encircling the room with compliments, Kate and Carlos hugged while their guests clapped. "Encore, encore," someone shouted. They hugged again. Peter was pleased the game had been such a success—until he talked with Molly after dinner.

"What's wrong?" he asked, reading her body language.

"How could you play a ridiculous game like that?" she seethed, barely controlling her fury. "With every step Kate and Carlos took, I felt worse. Peter, if this is what you expect me to do before our wedding, you can forget it. My mind would go blank with people staring at me, hanging on every word. Besides, my relationship with you is too private to talk about. I can't be all lovey-dovey in front of a group of people."

Peter wished he had said nothing—or at least found something to say that would have defused their growing tension. But he stupidly said the first thing that came to his mind. "I don't think you need to worry about our rehearsal dinner, Molly. You aren't even willing to set a date for our wedding." She gave him the silent treatment throughout the entire drive to her apartment.

"What are you thinking?" he asked. Her frown spoke volumes, but his guess about what was bothering Molly was far from the mark. She wasn't thinking about the rehearsal dinner at all.

Staring out Peter's car window, Molly felt increasing terror. *I'm not ready for marriage. I don't feel 'in love' like Kate does. Peter deserves someone who can give him what I can't.*

Peter's smile usually helped Molly's dark moods. He held up his hand in salute. "Scout's honor, I promise we won't play any games like that."

Her stonewalling continued.

"Want to stop for ice cream before I take you home?"

"No, I have to be able to fit into my bridesmaid dress tomorrow," she smiled, trying to defuse the tension.

"You'll be gorgeous. You always are."

"Thanks. I can't wait to see you in your tux."

Though words were beginning to flow, communication was nonexistent. Peter had no idea what his fiancée was thinking or feeling.

CHAPTER EIGHT

Molly wished she could push time back so everything could be like it used to be. Instead, she and Kate had another argument that night, the night before Kate's wedding. The last night they would ever be roommates.

"Please be happy for me," Kate begged. "I know you think I'm rushing into marriage but I'm not. Really. I've prayed for the right man for so long that it's only natural I'd know him when I met him. My whole family loves Carlos. But it's important to me that you do, Mol. Please? We always want you to be part of our lives."

"How can I be part of your life when you're constantly shutting me out of it?"

"You're the one shutting everyone out!" retorted Kate. "Even Peter, *your* fiancé! You hardly spend any time with him. I spend more time with my brother than you do!"

Recalling her response, Molly sighed, wishing she were with Kate instead of in a plane. The man next to her was asleep. Uninterrupted by human distraction, she continued to replay their argument, hearing herself accusing Kate of being selfish, of not caring, even of abusing her. "You are always trying to control me, Kate. You're manipulative, abusive…"

"You think I've abused you?" Kate looked incredulous,

44

shocked, as though Molly hit her.

"*Emotional* abuse. The things you say are cruel."

"That is simply not true, Molly," Kate said. "You know I've done nothing but show you love." Molly remembered her friend pausing, tenderly reaching to hug her. She remembered Kate's soft comment, "I think you're distorting reality because you're scared."

Molly twisted out of Kate's hug. "There's something else we need to talk about," Molly said, her anger cold, intense. "It's not too late."

"Too late for what?" Kate looked confused.

"To back out."

"What are you talking about?" Kate asked.

"I'm talking about you and Carlos. You're not a fit. You keep saying you're not rushing into this. But you are, believe me. You're making a huge mistake."

"I thought you would support me, Molly. This should be the happiest time of my life, but you seem determined to ruin it." Kate's eyes filled with tears; her cheeks were turning red.

"I'm trying to protect you." Molly was genuinely perplexed that her friend wouldn't listen. "I don't want to believe you're making a mistake—really, I don't."

"Then don't. It's your choice. I've made mine," Kate told her, slamming the door and leaving their apartment to walk off her anger. When she returned later that night, she told Molly she was sorry for losing her temper—and Molly said she was sorry, too. Though they hugged and prayed, Molly was sure their friendship would never be the same.

* * *

How could I have done that to Kate the night before her wedding? Molly wondered. Overwhelmed with guilt, she did a tremendous job of pretending all was well between her and Kate during the wedding. She looked like a model maid of honor. Now, flying farther and farther from her life, she could barely remember the event that occurred—she looked

45

at her watch. *Four o'clock AM—Kate got married yesterday.*

Kate and Carlos were married in a morning ceremony in the beautiful campus arboretum, overlooking the Pacific Ocean. Seven varieties of white flowers covered an arch over the couple. Molly could remember Kate's elation at the florist's shop months before, enthusiastically choosing her wedding flowers. "White, representing purity, and seven, the perfect number. I have to have seven varieties of gorgeous white flowers." Looking at the glowing bride and groom, Molly felt sick.

As the minister pronounced them man and wife, Molly glanced at Peter, beaming beside his sister's new husband. Molly felt like she was suffocating. *We could be next. I'm not ready.* At another level, she wished she *were* ready to be Peter's bride.

Peter, Carlos' best man, led Molly down the aisle behind the bride and groom. "You are the most beautiful woman here, Molly," he whispered. His arm gentle, his smile enveloping her, Molly knew Peter wished she were his bride and not his sister's maid of honor. He had told her that much the week before. She forced a smile in his direction.

I should feel like he *does. But I can't. What's wrong with me?* Seven varieties of white flowers—*for Kate's purity*—seemed to strangle Molly as the wedding transitioned to brunch. Tables decorated with the wedding favors Molly helped make besieged her mind when she saw the tables covered with seven varieties of white flowers. *Am I going crazy?* Molly smiled with her mouth; her eyes were bleak.

After the ten o'clock ceremony, the brunch kept the wedding party busy for the rest of the morning. While guests enjoyed tropical fruits and a vast assortment of pastries, with a chef making omelettes to order, Carlos guided his beaming bride to talk with guests gathered throughout the arboretum.

* * *

After an ecstatic Carlos and Kate left the reception for

their afternoon flight to Hawaii, Molly helped Peter and his family deliver a mountain of wedding gifts to the apartment Carlos and Kate would share after their honeymoon. She carried packages in from Peter's car without saying a word.

Locking the door of Kate's new home, Peter turned to Molly, smiling, hoping to break their uneasy silence. "Kate and Carlos want the whole family to come for dinner here the Saturday after they get back—so we can all be with them when they open their gifts. You're family, too, you know, Mol," he added, needing reassurance.

"I'll, uh, have to see. Classes start in two weeks, and I'm taking nine hours—all tough classes for summer school. I might be buried in books," she said, silencing him with a look.

"You don't have time for that?" Peter opened her car door, trying to keep himself calm, hoping being in his familiar old Honda would somehow change her mood.

She said only one thing. "Peter, I know everyone is going back to clean up after the reception, but I...I'm not feeling well. Please take me back to my apartment now, OK?"

He exhaled, forcing his voice to stay calm. "Please come with me. Everyone wants to see you. It has been so busy that people haven't really had time to talk. And a lot of the family are leaving tomorrow, Molly."

She shrugged. "I'm really sorry Peter, but I need to go home. I need you to be sensitive to my needs."

* * *

Something about flying forced Molly to face hidden motives. Maybe it was seeing how small the world was from another perspective. Or maybe it was getting a glimpse of the enormity of God's creation. She squirmed in her seat, leaning forward to get a better look at the city lights below. The clouds lifted, but her spirits did not.

For the first time in a long time, Molly admitted the truth. She *was* terrified. Afraid she'd fail as Peter's wife. Afraid

Peter would abandon her like her dad did. Tears streamed down her face as she realized she'd destroyed everything that mattered to her. Her body shook with silent sobs. Noticing, the man next to her shifted in his seat and looked across the aisle, but Molly couldn't stop her lonely mental journey. *Why didn't I see this before I made such a mess of my life?*

CHAPTER NINE

Descending into O'Hare Airport, Molly was numb.

She checked her cell phone as the plane pulled into the terminal. A text from her mom. "Plz cab home. Busy packing. See you soon."

Nothing changes with her, Molly thought, scowling. When she arrived at her childhood home, Molly barely noticed when her mom reneged on yet another promise.

"Mol, you can use Jenn's car; she left it here when she moved to London. I forgot my new car had to go to the garage." Babs didn't tell her daughter she hurriedly took it to her *boyfriend's* garage. As soon as she bribed Molly with the promise of driving it, she realized how silly that idea was; she asked Harry to help her get out of it. She wasn't about to let her daughter scuff up her Quattroporte's gorgeous Italian leather seats.

Earlier that evening, when Babs arrived at his place with her vehicle, Harry had made the mistake of asking, "Isn't your daughter a music major? She'd probably love your S Q4's upgraded Bowers and Wilkins sound system. Don't you always say it's concert-hall quality?"

Babs silenced him into compliance with a stern look. All during their cab ride back to her house, she showed Harry pictures of the Maserati on her phone. "I took these today, because I am going to miss my coupe so much," she said. "Isn't the Radica wood trim on my baby gorgeous, Harry? I can't believe how much I love this beauty."

In those moments, Harry realized why Babs rarely talked about her three adult children. Her possessions were her family. And when he met Molly early the next morning, Harry was careful not to mention her mother's new car.

Molly didn't stay up talking. She went to the guest suite, took a quick shower, and went to bed, grateful her old bedroom had been converted to a media room so she didn't have to stay in it. But she couldn't sleep. The old thoughts reverberating in her mind wouldn't allow her body to rest.

CHAPTER TEN

Even with the cumulative exhaustion of finals and his sister's wedding, Peter slept so restlessly that he finally gave up and got up. He looked at his phone. It was only seven. And no missed calls.

Stumbling groggily into the living room, the first thing he noticed was Jeremy sprawled on the couch, an empty beer bottle on the floor beside him.

This was the second time Jeremy had violated their agreement in as many months. Peter frowned, knowing he would have to follow-through on his promise to evict him. But he didn't want to—not when Jeremy had been making so much progress. Not when he was so close to a new start.

Before he could deal with Jeremy, Peter had to talk with Molly. He tried her phone and got voice mail. "Molly, where are you? Call me, I'm concerned about you." He tried again. No response. *Maybe Kate knows where she is. But Kate said her phone would be off all week.*

Several times in the past, Molly left notes for him under his welcome mat. He stepped onto the front porch to check, but had to move more of Jeremy's empty beer bottles before he could lift the mat. His face flushed with unexpected anger. No note.

Peter went back inside and shook Jeremy awake. "What do you think you're doing? You promised you'd stay clean. You've let me down big time Jer."

Jeremy's eyes were red, and his speech was slow. "Hey, it's not my fault. I got so depressed thinking about your sister's wedding I couldn't help myself. You know what I mean?"

Peter chose not to answer him. "Did Molly come over last night?"

"I don't know, man. I don't think so." Jeremy sat up, rubbing his eyes, trying to remember. "Maybe."

Peter had never felt like punching someone as much as he did Jeremy at that moment. "Was she here or not?"

"Yeah. She had a bicycle, I think. Yeah, she was riding her bike."

"Did she say anything?"

"Uh, wait. Yeah, she gave me something."

"What? Tell me what! Where is it?" Peter shouted.

"I, uh, I don't know," Jeremy fell back against the sofa, groaning, holding his head. His breath smelled rank.

Peter shook him. "Jeremy, you have to know *something*. I don't know if she's OK. I can't reach her." Afraid of what he would do, Peter turned and went to the kitchen to begin making coffee. *Maybe this will wake him up.*

Smelling the coffee, Jeremy sat up. "She had something in her hand. I think it was important. She told me to put it somewhere."

"Where? Do you still have it?" Peter was tearing the living room apart, looking under sofa cushions, moving chairs. Nothing.

"No, no, not in here. I remember!" Jeremy walked toward the bedroom, still holding his head.

Peter followed him.

"Here it is."

Peter's heart sunk when he felt the small bulge in the padded envelope. "Give me a minute, Jer, please. I'm sorry I lost my temper."

"No worries, Man. I deserved it."

"Yeah, but I promised I'd show you what real love is. I blew it." Knowing what he was holding in his hand, Peter began to cry. "Please just give me a minute, OK?" He closed the door.

Opening the envelope, Peter collapsed on his bedroom floor, sobbing. *Why didn't I see this coming? What could I have done? I've got to talk with her!* He pressed her number.

CHAPTER ELEVEN

Molly awakened at eleven, and her first instinct was to check her phone. Twenty-five missed calls. All. From. Peter. And here he is again. Molly refused the call. She knew what he wanted, and she couldn't give it to him. Marrying him was out of the question. She went downstairs to say goodbye to her mom.

Instead, she read the note pinned to the fridge. "We had to get to the airport; grocery money is in an envelope on the table. Anything else you need, use your debit card. Have fun (I know we will!). See you in August."

She shrugged. *What else is new? No tender goodbyes from mommy.* Without thinking, she shivered, not from cold but from—the house. Memories, bad memories, seemed to crawl out of the woodwork. Her parents' fighting; her mom screaming at her; her dad leaving; her dad's remarriage; her dad's suicide—and Jeremy.

She had to think about something—anything—other than this house and the sadness in it.

Her phone was ringing again. She picked it up, desperate to hear Peter's voice. This time, she answered without looking at caller ID. "Hi, it's Molly."

"Molly? I can't believe it's really you!"

Bewildered, it took Molly a few seconds to register. It wasn't Peter. It was her sister, Jennifer. They hadn't spoken with each other in months.

"Jenn, where are you? You won't believe where I am."

"You first."

"No, you."

"I'm in London. I just bought a flat in Greenwich!"

"How...are you kidding me?"

"I am based here now, with United Airlines."

"Wow, I hadn't heard. I've been crushed with, well...with a lot of things, this last semester."

"Like what?"

"School, school, school...trying to finish grad school by next semester."

"I'm glad one of us loves school. It's just not for me. But I love being a flight attendant. It's one career that doesn't require a college diploma." She laughed. "I've finally found my niche, traveling the world."

"Good for you, I'm glad one of us *has* a niche." Molly choked, barely able to find words. "I don't think I've found much of anything. Right now, I've pretty much ruined my life."

"You? Miss Perfection?" Jennifer suddenly stopped laughing, her tone serious. "What are you talking about?"

"I am a current grad school dropout, standing in our mother's kitchen in Illinois, housesitting while she and her man-of-the-month are vacationing in Europe."

"You're kidding. Why aren't you in school? And aren't you engaged?"

"It's a long story."

"I have time."

Molly sighed, then explained how she broke her engagement without talking to Peter, how she rushed to the airport last night when their mom called, and how she felt like dying now that she was in what the two sisters had once dubbed their family's Big Ol' House of Awfulness, or BOHA, for short.

"You absolutely cannot spend the summer in BOHA," Jenn ordered, her volume rising, Big Sister voice at full alert.

"I am pretty much committed to doing just that."

"Get uncommitted—and that's an order!"

"Mom said they have to have someone here."

"Well, one reason I was calling was to give you the scoop that Jeremy is on his way to Illinois right now, courtesy of one of my United Airlines' Buddy passes. He apparently doesn't know you're there. I just got off the phone with him before I called you. He was really weird when he called. He said I was the only one left to ask for help because he has hurt everyone else who cares about him. I told him he should visit Mom for a few months, and he said he would surprise her. Apparently Mom didn't clue him in about her trip."

"Apparently not. So, let me get this straight…he is on his way here?"

"Yes, his flight arrives in Chicago at seven tonight. He'll cab there from the airport, I imagine. Mom will be more than surprised to find him there when she gets back."

Molly suddenly felt like she couldn't breathe. Her fingers were tingling. "I can't be here with him. Not now. Not ever." She felt like she was having a heart attack. She began pacing the kitchen, opening and closing drawers.

"What is going on?"

"I am freaking out. I feel like I'm suffocating. I cannot be alone here with him. You know that, Jenn."

"Hold on. Take a deep breath, OK?"

Molly breathed. Inhale, inflate lungs; exhale, empty them. She felt herself beginning to relax, ever so slightly.

Jenn was talking faster than Molly could think. "What's your passport number, Molly?"

"Why do you want that?"

"So I can give you free flights."

"OK…I actually have it with me. I am surprised that I grabbed it in my rush to pack." Molly found it in her purse. Her breathing relaxed as she focused on reading the number to Jenn.

"Better now? All righty, I'm looking at flight openings. There we go. This is great! I can get you on a flight to Heathrow this evening at 7:25."

"Tonight? Are you kidding? I just got to Chicago."

"No, I'm absolutely not kidding. So, can you be back at O'Hare by 4 PM Central Time to check in? You would check in at the International Terminal, so it's highly unlikely you'd run into Jeremy. I know that's a little early but when you fly standby, it's good to get there earlier than usual."

Jennifer quit talking. The only sound was the rapid click click of her computer keys.

"Are you there?"

"Yes, I just added you as my family member who flies free. Remember it's stand-by, so you need to get to the airport ASAP, OK? But it looks like there are plenty of seats left on tonight's flight. And I just booked you for first-class stand-by, so that should be a shoe-in, or sister-in." She giggled, a sound Molly hadn't heard from her sister since she was in grade school. "All you have to do is check in at O'Hare; I'll take care of everything else."

A hint of a smile played on Molly's lips. "But I can't leave. I told Mom I'd stay here."

"Who is the Big Sister? I am. Your circumstances have changed. I'll email Mom and explain to her that I flew Jeremy home to house-sit because I need you here to help me get settled in my new flat. I am not taking no for an answer. Besides, you haven't unpacked yet, have you?"

Molly felt her sister's smile, and responded with, "But what about school?"

"You already told me you dropped out of all of your summer courses."

"Oh, right."

"Hey, I noticed there's a college in Greenwich, just two or three blocks from where I live. We can check it out. Maybe you can pick up some classes there this summer."

"Jenn, I feel sick. I don't know if I can do this."

"Before you do anything else, you need to call Peter and

tell him what's going on. You'll feel better if you're not running away. You're running to something, Molly. To your sister. I need you; it's high time we reconnect. It has been far too long."

Molly's head was spinning. "Yeah, about two years?" The last time she and Jennifer were together was when they both were in Illinois for their dad's funeral. And Jenn had been totally different then—critical, angry, harsh. Since then, they'd spoken on the phone about once a year, sticking with superficial topics, never really communicating. But this sister was someone she wanted to get to know again. "OK, I'll come."

"I'll meet you at the airport. It's a direct flight and should arrive about 9:05 tomorrow morning. And if for any reason you don't get on this flight, message me and I'll get you on the next one. We can take the tube home together from Heathrow. But promise me you'll call Peter right now."

Molly didn't have to call Peter. He was calling her. This time she answered.

He could barely speak through his tears. "Molly, you're safe. I love you. I couldn't find you. I, I didn't know what happened."

"I'm so sorry. I'm a mess. I don't know why I've been so rude to you, to everyone."

His voice choking, Peter could only say five words. "You broke our engagement. Why?"

"Like my note said, you deserve someone better. Like my email said…"

Peter found his voice, and it was exasperated. "What email? I didn't get an email. I woke up to your brother, hung-over, finally remembering under duress that you'd been here but not remembering what you'd said or why you came…he thought you brought something. So I, I found the ring this morning." He sobbed. It was several moments before he could speak again. "Where are you, Molly?"

"I'm in Chicago, at my mom's. My email, the one you didn't get, told you I'd be housesitting for her this summer.

She called right after you dropped me off at my apartment yesterday."

"I don't understand. You have classes this summer..."

"I went online after my mom called and dropped all of them. I am so confused that I thought it might help to put some space between us."

"But we are—or were—engaged. I don't want space."

Molly paused, unsure what to say.

Peter continued. "I love you, Molly. Do you still love me?"

She pictured him, his eyes shining, earnest, full of love. The intensely tender sound of his voice took her back to why she had wanted to marry him in the first place. "I do love you, Peter."

"Good, then come back to California, please. I'll pay for your flight."

"I can't."

"You can't, or you won't?" He felt so hurt that his voice had a hard edge.

Molly paused, startled by the change in his tone. "Um, I told my sister I'd help her in London. She just booked a flight for me out of Chicago. I'm leaving later this evening."

"Is this a sick joke? I don't get it. Last night, you were too tired to talk with me for ten minutes. You were too tired to hang out after your best friend's wedding but you had enough energy to fly to Chicago. And today you're jetting off to London? Come on, Molly, what's really going on?"

"I wish I knew. I haven't felt this confused since high school."

"I want to be here for you, Molly. I feel like I've failed you somehow," Peter said, sobs punctuating each word.

"No, Peter, you haven't failed me. I'm the failure." Molly wanted to cry with him, but she couldn't feel.

"And I, I've also failed your brother. I kicked him out this morning because he was drinking again. I know *he* made the choice to drink...but I still feel horrible about not being able to help him stay sober."

Molly felt a relief she couldn't understand. Jeremy wasn't

staying with Peter! "You're right, Peter. It was his choice, not yours. And that explains why he called our sister. Nowhere else to go. Jenn is flying him to Chicago even as we speak. He is going to stay here instead of me. She came up with the idea to fly me to London, so I won't be here when he arrives."

"Why London?"

"Jennifer is based there with United Airlines. I knew she became a flight attendant a couple of years ago, but she used to be based somewhere in the States. I think it was in New York or San Francisco, but I'm not sure. I didn't even know she'd transferred to Heathrow. But she recently moved into a flat in London and asked me to come help her get settled."

"What about us?"

"I want there to be an 'us,' I really do, Peter. But what if there *is* someone better for you? I want you to be free to find her, and that won't happen as long as you're stuck with me."

"I absolutely do not agree with your opinion. I don't believe I am 'stuck' with you. I love you, Molly. I want you. I miss you so much that I can barely function."

"Will you give me the freedom to figure out *life* this summer? Then we can reevaluate everything this fall."

Peter sighed. "I will respect your decision, even though it hurts." His voice broke up. "Could we pray together now?"

Molly nodded, forgetting he couldn't see her.

Sensing her inability to speak, Peter prayed for both of them. "Lord, we need Your help. Thank You that You see both of us and that London and California aren't too far away for You. Help our relationship flourish again, if that's what You want." For several moments, he couldn't speak. The only sounds Molly heard were his quiet sighs. "Help me love Molly the way You designed her to be loved. And help me let go of her if that is what is best for her." He sobbed, grasping for words. "I'm sorry, God, this is so hard. I don't know if I *can* let go."

CHAPTER TWELVE

After his call with Molly, Peter's mind was spinning. On autopilot, he began to pick up the beer bottles Jeremy left scattered around the living room, alternately moaning because he couldn't do anything to help Jeremy, then weeping when he considered that his relationship with Molly could be coming to an end. He didn't know what to do.

His aunt's unique tap on his front door interrupted his painful deliberations. Her knock always reminded him of a high school band's drum corps, like the rat-a-tat tapping of a snare drum. He opened the door, wondering if she'd been standing there long enough to hear his sobs.

"Hi, Aunt Zoë. Come on in."

"Peter, I saw Jeremy get into a cab and thought I'd come see what happened. Are you OK?"

"No, I'm not OK. Not even close."

Zoë waited quietly.

"See this mess?" He nodded at the remnants of Jeremy's solitary bash. "I had to ask Jeremy to leave. But this chaos is nothing compared to what's happening with Molly."

"Molly?"

"She's gone."

"Gone? What do you mean...where is she?"

"Illinois now. But on her way to London."

"I'd better sit down. Or do you want to come over to the house so you only have to tell the story once? Your parents are still there."

Peter's parents were staying with Brandon's brother Dan and sister-in-law Zoë—first to prepare before and then recuperate after their daughter Kate's wedding. Wanting to take advantage of the time with family, the brothers and their spouses had planned a few day trips together and would be back in time to celebrate Carlos and Kate's return from their week-long Hawaiian honeymoon.

"Oh, I forgot. They spent the night with you and Uncle Dan. After my sister's wedding. Yesterday. It seems like a year ago."

"But Molly was at the reception last night! How did she get to Illinois?"

"Walk me over to your house. I need everyone's collective wisdom right now."

Peter crumpled into his aunt's arms. She hugged him, then supported him on the short walk to her back door.

"Hey, Peter!" His dad greeted him with a bear hug, then stepped back when he noticed his son's red-rimmed eyes. "What happened?"

Peter reached into his pocket and pulled out the engagement ring that, for the past seven months, had symbolized hope and promise of a shared future with the woman he loved. "Molly dropped this off last night while the rest of us were cleaning up after the reception."

His mom was shocked. "Molly's engagement ring! What happened? I don't understand..." She began to cry. "I love Molly. She's already like one of our family...."

"I know, Mom." His sobs were loud enough to bring his uncle into the kitchen.

"Did something happen to Molly, Peter?" Dan's eyes were filled with compassion.

"I, it's just that, I don't know what to say."

"Take a deep breath. Take your time." Dan's voice, always

calming, helped.

"I tried to call her last night after I got home. She didn't answer. She said she didn't feel well. She had me drop her off at her apartment before the rest of us met to clean up. I tried to call her again and again and again. Finally, this morning, she answered my call…and told me her mom called after the wedding and needed her to housesit in Illinois, so she flew to Chicago late last night."

"I thought you said she wasn't feeling well." His mom looked as bewildered as Peter felt.

"Right." He paused. "There's more. After Molly got to Illinois, her sister Jennifer called from London, and asked Molly to fly there to help her get settled in her new flat in Greenwich. When I talked with Molly just a little while ago, she was planning to go back to O'Hare…"

Zoë interrupted. "Wait, let me get this straight. Molly is on her way to London, as in England?"

Brandon interrupted, "How can she afford all of this traveling?"

"Apparently her sister is a flight attendant with United, based in London…she was going to fly Molly standby, I guess…"

Zoë spoke so softly no one heard her. "I didn't think Molly and Jennifer got along. This is astonishing." She raised her voice to ask, "When is she coming back?"

Peter's words came out choked, almost garbled. "I, uh, I…I don't know. Maybe never. She dropped all three of her summer classes before she flew to Chicago last night."

Zoë spoke again. "This is my fault. I should have spent more time with her. I should have talked with her. I saw her isolating; distancing herself from all of us from the moment Kate and Carlos got engaged. But I was so excited with all of the wedding plans that I didn't pay attention to what was right in front of my eyes."

Dan said, "It's not your fault, honey. It's no one's *fault*."

Zoë's words tumbled out. "Did any of you know that Kate was crying before her wedding? She told me Molly was angry with her after the rehearsal dinner. I can't remember exactly what she said…"

Kelly continued, "Kate said Molly told her she should call off the wedding, that it wasn't too late—this, on the night before her wedding! She said Molly doesn't like Carlos and that she kept saying they're rushing everything. I wish I'd tried to talk with Molly, but I was so busy helping Kate that I didn't notice how much Molly was hurting."

Zoë nodded. "Kate said Molly told her nothing would be the same with their friendship after she married Carlos. I am sad I missed what was really going on."

"We all seemed to miss it. The story of Molly's life," Kate's dad sighed.

Dan seemed lost in thought. "Typical, so typical, and I was not alert to it at all."

"To *it?* What do you mean?" Brandon asked.

"Survivors of incestual abuse often isolate when they're faced with significant changes in daily life or in their relationships. Kate was Molly's emotional anchor, so to speak. When Carlos came into Kate's life, Molly didn't know what to do. And especially since Kate and Carlos fell in love quickly and decided to marry rapidly, Molly didn't know how to adjust. Trust is extremely difficult for incest survivors."

"But I thought she was healed a long time ago," Peter interjected.

"Healing comes in stages, Peter. Anything can 'trigger' survivors—anything experienced with any of the five senses. It only takes about a twelfth of a second for the trauma stored in the brain's amygdala to literally 'hijack' the brain's prefrontal cortex, where the brain's executive functioning occurs."

"Wait a minute. I don't get it," Peter scratched his head, trying to understand.

"Someone sees something, hears something, touches something, etc.—anything that reminds the person of trauma incidents—and, often the person isn't even aware of whatever *it* is that has triggered old trauma memories. It might feel like either a vague or an overwhelming sense that *something* is wrong. The amygdala is like a fire alarm in the person's brain; when it 'goes off' like a warning flare, it can rapidly send a surge of adrenalin that overtakes the brain's normal processing. Like the 'fight or flight' process…it's helpful when one needs a surge of adrenalin to combat danger, but not helpful in everyday life."

"Um, OK?"

"So in a twelfth of a second, the amygdala literally takes over the brain, sending it into what we in psychology refer to as the 'Five Fs' of Fight, Flight, Freeze, Fornicate or Feed."

"Now I really don't get it." Peter sat down, dazed. "I'm in grad school, studying psych. How did I miss this?"

"We all missed it." Dan continued. "What I'm trying to say is that something triggered Molly to feel so overwhelmed that she felt like she had to fight with Kate, flee the situation, freeze her complex emotions—and break off her engagement with you, Peter. Fight, flight, freeze."

"Are you saying she might not continue to feel this way?"

"Not if she can get stabilized. That happens when we do something called 'grounding,' and there are practical steps a person can take to rapidly move out of an amygdala hijacking and get back into the prefrontal cortex of his or her brain. Those steps can be completed in a fraction of a second if the person knows what to do—or chooses to do it. Or if the person knows *how* to do it."

"Does Molly know how to do this?" Zoë asked softly.

Dan sighed. "I'm not sure." He groaned. "I wonder if Jeremy being here triggered her."

"She said she'd forgiven him a long time ago," Peter said, a hint of defensiveness in his voice. "I never would have let him stay with me if I thought it would bother Molly."

"He molested her for years, from the time she was about four, I think," Zoë said. "Could those memories stored in her brain trigger her now?"

"When someone's emotional memories are stimulated, it can feel like the trauma is happening now. Emotions don't necessarily have a sense of time," Dan added. "Though the emotional response to the trauma can be stopped, a person can easily forget to do so, simply due to the intensity of the emotions in the present moment."

"This is all my fault!" Peter groaned, pacing the kitchen, wringing his hands. "I should never have let Jeremy stay with me. I should have found somewhere else for him when he was in trouble."

His dad spoke. "Peter, how could you know what was going on inside Molly's mind and heart?"

"I'm her fiancé, or at least I *was* her fiancé. I should have noticed something. I should be able to tell what she's feeling."

"Honey, you told me she hasn't spent time with you for months, that she has been so busy with school and other things that she never had time to go out with you or talk on the phone, even. You're not a mind reader," his mom added.

"But don't we express over 60% of what we're communicating with our body language, not with words?" Peter asked his family, all who knew the answer to his rhetorical question.

No one spoke, waiting for Peter to continue.

"I could tell she was upset; I guess I didn't know the right way to ask her what was wrong. I also knew she was avoiding me, but I didn't want to demand that she spend time with me. You know the verse, 'Love doesn't demand its own way.' I was trying to be loving, to wait…" He wept. "What do I do now?"

His dad broke the uneasy silence. "This is a time when I don't think you can wait it out. She's making major life decisions at a point in time when she doesn't seem to be thinking clearly."

Zoë spoke again. "Another thing I've noticed every time we've been around her is that she's losing weight. I don't think she's eating much at all."

Dan sighed, his psychology training kicking in. "When someone is traumatized, eating can be a problem. The 'Feed' of the Five F's. Either the person overeats, or undereats. In a weird psychological twist, when circumstances feel out of control, the person feels like he or she is in control by how he or she eats—or avoids eating. I'm not speaking specifically about Molly, just wondering out loud. Sometimes people will even binge eat, then purge…"

Kelly spoke. "My doctor calls the gut the emotional brain. She says any time anyone comes to her with gastrointestinal problems, she asks if something emotionally challenging is happening in that person's life." She paused, waiting, whispering her thoughts. *But, we shouldn't speculate about what might be going on. And we certainly don't want to gossip.*

Zoë interrupted, her strong, commanding voice bringing Kelly out of her reverie. "I don't think it's gossip if we're seeking to be part of the solution."

Kelly nodded. "Good point. All of us certainly want to be part of the solution, for both Peter and Molly's sakes. And for Kate, too." She turned to her husband, grasping his hand like a lifeline. "Could we all pray together, honey?"

The Johnsons stood next to each other, holding hands, forming a circle in Dan and Zoë's kitchen. Brandon prayed first. "God, thank You that You're with Molly right now. You know we love her—yet we know You love her more than we ever could. Please protect her. Please guide us in what, if anything, we need to do to help her."

Kelly added, "You know we love her like she's already our daughter. Help us. Please help Peter know what to do."

Peter finished for all of them, "God, thank You that You haven't failed us and that You never will. So we trust You, even though this feels worse than an appendectomy."

Dan laughed out loud. "How would you know how an appendectomy feels?" he asked his nephew. "You've never had one."

"It was the first painful thing that came to mind. But this is much, much worse."

Zoë's kitchen timer went off. "The blueberry French toast is done. Would it help to eat?"

CHAPTER THIRTEEN

Kate and Carlos were settled in their villa on the Maui coast, their honeymoon trip an incredible gift from his relatives who owned the property for their family to share.

Carlos' aunt and uncle had their property manager stock the vacation home with more than enough food for their entire week. Since their arrival, Carlos and Kate had been feasting on more than food, exploring a part of life neither of them had known before.

Their families had thought of anything they might need besides each other. In a beautiful silver tray on the dining table were gift cards for couples' massages, surf lessons, and even a luau with a six-course meal. In a basket on the kitchen table were gift cards for dinners at nearby restaurants, just in case they wanted to eat out.

Their first morning in Hawaii, they sampled fresh pineapple before taking a walk on the beach.

"Want to go surfing or paddle boarding later today?" Carlos asked as they watched the people already enjoying the ocean.

"Um, sure, either would be fun," Kate responded without her characteristic enthusiasm.

"Kate, what's wrong?" Carlos asked.

"I feel like nothing *should* be wrong. This place is perfect—we are right on the beach, your aunt Patty and uncle Jorge Mario gave us this incredible gift of their vacation home. And our other relatives gave us more gift cards than we could begin to use. It's the perfect honeymoon. Most importantly, I'm with you, the man I love. How can I be sad?"

"But your eyes are sad."

Kate began to weep. "You know me so well, Beloved. I can't believe you are my best friend and my husband. Everything is great—except I *am* sad about Molly. She has been my best friend since grade school. I don't want to lose her friendship, but I have. And I feel like it's all my fault."

"Did you change? Did you do anything to fuel her anger at you?"

"I married you. She told me not to marry you."

"And…"

"Well, you know that wasn't an option. I didn't mean to replace Molly with you as my best friend. I know I have room in my heart for both of you. But apparently she doesn't know that. I don't know what to do."

"When we get back to California, we'll start a "Win Back Molly" campaign." His smile reassured his bride. "We'll show her we love her every way we can. Remember when I tried to do that by giving her Guatemalan coffee?"

"I know. But she didn't get it."

"We'll try new tactics. She won't be able to resist our love." He smiled.

Kate picked up the fragrant lei her family placed around her neck before she and Carlos left for their honeymoon. Inhaling the sweet aroma of its fading white orchids, she wondered aloud, "See how these flowers are already turning brown? They're never going to look like they did when they were fresh. What if our friendship is like this—wilting, dead, beyond repair?"

Carlos gently held his own fading lei, its single strand of white orchids entwined with a braided ti leaf. "The flowers are beautiful, but they were dead from the moment they were cut. People are not flowers. I don't think your friendship with Molly is dead. Let's give it some time…"

She kissed him, intensely.

"I love it when you change the subject."

CHAPTER FOURTEEN

Arriving at O'Hare's international terminal, Molly checked her bag. The gate agent told her, "You're on the standby list. You should be OK, because there are still four first class seats left. But you don't have much time to clear security."

Molly made it to her gate just as her name was called. The agent handed her a ticket, and it was time to board. It helped that she didn't have time to think. *Just put one foot in front of the other and keep going.*

The flight attendant helped her settle into her first class berth, and Molly declined her offer of orange juice, accepting a bottle of chilled water instead. She noticed her flight attendant's name was Ingrid. Tall, elegant, with perfect skin and sleek black hair pulled into a chic knot at the nape of her neck, Ingrid looked like the quintessential world traveler.

Molly's seat was in an area that was blissfully compartmentalized, with well-defined separation from the other first-class passengers. After takeoff, Ingrid brought her pillows and a comforter, and helped her transform her seat into a bed. Molly immediately took two melatonin, put on her headphones, tuned to one of her Bach playlists and fell asleep, her body finally able to succumb to utter exhaustion.

The next thing Molly noticed was a gentle tap on her arm.

It took her a moment to remember where she was and another moment to realize it was the flight attendant speaking to her.

"Would you like breakfast? You missed dinner, and we'll be landing in two hours," the voice held kindness and genuine concern.

"Um, OK," Molly mumbled, smelling food and realizing her stomach was rumbling.

"Would you like coffee or hot tea?"

"Coffee would be great."

Ingrid brought Molly a pot of coffee, fresh cream and a warm washcloth to wipe off her hands and face.

The washcloth felt wonderful. She let herself savor its citrus fragrance and soft texture. Then, Ingrid was back, pouring steaming coffee into a mug.

Molly sipped slowly, hoping caffeine would enliven her dull mind.

In seconds, Ingrid returned with a basket of assorted pastries and a plate overflowing with scrambled eggs, bacon and a bowl of fresh fruit.

She picked at her food, feeling her stomach cramp with the dread of eating.

Ingrid came back. "Would you prefer something else? We also have oatmeal, or cold cereal, or…"

"No, this is fine," Molly said, pretending to eat. She covered the food with her linen napkin and closed her eyes, unwilling to face additional questions.

Ingrid silently removed the tray.

Molly looked at her watch, still on California time, and wondered what Peter was doing.

As the plane landed at Heathrow, she texted Jennifer. "Here, just landed."

Her phone lit up. "Can't wait to see you. I'm waiting just outside customs. Text if you don't see me as you exit."

* * *

Jennifer saw Molly before Molly noticed her. She ran to her sister, enveloping her in a bear hug. She felt Molly's body stiffen. "Oh, I forgot. You don't like hugs."

"Sorry. Let's try again." This time, Molly reached out to hug her sister back.

"Is that all the luggage you have?" Jenn asked, picking up Molly's backpack. "You travel like a flight attendant."

"I packed in about fifteen minutes for Chicago, and this is it," Molly said, pulling her roller bag behind her. "It will be interesting to see how much I forgot," she grimaced.

"We're about the same height, even though you're smaller than I am. Do you ever eat?" Jenn asked, only half joking. "Hey, I'm happy to loan you any clothes you need," Jenn told her, meaning it.

"Has it really been two years since we were last together?" Molly asked.

"And we weren't really 'together' then. Dad's funeral was one of the worst days of our lives," Jenn responded, guiding Molly toward the Tube station as they walked. "I got an Oyster Card for you already," Jenn told her, pressing something that looked like a credit card into her hand. "We just swipe these here, like this, and then we can enter."

Molly followed her sister's example, joining the throng pressing toward the underground entrance. "We call this the Tube," Jenn said, pointing toward the train. "We take the Piccadilly here and then change at Green Park to the Jubilee Line. Then we get off at Canary Wharf and take the DLR."

Molly smiled, her first smile of the day. "This sounds like a foreign language."

"Oh, trust me, it is."

When they exited the Tube at Canary Wharf, Jenn said, "Let's just have a bite to eat at Pret a Manger."

"Oh, you can eat. I'm not really hungry."

"You look like you need to eat, Mol. Have you looked in a mirror lately? You're really pale."

"All right, I'll try."

"Here, this soup is my favorite. Coconut chicken curry.

You'll love it."

Molly was surprised when the soup smelled so tantalizing that her stomach relaxed enough to eat a small bowl of it. "Thanks, Jenn. Food helps."

The rest of their trip to Jenn's new flat was via the DLR. When they exited in Greenwich, Jenn said, "Let me pull your roller bag. I'm definitely experienced at that!"

"OK, I can carry my backpack now." Molly reached to take it from her sister.

"Watch this," Jenn said, adeptly sliding the backpack over the roller bag's handle. "I've got it! It's less than a ten-minute walk from here," Jenn said, picking up the pace.

When they arrived at Jenn's building, Molly exclaimed, "You live here?"

"Absolutely. After traveling the world for the past ten years, I've finally found my favorite place. Right here on the River Thames. The area is called New Capital Quay."

The seven-story building was situated in a contemporary development near Dowells Street, close to the shops and restaurants of central Greenwich. As they entered, a concierge greeted them. "Hello, Jennifer."

"Hi, Adrian. My sister Molly will be visiting me for awhile."

"Lovely," he said. "Will there be anything you need?"

"We're good," she said.

He pushed the up button on the lift for them.

"This is gorgeous," Molly said, gazing around the expansive modern lobby. "You're renting?"

"No, I bought it. Closed two weeks ago." The lift doors closed, and Jennifer pressed the button for the seventh floor. "I was looking for a place that was secure, with a concierge, CCTV monitoring and, of course, it had to be cozy and comfortable. It was time for me to have a home. I've been staying in temporary places for far too long. Do you know I only had a hot bed when I started working for United and was based out of New York?"

"A hot bed?"

"A hot bed is a place for sleeping between flights, sort of like a pied-à-terre—'crash pad' is a more accurate way to describe it. Basically, a hot bed is a temporary place to stay, like a motel, only it costs far less than a motel because it is in a room shared with other frequent travelers, to save money. The main thing I didn't like about having a 'hot bed' was that other people slept in it when I wasn't using it. I thought it might work when I found out I could keep my own clean sheets in a cubby so I wouldn't have to sleep on someone else's dirty sheets. But sometimes I arrived at the location after a really late flight only to find there wasn't even a bunk bed left. Sometimes I had to sleep on a sofa, other times in a chair. Finally, when someone stole my sheets, I switched to a cold bed."

"A cold bed?"

"A cold bed is a bed set aside for only one person. It costs more than a hot bed, but it was definitely worth it to have my own bed. It is just a bed, though, in a very tiny room with absolutely no amenities. It never felt like home to me."

"I'm glad you have a home now." Entering the spacious flat, Molly exclaimed again, "This is really yours?"

With a flourish, Jenn said, "Welcome to the reception room, what we Brits call our living room!"

Molly admired the room's exquisite furnishings. "Your leather furniture seems perfect, something warm and comfortable for you to come home to! And I love your Oriental rug. The colors are so rich...oh, here's your kitchen. It's just the right size."

"The kitchen is where I need your help," Jenn said, pointing to a stack of boxes, many with IKEA delivery labels on their sides. "I have only the bare necessities in the cupboards. Everything else needs to find a home."

Molly studied the pile. "You have IKEA here? My favorite."

"I make it a point to visit IKEA in every country I can! Do you want to get settled—or come see the master suite?"

"A shower would feel good after flying all night, but show

me your room first. Wow, Jenn! It looks like you've lived here for years. Everything is so elegant and put together. And I love your canopy bed!"

"No more hot or cold beds for me!" Jenn laughed.

"But how did you get all of this heavy furniture up here?"

"Oh, I had help, lots of help."

"You know someone in London already?"

"You're going to be surprised when I tell you. But I'm going to let you get settled before we have that conversation. First, come look out on the balcony. Isn't this an incredible view of the Thames?"

"Your balcony overlooks the river! You have water on three sides! This view is amazing." They stepped back inside.

"And your wood floors are gorgeous!"

"Your room has an en suite, too," Jenn showed her. "And I also have a third bedroom, which I currently use as a den."

"I guess flight attendants get paid more than I imagined," Molly said, incredulous.

"Uh, not really. Do you not know about our trust fund?"

"Huh?"

"Why don't you take a shower so we can sit down and have a nice long conversation? I think there are a few things I need to tell you.

CHAPTER FIFTEEN

Peter staggered into the bathroom to splash his face with cool water, hoping it would help him wake up. It didn't. He looked at his phone. Seven AM. *I probably slept a total of three hours. I can't keep this up.* He looked at his phone again, just to be sure. *No calls. Where is she?*

He picked up the workout clothes he'd thrown on the floor the day prior, quickly putting them on for another day without caring how he looked. He found flip-flops by his front door, then made the quick walk across his tiny front yard to Dan and Zoë's back door, tapping his trademark three times before entering. His aunt was already in the kitchen, frying bacon. Dan was preparing to make poached eggs. "One egg or two, Peter?"

"I'm not hungry."

"You need to eat. What sounds good?"

"Finding Molly."

"We're going to talk about that today—after breakfast." Dan squeezed Peter's shoulder lightly, smiling reassuringly. "So what do you want to eat?"

"If I must, I'll have one egg, medium." Succumbing to the tantalizing smell of bacon, he added, "Maybe I am hungry, after all."

"One poached egg, medium, coming right up," Dan grinned. "Glad you changed your mind. Trust me, you'll thank me later."

"If you have a way for me to reach Molly, I'll definitely thank you."

His dad walked into the kitchen. "Did Dan tell you our idea?"

"You have an idea?" Like a drowning man, he grasped his dad's arm.

"After breakfast." His uncle interrupted. "We'll all think better when our blood sugar is up."

"Then let's eat fast."

"It's almost ready," Zoë said, walking over to give her nephew a quick hug.

"OK," Peter said listlessly. Needing something to occupy his mind, he walked into the dining room to help his mom set the table. "Mom, am I crazy?" he asked, his voice intense. "I don't think I can function without Molly. Do I love her too much? Am I too dependent on her?" He set plates next to his mother's carefully placed silverware and napkins. After years of practice, they worked comfortably together.

She paused, thinking, praying for the right words. "Son, you've mentioned several times that you've barely seen Molly during the last semester. I think you've functioned just fine. But you knew you were engaged then, and you were willing to wait while you both focused on school."

His eyes were bleak. "I *thought* she was focusing on school, but what if she never loved me? How could she just leave town without even talking with me if she actually loves me?"

"Peter, really? Don't look so hopeless," his mom teased, trying in vain to lift his mood. "Have you noticed the way she looks at you? She loves you."

He moaned, gripping the back of a chair like a life preserver, his eyes downcast. "Well, she's not looking at me now…"

Kelly stopped setting the table to make eye contact with her only son, usually the most upbeat of her five children.

"Peter, I've never seen you like this. Please remember you're not alone. Have you asked the Lord what to do next?" She paused, giving him time to think.

He let go of the chair, mumbling, looking at her at last. "Maybe there's nothing I *can* do." He shrugged. "But it's probably a good idea to pray."

His mom's eyes mirrored his concern. "Want to pray with everyone after breakfast?"

He nodded, mute.

Still trying to offer hope, Kelly continued, "The four of us stayed up last night talking about the, um, situation."

"The four of you, as in you and Dad and my aunt and uncle? Where are the girls?" Peter turned abruptly toward the living room, suddenly realizing he hadn't seen his younger sisters since the wedding. "Do Sarah, Mary and Grace know about this?"

"No, they went home early yesterday morning, right before Zoë came to look for you. Sorry they couldn't stick around to talk with you before they left. Mary and Grace have sports camps all week. And Sarah is staying with them while we're here. She decided not to take any classes this summer."

He sighed. "Well, at least they don't have to go through this nightmare."

"We're a family, so we called to let them know what's happening. They're praying for you and for Molly. Grace told us adamantly, 'There's no way Molly is leaving this family! We love her too, too much!' She said she wasn't going to eat all day today so she could focus on praying instead."

Peter took a deep breath to calm his emotions. His voice choked up. "Grace loves food. That's a huge sacrifice for her." It was a family joke that Grace could eat more than either her dad or her brother. He smiled faintly, thinking of his adorable, earnest little sister, then changed subjects when he recalled his mom's other comment. "You said all four of you stayed up last night talking. What did you come up with?"

Before Kelly could answer, Zoë walked into the dining

room, followed by Brandon balancing a huge tray loaded with bacon, fruit salad, and a pan of cinnamon rolls. Dan came next, carrying a plate of poached eggs, each marked with a colored toothpick to indicate the type of egg ordered.

"Let's eat!" Zoë's cheery voice contradicted her somber expression.

For several minutes, the dining room was filled with the sound of people sitting down, filling plates, preparing to eat. An uneasy silence infiltrated the room.

Dan spoke, breaking the tension. "Brandon, would you pray for our meal and our morning?"

Brandon nodded, then began. "Lord, we're thankful we can bear each other's burdens. We're grateful for Kate and Carlos and their new life together. Help them enjoy learning how to live as husband and wife. And protect Peter and Molly. Please bring Molly back to us. You know we've loved her since she was a little girl…we just don't know what is going on in her mind to make her think she needs to run away. Please help her come back to us…if it's Your will. But, how can it not be Your will? I don't know…" And with that, Brandon Johnson broke down, his shoulders heaving.

"Dad, are you OK?" Peter had never seen his dad sob before.

"Son, I'm sorry…I should be the one who's strong for you."

Dan waited for the tears to stop before he spoke, his quiet voice carrying authority and certainty. "I think this is one of those times when we can act in faith and trust God to stop us if we're making a mistake. If Molly is believing lies about herself or any of us, we need to lovingly show her the truth. Real faith walks, not just talks."

Zoë added, "So, we were up late, talking and praying…"

"I might as well have stayed here with you. I hardly slept all night."

"It was good you weren't here, Son. It took us a long time to reach this conclusion, and it was only after we prayed for two hours solid," his dad said. "Now we want your thoughts about the idea."

"OK, so what *is* the idea?" Peter's voice conveyed more than a hint of impatience.

"We want to fly you to London to talk with Molly and see if she'll come home."

He exhaled, loudly. "Tickets would cost a fortune, especially without advance purchase."

"I have enough frequent flyer miles to get you a round-trip ticket—and to get Molly a one-way ticket back," his dad said. "We've already checked LAX to London flights online."

"Wow."

"Are you willing to go?"

"Yes, of course! The sooner, the better! My summer internship doesn't begin for two weeks." His laugh was hollow. "I thought a two-week vacation after Kate's wedding would give me time with Molly."

"You just didn't know *where* you'd be spending time with her," his dad said, breaking into a smile. "Do you want to fly over this evening? You'd get to London when it's morning there. You could sleep on the flight."

"Mom said we were going to pray together. Can we do that before we decide?"

"Absolutely!" Brandon said, reaching to hold hands with his son, seated on his right, and his wife, on his left. After they all clasped hands, the family took turns praying.

Peter began, "Lord, forgive me for throwing a pity party for myself," he prayed, punctuating his words with tears. "I know You're good. I know You'll never fail. But I forgot it when," he paused, floundering.

Brandon continued, "Father God, forgive me, too. I forgot Your goodness when I thought we lost Molly forever. Help all of us trust You with her decision. Help her trust You, too," he added, his face illumined with nascent hope.

Dan prayed, simply. "Lord, our hope is in You."

Kelly added, "Yes, in You. Thank You, Father, that even though Molly is missing from us, she's not far from You. Thank You that You're right there with her, even now."

Zoë prayed, "Jesus, we don't even know what to say or how to pray. We trust You to help us, and to show Molly Your love. Help Peter, too. Give him Your wisdom and hope."

The room was quiet. In unison, everyone turned, looking expectantly to Peter.

"Well, what do you think?" Dan asked.

"I like the idea," Peter said quietly, tentatively. "But, even if I can get on a flight tonight, how will I find Molly when I get to London? Her phone doesn't likely have an international plan."

"You could call her sister," Zoë suggested.

"That could be a problem, since I don't have Jennifer's number."

"I have it," Zoë said, surprising everyone. "When their dad committed suicide I got all of her family's numbers to keep on hand, just in case another emergency occurred sometime."

"What if Jennifer doesn't have the same number any more?" Peter wasn't feeling optimistic.

"We can at least try," Zoë said, picking up her phone.

"Wait, what time is it there?" Peter stalled, looking as anxious as he felt.

"Hello, is this Jennifer Montgomery?" Zoë beamed, triumphant.

"Yes, who is this?"

"Zoë Johnson. I'm a friend of Molly's, and I'm also Peter's aunt. Molly gave me your number some time ago."

"I imagine you want to talk with Molly, but she's in the shower."

"Actually, Peter would like to speak with you," she said, holding the phone out to him.

"Sure." She paused, waiting.

Hesitating, he said, "Hello, Jenn? Sorry it's been such a long time…"

"I think you were in grade school the last time we spoke, Peter," Jenn chuckled. "But, you're not calling to talk with me, are you? I think I know why you're calling."

"Maybe not. I'm wondering if it's OK with you if I fly to London tonight? I really need to talk with Molly."

"Could you wait a few days? She just got here, and I need some time with her. We haven't been together since our dad died. But I totally understand your need to talk with her. Do you want her to call you back?"

"I…uh, I don't know. What do you think?"

"Maybe it would be good to wait until she has some rest. OK?"

"Sure, I understand. When could I come?"

"Let's see. It's already Monday afternoon here. We're eight hours ahead of you, by the way. How about Thursday? That's usually a good day to travel. You would leave California Thursday night and arrive here Friday. You can stay at my place when you come; I have plenty of room. What's your email? I'll send directions for what Tube to take; you'll also need to take the DLR."

"Um, OK. Will your directions tell me what the DLR is?"

"Oh, sorry. It's the acronym for Docklands Light Railway, the metro system that comes into Greenwich, the part of London where I live. You can take the Tube—you'll see the red and blue sign that says 'London Underground'—from Heathrow to Canary Wharf and pick up the DLR to Cutty Sark. I'll email you directions."

"And I'll email you my itinerary." Tentative, he asked, "Do you mind if I surprise Molly?"

Jenn's voice was upbeat. "Actually, I think surprising her is the only way to go. I don't want her to leave here and travel to another part of the world." She laughed lightly.

Peter's fear tumbled into words. "You don't think she'd do that, do you?"

"No, Peter, I was teasing you. I think she wants to see you, but right now she wouldn't be able to *say* she wants to see you. That's why a surprise could be a good thing."

He let himself exhale. "OK."

"You should be able to go to your phone provider and get

an international text plan added for thirty days. It doesn't cost much, and it would be worth it, because you and I can coordinate your arrival here so we know exactly where to connect, and when."

"I don't want to do anything behind Molly's back."

"Trust me, we're *not* deceiving her. We're teaming up to help her through a dark time. She has had more than enough of those already."

"As I understand it, you both have."

"Yes, but Molly had it far worse than I ever did." She paused.

Peter heard the sound of a door closing.

"OK, I need to go," she said, her voice clipped but friendly. "Do keep me updated."

Peter sighed when he realized how close Molly was just then. She had to have been right next to Jennifer when she said goodbye. *At least I know my love is safely in London.*

He turned to his family, ebullient. "I can't go to Molly until Thursday." He paused, observing his family's evolving expressions of relief, joy, and hope. "But I can go!"

* * *

Molly, drying her hair with a large Turkish towel, didn't ask who was on the phone. She never could have imagined Peter calling her sister.

Jenn quietly folded a small piece of paper and put it into her jeans pocket, then turned to Molly. "Now that you've showered, want to go do something fun? There are some great little restaurants near here."

"I'm not too hungry, but a walk would be nice." She removed the towel. "OK if I just pull my hair into a ponytail? I don't feel much like fixing it."

"That's great," Jenn responded, returning to her question. "Feel like getting something to eat? You only had soup when we stopped en route to my flat."

"I don't eat much."

"I can tell. You got like this when you were younger. Every time you were upset, you quit eating."

Molly didn't comment. Instead, she went back to the guest room to quickly dress in jeans and a T-shirt. "Ready!"

They left Jenn's flat and walked toward the quay. "This look OK?" Jenn asked, pointing toward a restaurant on the water.

Molly read the sign. "The Sail Loft. Sure, looks perfect."

As soon as they were seated, Jenn resumed her gentle probing. "Do you feel like you can eat now?"

"I'll try," Molly grimaced. "But I'm not used to someone bugging me about food."

"I didn't mean to bug you," Jenn apologized, clearly meaning it.

"No worries," Molly said, looking down. "I guess that's your big sister privilege." She paused, adding, "I usually order a salad." Unaware of what she was doing, she folded her napkin into a fan, then unfolded it and nervously twisted it into a knot. Staring out the window toward the River Thames but not seeing it, she responded to Jenn's earlier observation. "I don't remember much about childhood."

They were briefly interrupted by a waiter, who efficiently took their order and left. Unconsciously avoiding being overheard, both sisters leaned toward each other, speaking just above a whisper.

"You really don't remember childhood? Some things I remember all too well," Jenn said, wiping a tear from her eye. "Like on your sixth birthday when our parents wouldn't believe me when I tried to tell them about Jeremy molesting you. Instead of listening to me—or trying to protect you, they *punished* you by taking all your birthday presents away."

Molly felt like someone had punched her in the gut. "I forgot about that. That really happened? I mean, I do remember Jeremy—hurting me from the time I was four. I remember hiding from him in the trees behind our house."

"I didn't know you did that."

Molly continued, not hearing her sister's response. "I

85

don't remember much about any of my birthdays. Sometimes I get a little sliver of a memory, sort of like seeing only part of a snapshot, with most of the picture cut off. I *think* I remember we went out for pizza with the neighbors to celebrate my sixth birthday, but I can't quite picture anything that happened before or after we got home."

"Really? That's astonishing." Jenn groaned. "Let's back up. Do you remember me walking into your bedroom first thing that morning? I came in to say 'happy sixth birthday' before school, but you seemed upset and wouldn't tell me what was wrong. You were still in bed, desperately trying to pull the covers up over your body. That's when I noticed you had bruises all over your arms. Shaped like fingerprints. And you told me you got them by falling out of bed. You were so adamant about it that I almost believed you—until I tripped over Jeremy's belt when I was leaving your room."

Molly's hands were trembling. Jenn reached to touch her, but Molly turned away, numb.

Not knowing what else to do, Jenn continued. "So I kept begging you to talk, and you finally told me what happened. You were terrified and said Jeremy would kill me if I told Mom and Dad. Before I could talk with them, though, he'd called them at work and told them we were making up lies about him. They believed him instead of us," Jennifer wept.

Molly's emotions took her far away, to a place where she couldn't feel, couldn't talk, couldn't remember.

"Are you with me, Mol?" Jenn asked, concerned by her sister's detached expression.

"What?" Molly slowly forced herself to grasp where she was. "I'm sorry, Jenn. Sometimes I sort of check out."

Jenn, sniffling, paused to wipe a tear from her cheek. "You really don't remember that horrible birthday?"

"Listening to you describe it feels kind of like discovering pictures to illustrate a long-forgotten nightmare." Molly stared out the window, unseeing. "I think I remember all of us having dinner at a pizza restaurant—Giuseppe's, where we always went for birthdays. And our neighbors were there. The

Wendhams. Did you and I ride home with Dad that night? And Jeremy rode home with Mom?"

"Yes, we rode home with Dad, and he was utterly silent all the way there. It felt creepy, like something really bad was about to happen. When we got home, Mom was so furious that she threw all of your birthday presents into big black garbage bags and put them in the garage."

Molly closed her eyes, trying to force herself to remember. "I really can't recall that part. I think I hid in the basement right after we got home. I could hear Mom yelling at you in the kitchen. It was scary."

"I was scared for *you*, Mol. Do you remember our parents coming down to the basement? I stood at the top of the stairs and listened to Mom scream at you. I still remember *every* raging word. She shrieked, 'Look at me when I talk to you! I hope you'll always remember how you ruined your sixth birthday by lying. Start treating your brother with respect. And don't repeat any more of your hideous lies.'" Then she made you go to your room.

Molly stared at the floor, her voice barely audible. "All I remember is Dad standing in the basement, looking at a magazine from the recycling bin while Mom was yelling something. I kept looking at him, hoping he would make her stop. But he didn't do anything; he didn't say anything."

"Typical. Do you remember Nana Montgomery calling to talk with you after Mom sent you upstairs?"

Molly's brows furrowed in concentration. "Was I in my room then? I kind of remember Nana's call—but she always calls on our birthdays. I don't remember what she said."

"I stood at my bedroom door, watching our parents make you talk on the phone and pretend everything was fine. Your eyes were so solemn, so sad. You didn't say one word about your presents being taken away. Oh, you did say one really *funny* thing."

"Funny?" Molly's look was blank.

"Well, not 'funny' in the sense of 'humorous.' In retrospect, it shows how quickly you think. I heard you say,

'Jeremy gave me some colors.' I don't think he actually gave you *anything* for your birthday, but I'm sure Nana asked what he gave you, and you had to think of something, since Dad and Mom were standing there listening, so you thought of the colored bruises on your arms. Thus, he gave you 'colors.' Your performance was Oscar-worthy."

Molly sighed. "That's really sad."

"Yeah." Jenn's sigh echoed Molly's. "I think Mom gave you back the tea set from Nana the next day. She was probably worried that Nana would come and want to have a tea party with you, using your new tea set." Jennifer's laugh was bitter. "I never could figure out what happened to the rest of your birthday presents."

"Oh, here's our food," Molly said, nodding her thanks to the waiter. When he left, she turned back to her sister. "It's OK, Jenn. Really."

"No, it's not! I hate it that you were hurt." She picked up a napkin to dry her tears.

Molly thought, *That was nothing compared to what happened in high school.* She had to change the subject. "Hey, Jenn, I thought you were going to tell me how you got your furniture moved into your apartment."

"Remember Analese, the one who cleaned our house in Illinois when we were kids?"

"Of course I do! She drove that cool little sports car, a Fiat X 1/9. She also was the one who convinced Mom to let me go to California to see the Johnsons—after Kate and her family moved there. Analese even traveled with me. That's probably why Mom let me go. We had the most incredible time together."

"Yes. Well, Analese lives in London now, in Greenwich, to be exact."

"No way!"

"And Analese had another life we didn't know anything about."

"Another life? What do you mean?"

"We thought she was a cleaning lady, but she wasn't, not

really."

"Come on, Jenn. She *was* a cleaning lady. She cleaned our family's house every week."

"Yes, but she did that for her amusement, sort of her own little sociological experiment."

"I'm not following."

"She cleaned houses for fun, usually accepting only one or two 'clients' each year. She did it more to observe people and pray for their needs than to make a living. She inherited a fortune from her parents. They died in a car crash when she was ten."

"I remember her telling me her parents died. But not how—or that she inherited anything."

"At the time she was cleaning houses, she also owned a rather impressive financial firm, Harper Enterprises."

"Wait. I tried to call her once; it was after I'd finished high school. And Analese didn't answer the number I called; someone else answered and said what you just said, 'Harper Enterprises.' The person who answered told me Analese was in Russia for six months, doing some kind of volunteer work. I'd forgotten all about trying to reach her then. I totally lost touch with Analese after that."

"Did you know she used to work as a stockbroker and that she has a Harvard MBA?"

"No, I didn't have a clue. You're speaking in past tense. Did she sell her company?"

"Her priorities have changed."

"Well, I miss her. She taught me so much."

"She wants us to come for dinner while you're here, but they're out of town now. They asked if Saturday night would work. She's married, to a man she knew when she was an undergrad at Oxford."

A smile slowly dawned, lighting Molly's face. "We get to see Analese? That's incredible! And she went to Oxford *and* Harvard?" Her words tumbled over one another. "How in the world did you find her in London? And she's married?"

"Her husband Sam works at Foxtons, the real estate

company I contacted when I was ready to purchase a flat here in Greenwich. He told me his wife is American; I told him I was originally from Illinois. He told me his wife lived there for a number of years. One thing led to another—and that's how Analese and I reconnected."

"Amazing! And they helped you get your furniture moved?"

"Not only that; they helped me find every piece of furniture I now own. They have an incredible network of friends, business associates, you name it." Jenn paid their check, then became uncharacteristically quiet. "Want to sit by the water?" They walked to a nearby bench and sat next to each other, taking time to simply notice boats of various shapes and sizes gliding past them on the River Thames.

"Being with you is incredible—it's just what I needed," Molly said. When Jenn didn't respond, she asked, "Are you OK?"

Jenn's head was in her hands; her shoulders heaved with emotion. Though it was only seconds, it felt like minutes before she finally looked up.

"I need to apologize to you, Molly, but I don't even know how to begin. I wanted you to come here so I could try to tell you 'I'm sorry' in person. I was a total jerk to you when Dad died."

Molly paused, trying to understand why her usually calm sister was so agitated. "You weren't a jerk."

"Yes, I was. You lovingly talked about the most important thing in your life, your relationship with God, and I mocked you, criticized you, talked behind your back…"

"I didn't take it personally."

"I've changed my viewpoint since then," Jenn said, meaning it.

"How so?"

Jenn stared at the water, speaking slowly, her voice distant. "I've traveled the world for years—first, trying to find myself through short and long-term relationships with men, visiting different cultures, staying in youth hostels, getting odd jobs at resorts and restaurants to survive—then, trying to succeed in my career as a flight attendant. All of that left me feeling empty. There weren't enough men in the world or countries to explore to fill the void in my soul."

"What changed your perspective?" Molly looked confused.

Jenn, her face animated, turned to face Molly. "God. One day I decided to kill myself. It was about a year ago, on the anniversary of our dad's suicide, to be exact. I had decided there was absolutely nothing left to live for. I was in Switzerland and planned to jump off a cliff. I stood there, waiting until there were no people around to stop me."

Molly gasped. "No! What stopped you from jumping?"

"Molly, I am not making this up—God literally *spoke* to me—not with a voice anyone else could hear, but in my mind and heart." Her smiled broadened. "Jesus said, 'I have loved you with an everlasting love. Come to Me and find rest. I am the way and the truth and the life. You can come to God the Father, through Me. Believe in Me and be saved.' And that's exactly what I did."

Molly nodded, her smile tentative.

"That's all there is to it. I believed in Jesus as my Savior." Excited, Jenn continued talking, oblivious to Molly's misgivings. "After that, I began devouring the Bible, like it was God's love letter written just for me. I wanted to fall in love with Jesus like you did. I've been waiting to tell you this in person, Mol. I want you to know that I heard everything you said after Dad's funeral. I just acted like your new relationship with God didn't mean anything to me. What you said then about loving God planted a seed in me that kept growing."

Molly stared, unseeing, at the river. "I'm afraid my love is flickering, like a candle being slowly extinguished by the winds of life," Molly said, bleakly.

"Are you reading the Bible every day?"

Molly hung her head. "Not for a long time."

"Praying?"

"Not at all."

"Why did you stop?"

Molly paused, thinking, wondering. "It was last year, around Christmas. I went to Illinois instead of going skiing with Peter and Kate and their family. They invited me, but I just didn't want to go, because Carlos was going. And I was jealous of how he consumed Kate's time and attention."

Jenn nodded.

"When I went to Chicago, Mom didn't have time for me, even though she pretty much demanded I come 'home' for Christmas. Ha. We both know her *house* will never feel like *home*." Molly's laugh was a crater. "Then Mercedes asked me to spend the holiday with her. When I was with her, it felt like Mercedes was the first person who understood me. She listened to me explain how frustrated I was with Kate and her family. And she helped me see I couldn't trust *any* of the Johnsons—especially Kate or Peter."

Jenn's voice had an edge. "Mercedes showed you who *not* to trust? And when did 'trustworthy' ever describe her?"

"Touché. I guess I had relational amnesia." Molly sighed. "During that time, I also stopped trusting God, because every person I chose to distrust was somehow associated with Him."

"So you basically shifted your trust from God to Mercedes?" Jenn was the master of pointed questions.

"Ugh," Molly's eyes narrowed. "That's one way of looking at it, I suppose. I hate to think that's what I did, but—well, you're right."

"Sad to hear it."

"It gets worse, Jenn. After Christmas break, when I went back to school, I started lying to everyone in California. When Peter wanted me to visit his family over spring break, I told him I couldn't go because I had a project to do. Mercedes thought that lie was wonderful, and she rewarded me by inviting me to meet her at a spa near LA that week instead. It was a gruesome experience."

"Gruesome, how?"

"Oh, this is a long story. Are you sure you want to hear

it?"

"We have all night. You're still on Pacific Time; I'm a flight attendant, so my biological clock is usually confused about what time it is. Let's walk back to the flat…"

* * *

They changed into pajamas before sitting down in the living room, Molly on the leather sofa and Jenn on the oversized leather chair adjacent to it.

Jenn poured a cup of tea for each of them. "Lemon?"

"No, my story has plenty of sour parts without adding lemon." Molly smiled at her weak attempt at humor, and then slowly took a sip of tea. "This sad story goes back to high school, before dad died. Mercedes kept trying to befriend me then, basically because she wanted me to become a model. I think she hated it that her own modeling career had tanked, and it seemed like she was trying to live vicariously through me. I didn't want to model, but she wouldn't stop badgering me about it. And Dad wanted me to get a job, too. Finally, just to stop them from haranguing me, I said I'd try it. She eventually took me to the agency she loved most, the one downtown. Years prior, she'd dated the original owner, Anson Greeb, Senior. When he died, his son took over running the agency. Anson Greeb, Junior." Molly shuddered involuntarily.

"What's wrong?"

"I'm not sure I can talk about this."

"You don't have to."

"No, I want to tell you. I need your perspective." She took a deep breath, then slowly continued. "So, Anson, Junior, kept reaching out to me, taking me under his 'wing,' so to speak. And, trust me, it was *not* an angel's wing. At first, he seemed really caring, more caring than anyone I knew. He was always complimenting me on what a great job I was doing, how photogenic I was. At that time, I was confused about everything and everyone. First, Dad had that affair with his colleague Beth, then he married Mercedes—and Mom was a train wreck when it came to men. I'm not blaming this on them, though."

"They weren't there for you."

Molly, pensive, slowly sipped her tea. "I made some really stupid choices the summer before my senior year. Dad and Mercedes went out of the country on a long vacation—I think they went to Spain, but that part isn't relevant to the story. What is relevant is that Mercedes arranged for me to stay at their huge apartment alone, during the entire time they were gone."

"I'm not surprised Mom went for that. It gave her freedom to do anything she wanted."

"Actually, I don't think Mom even knew I was there alone." She sighed. "Even before Dad and Mercedes left on their trip, Anson started spending time with me. For the first few weeks, it seemed thrilling to spend time with someone older and more sophisticated than me, someone who wanted to hang out with me. I even thought he liked *me*."

"I don't like where this is going," Jenn said.

"It gets worse. After Dad and Mercedes left me alone, the first time Anson actually came into the apartment, he wanted to express his 'love' for me in bed. He said he had 'protection,' and I thought that was enough. By the time Dad and Mercedes got back from their trip, I was having morning sickness. I didn't know I was pregnant, but Mercedes immediately figured it out." She smiled ruefully; twisting a pillow's tassel so forcefully that it came off. "Oh, I'm sorry, Jenn! I didn't notice what I was doing. I'll get you another pillow."

"No worries, Mol. I can mend it."

"You know how to sew?"

"I've learned a few things in all my travels," Jenn shrugged. "You were saying?"

"I guess my continual nausea gave my *condition* away. Anyway, without understanding what I was doing, I went with Mercedes to have the abortion she scheduled. Actually, she paid cash for it and left me there to go through it alone. And Anson was totally out of the picture after that. He didn't care what I was going through at all. I quit modeling then and haven't gone back. My senior year of high school was a total blur. I moved back with Mom. She never noticed anything was wrong."

"Of course she didn't. Oh, Mol, I'm so sorry I was gone then." Jenn encircled her sister in a hug. Abruptly, she stood up. "Something just occurred to me, Molly," she said, agitated. You weren't even 18 yet that summer. Your 18th birthday wasn't until October 12th of your senior year, right?"

"Yes." Molly's eyes seemed hidden by a cloud of confusion.

"In some states, what Anson did would be *criminal* behavior. I don't know the laws in Illinois, but in my opinion, at least, he should have gone to jail for molesting you."

"But I think I said 'yes.'" Molly looked as puzzled as she felt.

"Molly, in many states, someone under age 18 cannot even legally give consent." She grabbed her laptop, then sat down, searching for Illinois' age of consent. "OK, it looks like it's age seventeen in Illinois. Still, Mol, what he did wasn't *right* on any level. He took advantage of you. I've been learning about this, because many of us flight attendants are being trained how to be alert for human traffickers—and ways we can find help for victims." She wept. "I didn't know this happened to you, Mol. I am so sorry I wasn't there for you then."

The pain stored in Molly's soul poured out like lava, hot tears flowing down her cheeks, unchecked. "You couldn't have known. And I wouldn't have known how to tell you," she moaned. "I numbed out everything—and stopped trusting anyone—after that happened."

"I can see why." Jenn stood and walked to the kitchen. "More tea?"

Molly stood next to her, adding fresh boiling water to her cup, ready to reuse her tea bag.

"I can afford to give my sister a fresh tea bag," Jenn teased. "Earl Grey again?"

Molly nodded. "I didn't talk with Mercedes again until our Dad's funeral. Do you remember that he killed himself just before my college graduation?"

"I'm sorry, Molly. I was so focused on finding *myself* at that time that I totally lost sight of anything going on in your life—including your college graduation. Maybe because I opted out of college after the first two years, I didn't want to celebrate your accomplishment. I don't know…I was so selfish then."

"Well, do you remember me leaving everyone at Mom's house and going for brunch with Mercedes the morning after Dad's funeral? At brunch, she brought up the abortion, telling me how great it was I didn't have a kid to lug around like our dad's former mistress, Beth, did."

"I am so sorry," Jenn said, twisting a strand of her hair. "I don't remember your brunch; what I do remember is that was the time when I was being so cruel to you. Please forgive me for not being there for you when you needed my encouragement. You were trying to lead what was left of our family into something positive—and no one wanted anything to do with you or your spiritual message."

Molly smiled at her sister. "You used to twirl your hair like that when you were growing up, Jenn, especially when you were upset. Please don't be upset about what happened then. God gave me comfort by having Beth be at our dad's funeral. She provided the one bright spot of the day. I think Mercedes invited her to hurt us, but it ended up helping me."

"What do you mean?"

"Beth and her husband—someone she'd known in college, who married her even though she had our dad's child—were kind to me. Before the funeral, Beth told me being pregnant with our dad's daughter was what it took to make her see her need for God. She said she grew up in a Christian home and rebelled against everything her parents taught her. She was sad that our parents' marriage failed, and she thought it was because of her."

"We both know *that* wasn't her fault," Jenn interjected.

"I wish I'd stayed in touch with her," Molly mused. "Do you know she named her daughter 'Renae' because it means 'reborn'?"

"I didn't know that," Jenn said. "Maybe we can reconnect with her sometime. But, Molly, I want to say again how sorry I am that I wasn't there for you then and haven't been there for you since. Will you forgive me?" Jenn wept.

"Of course I forgive you, Jenn. I love you. I've missed you so much." Molly wept with her, surprised by her tears. "I almost never cry. You are helping me in ways I don't even understand."

"I want to be here for you now. I am glad *we* are reconnecting."

"I'm sorry I ever let myself reconnect with Mercedes; I feel like I've been duped by her—again! After that brunch the day after Dad's funeral, I carefully avoided her, until last Christmas. Then, it was like I had amnesia about *everything* bad that had ever happened with her. I was desperate for family, and I thought I should be nice to her. She is our stepmother, after all. It backfired big time. When we went to the spa over spring break, guess who else was there? Anson Greeb. The worst part about that is that Mercedes knew he was going to be there. I think the whole spa trip was Mercedes' Machiavellian plan to get us back together."

"At least her plan didn't work that time…"

"Right. Because when I saw him, I packed everything, pronto, and drove back to college. I felt utterly betrayed by her—again."

"Sounds like what the Bible describes as a spiritual attack. Do you know Ephesians chapter six? It describes how our enemy, Satan, tries to get us to focus on anything—or anyone—besides God."

"Is that the passage about spiritual armor?" Molly asked.

"Yes, in verse 12, it says we need to wear the armor of God because we don't wrestle with flesh and blood but with powers, principalities, spiritual forces of darkness. There's specific spiritual armor to protect our mind, our heart—even our feet, so we can keep going and doing what God wants us to do! Besides the defensive armor, we have offensive armor—God's Word, the truth."

"You're new to the Christian faith, Jenn. How do you know so much about the Bible already?"

"Ever since God literally saved my life, I can't get enough of it! Now I read the Bible every day, not as much to learn things but to fall more deeply in love with God. And, the more I understand the truth, the more freedom I experience."

"Do you think that's why I started lying so often? Because I wasn't walking in the truth any more?"

"There's a verse in the Bible that says the truth sets you free."

Molly sighed. "I have definitely *not* been living as someone who is free! Instead, I've made a total mess of everything good in my life! I'm not sure *anything* can be redeemed."

"I wouldn't be so sure about that," Jenn responded, her teasing grin unexpectedly reminding Molly of Peter.

"Come on, Jenn," Molly said, tapping the floor nervously with her foot. "How can *you* be so sure? I've broken my engagement, alienated my best friend and dropped out of grad school—all in a few short days."

"Our God is a redeemer and a restorer." Jenn smiled earnestly. "See what He's doing for us? He's restoring our relationship, isn't He? That's a good start."

"You're not only my big sister, but now you're also my spiritual mentor!" Molly laughed. It felt good.

"Hey, it's about time I resumed my role as your big—as in older, wiser—sister," Jenn laughed with her. Then she became serious again. "So much has happened to both of us in the years we've been apart. I hope we never let anything come between us again."

A comfortable silence filled the room. Molly sighed. When she spoke, her voice was barely above a whisper. "It has been easy for us to bridge the years and the space between us. I'm still not sure there's any way I can restore the relationships I've destroyed in California."

"Molly, do you really think you could have *destroyed* the love the Johnson family has freely given you ever since you were a little girl?"

"You have no idea how rude I was."

"OK, help me understand."

"Here's one of many examples," Molly said, looking at the floor. "Kate was obviously excited when she told me about falling in love with Carlos. Instead of being happy for her, I lashed out at her, criticizing his entire Guatemalan culture, even though I'd never even met a Guatemalan. I condemned their relationship and said, 'Don't you know better than to trust him? Latinos are known womanizers. He's probably just trying to get you into bed!'"

"I see what you mean. You were sounding more like our mother than yourself."

"Ouch. That hurts to hear, but you're right. I can't blame it on Mom, though, because I made every lousy choice all by myself. I'm the one who delivered an ongoing barrage of cruel words to my best friend. From the moment I decided to believe lies about others, and myself, I forgot about the amazing gift of new life in Christ. I lived in bondage rather than freedom."

"It is never too late to tell God you're sorry, then say the same thing to the people you've wounded."

Molly looked into her sister's eyes. "Thanks for reminding me that there's hope."

CHAPTER SIXTEEN

Kate tried to get out of bed without disturbing her new husband. Carlos moved slightly but stayed asleep. It was still dark outside.

Tiptoeing, Kate made it to the living room and knelt by a wicker chair. "God, please help Molly. You know how upset she is. I don't know what to do to help her. Please help me be a good friend." She waited listening, then recalled Psalm 46:10, "Be still and know I am God," and Psalm 27:1, "The LORD is my light and my salvation, whom shall I fear? The LORD is the strength of my life, of whom shall I be afraid?"

"God, what am I afraid of? Am I afraid of losing Molly as a friend? Or losing her as my future sister-in-law? Or worried she'll always reject me? Help me trust You." Though some of her questions didn't have clear answers, Kate's heart was at peace as she trusted God with her concerns. She went back to bed.

She and Carlos spent the day outside, Kate's freckled fair skin lathered in sunscreen. The humidity turned her red hair into a mass of curls. "My own Little Orphan Annie," Carlos quipped when they went back to their villa. She laughed.

"Doesn't Peter's internship begin this week?" Carlos wondered.

"No, he had two weeks off. Then he starts seeing clients."

"Does he know where he wants to work after that?"

"He hopes he can continue at the church where he'll be counseling clients all summer. He wants to specialize in seeing adolescent males, but he's going to be seeing clients of all ages during the internship. Did I tell you he's actually doing his internship at two sites?"

"Right, he's going to work part-time at a drug treatment facility?"

"His hope is to work more than full-time between the two sites, so he can finish his master's degree by December."

"I hope he doesn't burn out."

"I know. He'll be doing group counseling at the treatment facility and individual and family counseling at the church."

"Are you ready to get back to classes?" Carlos asked. "I'm not. Let's just stay here."

"I wish. At least we have the summer off. Then, only one more semester for you to finish your master's degree. Do you still want to go for your PhD? I'm glad I'm taking a break during the fall semester, since I have my master's degree, finally! But should I finish my PhD? The main advantage of both of us finishing our PhDs is that we could teach at the college level." She paused to breathe. "What do you think?"

"What I think, Mrs. Cordoba, is that you are beautiful," Carlos responded, gently pulling her close.

She smiled at her husband. "Are you sure it's OK with you that I didn't do my married name the hyphenated way, you know, because it could be Johnson-Cordoba. What do you think? Because I can change it if you want me to. Do you?"

"It's fine the way it is," he said, his kisses quieting her questions.

CHAPTER SEVENTEEN

Molly shuffled into the living room, rubbing her eyes.

Jenn, wide-awake, laughed. "Good morning, Sunshine!"

"Nana always used to say that," Molly smiled, then groaned. "Coffee. I need strong, very strong coffee."

"Coming right up." Jenn lifted the plunger out of her coffee maker, then poured not-quite boiling water over freshly ground coffee beans to begin the precise steps of making French press coffee. "Do you know what time it is?"

"No clue. I haven't even looked at my phone," Molly said, reaching for it, where she left it charging on the kitchen counter. She sighed. No calls from Peter.

"It's noon here in London. But only a very early four AM in California."

Molly looked at her quizzically.

"I saw you check your phone. It's too early for Peter to call."

"He probably *won't* call."

"Even though I've never met him as an adult, if he's anything like his family, he is not going to let you go this easily."

"I'm not so sure."

"Time will tell." Jenn poured more hot water into the

French press, then carefully pressed the plunger down, waiting.

Molly sighed.

Jenn misinterpreted her sigh as a yawn. "Your body will take awhile to get used to the time change."

"At least I was able to fall asleep with the help of three melatonin."

"Three! I could never take that many; I'd feel too groggy to help passengers. But I've heard melatonin can really help with jet lag," she said, handing Molly a cup of coffee.

"I hope so." She sipped from the tiny cup of French press coffee Jenn handed her. "This is cute. Where did you find it?"

"Paris. During a vacation."

"Not work? You actually take holidays to see the sights?" Molly grinned, sensing the initial effects of caffeine on her mind. "Nice you get to be a tourist sometimes."

"Speaking of being a tourist, do you want to do something in Greenwich today? There's a lot to see here in southeast London. The Prime Meridian, the Old Royal Naval College, the Trinity Laban Conservatoire of Music and Dance."

"They all sound good. But before we go anywhere, Jenn, I want to thank you for your help last night. You gave me hope that relationships...can heal."

"It might take time, but it will be worth it," Jennifer said, smiling. "Now, how about going to Costa for pastry and cappuccino? This little cup of coffee isn't enough to fully awaken either of us. And I'm pathetically short on food at the flat. We can stop at Sainsbury's or Waitrose for a few groceries after we do our sightseeing. "

"Let me take a quick shower. What's the weather like today?"

"It is actually quite warm." Jennifer turned toward her bedroom, motioning Molly to follow. "I forgot to show you my closet. Let's find something fun for you to wear! She held out a yellow sundress. How about this?"

"Sure, but I have jeans and T-shirts."

"You're not in college here. We're two urbane gals out to

see the sights!"

Molly was glad to be wearing a sundress, dressed inconspicuously, like the hundreds of other people walking nearby.

At Costa, the barista noticed their accents. "American?"

"I am," said Molly.

"I am, too, but I live right here," Jenn beamed, proud of her new home.

"What part of America?" the barista asked Molly, making conversation.

"California," Molly said slowly, thinking, *But at the present time, I don't know where I'm from.*

"Well, you picked the perfect time to be in Greenwich. Usually it's more like Seattle here. Enjoy the sunny day," she smiled. "It might be the only one we have for awhile!" The barista continued her work, holding a stencil over each cup of cappuccino, sprinkling cocoa on top of the foam in the shape a palm tree. "There you go!"

Jenn and Molly found a seat. Looking across the room, Jenn commented, "Her coffee-brown shirt says it right: 'Barista Maestro.' Always fabulous," she added, holding her cup in the air in mock salute. "We can find somewhere for lunch this afternoon, since we're having such a late breakfast."

"Yeah, noon *is* a bit late for breakfast," Molly smiled. "Even for me. But my body isn't sure what time zone I'm in."

* * *

It was surprising how much Jennifer and Molly looked alike. Molly was a natural blonde, her hair highlighted by the California sun. Jennifer's *chosen* color was blonde, too. Her natural hair color was what their Grandma Finster once described as "dirty blonde," terminology which helped fuel Jenn's decision to begin lightening her hair in high school.

As children, they looked like sisters; now they looked almost like twins. As they walked into Greenwich, the 5'10" women drew numerous stares from other pedestrians. Even with their hair pulled back in simple ponytails, they were unmistakably beautiful. The sisters were unaware of anything but how wonderful it was to be catching up with each other.

"Let's plan our day as we walk," Jenn said.

Molly didn't respond, noticing the sign marking the street they were crossing. She laughed, reading the street name aloud, "Horseferry Place."

"I think they must have ferried horses across the River Thames near here, once upon a time," Jenn guessed, smiling.

Intensely focused on the sound of children playing at the school playground on their left, Molly was strangely quiet.

"Are you OK?" Jenn asked.

Molly choked back a sob. "When I hear children playing, I sometimes wonder what my son or daughter could be doing. My baby never got to crawl, or walk, or play."

"I'm sorry, Molly. I am so sorry."

They continued walking in uneasy silence, passing shops, then the Cutty Sark before crossing a grassy area. Jenn finally said, "We're almost at Trinity Laban Conservatoire."

They paused next to the music building, listening to student musicians, practicing.

"This is nice," Molly said.

"Want to go inside?" Jennifer asked.

Molly didn't answer, her attention riveted on a sign depicting a woman playing a flute, emblazoned with, "Trinity Laban Conservatoire of Music and Dance Regular Free Recitals and Masterclasses Open To The Public."

"What's wrong?"

"Oh, no! I just remembered my flute is being repaired. How could I have forgotten that? I have to pick it up next week so it's ready for summer school."

"Um, summer school?"

"Oh, right, I dropped my classes. Let's keep walking. I can't think about music right now. Too painful."

"You don't want to see if they have any classes you could take this summer?"

"Um, no. I can always check online," Molly stalled, walking briskly to move away from the painful memories of her life as a grad student. "Tell me about those buildings," she said, changing subjects as quickly as she could.

"Have you heard of the famous architect, Sir Christopher Wren? He rebuilt St. Paul's Cathedral in London."

"I think we might have discussed him in a history course or something."

"He was the one commissioned by William and Mary to design these buildings when the Queen decided to honor her navy for their sacrifice and brave service. This housed over 2,000 veterans of the Royal Navy—only the men, though; if they married while they were staying there, they had to move out."

"Magnificent structures."

"The building on our right is the Painted Hall, where the retired royal naval personnel ate. Want to see inside? It's known as the 'Sistine Chapel of the UK,' but much of the art is buried under layers of grime. There's a big restoration process underway."

"Like my life?"

"Both of our lives. I have stories to tell you, too."

Molly didn't hear her comment.

They stood quietly, simply enjoying the beauty surrounding them—and of being together as sisters again.

"Shall we wander over to the next building? It's the Chapel of St. Peter and St. Paul."

"Sure. I could spend the entire afternoon right here."

"I think you'll like the chapel, too. It has superb acoustics."

They sat in the chapel, basking in the majestic sounds of a pipe organ. When the organist stopped practicing, both of them sighed.

"Beautiful," Jenn said. "It's always a treat to listen to music here, whether it's a musician practicing or performing a concert. Isn't this an incredible organ? Organ scholars use it almost daily; it was the largest in situ work of Samuel Green. I think 'in situ' means built on location."

"I didn't know you were such a history buff."

"Is that what I am?" Jenn smiled. "I find history interesting; architecture speaks volumes to me about the people who came before us. Like this structure," she began, reading from a brochure. "The chapel of St. Peter and St. Paul was designed by Christopher Wren and constructed by Thomas Ripley and was the last major part of the Royal Hospital for Seamen to be built. Work on the four main buildings began in 1696." She paused, trying to recall something. "I think they call the buildings 'courts.'" She continued reading. "Building was continued by Nicholas Hawksmoor, John James and others when Wren had to leave to work on St. Paul's Cathedral in London."

"Look at the ceiling," Molly said. "It's incredible."

Jennifer read again: "The ceiling was designed by master plasterer John Papworth in a neo-classical design...and a Wedgewood colour scheme." She smiled. "I like the way Brits spell words. English *is* a different language from the one we speak."

A guide noticed them studying the room and began talking, interrupting their conversation. "You are Americans? Have you noticed the vast 7.5 metre high canvas above the altar? The painting is by the American artist Benjamin West, the only one of his altarpieces that still remains in the place for which it was originally commissioned. It took him seven years to complete this masterpiece. Can you tell what the painting illustrates?"

"No," Molly responded, staring intensely at the altarpiece.

"It portrays Paul, shipwrecked on the island of Malta. Many of the sailors who lived at the Royal Hospital had also experienced shipwreck. The painting depicts Paul gathering firewood to warm the storm's victims. When a venomous snake bit him, everyone was sure he would die. Yet he did not die, because God protected him. Many of our old soldiers were comforted by the story of Paul, a fellow shipwreck survivor."

"Thank you," Jenn told the guide, steering Molly toward the vestibule, wondering why her sister looked even more troubled than she had earlier.

"Is there any hope for the shipwreck of *my* life?" Molly glumly asked her sister. "Unlike Paul, maybe I've been bitten by a snake and I won't survive."

"There's always hope," Jenn said, continuing to steer them out of the chapel and into the foyer. "My hope increases every time I read the inscriptions on the four statues here."

Another guide talked over them. "Here in the vestibule, life-sized Coade stone statues represent the four virtues of Faith, Hope, Charity and Meekness. Coade stone is an artificial ceramic, manufactured in Eleanor Coades' Lambeth factory in the 1780's, made of a mix of new and reused materials, resulting in a paste that can be placed into detailed moulds before firing. Coade stone was a superb way to affordably create beautiful neo-classical design with the limited funds available at the time when the interior of the chapel was restored after a major fire." She paused to take a breath, and Molly and Jennifer turned to study the statues on their own.

The stone *did* look like exquisite marble. Molly stepped away from other tourists, praying, focusing on a statue of a shepherd lovingly holding a lamb. *It is so difficult for me to trust You, God. I don't know how to believe You really care for me. Help me see You as my shepherd. Help me let You carry me.* She read the inscription at the base of the statue: "Blessed are the meek, for they shall inherit the earth," and silently prayed, *God, I've felt betrayed by almost everyone. Help me forgive everyone I need to forgive, and see the truth about others, like Peter. Help me forgive myself and learn to trust You. Help me walk in hope, not arrogance.*

She moved on to the next statue, quietly reading its inscription aloud. "Which hope we have as an anchor of the soul both sure and steadfast."

Jenn stood next to her, praying softly, *Lord, thank You for being the authentic hope and anchor for both of our souls.* She read the next inscription, her soft voice audible only to Molly:

"Whoever shall give to drink unto one of these little ones a cup of cold water only in the name of a disciple, verily I say unto you, he shall in no wise lose his reward."

Molly turned to her sister, smiling at last. "God's love is amazing. He sent me here to you, and you are giving me just the cup of cold water I need, to revitalize my soul and help me turn back to Him. Thank you, Jenn." She prayed, *Thank You, God. Thank You!*

Jenn smiled with her, then read the fourth statue's inscription. "Faith is the substance of things hoped for, the evidence of things not seen," then concluded, "We don't have to worry about the future! We can learn to trust God."

* * *

The sisters were comfortably quiet on their walk back to Jenn's new flat, except for when Molly almost got hit by a bus when she stepped off a curb to walk across the street. Jenn grabbed her arm, saying, "Remember, the traffic goes the opposite way here!" She pointed to the curb, where bold letters warned, "Look left."

"Thanks, Jenn."

"Glad to keep you in the land of the living!"

They stopped to pick up groceries before arriving back at Jenn's flat.

"Can I help you unpack a few boxes in the kitchen before we fix dinner?" Molly asked.

While they worked, Molly wondered aloud, "How do you know so much about the architecture here?" She took new glasses and dishes out of several boxes, and then Jenn put them in the dishwasher.

Almost apologetically, Jenn said, "They're a little bit dusty when they're new, you know?"

"I would wash them, too. But Kate would give me grief. She's a lot more relaxed than I am," Molly smiled wistfully. "But she was always a great roommate! I was the one who failed her."

Jenn stopped loading dishes to look directly at her sister. "Don't give up on your friendship with Kate. I remember how kind her family was to you in grade school; I can't imagine them changing so much that they would give up on you."

Molly grimaced. "I'm not so sure about that. I've been horrible to all of them."

"Then you can make amends. Just like I'm trying to do with you." Jenn loaded the last glass in the dishwasher and hugged her sister. "Our family never hugged much. Can we change that?"

"I'll try. Physical touch is hard for me. But I love you, Jenn. Hugging you feels OK."

"Good!" Jenn beamed. "Let's see, I was going to tell you about why I decided to live in London." The sisters could track with each other as though they'd never been apart. "I've been coming to Greenwich at least once a year for the past seven years. Enjoying everything about this area is why I decided to invest here."

"We talked about so many things last night that I forgot to ask what you meant about a trust fund paying for your flat. Was that a recent event?"

"Ah, yes. The trust fund. I didn't know anything about its existence until our father's attorney tracked me down about five years ago. I received an official-looking letter via registered mail that explained funds I would receive that same year, on my twenty-fifth birthday." She paused. "You have a trust fund, too, Molly."

Molly, disoriented, smiled wanly. "Me? I haven't heard anything about it."

"Let's sit down." Jenn sat on the sofa, motioning for Molly to sit on the recliner next to her. "I hadn't, either. I guess our dad had directed his attorney not to inform us until just before our twenty-fifth birthdays. Another contingency is that we are never to mention it to Mercedes. A hand-written letter from dad warned me that she would try to get my money, and said that 'under no circumstances' was I to fall for any ruse she used. The letter mentioned that she had spent all his liquid assets. He had a prenup with her so she couldn't touch our inheritance. I'm sure she doesn't know about the trust fund or I would have heard from her."

"Sad."

"Yes. And Jeremy also had a trust fund from dad, but he told me that two things ate up his entire bequest. One—both of his divorces—and two, keeping himself out of jail."

"Out of jail?"

"About the time of his second divorce, he was still a stockbroker, remember? Apparently he had some less-than-legal investments. When some of his clients discovered his scam and demanded payout, his trust fund provided just enough money to pay them off and stay out of prison."

"How sad, for him—and them."

"Be prepared, Mol. It *is* a lot of money. And you'll be twenty-five in less than a year. You need to be thinking about what you want to do with your inheritance."

Molly's stomach tensed. "*That* is too overwhelming for me to contemplate right now."

"I know," Jenn nodded. "I didn't do anything with my trust fund at first; then, I finally decided to invest in property because I think it will hold its value over time."

CHAPTER EIGHTEEN

Peter rapped lightly on his aunt and uncle's back door. No one answered. He started to open it; surprisingly, it was locked. That was when he decided to check his phone and realized it was only 6 AM. No one was up yet.

He went back to the cottage behind their house that had been his home since he began grad school in California. *I need some direction.* He sat on his sofa and began reading Psalm 46. "God is our refuge and strength, a very present help in trouble…be still and know that I am God." *That's my problem. I've forgotten You are always God, and You are always good. I'm wildly trying to figure out a way to fix this mess with Molly on my own. Help me stop striving and rest in your care.* He continued reading, then praying, then reading some more, for another hour.

* * *

The hours and days passed rapidly. His dad dropped him at LAX Thursday evening. "Are you ready for this, Peter?"

"As ready as I'll ever be. Keep praying for me—and for *us*, OK?"

"You know I will."

"Thanks for sharing your frequent flyer miles, Dad. You

and Mom could have taken several vacations with the number of miles this took."

"We agreed that giving you this opportunity is worth far more than any trips we could take, Son."

"Hopefully, I'll know something in the next day or two. I'll text you, OK?"

The international terminal was bustling, but Peter had plenty of time to get through screening and to his gate. Once on board, he found his seat. Thankfully, even though he was in coach, his dad had booked him on an aisle seat. He could stretch out and get comfortable. And, because he had offloaded his fears to God, he was able to relax and fall asleep.

It was time for breakfast when he awoke. The woman in the middle seat next to him clearly hoped to engage him in conversation. "Is this your first time traveling to London?" she asked.

"Is it that obvious?" Peter was normally gregarious and fun; his smile was contagious.

The woman misinterpreted his smile and pressed her hand on his arm. "I'd be happy to show you some sights," she said, her tone seductive.

He shifted gears, changing his demeanor from friendly to formal. "Oh, I'm here to spend time with my fiancée and her sister," his tone clearly ending their conversation. *I hope she'll be my fiancée again, anyway.*

She finally let go of his arm.

Until they touched down, Peter pretended to be engrossed in the in-flight magazine.

* * *

Clearing customs took very little time. He hadn't checked a bag, so all he needed to do was follow Jennifer's directions to get to her flat. After texting her to let her know he was in London, he reviewed her emailed directions. Step One: purchase an Oyster Card to prepay for the tube and DLR.

Step Two: at Heathrow, get on at the "Piccadilly Line."

Peter completed the first two steps and realized how excited he was. And the closer he got to Molly, the more his heart began to pound. *What if she hates it that I'm here, surprising her?* He quickly stopped his negative thoughts. *I've prayed. My entire family is praying. I'm not going to give in to worry.* He prayed the prayer that never fails. *Your will be done, God, not mine.*

There were at least twenty-five other passengers, most either listening to music or intently studying their phones. Two were reading papers. When one of them left the coach, he tossed his copy of The Metro on the seat next to Peter, who flipped through it, his eyes stopping on a column called "Good Deed Feed." Blake in London wrote, "THANKS to the person who handed in my mobile phone at Paddington Station." Another, Claire in Lancashire, wrote, "Thank you to the man and lovely lady who calmed me when I dropped my purse on the train track at Manchester Victoria Station and waited with me until help arrived." Peter smiled, amazed that a newspaper actually carried positive stories. It helped the time pass. He was almost to Molly.

* * *

Jennifer hadn't anticipated any difficulty getting Molly to the prearranged spot to meet Peter when he arrived Friday afternoon. But when Jenn said, "Let's go into Greenwich," Molly responded with, "I am too tired to do anything this afternoon. Couldn't we just stay in, read, and make a cup of tea?"

Jennifer wasn't sure she would recognize Peter; she needed Molly to be there. And she'd told Peter they would both be in Greenwich to meet him. "A cup of tea would be fine, but I have to run an errand, and I really need your help finding something to give Analese tomorrow, when we go there for dinner."

The mention of Analese gave Molly a surge of energy. "OK, but I'm not dressing up."

"That's fine. You always look great."

They walked to the Greenwich Market, where Molly felt overwhelmed by the sounds of different musical instruments and crowds of people talking; the smells of foods from all over the world mingled with the acrid smell of smokers everywhere—it was a cacophony, set amidst an eclectic variety of wares—everything from quality antiques to cheap souvenirs.

They stopped to look at jewelry. "We could each get a matching pair," said Jenn, laughing at a garish pair of chandelier earrings. They moved on, distracted by a woman in another exhibit, her bright red bouffant hairdo extending at least seven inches beyond her forehead, like the prow of a ship.

The crowd pressed in on them, making shopping almost impossible.

"What did you have in mind?" Molly asked.

"I'm not sure." Jenn looked at her watch, shocked to see that it was almost time to meet Peter. "I have to get out of this crowd and think. Let's grab some coffee—or that cup of tea you wanted earlier. There's a coffee shop just around the corner."

They walked to the Costa across from the Cutty Sark DLR station, where Jenn had instructed Peter to meet them.

"We were in another Costa near your flat, right?" Molly said, and then suddenly was unable to think. She saw a man who reminded her of Peter. Six feet tall, dressed in jeans and a shirt just like one Peter wore, his sandy hair tousled, his smile infectious. She gasped. "Peter!"

He walked toward her, still smiling, waiting for her response.

"What are you doing here, in London?" Molly asked, astonished.

"I would travel the world for you," he said, meaning it. "Wait, I just did," he teased, his voice the one she loved above all others.

Molly turned from him to her sister, incredulous.

Jenn shrugged. "Who knew?"

"*You knew* he was coming! And shopping today was a trick to get us here, to meet him. You never did plan to buy anything for Analese!"

Peter felt a tinge of fear, unsure whether Molly was mad or glad to see him. His fear evaporated when Molly gently took his hand in hers and said, "I didn't know if you would ever want to see me again, after how horrible I've been."

"I've always wanted you, Molly. I always will."

Jennifer guided them out the door and toward her flat, staying a few steps ahead of them, giving them time to talk.

Despite jet lag, Peter experienced a surge of energy simply being with Molly.

* * *

At Jenn's flat, Molly's respect for Peter grew, observing him graciously engage her sister in conversation, asking about her life as a flight attendant, wondering about the real estate market in London. Molly was surprised by Peter's grasp of diverse topics.

"Don't overseas investors have unbelievably high real estate taxes in the UK?" he asked.

"Yes, they are high, but the UK tax situation is generally more favorable for property investors than many other major world markets. I don't really know much about the tax laws here. I believe there is some kind of private residence tax relief that applies, since this is my primary residence."

"How do you know about British tax laws, Peter?" Molly wondered.

"We discussed the UK's property taxes in my international econ course last year—an interesting elective. But I didn't know I'd be able to discuss international real estate with someone who has actually purchased property abroad!"

"It's a pleasure," Jenn said. "But I definitely couldn't have maneuvered the unique challenges of investing here if I hadn't had incredible help from friends. You'll get to meet them tomorrow night, since Sam and Analese are having all of us over for dinner."

For the next hour, Molly simply observed Peter, especially his genuine interest in getting to know her sister. At the same time, he carefully included Molly in their conversation. "Hey, Molly, you're really quiet," he said at one point. "Doing OK?"

"More than OK. I'm thankful to be with you again—I'd forgotten how incredibly kind you are, how much you care about people, especially me. I'm also amazed at how much you know—about so many topics," Molly said, standing, then curtsying, looking at Peter with a shy smile. Being with him made her feel unexpectedly spontaneous.

"Thank you, Your Majesty." He stood and bowed, with a flourish. "Ah, but there is much more I still must learn…" He held Molly's hand, kneeling. "Mayest this poor knight who traveled far dare hope thou, fairest maiden, wilt accompany me for tea on the morrow?"

Jenn interrupted, laughing at Peter and Molly's antics. She yawned. "Sorry, but I can't stay up another minute. Last night, Molly and I were up 'til 2 AM talking. Mind if I go on to bed? You two can stay up as late as you want."

When Jennifer left, Molly was quiet at first, and then blurted, "Peter, I don't know how to begin to tell you how sorry I am. I have been incredibly rude for months—and especially before and after Kate's wedding. Will you forgive me?"

"I already have," he said.

"I, I stopped trusting you. I believed lies about you and your family…I listened to Mercedes instead of remembering who you really are…"

"What does your stepmother have to do with anything?" he looked confused.

"Remember when I went to Illinois last Christmas? Mercedes convinced me your uncle Dan isn't ethical as a psychologist because he met with me for counseling and he's also my friend."

"Wait a minute. You really believe he, of all people, could be unethical? Besides, I didn't even know he'd met with you in a professional capacity."

"Before I really got to know him and your aunt, I went to his office a few times."

"Well, you need to know he never says who his clients are. Ever."

"I know that now. I've always known that, really. But all this happened in my mind, not in reality. Somehow I distorted how I saw your family. Every negative thing I said to Mercedes about any of you was fueled by my own faulty beliefs; she simply expanded on my rotten misrepresentations." He tried to speak. She raised her hand, stopping him, then continued. "I need to say this, and I need to use the correct word. I *lied* about you—I lied to you, I didn't even see the *real* you for months because I lived in the lies I believed about you."

"I've missed you." Peter's eyes overflowed with compassion.

Her eyes flashed, reflecting the anger she'd expected from him. "How can you still care about me, Peter, when I've just told you I lied about you for months?"

"Molly, I love you and forgive you. I am not going to quit caring about you—ever. Can we make the choice to trust in each other again?"

Molly's heart quieted. "I hope so…"

His eyes looked puzzled. "You're still not sure? Do you still believe lies about me?"

"No, I want to be sure, Peter. Trust is so hard for me. I want to say again how sorry I am that I ever stopped seeing you as you are…"

"Shh," he said, his eyes smiling, then turning serious. "But there are things we need to talk about. Important things."

They talked into the wee hours of the morning. Finally, Peter's jet lag hit, full force. "I'm going to have to go to bed. But, before I do, I must ask one question." Molly's initial nervousness quickly changed to relief when Peter, with his lopsided grin, said, "Will you accept my invitation to tea tomorrow?"

CHAPTER NINETEEN

"I don't know what I'm more excited about—Kate and Carlos getting back from their honeymoon tomorrow, or what *could* be happening in London," Zoë said.

"Peter's group text said 'today's the day.' I think we all know what he means," Kelly added. Brandon, Kelly, Dan and Zoë—the four Johnsons seated around the breakfast table nodded in unison.

"Since it's a lot later in the day there…"

Kelly interrupted, "Something could have happened already. Maybe it's something good and that's why Peter is too distracted to text."

Brandon said, "…or it's something bad and he doesn't know how to tell us."

"Let's go do something, anything, rather than just sitting around waiting for a call," Kelly said.

* * *

Peter had invited Molly to go with him for tea Saturday at 10 AM. Afterwards, walking next to him, Molly said, "I hear music."

"So do I, but it's the kind of music that's spilling out of

my heart," Peter said, his face enveloped in a smile. "I'm the happiest man in London."

Molly held up her left hand, the early-afternoon sun causing the diamond and rubies to sparkle. She sighed. "I didn't know I could be this happy."

"God sent sunshine, like a blessing on us," Peter said emphatically, taking her hand in his. "Thanks for saying 'yes' again."

"And I promise that this time, my 'yes' will never change to a 'no.' This time it's for the rest of our lives. Are you OK with that, Mr. Johnson?"

"That's why I flew all night to find you, Mrs. Johnson-to-be."

Without realizing it, they had gravitated toward the sounds of a choir rehearsing at St. Alfege's in Greenwich. No one seemed to be there but the musicians. The director turned, nodding a greeting to Peter and Molly, who sat in the sanctuary to listen. Peter reached to hold Molly's left hand.

Savoring the sensation of his hand clasping hers, Molly whispered, "Peter, I am so sorry. I didn't know how much I'd miss you. Or 'us.'"

The choir seemed to express their thoughts in music, singing, "Glory be to God on high…soul, sweet peace He offers you…. perfect gifts, each day anew."

They eventually wandered back toward Jenn's flat, stopping to sit and talk on a bench by the water, listening to the peaceful sound of the Thames lapping the shore. Peter noticed the smell first, wrinkling his nose in mock anguish. "Does it always smell this fishy here?"

"I don't know," Molly said, giggling at his silly expression. "I think Jenn said it's worse at low tide. It's amazing to see how much the water levels change between high and low tides."

"Should we get back, in case your sister's wondering where we are? Anyway, I'm sure her flat smells better than this!"

Molly looked at her watch, and then grabbed Peter's hand,

playfully pulling him up from the bench. "We've been gone five hours! Yes, it's definitely time to let Jenn know what's happening—and get ready for dinner with Analese!"

* * *

Adrian recognized Molly and let them into the building before she had time to buzz for Jennifer. Trained to notice details, he smiled, nodding at Molly's hand. "Brilliant, you two!" As the elevator opened, he smiled again. "Simply brilliant!"

"Adrian is the first person to know about our engagement," Peter said. "Brilliant," he enthused in an attempt at a British accent, "especially since his name begins with 'A.' Now we just need to find twenty-five other people to tell!"

"Twenty five?" asked Molly, bewildered, then her face relaxed. "A to Z. Now I get it," she laughed; glad she could figure out their first inside joke. They didn't notice the elevator whisking them upstairs until it stopped on Jenn's floor.

Jenn opened the door of her flat when they knocked. Talking intently on the phone, she motioned them in. As soon as she got off her call, Jenn noticed Molly's ring finger. "Just what I hoped I'd see! Your ring is absolutely gorgeous!" She held Molly's hand, studying the emerald-cut diamond and two rubies set perfectly on either side of it. "Tell me everything!" she enthused.

"Well, you heard Peter invite me to go with him for breakfast, right? He actually surprised me with a tea party, because he remembered me talking about the tea parties I used to have with Nana." She turned to Peter. "I don't even remember telling you about that."

"It was when we were both undergrads and Kate invited you on a ski trip to Colorado with our family. One night while we were there, you and I stayed up late, talking. It was the first time we really got to know one another. Before then, you were always Kate's best friend." He turned to Jennifer, grinning. "That was when I decided I wanted to marry your sister."

"It's a good thing you didn't tell me. I would have run away. Instead, I always thought you were like a brother, a very nice *kid brother*," she laughed.

"I *was* like a brother—Kate's brother. But I never wanted *you* to be my sister." He grinned again.

"So, he took me to the Cutty Sark. Thankfully, it's easy to find. He had done his homework, because he'd already made reservations for our tea and scones."

"I haven't even toured the ship yet," Jenn smiled. "OK, and then...?"

Molly took a deep breath, excited to tell her sister their story. "When we were seated, he asked, "Did you know this ship is the world's sole surviving tea clipper and the fastest ship of the 19th century?"

"I told him, 'No, I didn't know either of those facts.' And he said, 'Because you've always loved tea parties, I wanted to have one for you now.'"

"Then a waiter delivered a tray of pastries and a pot of tea—and tiny sandwiches, too."

Peter beamed, loving to hear his fiancée tell their newly revised story.

"I reached for a scone, and Peter said, 'Mol, wait, there's something on that.' I was so startled that I dropped the scone on the floor, thinking it must have a bug on it." She looked at Peter, giggling.

Peter smiled triumphantly. He hadn't heard Molly sound happy in a long time.

"You have teased me since we were in grade school!" Molly pretended to frown, then turned back to her sister. "While I was distracted by *that*, Peter reached across the table, held my hand and said, 'I had to make this trip because I have something that belongs to you.' Then he asked me if I were willing to accept *this* for the rest of my life." She held her ring next to the light, her eyes sparkling with it.

Peter continued, "At that point, I reminded Molly of the name of the tea room where we were seated: 'The Even Keel Café.' I asked her if that could be the name of our relationship from this day forward." He grinned.

"I told him, 'It's fine to call our relationship *Even Keel*, but I won't guarantee everything will be easy. All sailors know there are occasional storms.'" She smiled. "However, I promised not to jump ship the next time we face one."

"I'm so happy for you both!" Jenn enthused. "Now we need a brief intermission, or 'interval' as they say here in London, to talk about what's happening tomorrow."

"What do you mean?"

"I have sad news. I don't know if you noticed I was on the phone when you got back, but it was work calling. I keep forgetting to tell you that I'm on reserve this week. That's airline jargon meaning I'm on call, which means I have to be able to fly whenever I'm needed, with as little as four hours' notice. Thankfully, they gave me twenty-four hours' notice this time, so I still have some time left to spend with you."

"But I've hardly done anything to help you get settled," Molly lamented.

"Oh, yes, you have," Jennifer assured her. "What I needed to get settled was our new relationship as sisters—in Christ."

"All sorts of new relationships are beginning here," Peter said. "Isn't Greenwich known as 'the home of time'? A great place for *all* of us to find new beginnings." He looked at his watch and groaned. "Speaking of time, I was supposed to let my family know whether you said 'yes' or 'no,' Mol. I'd better text now and apologize for making them wait." He sent a group text. "Yes! Sorry forgot to text 7 hrs ago." Immediately his phone blew up with responses of joy.

In California, his dad turned to his mom, a lopsided grin on his face. "That boy never has had a great sense of timing."

"Good thing he's marrying a musician," his mom laughed.

* * *

124

Dinner with Sam and Analese Craig that evening was like being with long-lost friends.

Sam didn't look at all like what Molly expected. She thought an Oxford scholar might have a bushy beard, tortoise-shell glasses, a Harris Tweed jacket with leather patches on the sleeves—something like that. Instead, his beard was only the end-of-day stubble sported by many of the men she'd noticed on the Tube. His jeans and shirt were the latest London fashion—but his overall look was casual, unassuming.

And Analese—was Analese. Her chestnut hair now had touches of grey, but her eyes were the same crystalline blue Molly remembered. Her voice, though soft and sweet, carried more than a hint of playfulness—especially when she introduced her children. "Peter and Molly, I'd like to introduce our children, Andrew and Molly," she said. "Andrew will be three in July—and Molly was seven months old last week."

For a moment, Molly felt dazed. "Her name is *Molly?*"

Analese smiled. "She's named after *you*. I've prayed for you every day since I met you—and for you, too, Jennifer," she added. "Want to hold your namesake, Molly?"

Molly's shoulders tightened and her facial muscles tensed. She didn't know how to hold a baby.

Analese noticed her hesitation and smiled. "Trust me, she's not fragile. She is able to hold her own with her energetic big brother every day."

Baby Molly held her arms out, then clapped her hands from her perch on Molly's lap. The feeling and smell of her soft skin amazed Molly. When Baby Molly gave her a spontaneous hug and kiss, Molly could barely breathe. What sweetness. Her golden curls bounced as she moved her head, bobbing in time to the classical music playing in the background.

Jennifer turned to Baby Molly, who remembered her from previous visits and held out her arms to be held by her, too. "You won't believe what her middle name is, Molly!" she said, bouncing the baby on her lap.

"No clue."

"Annette—she has my middle name." Jenn beamed.

"Wow. Thank you for remembering us," Molly said softly.

Peter was already on the other side of the room, earnestly engaged with Andrew, whose tousled sandy hair topped a wiry body that was continually in motion, his eyes dancing as he spoke. "This is my big truck," Andrew said. "It makes big sounds. Vroom! Vroom!"

Baby Molly, wanting in on the action, climbed down from Jenn's lap to crawl across the floor and join her brother. Then she held her arms out to Peter. Laughing, he picked her up. "Girls named Molly seem to like me."

Sam helped Analese bring their meal to the table, everything a happy hubbub of activity. The food became a minor part of dinner, with the children busily involving all five adults for the next two hours.

As soon as the dishes were cleared from the table, Andrew carried a book to Peter and asked him to read a story. Peter used different voices for each character in the story, reading book after book until Andrew's head began to nod.

"Time for bed," Sam said, holding out his arms for his son. Analese followed him upstairs with Molly, who wiggled a chubby fist to wave goodnight, her head nestled on her mother's shoulder.

"This room is so warm and inviting," Peter said as their hosts went upstairs. He looked at a picture on the wall. "Is this a Scottish crest?" he asked. The picture depicted a chevalier on horseback in full charge grasping a broken lance.

Jenn responded. "I asked that same question the first time I was here. And, yes, it is a crest, or coat of arms. The words under the crest, *'Vive Deco et Vives,'* mean *Live for God and You Shall Have Life.'*"

"You speak Latin?" Molly asked, amazed.

Jenn laughed. "No, I finally learned the meaning after asking them two or three times."

"Anyone for coffee?" Sam asked when he and Analese

returned.

"We noticed your coat of arms—are you Scottish?" Peter asked him.

"Yes, my family is originally from the Scottish Lowlands. One of my ancestors, John Craig, actually co-pastored in Edinburgh with John Knox. But my parents moved to London when I was ten, so England is home."

"Do you have any family left in Scotland?"

"Oh, yes. Aunts, uncles, cousins. And, my parents moved back to Edinburgh two years ago, so all of my family is there now, except us." He gazed lovingly at Analese and their children.

Conversation flowed easily, as though they'd always known each other.

"Your children are adorable," Molly said. "What a surprise to go from seeing you as a single working woman, to a wife and mother of two!"

Jenn intentionally hadn't told Molly about Sam and Analese's son and daughter, knowing Analese wanted to introduce Molly's namesake that night at dinner.

"What I still don't understand, Analese, is why you ever cleaned houses, when you didn't need income," Jenn said.

"But I did need people. After my parents died, I felt lost without family connections. I had the aunt and uncle I went to California to see when we traveled together." She looked at Jenn, then at Molly, smiling. "I began my company in Illinois because my parents had lived there, but I wasn't close to anyone in that area. I know it was a little unorthodox..."

"A little?" Jenn laughed. "Has anyone here ever thought of cleaning houses for fun?"

"It all has to do with perspective," Analese laughed with her. "I didn't look at it as work. It actually was relaxing to do a menial job when my brain was working overtime the rest of the week. No phones interrupted my work, and I could pray while I worked." She turned to Molly. "I think those prayers for your family were what gave me the idea to take you to California all those years ago."

Sam brought a tray of cookies and fruit into the reception room while Peter helped him serve the coffee.

"Analese, have I ever thanked you for taking me to visit Kate's family when I was 13?" Molly asked.

"I'm sure you have."

Peter took a bite of shortbread. "This is delicious!" He paused, analyzing flavors. "What is in this…butterscotch?"

Sam responded. "It's my mother's family recipe. And, yes, the shortbread is topped with butterscotch—also a family recipe, and on top of that, drizzled chocolate. And the shortbread itself is made mainly with butter, flour and sugar."

"Do you share this recipe? My mom is from Wisconsin, and she loves *anything* that has lots of butter!"

"Absolutely. I'll copy it for you right now, so I won't forget." He walked to the kitchen and returned, carrying a treasured family cookbook. As he began writing on a coloured recipe card, he looked up, explaining, "Even our recipe cards are Scottish—see the plaid in the background? My mom designed these with the green and orange colours of our family tartan."

"Thanks, Sam!" Peter paused to study the recipe.

"You'll have a wee bit of Scotland to take home with you!"

"We'll think of you every time we make this, Sam. And Analese, I also want to say thanks to *you* for bringing Molly from Illinois to visit our family in California, back when we were kids. Molly thought she was coming to see my sister, but that was the Christmas I fell in love with an older woman." He took a sip of his coffee, his eyes teasing.

"You told me you fell in love with me years after that, during the Christmas vacation when we all skied in Colorado!" Molly said, pretending to be offended.

He grinned sheepishly. "After thinking about it, I've decided it really began in California, when we were much younger."

"You weren't even 13 then! And how can you refer to me as an 'older' woman? I'm not even a year older than you!"

Molly teased him back. "Just because you're an overachiever who finishes college in half the usual time..." she added.

"Hey, I started taking college courses in high school. Lots of people do that nowadays," he finished lamely, turning to their hosts. "As I was saying, Analese, thank you for getting all of this started."

Analese laughed at their banter. "Who knew we'd meet again, here in England? God works in mysterious ways!"

Jenn spoke up, her voice tentative, voicing a question that had been on her mind ever since she and Analese first connected in Greenwich. "Were we some kind of a sociological experiment for you—I mean, were you in our house *studying* us?"

"No way!" Analese reacted, leaning forward in her chair, her blue eyes intense. "If anything, I was studying *myself*. From the time I was in grad school, all I did was study and work, work and study, with no time to get to know anyone. My parents raised me in a church, but I didn't feel comfortable in any of the churches I visited. I did remember my mother praying when she worked around our house, so I thought I could do something that freed my mind to pray— thus the housecleaning 'experiment' began! I hoped being in people's homes would help me know how to pray for them, would somehow bring back something of the sweet times with my own parents. I know it wasn't a substitute for family or church, but it was all I could think of doing at the time."

Peter spoke slowly, thoughtfully. "I'm in grad school now, and I know what you mean about spending all the time working and not connecting with people. Although I don't think I'll choose your housecleaning option," he turned to Analese, laughing, "I do want to figure out a better way to make time to be with the people who matter the most to me." He gazed at Molly as he talked.

Analese said, "Church has changed since I was a child. What I remember from church then was being taught the Bible in a happy atmosphere, with music people enjoyed. And my parents spent time after church enjoying being with friends, having dinners together as families, looking out for each other." She set her coffee cup on the table next to her. "Now church seems like a place where people go to be entertained by professional musicians and listen to platitudes they'll never apply to their lives. The same complexities I've observed in the corporate world are happening in the church. It seems more like a political organization than a place of genuine compassion. It's discouraging! I need a place to go to be challenged to grow in my faith, a place where people build each other up instead of tearing each other down." She paused. "Sorry, I didn't mean to stand on my soapbox. I could go to Hyde Park if I want to do that."

Sam noticed Peter and Molly's baffled expressions. "Hyde Park in London has an area called 'Speakers' Corner' where people can express themselves publicly on any lawful topic. It's a great place to have challenging discussions and hear new perspectives." He smiled at his wife. "But you'll have to take your own soapbox there, Analese."

"I wish we had time to go," Peter said.

"On your next visit. You're always welcome at my flat," Jenn said.

"Is it OK if we go back to the discussion about church?" Sam asked. "One thing that drew Analese and me to study at Oxford was our mutual love for the writings of C. S. Lewis. In 1931—long before we were there—Lewis converted to Christianity, during the years he was a tutor in English language and literature at Magdalen College. He once said, 'It is easy to think that the Church has a lot of different objects—education, building, missions, holding services. Just as it is easy to think the State has a lot of different objects—military, political, economic, and what not. But in a way things are much simpler than that. The State exists simply to promote and to protect the ordinary happiness of human beings in this life. A husband and wife chatting over a fire, a couple of friends having a game of darts in a pub, a man reading a book in his own room or digging in his own garden—that is what the State is there for. And unless they are helping to increase and prolong and protect such moments, all the laws, parliaments, armies, courts, police, economics, etc., are simply a waste of time. In the same way the Church exists for nothing else but to draw men into Christ, to make them little Christs.'" He paused, embarrassed. "Sorry that was such a long quotation. As I said, I *really* like Lewis."

Everyone paused, still thinking about what he'd said. Analese spoke first. "I like that quote, Dearling."

Jenn turned to Molly, "Don't you love what they call each other—'Dearling'? I've never heard anyone say that." She turned to her host, "I like your quote, too, Sam—and this conversation. It's refreshing to talk about something besides the weather. Another thought-provoking statement is in the book you loaned me, Analese…"

"*Mere Christianity*?"

"Yes. In that seemingly short but profound book, Lewis says, 'If I find in myself a desire which no experience in this world can satisfy, the most probable explanation is that I was made for another world.' Is that what he means when he says the Church exists for making people into 'little Christs'?"

"It would seem so," Sam said thoughtfully.

"Becoming so-called 'little Christs' doesn't mean we're trying to be better than anyone else but that we're following our Shepherd, right?" Peter inserted. "Instead of living without regard for others or being focused on personal success, we can follow Jesus as part of a caring Christian community, learning to show the world His love."

"Unfortunately I haven't met too many Christians willing to sacrifice their desires for His," Analese interjected.

"How do we change that?" Peter asked.

Sam responded. "Doesn't it go back to Matthew 6:33? 'Seek first the kingdom of God.' We need to change our focus to God, not people. King David said we can 'taste and see that the Lord is good.'"

Analese looked at each person, smiling. "This moment—with all of us relaxing, enjoying conversation, food, and each other—makes me wonder if that's what God means when He says to 'taste and see' He is good. He gives good gifts, like all of you—I want to remember to take time every day to savor His goodness." She sighed, content.

Everyone continued talking, engaged in sharing ideas and hope. It was well after midnight when Jennifer yawned, then said, "I hate to cut this short, but I have to get some sleep before flying to Spain tomorrow—and Molly and Peter have to head back to Cali."

Analese said, "This has been a wonderful reunion. Let's stay in touch, OK?"

"Absolutely," Molly said. "But I need your contact info."

Analese handed her a card. "Here you go. And my prayers go with you all."

"Thanks for everything, Analese." Molly sniffed, surprised by her tears.

Analese grabbed a tissue for her and one for herself, since her eyes were also filling with tears. "Will you write down your address and phone number for me?"

"Here you go," Molly said, writing.

"No one wants my contact info?" Peter pretended to be offended.

"Sounds like we can find you wherever Molly is," Sam smiled. "And, Jenn, you're welcome to come to church with us whenever you're in Greenwich. We always invite a few people over for dinner afterwards…"

"Like my parents did," Analese smiled.

"I will take you up on that. Definitely."

Jenn, Molly and Peter walked the mile back to Jenn's flat, still talking, enjoying the brisk night air.

"If you want to spend some time seeing London, you two can stay here when I leave tomorrow afternoon."

"There is no way I could stay alone with Molly here—or anywhere," Peter said, meaning it. "Not until we're married, that is." He stammered. "Not because I don't want to be with her—but because I *do* want to be with her—too much." His cheeks reddened. "Can we take you up on your offer later?"

"We appreciate everything you've done, Jenn," Molly said, smiling, silently mouthing "Thank you" to Peter.

The sisters continued talking while Peter was at his laptop, applying years of his dad's frequent flyer miles to reserve their flights home for the next day.

CHAPTER TWENTY

Peter awakened, taking a moment to remember he was in England, and then wondering what delicious food he smelled. The sweet fragrance drew him into Jennifer's kitchen.

She was so engrossed in taking a pan from the oven that she didn't notice him.

He spoke softly so he wouldn't startle her. "Smells great!"

"Oh! Good morning, Peter! I don't cook very often, but I found these at the store and wanted to try them." She picked up a box on the counter.

He read the label out loud. "Jus-Rol. Bake-It-Fresh. Pain Au Chocolat."

When I lived in France a few years ago, a little pastry wagon—similar to an ice cream truck—came to my home every morning with fresh pain au chocolat. It was a buttery croissant, with chocolate that was melt-in-your mouth delicious! I'm sure this won't be as good as that, but I thought it would be fun to give it a try." She turned to Peter, checking to be sure Molly wouldn't overhear. "I hope Molly is OK. I don't think she eats much, and she seems sad—maybe even depressed. Please take good care of her."

"I promise to do just that," he said, careful not to voice his own fears, changing the subject instead. "Want me to set the table?" Jenn directed him to a box marked "plates," and he happily became engrossed in unwrapping and washing dishes for breakfast. "We could easily get some more of these boxes unpacked before we leave today."

"Are you sure? I thought you might want to do some more sightseeing, go for tea, or something like that."

"With what little time we have left in London, I'd rather you and Molly get to be together."

Molly appeared, her eyes bleary, her hair askew. "Did I hear my name?"

"I love your bed-head look," Peter looked up from the sink of sudsy water. "Yes, you did. I was just wondering if the three of us could get Jenn's kitchen organized before we all leave this afternoon."

"Perfect," Molly said. "But first, I need to wash my hair—and brush my teeth!"

* * *

Though Peter was ecstatic that Molly was once again his fiancée, he was troubled by how abruptly she'd ended their relationship, dropped her summer classes and run away from everything that mattered to her, without warning. A psych major, he recalled the axiom, *People do things for their reasons, not your reasons.*

He wanted desperately to tell her, "Don't ever leave me again; don't be afraid, your past doesn't have to dictate your present life," but he knew *she* would have to figure out whatever root issues triggered her choice to run away from life. It seemed like she believed everything was due to her stepmother's recent influence, but he didn't believe it was as simple as that. He could see she was exhibiting PTSD symptoms, but he wasn't the one to diagnosis her. *I love her, and I want to show her what real love is.* He just hoped she was willing to experience his love for the rest of their lives.

* * *

Jennifer noticed an unpacked box marked "high tea," and decided to transform their final morning together into a surprise tea party for her sister. "Peter, why don't you go ahead and shower? I'll just finish up here, and we can eat when you and Molly are ready."

When her guests came into the reception room a half-hour later, it was transformed into a tearoom, a lace tablecloth on the coffee table, with elegantly folded linen napkins set next to china cups and plates. "Do I smell scones baking?" Molly asked.

"You do, and there's more," Jenn said, serving the pain au chocolat, tiny cucumber sandwiches, hard-boiled eggs, scones and biscuits with a flourish.

Molly poured tea out of her sister's antique Limoges teapot into three matching cups. "Earl Grey, of course," she said, savoring its sweet citrus scent before sipping from her delicate china cup. "Delicious, Jenn!"

"Thanks! Brewed with tea leaves, the British way."

"*Everything* is delicious," Peter said. "Great cookies!"

"We in the UK call them 'biscuits,' not cookies," Jenn corrected, smiling. "Glad you like them!" She bit into a chocolate pastry, then frowned. "But I'm not sure I like this pain au chocolat. It *looks* right and the texture is right, but something is missing in the flavor. I guess I shouldn't have expected something I make from a box in the fridge to taste anything like France's fresh pastries." She wrinkled her nose in mock consternation.

Peter took a bite of pain au chocolat, chewing slowly, thoughtfully. "I think I know what it is. May I see the box?"

"Um, sure. It's on the kitchen counter."

He held it up, reading aloud. "Third ingredient is margarine. Are you used to having pain au chocolat that's made with butter?"

"Oh, judging by how flakey and delicious it usually is, yes. I probably do like it better with butter."

He smiled. "My mom would like how you said that, Jenn!

She always told us about her mom growing up when it was actually *illegal* to sell margarine in Wisconsin—they called it 'ole' or 'oleomargarine,' and people would drive across the state line into Illinois and *smuggle* margarine back into Wisconsin. Criminals making oleo runs," he said, laughing. "But not my mom's family. They only ate butter. And, to this day, I still prefer butter."

Molly was pensive. "One thing I always notice about your family, Peter, is how positively you speak about each other. You never say critical things behind each other's backs."

"Ouch." Jenn said, grimacing. "That's something I definitely need to work on. More often than not, I've said negative things about our family. Present company excluded, of course," she added. "Although, as you well know, Mol, I have said critical things about you in the past. And I want that behavior to stay in the past."

"I learned a quote in one of my classes last semester," Peter said. "It's something like, 'Be kind to everyone you meet, for everyone is fighting a hard battle.'"

"A hard battle," Jenn said. "Yes, that's true. Who said that?"

"Some say Plato did, but others think it was someone named Ian MacLaren."

"How does your family stay so positive, Peter?" Molly asked.

"We have our moments, especially if our blood sugar drops, like when we're traveling and forget to eat. But, usually, we simply seek to live in God's love, treating each other the way we want to be treated."

"Being kind…aware everyone is fighting a hard battle." Molly sighed. "What if I can't get beyond the flawed thinking that led me to escape life?"

Jenn said, "Molly, I should tell you what I did after I realized I was depressed, after I'd considered suicide…I met with a counselor for awhile to help me grieve our dad's suicide, and also to learn how to change my long-standing negative thought patterns. And there were other things, too…" she stopped, not quite ready to talk about them.

"Maybe that's what I need to do when I get back to California?"

CHAPTER TWENTY-ONE

When Peter and Molly got on the Tube to Heathrow with Jennifer that afternoon, Jenn motioned for Molly to take the one available seat while she and Peter stood, making sure their luggage didn't roll into other passengers.

Peter turned to Jenn. "Why is the train called the Tube?"

"I think it's because of the shape of the tunnels."

Molly tuned them out, focusing instead on the woman seated across from her. Sixty-ish, her mouth turned downward, the woman's lips twitched as though she were either stifling a cry or biting her tongue. Under her eyes, terraces of skin spoke of chronic sleepless nights. She looked down, reading, her mouth moving in rhythm to the train until it stopped for new passengers. Glancing at a grey-haired man standing near her, she nodded emphatically toward the seat that emptied across from her. Her shoulders heaved as she sighed. He wasn't quick enough to snag it.

A twenty-something bounded into the empty seat, her smile triumphant, savoring her conquest. The sign above her read "Priority Seat. For people who are disabled, pregnant, or less able to stand."

Molly frowned, then looked elsewhere. A man seated two people over from the new arrival seemed oblivious to the crowd pressing in around him. Light brown curls spilled from beneath a well-worn leather duckbill cap, his bulbous nose no distraction to his earnest reading of the Metro. She tried to read the headline. Did it say, "England's Population to Soar…" or "England's Population Uproar"? The man pinched his eyes between his thumb and finger, perhaps trying to stay awake.

Molly attempted his technique. It didn't help. She still felt tired, but it wasn't just the time zone. She felt herself checking out emotionally, drained from the series of choices that led her to London. *My entire life is in the Tube. How am I going to climb out of this mess?*

Peter, noticing, tried to find a way to cross the crowded train car to sit or stand next to his love. When the car stopped, as other people jockeyed for seats, he quickly moved to stand right in front of Molly. "Doing OK?" he asked softly.

She didn't notice him.

He tapped her arm, gently.

She jumped, startled out of her mental gymnastics.

"I'm sorry, Mol," he said, meaning it. "I didn't mean to scare you." A seat opened up next to her. He set his backpack on it, then quickly reached to grab Molly's roller bag so Jenn wouldn't have to continue struggling to keep it and her own bag from rolling into someone. When he returned to sit next to Molly, she looked up, distraught.

"I'm, I'm sorry, Peter. I don't know what's happening. I can't focus. I feel like I'm not here, like my mind is out of my body somewhere else."

"Dissociating," he said simply, so only she could hear him. "It's what people do when the stress of life is overwhelming."

She leaned into him. "Peter, am I going crazy? Am I going to be able to function at school?"

"You're not going crazy. Absolutely not. There's just a lot of junk stored in your brain, in the amygdala." He smiled. "That's the Greek word for almond; there are two almond-shaped groups of neurons in the brain."

"Huh?"

"That's where trauma memories are stored. And, when they're triggered, they can 'hijack' your brain's prefrontal cortex so you can't think clearly."

She sighed. "If you say so."

He smiled, his eyes filled with compassion as he looked into her troubled eyes. "It happens to everyone, at times."

"I don't know anyone else who is...um, hijacked," she gave Peter a faint smile, trying to respond to his love. She whispered into his ear, "Do you think anyone can hear us?"

Peter shook his head no, glancing at the people standing near them. All were clearly engrossed in sounds coming from their headphones, oblivious to Peter and Molly.

"Hey, guys, we get off at the next stop," Jenn called over the hubbub.

* * *

They had a few minutes to stand talking before Jenn said, "I need to head to Terminal Two. You guys are going to Terminal Three." She nodded toward the sign directing them there.

Molly held her sister's hand, something she hadn't done since preschool. "I can't leave you, not yet."

Jenn's eyes were brimming with tears. She forced herself to smile. "Now that you know how easy it is to fly here, let's do this again sometime, OK?"

Peter sighed. "I don't think my dad has any miles left for us to use."

"I can get buddy passes for both of you next time. I'm sorry I didn't think of getting you one this time, Peter."

* * *

Peter and Molly walked in silence, Peter pulling Molly's bag with her backpack hoisted over its handle and carrying his own backpack, too. "I could carry something, Peter."

"No, I've got it. I'm fine." He smiled. They checked in,

went through security, then had time to stop for coffee at Heathrow's Café Nero.

"Your dad certainly was kind to give up all of his years of saved frequent flyer miles just so you could come..." Molly didn't know how to finish the sentence.

"I wish you could have seen my family, Molly. Dad was crying. I've never seen him like that before. They love you so much." Peter's eyes filled with tears.

"I don't deserve *anyone's* love," Molly moaned. "How am I ever going to face your family after my ridiculous choice to drop out of life?"

"I know everyone in my family—including me—has made stupid mistakes. Which reminds me—I want to tell you how sorry I am that I invited your brother to stay with me. I know you told me it was OK, but I should have been more sensitive. Will you forgive me, Mol?"

"Forgive you? I'm the one who messed up here. And he needed your help. He had no one else."

"No, I mean it. I was wrong to expect you to want me to help the one who molested you for years. I could have found somewhere else for him to stay. And, even though you told me you forgave him, I have to wonder if having him around triggered you, made you relive the trauma somehow. I am sorry I was insensitive to that. You know that amygdala stuff I explained to you on the Tube?"

"Almond-shaped set of neurons or something like that?"

"Uncle Dan explained that to me after you left. He felt horrible that he hadn't stopped Jeremy from staying with me."

"Peter, it's OK."

"No, it's not OK. It's my fault that you were reminded of your childhood pain. Please forgive me. From now on, I'll try hard to be more aware, more encouraging, more..."

"Shh," she said, smiling. "You couldn't be more kind to me than you already are."

Even after they boarded their flight, their conversation continued.

Molly sighed. "I don't know why I have such a hard time trusting God with my life. Or why I feel like I don't belong anywhere."

"You feel like you don't belong?" Peter was incredulous.

"Like last night. Even though it was an incredible time, and it was wonderful to see Analese and meet her great husband, I had the feeling I was the outsider there."

"You—the outsider? With their baby named after *you*?" He smiled, his lopsided grin reminding Molly he was teasing again. "Seriously, though, feeling like you don't belong isn't your fault. And even though it isn't an accurate feeling, it probably feels more real than me trying to convince you that you *do* belong."

"Anywhere I go, I feel that way. Like I might say or do something so stupid that people will see through me and know I'm not really a part of whatever group I'm in. I think I'm tired of feeling this way."

Peter held her hand. "I have an idea, but I don't want to push anything on you."

"You're not pushy, ever. What's your idea?"

"Since I'm a counseling psych major, this idea probably won't come as a big surprise—but what if you do meet with someone for counseling when we get back? It could be helpful to talk with someone about your concerns."

"I've been thinking about that since last night, when Jenn talked about how much counseling helped her. And the one thing this fiasco proves is that I need some practical help."

"Molly, I don't think of this trip as a fiasco at all. Remember Romans 8:28, 'God causes all things to work together for good...'?"

She nodded, trying to believe him.

"Our relationship was going nowhere, fast. We weren't communicating, there were a lot of things that needed to be addressed—and if it took us meeting in London to start working through them, then it's definitely worth the trip! Plus you got reconnected with your sister—and Analese!"

CHAPTER TWENTY-TWO

Molly had been back in California for two weeks, and she still hadn't seen Kate.

Every day, Peter asked her if she'd connected with Kate yet. And every day, she had an excuse. *I have to meet with my advisor. I'm crushed with homework for the three classes I'm taking. I have to prepare for my graduate recital this fall. And I don't know what to say to Kate.* She even tried joking around with him. *I have I to figure out the title for my original flute composition. I can't have a recital without a title.* He wouldn't stop asking.

One day, Kate simply showed up at her door. Molly heard the doorbell and thought it was UPS, delivering the new flute chamois she'd ordered. Opening the door, she gasped.

Kate reached to hug her.

Molly hugged her back, like a drowning person clinging to a life preserver. "Can you ever forgive me for being such a jerk?"

"I love you, Mol, and I forgave you a long time ago."

"But the night before your wedding—the horrible things I said. I keep hearing myself, and I can't believe I said those cruel things about Carlos."

Tears welled in Kate's eyes. "It did hurt."

"I know. I know. My sister said I sounded more like our

mom in the way I was describing him…"

"Like your mom? Does she know about Carlos?"

"No, no. I mean like the way she talks about people behind their backs. But I'm not making excuses. I'm not blaming my mom or anyone else for how awful I was to you."

For the first time since Kate's wedding day, they were together in the living room they'd shared as roommates. Kate sat in her favorite chair; Molly sat on the sofa, across from her.

"What happened, Mol? I want us to be friends, if you do…" She sighed, her eyes overflowing with tears.

"Yes, I do!" Molly's voice and smile were earnest.

"OK, what happened?" Kate asked.

"That's the problem. I don't know, and that's why I haven't called. Will you forgive me for how I treated you and Carlos?"

Kate smiled. "Of course. But let's figure out what happened so it doesn't happen again."

"I don't know. Maybe I was jealous because relationships seem so easy for you. Or maybe I thought you didn't want me as a friend anymore."

"That's just plain silly," Kate said, with the same lopsided smile her brother had when he was teasing.

"I see that now. But then, I started believing lies—about you, about everyone."

"Why didn't you tell anyone—like me, your best friend—what you were feeling?"

"Well, that's part of the problem. I did talk with someone. But it was the wrong person."

"Who? I don't get it."

"My stepmom."

Kate gasped, incredulous. "No! Mercedes? The one who hurt you in high school?"

Molly opened her laptop. "Maybe an email will show you. Mercedes doesn't like to text, so we mostly communicated by emails. Here's one I wrote: 'Hey, Mercedes, it's another rotten day here. The Love Birds are out twitterpating somewhere, having a disgustingly romantic picnic. The last thing Kate said before she left was, *Oh, Carlos is the kindest man I know. He is making sandwiches and my favorites—chocolate covered strawberries.* I want to throw up.' And Mercedes wrote back, *You have to be the bigger person. Just let them do their thing and ignore them. That's the best way to show them you can't support them in this fiasco.* Then I wrote back, *Yeah, them getting married is the dumbest thing I can imagine.* And Mercedes responded with, *Be sure you don't emulate their mistake.*" Molly looked up, expecting Kate to reject her.

Kate said only, "She was pushing you to break your engagement with Peter?"

"That's one of the most direct statements she made about that. Usually she suggested negative things based on my complaints. She could take one remark of mine and spin it into an entirely different scenario."

"So you were being fed a steady diet of lies."

"It wasn't just her. I need to tell you I lied, too. I lied *to* you and *about* you."

"I'm confused…"

"One of the lies was last spring, when I told you I couldn't go with you, Carlos and Peter to visit your family because I had to stay here and work on a project. Remember?"

"Sure. I baked cookies to help while you studied." Kate smiled. She knew Molly loved chocolate chip cookies but would seldom eat them because she avoided carbs. "I was hoping I could show you that I loved you no matter how you treated me. Did it work?"

"Maybe what you did then is starting to work now." Molly forced herself to smile before she looked down, twisting the navy tassel on the striped denim pillow in her lap. She spoke, staring at the floor. "I didn't eat them here, because I didn't have a project to keep me here. I took them with me to a resort a couple of hours away. When Mercedes found out I'd lied to you, she invited me to meet her for spa time together."

"You didn't have a project?" Kate asked, bewildered.

"No, that was *one* of the times I lied to get out of going home to be with your family. Another was before then, at Christmas. I told you and Peter that my mom insisted I come home. But I hardly saw her during my time in Illinois; I spent most of the Christmas vacation with Mercedes. That was when Mercedes and I really began to click, over a shared condemnation of anything connected to you all."

"I don't get it, Molly." Kate stood and paced around the kitchen.

Molly looked down. "It didn't matter what any of you, Carlos or your family did. I twisted your words and actions to convince myself no one cared. It doesn't make sense now. All I wanted to do then was get away from you."

"I still don't get how you went from *knowing* my family cares about you to thinking we didn't care. Really, Mol?"

Molly looked up at Kate, shocked to see her smiling at her. "I know. It doesn't make sense because you all showed me real love—from the time we were in grade school together!"

"So, even though we never stopped being loving and kind to you, you started believing the worst about us. I'm not saying we never fail. We do fail, in many ways. Only God never fails." She was still smiling, though her voice was firm. "But we absolutely did not do the things you believed about us."

"You're right. I now know my thinking was based on lies I *chose* to believe, on lies that multiplied with each telling, until I couldn't even remember the *real* you. Every time I looked at you or thought about you, it was the fake you, that imaginary person who was a product of my own hideous imagination." Molly exhaled, frustrated with herself. "So what do I do now?"

"For one thing, it's time we go back to honestly loving each other. Remember that verse? 'Love expects the best'? I'll expect the best from you. Will you do the same for me?"

"Of course! Will you tell me if I start acting like a jerk again?"

"Molly, you don't ever have to go there again." Kate's grin

showed Molly she wasn't criticizing her. "You can simply allow God's love to pour through you."

"Next I need to meet with Carlos and ask him to forgive me."

"Funny thing. We were praying you'd want to do that. He's waiting outside."

"In this heat?" Molly ran to the door. "Carlos, please come in."

"Special delivery," he said, handing her a bag of Kona coffee.

Clutching the bag, Molly inhaled its sweet rich fragrance, gathering courage to continue.

Sensing her tension, he spoke softly, explaining, "We bought the coffee for you on our honeymoon. Hawaiians say it's the best coffee in the world. It's good, just not as good as my Guatemalan coffee. But, then I'm biased."

"I'm the one who has been biased," Molly said, trying to find words to express how sorry she was.

Carlos' smile helped her continue.

Before he even sat down, her words tumbled out like an unrehearsed Cirque du Soleil routine. "Will you forgive me for all of my unfair criticism, cruel, stupid comments, and for not welcoming you as Kate's best friend?"

He spoke slowly, calmly, his eyes mirroring the kindness he felt. "I'll never replace *you*, Molly. You'll always be Kate's *first* best friend."

Molly continued as though she hadn't heard him. "I've been rude, inconsiderate—and wrong about you—in just about every way I could be wrong. Please forgive me for everything I said, did, and thought that was untrue and unkind," Molly said, her eyes pleading.

Gently, Carlos reached and lightly touched Molly's hand.

She felt safe with him, almost as safe as she did with Peter. The tense muscles in her face visibly relaxed. "Oh, I was so wrong about Guatemalans."

Smiling into her eyes, he said, "I've never held anything against you." Then, showing his true personality, he added,

"Besides, I always knew you'd love me when you got to know me."

Molly laughed, and the tension in the room began to fade. But the struggle in her mind would take time to heal.

CHAPTER TWENTY-THREE

Zoë dashed back to the cottage behind her home, hoping to talk with Peter. When he didn't respond to her unique knock, she sighed, remembering why he wasn't home. *He started his new internship today.* Walking into her own back door, she called her husband at work instead.

His voice mail was not what she wanted to hear. "Dr. Johnson is unavailable at the present time. If this is an emergency, please hang up and dial 911. Otherwise, please leave your name and number, and I'll be happy to get back with you as soon as I can."

"I need to talk with you, honey. Please call, I really need your input," Zoë didn't like the tone of desperation in her voice. She sat down in her favorite chair, praying. *God, help me know what to do. Help me not rush into something I shouldn't do.* Her phone vibrated. He wrote, "Teaching class now. Can I call back in an hour?"

"Sure!" *I can't believe I forgot he's teaching!* Zoë collapsed in the overstuffed chintz chair in their den where she spent time renewing her soul every day. Silently, she began to pray. *God, You know I'm impatient. You know I can't bear to see the people I love suffer. Help Peter. Help Molly. Show them how to heal their relationship. Show me if there's anything I should say or do. Or do You want me to be quiet?* Aloud, she exclaimed, "But I don't want to be quiet!"

Her Bible opened to Daniel chapter six, right where she'd left off the day before. *It was unfair when Daniel was thrown into the lion's den. His colleagues looked for a way to attack him, and they used his faith as a way to get him to disobey the king's order—but they were the ones who manipulated King Darius to sign into law an edict banning prayer to any god except the king! They knew Daniel's custom of praying three times a day to God. And their trap worked! When Daniel was found guilty of praying to someone other than Darius, he was thrown into the lion's den—a certain death sentence.*

She read how King Darius spent a sleepless night fasting for Daniel's protection from a law even a king couldn't undo. When King Darius' troubled voice called to Daniel at dawn, Daniel responded with, "O king, live forever! My God sent His angel and shut the lions' mouths, and they have not harmed me...I have committed no crime." Zoë suddenly realized the answer to her concerns. *The same God who shut the lions' mouths then can keep my mouth shut now! He can keep me from trying to fix things at my pace instead of His.*

She heard a tap at her back door and thought it must be a neighbor. It was Molly! Zoë breathed a prayer, reminding God she wanted Him to close her mouth as needed.

While Molly waited at Zoë's back door, she worried Zoë wouldn't even want to see her. The door burst open, and she knew her fears were unfounded. Zoë's smile was as wildly articulate as her red hair, unrestrained by a flowered silk headband vainly attempting to keep her curls in check.

"Just the person I've been hoping to see!" Zoë exclaimed.

"I came to say I'm sorry. For everything." Molly choked out the words, her cheeks and neck flushing with embarrassment.

"Please come in. Do you want iced tea? Or lemonade? Coffee?" She motioned to a chair in her cozy kitchen.

"Nothing, thanks." Molly said, sitting on the edge of the chair. "I just need to tell you I'm sorry."

Zoë nodded, her eyes giving Molly what she needed—

acceptance.

"I don't know what is wrong, but I want to tell you I'm going to get help so I can fix it."

"Molly, we love you."

"I know, and I also know I've been a jerk."

"We all have our moments." Zoë's wry smile broke the tension. She started to tell her, "When I was your age," but stopped, giving Molly time to say what she wanted to say.

"Do you know a female counselor who could help me heal from my dad's suicide and my brother's abuse? I need to get serious about healing so I don't take out my frustration on everyone who cares."

"I can give you a few names and you can check them out. Did you know there are hundreds of different kinds of counseling?"

"No clue."

"Some counselors are direct, others just try to get people to talk about their feelings. Some will respect your faith; others will try to redirect your beliefs."

"How can I choose the right one?"

"Basically by asking questions—and, if the counselor has a website, check it out to see if you think you're a fit. You could also interview the therapist on the phone briefly to see if you like her."

"I can interview a therapist? I thought *they* were the authorities!" She paused, changing the subject. "By asking you for someone else's information, I'm not saying you and Dan haven't helped me."

Zoë nodded. "I know."

"After my brief escape from reality, I want to be sure I don't ever have a repeat performance. That's why I'm looking for a counselor."

"I got it. In the meantime, can we start meeting again, as friends? I've missed you—more than words can say…" Zoë's tears finished her sentence.

Molly paused, unable to find words. She swallowed, then forced herself to speak. "How can you want to be my friend?

I lied about you, I lied to you. I mistrusted you. I rejected every idea you had about helping with our engagement. You said you'd host a party, and all I did was criticize you."

"Love expects the best," Zoë smiled.

"And I expected the worst—from everyone who cares."

"And we all still care. But to answer your question, I want to be your friend because you are a joy to me. I love talking with you. I have failed people who matter to me, too. And one of the beautiful things about a true friend is that she keeps on accepting you, no matter what."

Molly sighed. "I have a lot to learn."

"One of my favorite quotes, attributed to both Dinah Mulock Craik or George Eliot, is 'Oh, the comfort—the inexpressible comfort of feeling safe with a person—having neither to weigh thoughts nor measure words, but pouring them all right out, just as they are, chaff and grain together; certain that a faithful hand will take and sift them, keep what is worth keeping, and then with the breath of kindness blow the rest away.'"

"I *really* have a lot to learn."

"But that's how we learn, when one person chooses to love us as we are. And look how many people love you, Molly. Dan and I, Peter—of course! Kate…"

"Even Carlos loves me after all I've said and done to him."

"I think I need to tell you about some of the horrid things I did BC."

"BC?"

"Before Christ. Before I knew God sent Jesus to love me, forgive my sins and give me new life, I tried just about everything I could to find some sort of peace in my life. Drugs, sex, betrayal."

"You don't strike me as someone who would betray anyone," Molly said adamantly.

Zoë laughed. "Oh but I *do* strike you as someone who would do drugs?"

"Well, you told me about that a long time ago, that you'd

experimented with marijuana and alcohol in college."

"Until I found out there are a number of really bad consequences from both," Zoë's laugh was hollow. "I think we need some lemonade," Zoë stood up, suddenly wishing she hadn't begun to divulge a part of her past she wanted to stay there.

"So who did you betray?" Molly asked, filling their glasses with ice.

Tears spilled from Zoë's eyes. "Someone who helped me more than anyone else up to that point in my life. My mentor, my best friend. I started a campaign of lies about her that destroyed her career."

"How could that even happen?" Molly's face mirrored the shock she felt.

"Pretty easily, actually," tears splashed down Zoë's cheeks. This was a story she had only told her husband Dan, the memories still too painful. "Heather and I went to college together, so I knew her weaknesses; I knew her strengths. And one of her strengths was meeting people. She taught me so much about making friends. That's why I call her my mentor. She had this incredible ability to walk into a room and reach out to just about everyone there. She literally was the life of every party. And she genuinely cared about people. She taught me how to listen more than I speak. When we graduated college, we began teaching at the same elementary school. And everyone there loved her. I felt left out."

"You? I find that hard to believe. You are so open and caring."

"Anything I am now was because of the colossal lessons I learned after I wounded my dearest friend and destroyed our friendship forever."

"What happened?"

"When she wasn't around—whether I was at a staff meeting or in the teachers' lounge—at parties, whatever—I would drop little hints about her past to get people interested in *me*. I discovered that people love hearing dirt about other people. Especially someone as popular and friendly as

Heather. I was so jealous of her that I secretly wanted to destroy her."

"I don't like where this is going. It sounds eerily like what I've been doing."

Zoë didn't hear Molly. She took a deep breath, agonizing over each word that propelled her back in time. "It was at a faculty holiday party. Everyone was dressed in funny Christmas sweaters and having a blast. I walked over to Heather and said, 'This party reminds me of that fraternity party we went to in college where you were so drunk, you know, before you hit bottom.' Heather's eyes begged me to stop talking. She even tried to change the subject, saying, 'Oh, I don't know what you're talking about.' But now I was finally the life of the party and I wasn't about to stop talking. I kept going."

"Is this when her career was ruined?"

"Pretty much. When I was sure I had everyone's attention, I told about how, at that party, she got up on the table to dance. And how that began her life as a stripper."

"Not really, right?"

"Actually, she did *dance* at a few other fraternity parties after that. But she wasn't ever a 'stripper.' But, the faculty had already labeled her a 'former stripper.' And, after that, it only took a few weeks for parents to start complaining about the character of the young woman teaching their second graders. Heather was totally broken. No one wanted to hear her 'side' of the story. And the 'story' kept growing. Parents and teachers added to my gossip, and before long she was known as a former drug addict and prostitute, none of which was true, of course. She could do nothing to rebuild her reputation. She eventually had to move out of state and start a new career."

"Have you told her you're sorry?"

"Oh, Molly, I've tried. I called her parents to get her new address; they won't give it to me. Before she moved away, I sent letters, flowers. I wrote the school and told them I was wrong, that she was never a stripper. I even admitted that I was exaggerating to make her look bad because I was jealous. But the damage was irreparable. The school board preferred to believe my lies rather than the truth. Heather will never trust me again."

"I'm sorry, Zoë."

"It is amazing how a few words, carelessly spoken, can destroy a person's stellar reputation. Honestly, Heather was one of the most caring, competent teachers in that school. And my jealousy robbed me of a precious friend." Zoë put her head in her hands, exhausted. Speaking her memories aloud took her back to a time she wanted to forget.

"I was doing the same thing to you. You've only been good to me, and I spoke about you to Mercedes as though you didn't care at all."

"But your words weren't to work colleagues. They were limited to one person."

"That's no credit to me. It's only because I don't have a lot of people I could tell," Molly smiled ruefully. "My heart was in the same jealous place yours was."

"Well, neither of us has to stay in those places," Zoë said, shaking her head, trying to forget again.

"You said that happened BC?"

"Yes, it was shortly after that I went to a group where single adults met to encourage each other. Actually, one of the other teachers invited me. She said I seemed depressed; maybe this would cheer me up. It did."

"How?"

"First of all, there was no alcohol involved. So there was no opportunity for me to get into a boastful, drunken state."

"You didn't say you were drunk when you said those things about your friend."

"Yeah, I didn't because it was no excuse. Because there *is* no excuse for what I did."

"So you went to a singles' group…"

"What I didn't know was that they were Christians. I mean *real* Christians. They lived what they talked about. When they said 'God is love,' they followed their words with loving actions. They read the Bible like it could change their lives."

"Kind of like you and Dan do?" Molly smiled, trying to gently push her friend back to the present.

"Thanks, Molly. Yes, I've changed a lot since that horrific time with Heather. When I fell in love with Jesus—I quit acting like I did BC, you know, *before Christ*." Refilling Molly's lemonade, she smiled. "I never want to go back to being the old Zoë."

"That brings up an interesting point. I was a Christian when I told lies about you. I had my spiritual epiphany, remember? You helped me come to know Christ."

Zoë nodded, remembering Molly's journey. She looked down at her phone. "I am so sorry. This is the third time Dan has tried to call. Do you mind if I take it?" She stepped into the dining room to talk.

Molly's thoughts traveled back to her junior year of college, when it felt like the worst problem in her life was all of the Christians talking *at* her, especially her roommate Kate. She remembered the time her flute ensemble performed at a campus chapel service, and she stayed to listen to the guest speaker, Tom Halden. For her, that was an unusual occurrence, since she never liked hearing anyone talk about God. But this speaker was captivating, especially when he talked about growing up without friends, his divorced parents unaware he was being bullied to the point of slavery in middle school. 'In LA,' he'd said, 'if someone tells you to do something or else, you know what they mean.' She remembered him describing how a gang forced him to deliver their punishment to other junior high students—putting eggs in kids' lockers, smearing paint on their clothes, throwing rocks at their houses.

Tom talked about Nate, one of the kids he'd hurt over and over. There was a year they didn't see each other at all. But when they were both in high school, Nate invited him to his family's cabin on Lake Arrowhead, where Tom had the time of his life. He thought the guy must have forgotten all of the cruel things he'd done to him in junior high. So, he finally asked him if he remembered, and was shocked when Nate said, simply, 'yes.'

Molly could still hear Tom's next words. "A few weeks later, when Nate and I went with his parents to the lake again, I worked up my courage to ask, 'Have you ever done anything bad like I did?' And Nate said, 'I did something so bad that my best friend had to die for me.'"

Still traveling back in time, Molly didn't hear Zoë talking softly on her phone to Dan in the dining room.

"I can't believe I told her about Heather, Dan. I promised myself I'd never tell anyone about that dark season. Talking about how I ruined Heather's life makes me feel like I'm back there again," she sobbed. She paced back and forth across the dining room, intently listening to her husband, her sobs beginning to quiet.

Molly was oblivious to time, remembering being mesmerized by that speaker, who explained the 'best friend' his new friend was discussing was Jesus, who died on the cross to pay for all of our sins.

Zoë returned to the kitchen, unable to hide her red eyes.

"Are you OK?" Molly asked.

"Just talking about the awful things I did to Heather took me back almost twenty-five years. I feel as horrible now as I did when it happened."

"But you weren't even a Christian then, Zoë. What I'm struggling with is how could I treat all of you so horribly when I claim to *be* a Christian?"

Zoë sat down, slowly sipping lemonade, forcing herself to come back to the present before she spoke. "Christians can let themselves be controlled by old things in their lives—and behave just as badly, or sometimes even worse, than people who have no faith. There's a verse in Ephesians that says we're to throw off our old way of life because it's continually being corrupted. In other words," she smiled faintly, "We're not getting better; we're getting worse."

"Sometimes I feel like the Christian life isn't just hard; it's impossible."

"It is when we try to live it in our own strength. John 15 explains that God sent the Holy Spirit to live in us, to give us His supernatural strength."

"Then I need to figure out how to exchange my weakness for His strength, because my weakness just took me on a long detour to London."

"And someone who loves you was willing to fly there and bring you back."

Molly exhaled. "Yes. That's true. And I need to live in truth, don't I?"

"So do I. As you now know, we *all* have painful things in our past."

"Well, a lot of people say everything happens for a reason, that God has a plan for everything."

"Yeah, and a lot of people would be wrong." Zoë's eyes flashed.

Molly's face reflected the surprise she felt at her friend's strong reaction. "What do you mean?"

"Think about it in light of the character of God—all loving, kind, merciful, just, true, and so forth. How could He either sit by and do nothing or actually *cause* horrible things that shatter people's lives? Like your brother abusing you for years, or a mother and child being killed by a drunk driver, or someone like me carelessly destroying a friend's reputation? Those things were senseless; there was no 'reason' behind them, no beautiful purpose in God's perfect plan. They are simply a result of what happened in the Garden of Eden, when Adam and Eve sinned. The result of their choice fuels all human misery."

Molly had never seen Zoë this morose. She didn't know how to deal with her mentor's pain. "I, um, should go."

"Oh, Molly, I'm sorry to be in such a foul mood. I need to figure out if there's something I can do to make amends for what I did back then. I hate knowing how I hurt my friend."

"I don't know what to say. I feel like a failure in comforting you," Molly groaned.

"You're doing fine, Molly. I just feel like I was hit with an emotional Mac truck," Zoë tried to smile.

"Could we pray together?" Molly asked, remembering the times Zoë had done the same for her.

"Yes, please!"

"I'll try starting. Bear with me. I'm inexperienced at this." Molly bowed her head. "Lord, You know and love us, and we're thankful You help when we ask! Please help Zoë know what to do. Help her reach Heather, if that's Your will. Help her trust You with this sorrow. Thank You for forgiving our sin when we ask you to, and for what You did on the cross…"

Zoë couldn't speak. "Amen," she finally said. "Amen."

Molly reached to hug her. "Let me know what happens. I will be praying for you."

Zoë blew her nose and hugged Molly back. "Thank you, friend. A true friend is someone you can trust with your secrets. You and Dan are the only ones who know about this."

"And it will remain that way," Molly assured her. She left through the back door, where she'd left her bicycle. She paused a moment, looking wistfully at the cottage behind Dan and Zoë's house, wishing Peter were home. But he was at work, where he would be most of the summer.

CHAPTER TWENTY-FOUR

As Molly waited for her first session with the psychologist, she was glad to be alone. A pleasant older woman had checked her in, then brought her to wait in a tiny room across the hall. Molly could hear her muted voice answering phone calls. She'd been afraid she'd see someone else from college, especially since she'd come to an office right across the street from campus. But the cozy waiting room felt safe. She picked up a magazine, flipping through pages she didn't see. *I hope I like her. I hope she can help me. I hope I can figure out what I need to say to her.*

The door opened and a tall, elegant middle-aged woman greeted her with a warm smile and caring brown eyes. "Molly Montgomery? I'm Dr. Holm. But please call me 'Brooke.' OK?"

Molly walked next to her, using her peripheral vision to observe the psychologist's style. Her dress, a navy crepe sheath, hit just below the knees; three primary-colored enamel bangle bracelets finished the look of simple elegance. Hearing the rhythmic "click, click, click" of Brooke's heels on the beige travertine floors, Molly noticed that her pedicure perfectly matched stylishly strappy red Italian leather sandals. Following her into the spacious office across the hall from the waiting room, Molly gazed at several shelves, each hosting an array of brightly-colored clay figures clearly made by children.

Dr. Holm noticed her interest and smiled. "My younger clients love making things with clay. It helps them express their feelings."

"That's a lot of dinosaurs." Every imaginable shape and color of miniature dinosaurs roamed the office.

"It's one way to help children talk. I ask them what they know about dinosaurs—which usually is a lot more than I do," Brooke laughed. "Eventually everyone describes dinosaurs as being 'extinct,' which is my segue to say, 'And that's what can happen to your problems.'"

"Every problem extinct? That seems like a big promise, Dr. Holm," Molly said, her voice laced with skepticism.

"Brooke," she smiled, ignoring Molly's insult. "Or would you prefer 'Dr. Brooke?'" She laughed. "That's what the kids call me." Her hands gently motioning, she said, "Sit wherever you're comfortable—the sofa or either chair."

Molly looked at the large recliner, and then sat on the edge of the brown leather sofa instead, reaching for a tapestry pillow to clasp in her lap. Determined to be open with her therapist, she forced herself to say what was bothering her. "Someone told me therapists aren't supposed to let clients call them by their first names."

"Someone?" Dr. Holm smiled.

"My stepmother. She was seeing a therapist in Chicago who told her that would make their relationship a double relationship or something like that. He said he wouldn't work with her if…."

Dr. Holm gently interrupted. "He likely meant a 'dual relationship.' Does that sound right?"

"Yes, that's the term."

"Sometimes when a therapist feels like the client wants to be best friends or even could have a romantic interest in him or her, using the formal title is appropriate. There are times when, observing someone's body language, I introduce myself as 'Doctor' instead of my first name."

"I think I understand. And I know you can't suggest it, but I can. It's likely that my stepmother was hitting on him. No wonder he wanted to be called 'Doctor.'"

Dr. Holm nodded to show she heard her, then continued. "If you're more comfortable calling me 'Doctor Holm,' please do. I usually offer 'Brooke' just because I like to have a comparatively informal working relationship. I believe you are competent, able to make good decisions about your own life. My role is to help you wonder and discover new insights and practical tools to experience profound healing." This psychologist seemed a master of segue, deftly shifting the topic. "What concerns brought you here today?"

Molly gulped. "I don't even know where to begin." She felt her mind check out of the office, abruptly reluctant to discuss her problems with a complete stranger.

"Would it help if I told you a little about myself?" When Brooke leaned forward, the light from her office window shimmered off ash-blonde highlights of her shoulder-length brunette hair.

Without thinking, Molly blurted, "I love your hair color. It is balayaged perfectly!"

She blushed, embarrassed, thinking *Kate would say something like that, not me.*

"Thanks, my stylist gets all the credit for that," Brooke smiled, her ease in accepting the compliment somehow bringing comfort to Molly. She continued, explaining, "There are hundreds of different types of therapy, so I'll only describe the ones I tend to utilize, OK?"

Molly nodded, glad for time to recoup.

"I am a cognitive behavioral therapist, which means we can work on how thoughts can influence feelings, and how actions are shaped by both. I am also solution focused, which means I believe there are proactive ways to deal with your concerns, so I don't plan for you to need to keep seeing me indefinitely. For my Christian clients who want to apply the Bible to their lives, we do some practical work there, too.

And besides all that, I'm kind of eclectic, using as many of the hundreds of forms of psychotherapy as are relevant to your concerns." She looked at the paperwork Molly had sent her before their appointment. "I see you're close to completing your master's in music. We can integrate music in our sessions, if you'd like that." She nodded toward a certificate on her wall.

Molly felt surprised that her passion for music could be part of the counseling process. She read the certificate aloud. "Brooke Holm, PsyD, Board Certified MT-BC by The Certification Board for Music Therapists."

"Shall we begin here?" Brooke turned her attention back to Molly's paperwork. "You wrote that your reason for seeking counseling is a 'recent break with reality.' Tell me about that."

"It was following my best friend's wedding here in California last month. Without telling anyone here where I was going, I took off that same night and went first to Chicago and then to London the next day."

"Do you know people in either place?"

As Molly talked about her mother's demands, her sister's invitation and her own broken engagement, Brooke seemed to get it. "So you felt overwhelmed and hopeless?"

Molly sighed. "That about sums it up."

"Sometimes people check out of reality because they don't know how to deal with their reality." She paused, watching Molly. "Do you ever notice yourself dissociating?"

"Um, what?"

Brooke's expression was serious, though it felt like she could easily smile again. "Dissociation occurs when a person temporarily checks out of current events, so to speak. Though her body is present; mentally or emotionally, she is somewhere else. There could be some memory loss—of events, people, and so forth. Some people say it feels like they're out of their bodies; others say they can't focus on reality."

"Oh, I do that all the time. Sometimes I play my flute for

hours and forget where I am. The music transports me to somewhere safe, somewhere no one can hurt me."

"Someone hurt you?"

Brooke was quick, Molly realized. "Yes, from the time I was four, my older brother molested me, day and night. I never knew when he would…"

Her deep brown eyes brimming with tears, Brooke sighed, remaining quiet, simply gazing at Molly.

The silence was comforting. Molly saw Brooke's tears and somehow felt accepted, understood.

Finally Brooke said, "I'm glad you're here. Did you know survivors of sexual abuse are often called 'numb survivors', or 'people with frozen emotions'?"

Molly was quiet, thinking, remembering. Her expression was sad.

"You *can* profoundly heal from that horrible trauma."

"Well, that's just it. I thought I *had* healed. I have great friends here at school—like Dr. Montgomery and his wife Zoë. Their niece Kate is—or was—my roommate. Their nephew is my fiancé. It was her wedding that started my spiral out of control."

"Yes, I know Dan and Zoë. Just so you know, though, our discussions here are confidential. I won't be sharing anything with anybody, unless you specifically direct me to do so—or unless there's a threat of harm to you or someone else. You probably noticed that on the therapy agreement." She held up a page Molly had signed prior to arriving.

"I noticed."

Brooke's warm smile helped Molly feel protected. "The thing is, Molly, with sexual abuse, a new situation can trigger old trauma. We need to explore tools that help you deal with triggers as they occur so you don't feel like you have to run away from life again."

"So does that mean I have to relive every horrible event that happened?"

"Does someone with physical pain have to re-experience a car crash or skiing accident to heal her internal injuries? No, they need to take time to discover and heal each wound, not re-experience them. And, God has designed your mind to know where it needs to go, which is where we'll go when you feel safe enough to address specific concerns. EMDR is one method of treatment that often is useful in healing from trauma."

"EM…what?" Molly felt confused again.

Brooke's smile enveloped Molly. "Eye Movement Desensitization and Reprocessing." She picked up two cords and handed them to Molly. "Do you feel anything?"

Molly noticed two small white lights, one at the end of each cord. Brooke flipped a switch and Molly felt a slight pulse emanating from the plastic ovals attached to the end of each cord. She nodded. "A slight vibration."

Brooke reached for the equipment, setting it back on a table beside her. She nodded toward it, "So that is some of the equipment we might use, if you decide EMDR is one way to go. It's an eight-stage protocol that helps your brain actually release trauma stored there. Some people find relief in just one or two EMDR sessions; others might want a few more. I've heard that it's the military's preferred treatment for PTSD. You can read about it on my website or at other online sites, if you're interested."

"Do I have PTSD?" Molly whispered, almost afraid to speak her fear of that diagnosis.

"I don't know. Many survivors of sexual abuse do develop PTSD. We'll look at that next time. The thing to remember is that it is only a diagnosis designed to guide treatment, not a definition of *you*. Therapy is designed to move you from being a numb survivor to one who can feel and ultimately, a woman who thrives. Sexual trauma does not have to rule your life."

They continued talking, developing an easy camaraderie. For the first time in a long time, Molly felt understood, safe.

"Do you want to come again next week?" Brooke asked.

"Sure."

"Are you willing to do some homework?"

"Wow. Homework. I'm taking three classes this summer, but I can try to get some of it done. And I'm thinking about dropping one or two of the courses, anyway."

"Do it at your own pace," Brooke said, handing her a workbook.

Molly read the title aloud. "Core Healing from Sexual Abuse. A Journey of Hope." She looked nervous. "I can't carry this across campus with *that* emblazoned on it."

Dr. Holm handed her a pale blue file folder. "Would slipping it inside this help?"

"Thanks."

"You can work at your own pace," Brooke reiterated. "And before you do chapter one, please review 'Grounding Exercises,' in the back, so you can manage an amygdala hijacking."

"I've heard that term!" Molly felt triumphant.

Nodding, Brooke continued. "Then you probably know it only takes 1/12 of a second for old trauma stored in your brain to take you back to all of the old traumatized, helpless feelings. Those feelings are so powerful that most people don't realize it's also possible to rapidly move out of the 'hijacking' and away from the intensity of trauma memories. 1/12 of a second." She smiled again. "So, this exercise offers practical tools, three kinds of exercises to help you come back to the present whenever you feel triggered by old trauma. After you feel confident that you can apply grounding techniques, you can begin the first chapter, which will help you understand some of what you're experiencing now. And if it causes you to feel overwhelmed, just stop and do grounding exercises, OK?"

"Do you really think I can do this? It's hard to imagine being able to heal."

"Have you heard of neuroplasticity?" Seeing Molly nod, Brooke continued. "It's great news for all of us. Our brains *can* continue changing and growing throughout your life. Dr. Earl Henslin says we can actually stimulate our neurons to multiply and connect and branch 'wildly in our brains' in several ways, which we can discuss next time if you want to.

"Let's see if I can apply even a fraction of what we've discussed today."

"I think you'll be pleasantly surprised, Molly. Now you have some tools to help you get where you want to go." Brooke smiled as Molly said goodbye.

Just to be safe, Molly stopped in the waiting room to put the workbook in the file folder, zipping it securely in her backpack before walking across campus to her first class.

CHAPTER TWENTY-FIVE

Shifting his car into reverse, Peter wondered what made him think he could do two counseling internships at the same time. He carefully backed out of his parking spot, checking traffic before entering the fray. *Twenty minutes to get to the church.*

He had spent the morning at Casa de Esperanza, the drug treatment facility where he worked four hours, three days a week. The intense demands made it feel like he was there more than twelve hours a week. Like this morning, when a flaaka addict arriving for detox attacked him in the hallway as he was walking toward his second group therapy session. Peter rubbed his arm, for the first time seeing—and feeling—multiple scratches and bruises. He was grateful that three of his colleagues were also walking down that hall during the 'event,' as staff referred to these routine angry outbursts. It took all four of them to subdue the thirty-year-old man.

The other staff joked about 'frequent fliers,' addicts who completed inpatient rehab only to return time and again for more detox and recovery. Peter was getting discouraged, wondering if his work were really helping anyone. Then, a man he'd met in the first group therapy session stopped him just before he reached the door for his second group. He said, "Hey, Peter, you're the first therapist who ever showed me I matter."

"What do you mean, Thomas?"

"You sit and talk with me like I'm a real person, not just your project or another addict. Thanks, man."

Remembering their conversation in the car, he smiled, aware he wasn't really the only therapist there who cared, and yet glad he'd gotten through to one of the men. *I guess it's OK to do two internships at once. Then I can still finish my master's next semester when Molly finishes hers. I just need a good night's sleep.* Traffic was light, so he drove into the church parking lot two minutes early. He ran into the counseling office complex, glad when the secretary told him his first client of five back-to-back sessions was running a few minutes late.

He always enjoyed being with fifty-year-old Ben. They had developed a comfortable working relationship, like two detectives working together to solve the mystery of Ben's chronic depression. But that session ran over, so Peter went directly from saying goodbye to Ben to greeting seven-year-old Nate and his mom in the waiting room. Nate, there because he'd been bullied at school, was too nervous to talk at first. They walked together to the play therapy room, where Nate said, "Hey, I didn't know you'd have such cool things in here." By the end of their appointment, Nate had begun telling his story via positioning action figures in a sand tray. He didn't want to leave. "Being here isn't as scary as I thought it would be. It's kinda fun, really."

After that, Peter met with a couple who began swearing at each other before they even sat down at opposite ends of the leather sofa. He motioned for a time-out. "Hey, this office is your safe zone, OK?" he said, smiling, hoping they'd stop volleying insults long enough to hear him out. He went from helping them learn new communication techniques to a quick break before an intake session with Wanda, a meth addict court-ordered to attend counseling.

"I hope they won't take this baby away," she said, patting her stomach as she eased her emaciated body into a chair, the smell of stale cigarette smoke floating from where she sat. "I lost all my other babies to the state. I had two others, ya know? They don't give a girl a chance."

"When are you due?" Peter asked.

"In about a month," she said flatly, handing him a packet of coffee-stained pages. "Here, I brought them papers they sent me in tha' mail and tol' me to fill out."

Peter thanked her, noticing her sad eyes, trying to ignore her brown teeth, misshapen stubs revealing habitual methamphetamine use.

Looking up from her paperwork, Peter said, "I see you have a job as a personal assistant?"

"Well, I jes put that there because it sounds fancy. What I really do is something else. But I didn't want to write down I meet with men." Her concave cheeks accentuated the hollow tone of her voice as she evaded labeling her work as prostitution.

He asked what she enjoyed doing in her spare time.

"Other than meth, I do like an occasional joint. But, I'm cutting down on all that, with this li'l baby livin' inside me, really I am. Sometimes I am," she muttered under her breath.

"What do you want?" he asked her.

"Huh?" she said, never considering she could want anything but what she knew.

"If a miracle happened and you were exactly where you wanted to be, doing what you wanted to do, what might it be?"

Wanda patted her stomach again, looking down. She whispered, "I'd live on a ranch back in tha' Tennessee hills and have two horses and a husband who really, truly loved me." A faint smile played on her face. "We'd ride those horses off across a river and laugh and take care o' our babes and they'd smile and laugh, too, real happy like, ya' know?"

He nodded, leaning forward to understand her soft drawl.

The smile gone, her voice tight, she continued. "But it's all a fairy tale. There ain't no place like that fer me." Her pace and volume increased, the words ricocheting, as though she had to release the memories before she could think about what she was saying. "My pa, he used ta tell me when I was growin' up in Tennessee, 'Girl, come here, and make yer pappy feel better. That's what ya were born fer.' He'd slap my behind and force himself on me, saying, 'This here's tha' mommy 'n daddy game.' She wiped a single tear from her cheek before continuing. "An' I had ta do what he said or he'd whup me. Sometimes I threw up because I didn't like ta do it. But he had a big ol' leather belt jes fer me. That's why I ran away when I was fifteen, cuz I met a man at the county fair who told me he'd be a *good* daddy ta me. He said I was too pretty ta be so sad. An' he got lots of work fer me, the same work I still do here in Caleefornya."

Peter noticed there was no light in her eyes as she spoke.

Wanda took a deep breath, then began coughing uncontrollably.

Peter gave her a bottle of water.

"Thanks," she smiled faintly, slowly sipping, catching her breath. She continued, a fierce look of determination on her face. "I had to work fer that man a long time to pay him back. So he was more like my pa. Ya know? But he tol' me I owed him big time fer the drugs he gave me to help me out ever' time I felt blue. They cost a lot. I finally paid him back but there was other men who told me I owed them a heap o' money, too, cuz I still needed to keep from feelin' so blue. I guess I'm still payin' everybody back somehow." She sighed, spent. "I never tol' no one 'bout any o' that," she said, looking down. "Yer a good list'ner."

Peter's next client was Deidre, there because she was anxious about her only child, a twenty-two year-old son, who told her he wanted nothing to do with either of his parents. "My husband and I tried to do our best. We paid for private schools, we took him on wonderful vacations, we laughed together. I don't know what went wrong. Now he says he hates us both."

Peter listened, then offered ideas to help her deal with the pain.

At the end of that session, Deidre thanked Peter and said, "This must be such a relaxing job. You get to sit here all day.

Maybe I'll go back to school. It seems like so much fun!"

Peter walked her to the door, thanking her for coming. Then he turned back to knock on the door of his supervisor's office. "Have five minutes, Dr. Keating?"

"Sure, Peter. Please call me Ed, now that we're colleagues."

"OK. Ed, I need your input. I feel overwhelmed after leading two groups at the treatment center this morning, then having five back-to-back clients here. Any advice on how to listen to everyone's problems without getting discouraged? Or how to be confident I'm giving them the right kind of help? I'm so young, and I feel inadequate."

"On a practical note, I notice your sessions running over...tell me about that."

"Well, when someone runs late..."

"Stop right there. If someone runs late, you have to end their session at the scheduled time or you won't be able to survive. If you don't have at least ten minutes between appointments, you're not being fair to yourself or your clients."

"Uh, I probably had a total of six minutes 'off' all day.'"

"That's a practical change you can make right away." Ed paused before continuing. "You need to let each of your clients know that sessions need to begin and end on time, in forty-five or fifty minutes."

"That is going to be tough. I've been pretty relaxed about that. What do I do if someone tells me he's suicidal in the last five minutes?"

"Obviously, you'll make an exception. We always put people's needs first."

Peter glanced at the clocks on either end of the room. "I asked for five minutes..."

Ed laughed. "I have more time. This is important stuff." He motioned for Peter to sit down. "After twenty years as a therapist, I still pray every day that I'll hear what everyone is *really* saying and offer wise counsel. Frankly, I still feel inadequate sometimes. The only way I feel safe helping people is to ask the God who intimately knows each one to lead in His wisdom."

"This afternoon, I listened to five different kinds of sadness. I didn't know there were this many sorrows in the world."

"Just wait; you'll hear more than you can even imagine."

"But I don't know if I'm going to get it right."

"Hold up your hands, Peter."

Dutifully, Peter lifted both hands.

"Now look at your palms."

"OK."

"See any nail holes?"

For a split second, Peter looked puzzled. His eyes lit up when he got it.

Ed nodded, smiling. "We only have one Savior. We can point people to him. And, if they don't want to hear about him, our job is to quietly, persistently respect their beliefs. We show his love by exhibiting compassion, kindness and openness to everyone who comes here, listening to their unique concerns—whatever they are, whoever they are, wherever they are. If you'll look at each person who comes into your office as the only person in the world, you will do OK. Because at that moment, that person *is* the only person in your world."

Peter headed home, stopping at Del Taco for a macho burrito, savoring each fragrant bit of grilled chicken smothered in their inimitable red and green sauces, as well as the sour cream and cheddar cheese. *Every bite seriously delicious,* he thought.

He planned to call Molly when he arrived home; instead, he fell asleep the moment he sat in his recliner. When he awakened the next morning, he stretched, stiff from sleeping all night in the chair, and looked at his phone. "Eight o'clock! I don't believe I slept 12 hours!" And it was already time to shave and begin the drive back to the church to counsel the eight clients scheduled to see him that day. *I'll try Molly when I have a break today.*

CHAPTER TWENTY-SIX

Molly had one semester left after her summer classes. She had planned to coast through summer school so she could concentrate on next semester's graduate recital. Then, her *Master of Music in Performance: Woodwind Emphasis* should be in hand. But she hadn't counted on the time and energy therapy would consume.

Her second appointment with Dr. Holm—Brooke—was a week after her first one. She sat down each morning before class to work on the counseling homework, as Brooke had advised. Remembering how rapidly her life had spiraled out of control was all the incentive she needed to stay on track. It was the day before her appointment when Molly had another scare.

When she got up that morning, she noticed more than a few strands of hair on her pillow and wasn't too concerned at first. It had been falling out lately, more than usual—but not in clumps. But as she was studying, absently twisting her hair, a substantial clump of hair simply fell out in her hand. She tried to focus on the Core Healing workbook, but all she could do was worry about becoming bald.

Brooke greeted her as warmly as she had on their first visit. Molly noticed Brooke's thick hair cascading luxuriantly onto a cream silk blouse. She couldn't bear to think about thick hair, so wondered instead whether Brooke's tailored slacks were linen or cotton.

Brooke interrupted her random thoughts. "Molly, are you with me?"

"Oh, I'm sorry. I...I guess I'm distracted. Did you say something?"

Brooke's eyes mirrored her concern. "How was your week?"

"It was OK until yesterday morning. I noticed then that my hair is falling out, in big clumps. I'm think I'm going bald." Molly attempted to laugh, but it sounded more like she choked.

"Hmm." Brooke became quiet for a moment, noticing. "Can you tell me what you ate this morning?"

"Oh, nothing. I mean, I drank a cup of coffee. And I have a protein bar in my backpack to eat on the way to class."

"And yesterday? What did you eat then?"

"Let's see. For breakfast, coffee. I didn't have time to eat a protein bar yesterday, but I had a carrot and some almonds last night."

"Is that your typical diet, Molly?"

"Pretty much. During the short time I was a model, I learned to watch food consumption carefully. Sometimes I buy a rotisserie chicken and eat that all week. And I often keep lettuce in my fridge."

"Mmm, hmm," Brooke said, opening a file and pulling out a piece of paper. She handed it to Molly. "Molly, you are presenting several indications of an eating disorder. We'll look at this more carefully in the weeks to come. In the meantime, please take this list of several dieticians. Will you make an appointment with one of them this week?"

"Wait a minute! An eating disorder? Me? How can that be?"

"You aren't eating enough food to maintain a healthy body. That could be why you're hair is falling out, Molly. You need to see a physician to find out for sure. Do you have a family physician here?"

"Student health."

"Would you like names of the doctors there who seem most knowledgeable about eating disorders? Oh, one more question about your diet, OK?" She waited for Molly's nod. "Have you ever experienced binge eating? It, like not eating enough, is often comorbid with sexual abuse."

Molly's eyebrows arched. "English, please."

"Comorbid? That basically means occurring at the same time as…"

"OK. So you're saying there are domino effects from what I experienced in childhood?"

"Yes."

"I saw binge eating and anorexia on the list of possible results of sexual abuse, here," Molly said, turning to page four of the Core Healing workbook. "Is that what you're saying I have?"

"We're not jumping to conclusions. At this point, we are simply wondering, making sure we don't miss important concerns. Anorexia nervosa, or anorexia, refers to self-starvation, lack of appetite and so forth. It is often related to feelings of fear and a loss of control."

"I don't understand."

"When someone is afraid of failing, or being abandoned—or of getting fat, there is a false sense of being in control when she restricts food intake."

"I've been doing that since high school, but I've never thought it was a problem…"

Brooke continued, "Binge eating is when someone rapidly consumes a lot of high-calorie food. It is difficult to stop the bingeing process once it begins. A typical binge is from 1,500 to 3,000 calories—but it can go higher, much higher, than that. And sometimes—not always—but particularly if someone is afraid of gaining weight, he or she will purge following the binge. Purging is making oneself vomit in various ways. About sixty percent of people who have anorexia are also bulimic, a condition sometimes referred to as bulorexia."

Molly checked out, her mind propelling her back to LAX, gorging on chocolates in the women's restroom.

"Where are you, Molly?"

Molly didn't respond.

Her tone firm and crisp, yet caring, Brooke spoke. "Molly, press your feet into the floor. Good, now wiggle your toes."

Molly complied.

"What do you notice?"

"That my polish is chipped."

"What did you sense?"

"My toes were moving."

"Good, good. And where are you now?"

"Here, in your office." Molly looked quizzically at Brooke. "Where else would I be?"

"You weren't here a moment ago, at least not mentally or emotionally. Where did you go?"

Molly felt her cheeks redden with shame. She mumbled, "In the bathroom at LAX, gorging on chocolates that I didn't even taste. Specifically, I was eating an entire one-pound box of See's Truffles."

"Is that the only time you can recall bingeing?"

"I think so. But there are pockets of time, especially during grade school, that I can't remember much of anything at all."

"I understand. That, too, is typical for survivors of sexual abuse. When trauma has been severe, survivors often suppress or repress memories."

"Am I going to *ever* get beyond this?"

"Absolutely! Did you notice what happened when we did the grounding exercise?"

"The toe-wiggling?"

"Right. You were able to move yourself back into the present by making a small physical motion. What you were doing was actually moving your thoughts away from the amygdala and the trauma stored there and into the PFC— prefrontal cortex."

"That seems too easy."

"When you know what to do, it *is* easy. The reason to practice grounding is so you can remember it in the midst of feeling triggered."

"Please explain…"

"Being triggered is when you're taken back mentally or emotionally to the feelings of trauma associated with abuse. It initiates feelings that are called 'flooding,' that cause you to feel out of control." She paused, noticing Molly didn't understand her description. "Have you ever seen the aftermath of a river flooding?"

"No."

"Hmm, well the rushing waters of the river can cause boulders the size of a car to tumble down the riverbed, destroying houses and anything else in their path."

"Sounds horrible."

"So when you think of your emotions 'flooding,' does that help you imagine how challenging it is to stop their cataclysmic destruction in your life?"

"Well, that's not good news. I feel helpless."

"And that's why many survivors of sexual abuse 'numb' their pain with drugs, alcohol, sex—which releases various neurochemicals—or develop eating disorders. When someone doesn't know how to *stop* the flooding, it can be as mentally and emotionally disastrous to a person's life as a flooding river is to everything in its path."

"OK, how do I actually stop the flooding?"

"When you notice any of the five F's, immediately do grounding exercises."

"Fight, flight, freeze, fornicate, feed?"

"Right. It's challenging, but definitely doable. So we just did physical grounding; let's review the other two kinds of grounding, so you can bring yourself back into the present any time you dissociate." Noticing Molly's confusion, she added, "When you check out mentally or emotionally as a result of being triggered—then flooding."

"OK, grounding exercises. That was the first homework I did, in the appendix at the back of the workbook, right?

Mental grounding is a way to focus—like when I count backwards from 100 by 5s, or when I notice specific shapes or colors wherever I am at the time of a hijacking."

"Great. You've got it! And the third kind?"

"That's harder." Molly turned to page 81. "*Soothing grounding*. But I don't think I can do that. I mean, talk to myself in a kind voice? Really? I only know how to condemn myself."

"It *is* challenging. Let me ask you this, Molly. Is learning how to speak to yourself with a kind voice worth the effort or do you want to keep talking to yourself in a voice full of shame, anger, and condemnation?"

"Ha, ha. I get your point."

"It's like talking to yourself in the voice you'd use to soothe a crying baby."

"OK, but what do I actually *say* to myself with this kind voice?" Molly felt irritated. She had rarely talked with any babies. Then she remembered her namesake in London and smiled faintly.

"Where were you then, Molly?"

"You can tell when I'm thinking outside this room?"

"I try to be alert." Brooke's smile was infectious.

Molly's smile broadened and included her eyes. They lit up when she said, "I was in London, meeting my friend's baby, who is actually named after me."

CHAPTER TWENTY-SEVEN

Analese was feeling overwhelmed. It happened every year at the same time in mid-June, the time when her parents were killed in a car accident. She knew she should be ready for it. But, this year, with the additional demands of a baby and a toddler, Analese was caught off guard.

I was only ten years old, she thought, remembering the police officer that came to her summer camp to notify her that both her parents were killed in an accident on their way to pick her up. She remembered how her maternal grandmother moved from California to her family home in Illinois so she could stay in her private school with people she knew. *Did I ever thank Grandmother for giving up her life to help me? And she is gone now, too.*

When Sam came home from work, he found her in the den, crying. "My dearling, what's wrong?" he asked, surprise and concern in his gentle Scottish brogue.

"It hit me this morning that I have no mother to call when Molly is teething or when Andrew does something adorable—which happens to be every single day," she smiled faintly. "I just wish I had a family sometimes."

"You have a family, Dearling—my parents, aunts and uncles—they all love you and are your family, too. You can take the kids to see them in Edinburgh any time you want to go. They'd love it."

Analese nodded. "I know I can talk with your mom—and I do call her, many days. But today, I'm missing *my* mom."

"I wish I could have known your parents."

Analese's sob was so loud that baby Molly looked up from the other side of the room where she was playing with colorful plastic blocks. Andrew stopped pushing his fire truck, his eyes filled with concern. He left the truck in the middle of the room and walked over to pat his mama's arm. "You be OK, Mama. Jesus love you," he sang sweetly. "You be all better."

"Oh, honey, you're right. Jesus does love us," Analese said, lifting him to her lap. Molly zoomed across the room, the fastest crawling she'd ever done. Her chubby hands reached for her mama. She didn't want to share. Laughing, Analese made room for her seven-month-old. Reveling in the sweetness of her little family, she smiled. "With these two, how can I stay sad?"

"What about calling your great-aunt in California?"

"Aunt Elizabeth! She would love to hear about the children, and I've been terrible about staying in touch. Oh, Sam, I don't think I've called her since Molly was a newborn."

Sam gave her a gentle hug. "It's not too late."

"Would you go with me to California sometime, to take the children to meet her?"

"Actually, I've been intending to tell you I have to go to Scotland in two weeks for work. What if you'd take the kiddos to California then? I was going to ask you if you wanted to come to Edinburgh with me, but I found out today my parents will be in Spain during that time, so you'd be on your own most of the day. I'll be there at least a week, maybe longer, depending on how long it takes to complete the ethics programme. I'll be training the Scottish personnel at several offices," he added.

"It would be fun to go," Analese began saying when Molly

squeezed out of her arms, flopping, laughing, onto the floor. At the same time, Andrew bounded off her lap, landing on his sister's foot. Molly wailed, more in anger than pain. Both Sam and Analese were immediately engaged in calming their children, making sure neither of them was hurt.

Sam laughed. "OK, so I'm guessing this is proof positive you won't want to travel to America alone with our charming wee ones."

"Can you imagine their antics on a crowded plane for—what is it? Eight or nine hours?"

"Something like that." Sam reached to hug Molly, who wiggled away from him, intent on crawling toward her favorite doll. He sang, his voice a rich baritone. "Let's fly away, oh fly away. Want to fly to Scotland one day soon?"

"Absolutely. It's a date," Analese smiled. One of their favorite inside jokes was Sam's spontaneous songs about where he wanted her to 'fly away' with him. So far they had traveled to twelve countries—but all before the children were born. Their only out-of-London travels since Andrew's birth were visiting Sam's family in nearby Scotland. "Do you think your mom will mind us taking over her house?"

"No, she already asked if you and the kids could come. And, depending on how long my work keeps us there, they might get home at the tail end of our visit."

"Just let me know when to start packing."

CHAPTER TWENTY-EIGHT

Zoë sat at her computer, trying every combination of names she could think of. Heather's maiden name, then her married name, which she discovered in a news article entitled "Colorado Teachers Plan Wedding to Include Students." It described Heather's husband as "Boulder Teacher of the Year," stating that Heather was already being considered for next year's title "because of her innovations in education."

Heather and Zach's wedding made news because of *how* they involved their students. Zoë smiled, remembering her kindness and creativity, captured beautifully in words by the reporter. "This bride chose all of her third-grade girls to be her bridesmaids and let them decide what to wear." The accompanying pictures showed a line of twelve third-grade girls dressed as every princess imaginable. All different. *Oh, that sounds just like Heather,* Zoë thought, reminded again of how much she missed her.

Heather's husband chose students as groomsmen from Heather's class rather than his own, so none of her students would be left out of the ceremony. The boys, naturally, were dressed as princes. The bride looked regal in her gown, its twelve-foot train rivaling that of any of the world's finest royalty. Her radiant smile gave Zoë hope that she'd healed from the horrific betrayal at her first teaching job.

Feeling a faint surge of hope, she googled Heather's married name—Heather Carmello—and easily found her Facebook account. Studying her friend's picture, Zoë felt anguish, wondering what could have been. She decided to send her a brief message, praying for just the right words to apologize. She longed for Heather to respond to her this time, at last. Zoë had finally stopped trying to reconcile about ten years prior, after she'd tried calling Heather at her parents' home, and they shrieked, "How dare you harass our daughter! You have done enough damage for a lifetime."

Zoë sighed, prayed, then wrote, simply, "Heather, it's Zoë. Please forgive me. Can we talk sometime? I know I was a jerk when we taught together, and I want to make amends. Please let me know what I can do. Here's my number..." As she pressed "return," she prayed fervently that her words communicated her deep regret for wounding her friend. *Former friend,* she reminded herself grimly.

When Dan came home, he noticed her distress. "What's going on?"

Zoë was uncharacteristically quiet.

He set his briefcase on the floor to give his wife his full attention. "You're trying to contact Heather again." It was a statement, not a question. He knew nothing that upset his wife as much as remembering that season of her life.

"Yes, I found her married name online."

"Honey, when you try to tell someone you're sorry and they don't want to connect, you might consider stopping." He put his arms around her. "God knows you're sorry. You've told her—what, about a dozen times, in about a dozen different ways? Flowers, a box of gifts, letters of apology..."

"But she has never heard me."

"What you're saying is you can't forgive yourself unless she does? Is that about right?"

"I guess so," Zoë murmured.

"Has God forgiven you?" It was a rhetorical question.

"Yes," Zoë said, not believing it. She opened her laptop and set it on the kitchen counter, clicking open the news article about Heather and Zach. She turned the screen to face Dan. "Here she is, honey. Wasn't her wedding beautiful? I could have been there…" She sighed.

"Zoë, every one of us has things about the past we can't change. What we can do is live in the present, and be the kind of loving people God created us to be *now*. If you keep going back to the past, you'll easily become depressed."

"And if I live in the future, I'll be anxious," Zoë finished for him, having heard Dan explain that to students countless times. "OK, Doc, I know what I need to do."

"Which is?"

"Live in the present. And pray." Distracted by the distinct tone of an inbound message, she clicked Messenger. "I don't believe it! Heather already wrote me back." Her heart rate increased as she clicked the message to open it. Her face fell and she began to sob. "Read it, Dan. I can't bear to say what she wrote."

He read aloud, "Zoë, how dare you think you can come into my happy life and wreak havoc again?!!! Stop trying to reach me. And don't EVER contact my parents to try to weasel your way back to me. They hate you as much as I do. I was afraid you'd find my new name through that article about our perfect wedding. But now that you have, I know you cannot rob me of my happiness or my wonderful career—ever again! Just seeing your name makes me want to vomit. Do not ever try to reach me again, on social media, through the mail—or any other way. No flowers. No phone calls; if you do try to reach me in any way, shape or form, I'll find a lawyer and sue you. And I am officially blocking you on FB as of NOW."

Zoë sighed, her shoulders heaving with sobs.

"You have an answer. Not the one we wanted, surely, but an answer."

"It is hard to accept that there's absolutely nothing I can do to make it right," Zoë moaned. She rubbed her wet nose with her hand.

Dan handed her a tissue. "You could pray she'll learn to forgive. But I wouldn't even 'park' too long on praying for her, if it takes you into these morose thoughts. It seems like she has developed what Dr. Fred Luskin calls a 'grievance story.' If that's the case, it means that every time she recalls you, she associates you with the pain, shame and embarrassment she experienced when you two were teachers together..."

"Thanks for reminding me, Dan," she groaned.

"I didn't mean to make it worse," he reached to hug her. "All of us have been wounded or betrayed by someone we trusted. And sometimes, we're the one who did the betraying."

Her eyebrows arched. "Not you."

"That's not true. Even when I've been too busy to be someone's friend, it can feel like a betrayal to that person. But when we stay in the blaming phase of any situation, person or concern, we become stuck in anger or bitterness. Can I read you what Frederick Buechner said about that?"

She nodded, needing redirection for her spiraling emotions, following him into the den.

He reached to a well-worn page in Luskin's book, "Forgive for Good," then gently motioned for his wife to sit by him on the leather sofa while he began to read. "Buechner wrote, 'Of the seven deadly sins, anger is possibly the most fun. To lick your wounds, to smack your lips over grievances long past...to savor to the last toothsome morsel both the pain you are given and the pain you are giving back—in many ways it is a feast fit for a king. The chief drawback is what you are wolfing down is yourself. The skeleton at the feast is you.'"

"That's a gruesome picture." Zoë paused, lifting her head from where it was resting on Dan's shoulder. "So Heather's hating me is hurting *her*?"

"Absolutely. And you keep hurting yourself every time you focus on that time in your past. Instead of continually beating yourself up for something you can't change, you can choose a different emotion toward her. Like pity. Or sorrow." He flipped through the book, then handed it to Zoë. "This might be something you'd enjoy reading. It offers practical ideas that could help you forgive yourself, too."

"OK, I'll read it," she said, sighing again. "In the meantime, I can pray more hopefully, choosing Bible verses to pray for Heather instead of reviewing the old, sad stuff over and over ad nauseum." She smiled sheepishly, raising her right hand. "My solemn promise to you is that, instead of focusing on what I did *then*, I'll ask God to show her His love *now*. Heather doesn't really need to know what I think, anyway. She certainly has made it crystal-clear that she has no desire to be in touch." Still seated, she pressed her feet into the floor.

"What are you doing?"

"Those grounding exercises you've been talking about to everyone who comes here. I pay attention," she laughed. "And now, sir, I'm trying to move back into my prefrontal cortex."

He laughed. "You're adorable."

"Ha, ha. But it really works. I'm already thinking more clearly."

"I'm proud of you, my love." He followed her example, pressing his feet next to hers, into the Persian carpet, then lifting his feet to wiggle his toes.

"Oh, you're trying to do the fancy kind of grounding and show me up, aren't you," Zoë laughed.

"Yeah, well I am the psychologist, after all."

"Not in this house, you're not. You're my boyfriend." Smiling, she let his arms enfold her.

CHAPTER TWENTY-NINE

Molly couldn't remember where she'd parked her bicycle en route to class. She'd been late leaving her apartment that morning and did everything on autopilot. She felt herself getting upset, then stopped. *I can pray,* she thought, remembering what she'd read that morning. "Even if my father and mother abandon me, the LORD will hold me close. Teach me how to live, O LORD. Lead me along the right path…" The words were from Psalm 27, and today was June 27. She and Peter had agreed to read one Psalm a day corresponding with the days of the month.

She looked next to her and noticed her bike, right where she'd parked it. *I know God isn't some wizard, waiting to give me what I want. But maybe I need to trust Him more—with the specific problems of every day,* she reasoned as she put her bike chain into her backpack. She decided to text Peter. *Hey, hon. Guess what? I learned something in our Psalm of the day!*

Perfect timing! He texted back. *I have a ten-minute break. Can you talk?*

She called him. "This is amazing. We're hardly ever free at the same time."

"So what did you learn?"

"I couldn't find my bike, and I remembered God's

promise to lead me on the right path, so I asked Him to—
and when I looked up, there was my bike!"

"Oh, that's cool."

She heard him sigh. "What's wrong?"

"I just wish it were always so easy. I'm praying, too, about
one of the guys in treatment who ODed last night."

"He died?

"Not so far. He's in the ER after overdosing on
prescription painkillers. Sometimes I can't take the
discouragement of this work."

"Peter, God promises to hold you close and teach you
how to live and lead you on the right path, too. He will get
you through this day—and He will show you how to help the
people you're counseling."

Peter's face brightened visibly as he heard Molly's words,
realizing she was comforting him for the first time, ever.
"Thank you, Molly. I needed that. You've just made my day."

"Could I make dinner for you tonight?"

"You cook now, too?" he teased her.

"Well, it might be something from the deli, or maybe I'll
call your Aunt Zoë for help with a recipe."

"Oh, could you ask her how she makes her meat loaf?
That is absolutely the best comfort food ever."

"Meat loaf it is. What time?"

When they ended their conversation, Peter was astonished,
realizing their relationship had just moved into the healthiest
place it had ever been. They were equals. He also realized he
needed to marry her *sooner* rather than later. *I need her.*

Molly's call to Zoë brightened Zoë's day, too. "This is just
what I needed, Molly."

"You needed to give me cooking advice?"

"No, something constructive to do. OK, so meat loaf is
the easiest recipe, ever. I learned it from my grandmother.
You get about a pound of lean ground beef, smoosh it..."

"Is that a special cooking technique?" Molly's question
was serious.

Zoë laughed. "I forget, this is your first solo cooking

adventure. All I mean by 'smoosh' is stir it up a bit, then add about a cup of fine bread crumbs."

"Do I have to buy those?"

"Do you have any day-old bread?"

"Yes, actually I do. Gluten-free. Typically, I wouldn't eat bread, but my therapist is encouraging me to eat regularly, so I've been having a piece of toast with almond butter for breakfast. She's having me keep track of what I eat all day, every day."

"I'm glad you're eating more."

"It's hard. I'm so used to telling myself not to get bigger than a size two."

"But you're tall. I'm glad you're eating. You'll look lovely no matter what! Back to the recipe: you just crumble two slices of bread in your hands, toss that into the bowl with the meat, and mix it together—with your hands, a spoon, whatever. Finely chop a couple of stalks of celery, and oh, maybe about a fourth of an onion—a sweet Vidalia onion if you can find it, but another kind is OK, too. Or, if you don't like onions, use only a tablespoon or so of chopped onion."

"Got it. What else?"

"Add about a tablespoon of Worcestershire sauce; one egg, lightly beaten; some milk."

"Some milk...how much?"

"Oh, let me think. I just do all of this by habit. About ½ cup of milk should work."

"OK, anything else?"

"A little bit of salt. I used to put in a teaspoon, but Dan and I are trying to cut back on salt, so I just put in about one-fourth teaspoon, and it tastes fine. See what you think. You might want a little more."

"One-fourth teaspoon of salt."

"Pepper, too, about one-half teaspoon. Then, mix it all together—add some ketchup, maybe two tablespoons of that. Do you have a loaf pan?"

"I'll buy one when I get groceries."

"Spray the pan with cooking spray. Pat the meat mixture

into that, and shape it into a loaf. Finally, score it on top with a fork."

"What?"

"Um, you know, make what you students call a 'hash tag' on top of the meat loaf." She laughed. "Then squirt ketchup liberally on top before baking it, uncovered, in a preheated 350 degree oven for an hour. You could bake a couple of potatoes at the same time. They are great with meat loaf."

Molly's voice was soft. "How do I bake potatoes?"

"All you need to do is scrub them a bit with a vegetable brush, while you rinse them with water."

"Um, what is a vegetable brush?"

Zoë chuckled. "It's just a small brush to scrub dirt off of vegetables; if you don't have one, you can use a paper towel to clean them."

"I'll add a vegetable brush to my list. Who knew I'd be brushing my vegetables one day?" Molly laughed.

"Very funny. Yes, now you have more than teeth and hair to brush! So, keep brushing your potatoes until they're shiny…"

"Really?"

"No, just kidding…just until they're clean. After that, you can either bake them as they are or wrap them in foil—if you want to doll them up, you can lightly dab on butter, then sprinkle them with garlic pepper before wrapping them in foil. Then you just pop them in the oven at the same time you put the meat loaf in. You could buy some sour cream, too, because Peter likes that on his potatoes, as well as butter."

"Thanks for the great ideas. Should I make a salad, too?"

"Perfect, Molly. Sounds like Peter's in for a treat!"

Molly's bicycle basket barely contained her groceries when she pedaled home from the store. She began preparing the meat loaf first, carefully following the detailed instructions she wrote as Zoë talked. She thought of the dinners Kate made when they lived together. *That would be all of them,* she realized. Even the times they had invited Carlos and Peter over for dinner, Kate had done the majority of the work.

Sometimes she had the salad ingredients, already washed, on the counter for Molly to put together when she breezed in from class. *I need to tell her I'm sorry I was never there to help*, Molly thought, pushing a strand of hair off her face.

By six, she had the meat loaf and potatoes in the oven. She set the table with extra care, digging out cloth napkins Kate gave her for her last birthday. "You'll enjoy using these someday. It makes a meal feel special," she'd said as Molly unwrapped her gift. She studied the napkins for a moment, then tied them around the forks with the same knot she used on her neck scarves. The table did look special.

Peter arrived at seven, right on time. As Molly opened the door, he handed her a bouquet of red roses. "For my love," he said.

"Beautiful," she said, hugging him.

He was surprised at her spontaneity—and also nervous, not about her but about himself and his incredible desire for her. "Everything in here smells great—you included," he grinned.

He walked into her tiny kitchen to help her finish the salad. Together, they set the food on the table, then Peter pulled out Molly's chair.

"The last meal we had alone was when we got engaged— for the second time, in London," Molly recalled, smiling faintly.

"I have something important to talk about at this meal, too," he said, not meaning to jump into his idea quite yet.

"This time, I think I already know what you want to say."

"No way. Really?"

"Try me."

"OK. What do you think I want to say?"

Molly's face wasn't easy to read. All the time she was preparing dinner for Peter, she had one thought, over and over again. It was time to say it aloud. "We need to get married soon."

Peter sat back in his chair, stunned. "I, uh," he stammered. "I didn't think you'd want to do it. I thought you'd want to wait."

"Peter, today was the best day I've had since we got engaged. All day I've had fun thinking about you, planning a meal you'd enjoy and anticipating just being with you. But we can't just spend a couple of hours now and then with each other. We're both too busy. How soon could we get married, really?"

"I don't know. I hadn't even let myself dream. But, you're right, that's what I wanted to talk about tonight. After dinner, we could do a computer search about getting a California marriage license."

"Absolutely," she beamed. "I love the way God is leading us! Now," she said, handing him his napkin with a flourish, "let's eat. I want to see how you like this, the first meal I've ever prepared by myself."

They bowed to pray. Peter began, "God, show us how to do this, when to get married—and how to live so our marriage will bring You joy. Thank you for bringing us together." He looked up, his smile as broad as the room.

"Amen," Molly added.

Peter, savoring his first bite, said, "This meat loaf tastes just like Aunt Zoë's. But it's even better."

"Better?"

"Because it's made with your love. If this is your first cooking attempt, I can't wait for the second!"

When they finished eating, he helped her do the dishes, both of them laughing, tossing bubbles on each other. But Molly's feelings were hurt when he asked, "Do you mind if we go to Dan and Zoë's to do our computer search?"

"Don't you like being alone with me?"

"That's just it. I like it too much. I'm afraid of how much I desire you."

She blushed, knowing what he meant. She felt the same way. "OK. Let me grab my purse."

As they drove, she asked, "Peter, are we crazy?"

"Oh, yeah, crazy in love," he quipped.

"No, really. I can't believe how easily I changed my mind.

And you do remember I'm in therapy and have a lot of healing to do?"

"Hey, we're all a work in progress," he smiled. Then, noticing her concern, he reached to hold her hand. "Babe, we've been engaged for more than a year. We've known each other since grade school. We know each other's history and have the support of friends and family. We love each other. I think we can do a better job finishing grad school when we're together rather than apart."

"It's going to be a nightmare with my mom. She'll probably want one of her boyfriends to walk me down the aisle."

"That's not happening," Peter said, protecting her.

"We need to figure out how to do this so it's not a major disaster."

"Elope?"

"Maybe. Let's ask your aunt and uncle. They know a lot more about life than we do. And let's call your parents, too."

"Want me to call now, so they know first?" He handed her the phone. "Will you make the call and put in on speaker?"

"Absolutely." Suddenly, inexplicably, she felt nervous.

He noticed her tension and mouthed, "Don't worry. Everything is going to be great," just as his mom answered. He shifted gears. "Mom!" he said. "I'm glad we reached you."

Her voice tight, she said, "Honey, is everything OK?"

"Better than ever," he said, his voice brimming with joy. "Can you get Dad?"

"Here he is."

"Hey, Son. Good to hear from you!"

"Molly is here, too."

"Hi, Molly! How are classes going?"

"Good. But we're calling about something much more amazing than classes…"

Brandon and Kelly looked at each other, both of their faces registering shock as they realized what Molly meant. They waited for Peter to say it.

"We want to get married right away, or as soon as

possible."

"Any special reason?"

"Yes, we're in love and tired of waiting to be together."

"I agree with Peter," Molly said. "And also, we think we'll both make it through life more easily if we're married rather than single."

Brandon, teasing, said, "That's a little counter-cultural, isn't it?"

"Stop it, honey," Kelly interrupted. "We don't want them to change their minds."

"We're not going to change our minds," Molly spoke decisively. "But we're not quite sure how to plan everything, especially so we don't upset my mom."

"Your mom is always upset, isn't she, Molly?" Peter asked, only half-teasing.

"Good point. OK, then, what do you think we should do, Mr. and Mrs. Johnson?"

Brandon said, "We still can't get you to say our names, but that's all right. Soon, I hope you'll be willing to call us 'Mom' and 'Dad.'"

"OK. And would you walk me down the aisle, 'Dad-to-be?'" she asked, surprising everyone, including herself.

"It would be an honor," he said simply.

"Dad, how soon can we do this?" Peter interrupted. "We have a one-week break between summer and fall semesters. Is that too soon?"

"Have you completed any premarital counseling?" Kelly asked, aware of the challenges young couples face.

"Sort of. The semester after we were first engaged, I was taking Marriage and Family. Part of our course work was learning how to use several marriage assessments. Molly came to six class sessions when we were learning how to use PrepareEnrich. It showed our relationship in ten different areas—like spiritual beliefs, communication, conflict resolution...."

"And what did it show?" his dad asked.

"Well, a lot has changed since then," Peter tried to redirect the question.

"And…"

"It showed we needed significant work on communication and conflict resolution."

"Have you done that?"

"We're willing to work on it," Molly said. "I'm in individual counseling so that I can deal with the root issues that caused me to temporarily drop out of life. I know I have a lot of work left to do, but at least I'm finally making progress. Before, I didn't let myself feel the pain so I didn't know there was any healing left to do."

"Thank you for sharing that, Molly—and for all the hard work you're doing. We're praying for you," Kelly said, her voice choking up. "I can't imagine how difficult it is to heal from—everything."

Molly looked at Peter, her face reflecting his grin. She said, "It's a lot more difficult *not* to heal than it is *to heal*. All I've been doing is trying to numb out the pain with activities, success, and a lot of other things."

Peter squeezed her hand and whispered. *I'm so proud of you, Babe.* To his parents, he said, "We're on our way to Dan and Zoë's now. Want us to Skype you so we can all start making wedding plans?"

"This is so exciting I can hardly stand it," Kelly said. "My mind is racing twenty different directions."

His dad spoke, "Before we get caught up in all kinds of big plans, Hon, we need to be sure the kids are preparing for *marriage,* not just a wedding."

"I really don't want a big wedding," Molly stated emphatically. "Could we just invite my mom and your family?"

"Will your mom want to help you two plan the ceremony?" Peter's mom wondered.

"Probably not. Anyway, I'm afraid she'd find some way to destroy it. Instead of being the sacred experience Peter and I want, it would be something to make *her* feel good." Molly hesitated. "Am I being selfish if I don't ask her to help us plan?"

Peter spoke, his tone serious and caring. "She has caused a lot of torment in your life. I want our wedding to be the first day of our marriage, a day for you to start an entirely new chapter of your life—and for us to begin our life as one. A life of joy. No, you're not being selfish; you're being wise." He turned the car into his aunt and uncle's driveway. "Hey, Mom and Dad, we're here. We'll take a few minutes to tell Uncle Dan and Aunt Zoë and then Skype, OK?"

"We'll check California marriage law online and be ready with some info when you call back," his dad said. "And I want you to think about getting some counseling to help you build your communication skills. That's one of the top two marital problems couples face."

Peter's aunt and uncle mirrored his parents' joy, then echoed his dad's concern that Peter and Molly complete premarital counseling prior to their wedding.

When the six of them connected by Skype, Brandon said, "There is no waiting period to marry in California. Should be, with the divorce rate what it is."

"Dad, I promise we'll sign up for premarital counseling this week." Peter's eyes twinkled, his mouth upturned where it always went when he was teasing. "So we can get married any time we get the license?"

"Looks like it," his dad continued.

"You'll need to decide where, and find a pastor to conduct the ceremony..." Kelly added. "And find attendants."

"Kate for me. Oh, wait. My sister will be the maid of honor. Kate could be matron of honor! But what about your other sisters, Peter? Will they feel left out?"

Kelly interjected, "They had fun being in their sister's wedding, but I really think they would understand if you tell them you're keeping this simple. Maybe they could help in other ways?"

"Absolutely!" Peter said. "What if Sarah, Mary and Grace are our musicians? I love it when they sing together. Grace could play the harp, too."

"Perfect," everyone said together.

"Who will your attendants be?" Brandon asked his son.

"It would be nice to have Carlos walk down the aisle with Kate again. But, Dad, would you be my best man? Keeping it simple, with only family," Peter smiled.

"Are you sure, Son? Think I can walk Molly down the aisle and do that, too?" He had Peter's same teasing grin. "Seriously, don't you want one of your college friends?"

"Remember, we want this to be simple. Just immediate family."

Molly turned to Zoë. "Would you and Dan be in charge of the reception?"

"How did you know I was hoping you'd ask me that?"

Peter was holding his sides, laughing. "Aunt Zoë, she knew because your whole body was saying, 'Pick me, pick me!' You're the most talkative silent person I've ever met!"

"At least I waited to be asked." She turned to Molly, laughing. "So, what do you want us to do? Hosting, organizing…what?" she asked, beaming in anticipation.

"Everything. Anything. Decide a menu, maybe sandwiches for after the ceremony—unless we should just have cake? And could you bake a cake like you did for Kate and Carlos?"

Dan said, "I can set everything up here, just let me know how you want it."

"Thanks, Uncle Dan," Peter said. "You all are going to make this easy for us."

Molly hesitated. "Could we invite Analese, too, if she and her family can come? Wouldn't her kids be adorable in the wedding?"

Peter nodded, vigorously. "Definitely!"

"Have you talked with your mom?" Brandon asked Molly.

She sighed. "That's going to be difficult, since she's still in Europe. The last I heard, she's furious that I didn't stay in Illinois and house sit." She sighed again. "But I think she gets back either this week or next."

"It will take more than a month to plan even a very simple wedding," Zoë said. "What if we have it in our yard? We have the gazebo, and we could put chairs around it, too…"

"It might be too hot," Dan said.

"We're only talking about a max of twenty people, right? We could even have the ceremony inside in the family room," Zoë enthused, watching Molly's face light up.

"I can't think of anywhere I'd rather have our celebration." Molly's face shone with joy. "Oh, I have to check with my sister and find out when she can make it." Her expression changed. "And I need to find out if my mom will even come."

CHAPTER THIRTY

For her summer semester, Molly had intentionally chosen classes that weren't too challenging. Only one of them was interesting to her. She finally made an appointment to talk with her advisor about the other two, wondering if she could switch to something else.

"Dr. Thomson, I'm sorry I didn't meet with you last semester. I know you tried to call me a few times. I've been so busy with, with everything..."

"I've also emailed you. Didn't you see my messages?"

"I'm sorry..."

"Here's why I've been trying to reach you. Do you realize you've finished all of your required course work except your final recital?"

"What do you mean?"

"You've completed all of the courses you need to graduate. Your graduate recital is the only unfinished requirement!"

Molly looked as dazed as she felt. "I, um thought I had to take three classes this summer. That's what I signed up for. You mean I don't need them?"

"No, you don't. You still have time to drop them, if you want the summer to get ready for your recital. I noticed something last week," she said, looking at her computer, "You already dropped these classes once. Why did you sign up for them again?"

"It's a long story. But you have no idea what wonderful news this is."

"There is one more thing. We had a student scheduled for her recital this summer who had to go home due to a family emergency. So we have one summer graduate recital opening, if you're willing to take it."

"Absolutely. I think I'm close to having enough music ready."

"I know you do." Dr. Thomson smiled. "All we need to do is set the date. You also need to go online and register for your master's graduation ceremony. The deadline is next week."

When she left the office, she called Peter.

"Molly! Everything OK?"

"You won't believe what happened, Peter. Somehow I messed up and signed up for three classes I don't need to graduate."

"And that's a problem because…"

Hearing his smile, Molly smiled back. "It seems like we're getting a green light for our wedding. Now I actually have time to get ready."

"Have you called your mom yet?"

Silence.

"I take that as 'no.' Want me to call her?"

"You would do that? Oh, Peter, that would help so much! She won't yell at *you*. At least I hope she won't! But should I drop all of my classes? My advisor told me I still can."

"What do you think? What about that music cognition class you've told me about? Would you enjoy taking that just for fun?"

"Yes, I could stay in *Music Perception and Cognition*. There's not much homework. No tests. And what I'm learning complements what I'm doing with Dr. Holm, I mean, Brooke."

"Sorry, my love, I have a group to facilitate in five minutes. Talk to you again soon."

* * *

Molly went to meet with Dr. Holm that afternoon. She couldn't wait to tell her the news.

"Brooke, I had something amazing happen since I was here last week. Actually, several amazing things!"

CHAPTER THIRTY-ONE

After her meeting with her advisor, Molly wondered how many other important messages she'd missed in recent months. *I need to check my phone more often*, she thought.

She found a message from Peter's mom, received several days prior. "Honey, Brandon and I are so excited you and Peter want to get married this summer. We're wondering if you two could come visit us this weekend or next, to make some definite plans. Let us know what works for you, OK?"

Peter was able to change his Friday appointments. Their two-hour drive to Glendale was the perfect time to talk. "Molly, I love you. And I'm so glad you're willing to spend the rest of your life with me."

"I shudder when I think I almost threw 'us' away."

"But God stopped you, just in time." He reached across the front seat to hold her hand.

When they reached the Johnsons' home in Glendale, Peter was surprised at his parents' brown lawn. "Water restrictions," his dad said. "This is the worst drought we've experienced."

"Come on inside. Let's get out of the heat," his mom called from the doorway of the four-bedroom bungalow.

The living room seemed different, somehow, with

bookshelves stretching across two walls and books on almost every table and chair in the room. Molly felt disoriented. "I know I haven't been here for awhile, but I don't remember these books."

Kelly spoke softly, her voice tinged with sadness. "When Brandon's mom died last year, we inherited part of his dad's library. He was a pastor in Pasadena," she added. "Dan has quite a few of their dad's books, too."

Molly felt a knot in her stomach. She hadn't been there for Peter when his grandma died. She remembered, now, him asking her to come with him to the funeral. She couldn't recall which of her standard excuses she'd given him. "I'm so sorry I wasn't with you then."

Peter hugged her. "You're with us now." He turned to his mom. "OK if we get our bags from the car?" He could tell Molly needed a moment.

"About your room...we need to talk about that," his dad said, clearly teasing. "How shall we say this? 'Your' room is now the den, or the 'library,' as your mom likes to call it."

Peter's hand was already on the front doorknob, but he turned to his dad, his laugh infectious. "Oh, yeah, Mom told me my old room has been commandeered. But I don't plan to need it ever again," he said, steering Molly outside. "We'll grab our stuff and be right back."

"You OK?" he asked, as soon as the door closed behind them.

"I feel like such a jerk. I haven't been here for you or your family. I've basically been a selfish pig."

"Molly, please stop apologizing, and go with me into *our* future, not the past." He kissed her cheek lightly, then stepped back, momentarily stunned by the intensity of his feelings.

"Help me," she whispered.

"At our wedding, they'll say something like, 'From this day forward, 'til death do us part.' There's a reason for that." He handed out her roller bag and grabbed his own, jumping from the car to the sidewalk with his bag in his arms. "I love you,

Molly Montgomery—soon-to-be Johnson!" He paused, suddenly serious. "I never asked. Do you even want to take my last name? I mean, a lot of women don't…"

"You'd better believe I want your name! I want all of you! And we'd better get back inside before I grab you right here, in front of all your neighbors!"

"Who is this woman?" Peter said, only half joking. "Thank God for answered prayer!"

Both smiling, they walked back into the house. "Let's get you two settled," his mom said.

His dad opened Peter's old bedroom door with a flourish. "Welcome to the Johnson Library."

Molly and Peter gasped. Books filled dark wood bookcases, literally floor to ceiling on every wall. Two leather recliners completed the space. "This *is* a library, Dad. You finally have a space for your books."

Brandon laughed. "Look closely. Many of these are your mother's finds. Like the entire collection of Oswald Chambers' books." She keeps telling me to read them, but I'm already reading ten different books. I believe Mark Twain when he said, 'The man who does not read good books has no advantage over the man who can't read them.'"

"Honey," she gently corrected. "Chambers didn't even write any of the books credited to him. He died when he was in Egypt as chaplain to the British troops, and his wife compiled his notes into these books later. An interesting story."

"Will you tell me the story?" Molly asked.

"Later, after everyone gets settled." She smiled, eager to build the connection between them.

Peter was studying the carved oak bookcases. "Weren't these in Grandpa's office?"

"Yes." Kelly smiled. "He found them at an estate sale in Beverly Hills over thirty years ago," Kelly said. "He always said they reminded him of an English castle."

Remembering what they were doing, she turned to Molly. "You get Sarah's room, OK? Since all three girls are at camp, we have extra beds."

"They're at Eagle Lake?" Peter wondered.

Brandon turned to Molly, "It's an incredible camp in Colorado, run by the Navigators—the highlight of every summer for them. This year, Sarah is leading a high school group at camp for the first time."

"And Mary and Grace are excited about being campers again. Do you mind having Mary's room, Peter?" his mom asked.

"Perfect, I've always loved pink," Peter joked. "But, I have to say, I'm glad it's just the four of us this time, Mom and Dad, because we have a lot to talk about," Peter said, hugging her. "It's so good to be home."

"We have lemonade and iced tea ready in the kitchen." Kelly, always a relaxed hostess, had glasses ready, as well as a plate of her amazing Snickerdoodle cookies.

After everyone was seated comfortably around the kitchen table, Brandon asked, "Where do you kids plan to live?"

"We don't know yet."

"I thought we could stay in my apartment, but now that I'm finishing my master's this summer, I'll have to move out of student housing."

"We're so proud of you, Molly!" Kelly enthused.

"We'll be there for your recital," Brandon added. "Peter has been telling us all about it."

"Thank you," Molly murmured, blushing.

Peter looked pensive. "I'm sure Uncle Dan and Aunt Zoë would let us stay in their cottage."

"I like it," Molly smiled, content.

"You're too easy," Peter said, poking her arm.

"It's about time, isn't it?" Molly teased back.

Brandon got to the point. "What about finances once you get married? The top two problems couples have are usually communication and financial management. Your internship doesn't pay you enough for the two of you, Peter."

Molly spoke up. "I need to tell you something." She turned to her fiancé. "Peter, I'm sorry I forgot about this until right now. It's, um, something my sister told me when I was with her in London. How do I say this?" She hesitated, embarrassed, looking down. Taking a deep breath, she looked up and around the room. "I guess I'll just say it. Finances won't be a long-term problem. Apparently I have a trust fund from my dad, which I'll receive on my next birthday." She hesitated, "That's on October 12, when I'm twenty-five. We'll definitely need to learn how to manage it, but we'll have enough money for quite a few years. It's four..."

"Four thousand dollars will disappear quickly," Brandon said.

"Um, not thousand. Million," Molly said so softly they had to strain to hear.

"Oh, my!" Kelly was speechless.

Peter looked momentarily stunned. "That is going to take a lot of financial planning. I keep hearing horror stories of people who inherit money, squander it—and waste their lives doing nothing. I don't want to be like that."

Molly looked hurt. "I didn't know it would be such a problem."

"No, Molly. That's not what I meant. It's an incredible blessing! I just meant I want to learn how to manage it wisely—not that it's mine to manage," he stammered. "I'm not trying to tell you what to do. I mean, it's your inheritance, not mine..." He stopped, embarrassed.

Molly surprised all of them when she started giggling. "I was so nervous to tell you about this. But I think you're more nervous about it than I am, Peter. And, by the way, it's going to be *our* trust fund, not just mine."

"Well, it's kind of a shock to a poor boy like me," he said, recovering his wit.

"You're not poor, Son," his dad chimed in. "But not a millionaire, either." I think we're just trying to process your news," he turned to Molly apologetically. "Not many couples have a financial advantage like that to begin with."

Suddenly grasping *why* Molly had a trust fund, Kelly spoke, tenderly. "I'm sorry you don't have your dad, Honey," she said.

"Thank you, Mrs. Johnson, um Kelly," Molly said, wishing she could tell her she felt like she never had a dad to lose.

"That will be 'Mom,' I hope, next month!"

Turning to Molly, Brandon asked, "By the way, what is *your* mom saying about all of this?"

Peter gulped. "Yeah, that. I made the call last week so Molly wouldn't have to. I didn't know a human being could be quite as enraged as Mrs. Montgomery became. I have never been called a 'turd' before."

"You're kidding," his dad laughed.

"No, and that was the mild moment of her criticism. When she got rolling, she told me 'hell will freeze over before you marry my daughter.' I asked her to explain her specific objections and she hung up on me."

"Does that mean she's not coming for the wedding?"

"She didn't even let Peter tell her when it was. So, to answer that, we don't really know."

"Hmm. This makes planning a little more challenging. Do you mind if I try to call her?" Kelly asked. "She might be more willing to talk with another mom."

"You can try," Molly hesitated. "But I don't want you to get hurt."

Twenty minutes later, Kelly returned from the kitchen. "Well, that was interesting. It helped that she thought I was a potential client at first." Kelly smiled.

"You didn't lead her on, did you?" Brandon asked, incredulous.

"Not at all. But she jumped in, noticing my area code, wondering if I were moving from SoCal to Illinois. I explained that I was hoping she'd come to California instead."

"What happened?" Molly and Peter asked in unison.

"She said she'll come if you call her, Molly, to go over details."

Molly sighed. "Might as well do it now." She turned back to them as she was walking toward the kitchen. "Pray the guillotine won't hurt too much as it chops off my head."

While Molly was in the other room, Kelly observed, "It's no wonder Molly gets confused sometimes. I was confused at her age, and I didn't have any of the complicated family relationships she has."

"Mom and Dad, you don't know the half of it. Could we pray together while she's calling?"

Molly returned five minutes later.

"How did it go?" Peter asked.

"I am amazed and astounded. Amazed. Astounded."

"What happened?"

"She said 'It's about time you get married. And if it's the brother of Carla—she never can get Kate's name right—he must be an OK guy. Just be sure you invite the Wendhams."

"Wendhams?"

"Sheldon and Lauren Wendham are my mom's next-door neighbors and probably her only long-term friends. So, I said, 'Sure.' Is that OK?"

"It's your wedding, Honey," Kelly beamed, turning to her son. "And yours, too, of course."

"Glad you added that, Mom. I was starting to think you'd forgotten your only son." He looked at Molly. "Did I just hear you right? Your mom said I'm an "OK guy"—so I'm not a "turd" anymore?"

"You heard me right," she grinned. There was a collective sigh of relief before the wedding conversation resumed. "Now we can go forward!"

"Hip, hip, hooray," Peter cheered. He picked up two sofa pillows and whacked them together like cymbals, marching around the living room. "Bring out the band. This is a huge moment! May the plans for our festivities begin!"

Molly laughed out loud, then paused. "I still want our wedding to be really simple," she said, emphatically. "Not a hundred people, please."

"And no games at the rehearsal dinner," Peter added, remembering.

"Where do you kids want the wedding to be?" Kelly

asked.

"Dan and Zoë's, if that's still OK with you. My mom would definitely *not* be OK with coming to a church wedding."

Brandon asked, "Are there any other relatives you kids need to invite? Aunts, uncles, anyone?"

Peter looked at both of his parents. "Uncle Dan and Aunt Zoë are it for us, right?"

Kelly's nod reflected the sadness that occasionally hit her when reminded she was an only child. Noticing, Molly said, "My dad was an only child. My mom, too."

"Are your grandparents alive?"

"My mom's mom, Grandma Finster, passed away. But I need to invite my dad's parents. They live in Florida now. I was waiting until I knew what my mom said," Molly exhaled. "I also have a half-sister."

"I didn't know that," Kelly said. "Where is she?"

"She's in Illinois. Her mom used to work for my dad, but they never married. She is married now, though, to a wonderful Christian man I met briefly at my dad's funeral. But I can't invite them. My mom would be livid."

"Did you talk with Analese?"

"I don't know what to do about that. I'm afraid Mom would see Analese as hired help coming, uninvited, to a family event. She won't like it."

"But what do you want, Molly?" Brandon asked gently.

"I'd love for her and her family to come, if they can. And I could prepare my mom ahead of time, or at least try to prepare her so she doesn't make a scene."

"She'd make a scene at her daughter's wedding?" Kelly asked, incredulous.

"You don't know her," Molly said. "She is *always* right."

"A narcissist?" Brandon muttered under his breath. Then, he said, "Sorry, I was thinking aloud."

Molly began to laugh. It started as a giggle, then became a full-on belly laugh.

"What is this?" Peter asked her.

"Your family! I've never heard so many psychological terms from any group of people in my life. I feel like I'm floating in a sea of people helpers. And your parents aren't even counselors!"

"With my dad being a pastor, I've always been aware of people's complex needs," Brandon said philosophically. "And you know what my brother does," he laughed.

"And what I'm preparing to do," Peter added. "Maybe you'd better run while you still can."

"I'm right where I want to be," Molly leaned into him.

"Speaking of that," Brandon said, deftly changing to a subject he needed to pursue. "OK if we speak candidly?"

"Um, Dad, I thought we already were."

"I mean even more candidly," his dad said.

Peter said, "Only if you're subtle."

"Seeing how much you two love each other—and want each other—can we talk about some precautions?"

"I know exactly where you're headed, Dad." Peter turned to Molly. "You OK with a frank conversation?"

Molly gulped. Her family never had any kind of conversations, so she had no idea where they were going.

Kelly saw her discomfort and said, "Honey, this will be short and sweet. Take a deep breath," she smiled.

"I'll try," Molly said slowly.

Brandon jumped right in. "All we want to say is this. Too many kids are having sex before their wedding night, and it can sabotage trust for the rest of their lives. We want you two to have a wild and crazy life-long honeymoon, with no regrets. A lot of young people are trying to spend time in groups rather than alone to prevent the physical stuff from happening before the wedding night."

"How does that work, realistically?" Molly asked.

"Well, you can come here any time you want to get away from campus. But, when you're at school, you could hang out with my brother and his wife. I'm sure they'd be happy to let you use their den or living room so you can have time to be together, but you wouldn't be totally alone—it helps keep 'things' from happening."

"You mean sex, Dad?" Peter laughed. "I've had tons of classes talking about this very thing, and while we were driving here, Molly and I were talking about it, too."

"You were?" Kelly asked. "Wait, of course you were. It's not like intimacy isn't something we've never discussed."

"But I never did, Kelly," Molly said, warming to this family. "It's good to know you care enough to bring up a topic most people ignore."

"Yeah. You're right, Mom and Dad. We need to be smart. Most college students—who am I kidding? Even most high school students are having sex before they're married. It's almost a 'given' in our culture."

"Which leads to confusion later," his mom said. "There are too many couples who have no intimacy by the second year of their marriage—sometimes by the second month."

Peter nodded. "You're right. I met with a couple last week who said they had great sex before they were married but that intimacy struggles began the first night of their honeymoon."

"We just want you kids to have a great marriage—and that's one step toward it," Brandon returned to finish his earlier comments. "There are some good books…"

Peter's lopsided grin reminded everyone he was teasing, again. "Like 'Sacred Marriage,' or 'Love and Respect,' 'The DNA of Relationships,' 'The Mystery of Marriage,' 'The Meaning of Marriage,' or…"

His dad laughed. "OK, we get the point. I have to remind myself you come from a family of thinkers, and also that you're in grad school studying to be a counselor."

"Dad, another thing to remember is this: Molly and I want to get this right. We don't want our marriage to fail."

"Another *rather* important step is actually knowing when the wedding is going to be," Kelly smiled. "Have you set a date or found a minister to perform the ceremony?"

"Kate said she'd check with her pastor. Let me text her and see," Molly quickly sent a message.

Her phone dinged almost as soon as the message left it.

"Kate says 'yes, it's all set for August 25.' Is that OK with everyone? My commencement is August 11, but I'm not going to walk at graduation. My graduate recital is the week before that."

"Yes, the 25th is perfect!" Kelly enthused. "But do you want to do *something* to celebrate completing your master's? We could have a party at Dan and Zoë's."

"They'll be in full-on wedding preparation by then. How about if I take everyone out for dinner after my recital and celebrate both at the same time?"

"Will your mom be coming for your recital?"

"She always seems to have something going on when I have a concert. The fact that she'll come to our wedding is surprising."

"Do you think she'll want to help you choose your wedding gown?"

"Um, no. She has never had any interest in shopping with me."

Kelly smiled. "Would you like me to take you shopping tomorrow?"

As soon as Molly said 'yes,' her heart started pounding. *How can I buy a wedding gown when I have to gain weight? If I buy one, and it doesn't fit on our wedding day, then what will I do? And how can I tell Peter's mom it might not fit later?*

The small talk continued, with Molly getting quieter and quieter. Peter couldn't help but notice Molly's angst. "Mol and I are going to grab coffee; we'll be back in an hour or two, OK?"

Once seated in Peter's car, Molly began to cry. "How can I go shopping for a wedding gown? In a month, I'll be fat."

"Fat? You? No way."

"You don't understand. I told you the dietician is checking my eating records twice a week; once when I see her, and once after I see Brooke. She told me she will check me into the hospital if I don't follow her basic eating plan. Thus weight gain is guaranteed."

"That seems intense. What *were* you eating, Babe?"

"Apparently not enough 'to keep a fly alive,' according to Dr. Rodriguez, the dietician. And Brooke won't meet with me unless I meet with *both* of them every week. I have not one, but two eating disorders—anorexia and bulimia."

"Molly, I should have known!"

"How could you have? I rarely ate a meal with you. If I did, I made sure you didn't see me wrap the food in a napkin and throw it away. This time, I'm serious about changing. I know I can't afford another emotional crisis like the last one. So, I'll follow what Brooke and Dr. Rodriguez recommend for me."

"So, what *were* you eating?" Peter took her back to his original question.

"No breakfast, sometimes a protein bar for lunch; sometimes two or three almonds for lunch or mid-morning. Sometimes a small piece of rotisserie chicken for dinner— with a lettuce salad, no dressing."

"It's no wonder you got depressed. If I ate that much, just for one day, I'd be depressed because my blood sugar levels would drop through the floor."

She sighed.

"So what are you eating now that the good docs are checking up on you?"

She laughed at his silly grin. "For breakfast, I have gluten-free toast with fruit spread or almond butter. Lunch is lean meat from the deli—like turkey, beef or chicken, paired with carrot sticks or something like that. Then, dinner, I'm supposed to have a vegetable, meat, and so on. I have pages and pages of ideas from Dr. Rodriguez. As she says, 'no two days' of my food intake ever have to be the same.' A variety of foods is supposed to make me want to eat."

"And is that working for you?"

"I can't say that I *want* to eat yet, but I am noticing I feel better. I also have relaxation exercises to do before every meal. Apparently the gut is called 'the emotional brain,' and every time I'm tense, I lose my appetite. The idea is that, by relaxing, I'll increase my appetite. And my moods seem more stable than they were." She sighed again. "But that doesn't help me with the wedding gown dilemma."

"My mom might have some ideas—you know, she has three daughters. Or, if she doesn't know, she has friends she could ask."

"Peter, you know how private I am. I don't want her asking her friends. But we could ask her for ideas. Maybe after we finish our coffee?"

CHAPTER THIRTY-TWO

"We need to invite Peter and Molly over for dinner, Carlos."

"Mmm, hmm."

"Did you hear me?" Kate asked, her volume rising.

He looked up from his book. "No, sorry."

"Do we have a free night to invite Peter and Molly over for dinner? They're with my parents this weekend, and the weeks ahead are going to be busy for them."

"How about Friday? Neither of us has classes this Friday, so we could cook together!" He smiled, excited to have a day working in the kitchen with his bride.

Five minutes later, Kate looked up from her phone. "She can come! She's checking with Peter but thinks he's free Friday night, too. So what shall we make?"

"What about pollo guisado with rice and tortillas?"

"That yummy chicken stew your mom makes?"

"Si, guisado," he smiled, teasing her. "Not stew."

"Guisado," she laughed with him. "Do you want me to call your mom and get the recipe?"

"That would be great. I have to keep prepping for this physics exam. It's Monday," he said, returning to his book.

Mrs. Cordoba was as affable as her son, and explained the

recipe to Kate step-by-step. "It's really a Spanish stew," she said. "You know Guatemala was ruled by Spain—the Spanish were our family's ancestors, on both my side and Carlos' Papi's side."

Carlos had told Kate his family descended from Guatemala's ruling class. She said, "That's wonderful. What a legacy, Mrs. Cordoba!"

"Please call me 'Mamita,' Kate. Now, back to the guisado. It's best served with rice and tortillas—*corn* tortillas."

"OK, Mamita. Corn tortillas."

"Not just any corn tortillas. *Guatemalan* corn tortillas. The best in the world."

Kate smiled. "OK, Mamita, Guatemalan corn tortillas. What should we make for dessert?"

"Well, you are aware of Carlos' favorite, si?"

"Is it moh-lay with plantains?"

"Si, plátanos en mole. The mole is a chocolate-spice sauce."

"Can I use bananas instead of plantains?"

"Oh, no. No. You can get plantains at the Farmer's Market. Plantains are the essential ingredient. You want your friend to know authentic Guatemalan food, si? This is the friend who used to have misunderstandings about our people, si? So you want this meal to be perfect."

"Oh, Mamita, she already apologized. She is so sorry she said cruel things before. It wasn't about Guatemala or about Carlos; it was some sad stuff she was going through."

"Hmmph," Mamita said. "People should know better than to say things about people they don't even know."

"I know, Mamita, I know. But I think Molly learned a huge lesson."

"We shall see."

"Please forgive her. Molly has been my best friend since childhood. She's never talked like that before."

"Yes, I will forgive her. We Guatemalans are a kind people. We forgive. Besides, I don't want to carry around a grudge; it's like drinking poison and hoping your enemy will die."

CHAPTER THIRTY-THREE

Molly awakened to the smell of coffee—and something else she couldn't identify. Whatever it was, the fragrance was incredible. She got up, brushed her teeth, pulled her hair back into a ponytail and dressed in sweats and a T-shirt. She couldn't get to the kitchen fast enough.

Peter and his parents were cooking together, their backs to the door, and didn't hear Molly's soft footsteps approaching the kitchen. "Dad, Mom, can you believe I get to marry the only woman I've ever loved?"

"Yes, we can," his dad said. "And we can't imagine you marrying anyone else!" his voice rang with the enthusiasm he felt.

"I can't imagine marrying anyone else, either," Molly said, reaching to give Peter a sideways hug. "And I don't think I've felt this hungry in years! What in the world are these marvelous smells?"

"Kelly is making her famous baked blueberry French toast, Peter made spiced apples, and I'm brewing coffee."

In minutes, they were seated in the kitchen. As was their custom, Brandon and Kelly reached to form a circle around the table, holding hands, then bowed to pray. "Hon, will you pray today?" Brandon asked his wife.

"Lord, you are so good to us. Thank You for bringing Molly back from London, for bringing her to our hearts and lives so many years ago. Help us find the perfect wedding gown today! In Jesus' Name, Amen." She looked up, turning to Molly, beaming.

"What, Mom? You look like you've just discovered penicillin or something!"

"Very funny, Peter," she said, turning back to Molly. "I have an incredible idea."

"I like incredible ideas," Molly tried to smile, wondering what could be so exciting.

"My friend Celia owns a bridal thrift store near Beverly Hills. They only sell wedding gowns, bridesmaid dresses, and bridal accessories. I called her this morning, and they have dozens of gorgeous wedding gowns in."

"A used wedding gown?"

"Kate's was used—and you didn't even know it, did you?" Kelly smiled.

"Well, I guess I'll only wear it once," Molly said, hesitating. She wasn't a thrift shopper.

"The only reason I suggest it is because Celia told me the most incredible gown there is a new designer gown. She said it looks like a princess would wear it."

"You're more beautiful than a princess," Peter said, meaning it.

* * *

The drive to the bridal shop went quickly. Its exterior looked like an elegant store on Rodeo Drive, not a thrift store in Burbank. When they walked in, the owner greeted them like long-lost friends. "This must be Molly. I'm Celia. How lovely to meet you," she said, meaning it.

"Thank you. It's good to meet you, Celia."

"What sort of gown did you have in mind?"

"Something with classic lines. And the lace needs to be real, not synthetic."

"Come this way." Celia had several gowns ready for her perusal in a large, private fitting room.

Molly's eyes were already riveted on the perfect gown. She had never even let herself dream of her wedding day, and suddenly this felt like a dream come true.

"We are already on the same page," Celia said. "When Kelly described you, this seemed perfect for you. Would you like to try it on?"

Molly turned to Kelly. "Will you help me, Kelly?" she asked, surprising herself. She realized she felt as safe with Peter's mother as she did with him.

Ten minutes later, Molly was wearing the gown, turning to see it from every angle. The vintage lace was more elegant than anything she'd ever seen.

Celia brought a veil. "What do you think of this?"

Molly beamed. "Perfect."

"I can't say for sure that this is a Galia Lahav dress, since someone, sometime cut out the label, but it certainly seems like other Lahav gowns we've had here. Did you notice the exquisite workmanship—and the French lace train?"

"Yes, the train is my favorite part. But I have a strange question," Molly gulped. "I am on a medical diet to gain weight…"

"And you want to know if the dress will still fit on your wedding day?"

"Oh, did Kelly already tell you my concern about finding a gown that will fit in August?"

"No, she only told me you're five foot ten and about a size two. The empire waistline complements your height beautifully—did you notice the dress is actually quite loose on you now?"

"Not really. But I'm used to wearing T-shirts and sweats to class most of the time," Molly laughed. "I don't usually wear fitted clothing, and I almost never wear dresses—the last time was for Kate's wedding."

"Kate's gown came from here, too!" Celia exclaimed.

"Hers was more fitted, though, wasn't it?"

"Yes, Kate's was a trumpet gown, with a mermaid silhouette and a court train."

"That's a lot to remember," Kelly said. "You helped Kate find exactly what she wanted."

"And Kate was a lovely bride." Celia turned her full attention to Molly. "You will also be a lovely bride. And I had hoped you'd like the fit of this gown. With its unique design, there is easily room for you to go up two, maybe even three sizes."

Molly breathed a sigh of relief. "Then I'll take it."

"You don't want to try on a few others?" Kelly asked, surprised.

"This is the one," Molly said without hesitation. She turned to Celia. Forcing herself to speak calmly, she asked, "Can you direct me to the powder room?"

The changing room compelled Molly's mind and emotions back to high school and to modeling, having to change clothes with strangers gawking at her body. Even though she felt safe with Kelly, she didn't feel safe in that room. She felt claustrophobic. Once in the powder room, she felt an intense urge to vomit. Then she heard Brooke's voice saying, "You have two eating disorders. And they rear their ugly heads whenever you feel out of control. The only way to keep them from controlling you for the rest of your life is to ground yourself in those moments and make the choice to stay in the present."

She clung to the sink, pressing her feet into the floor, noticing, and then saying aloud, "I'm here now. I'm not there." She splashed some cool water on her face, reminding herself, "This day is a new day; it's a gift from God."

Five minutes later, Molly joined Celia and Kelly. They thought her smile was because of the wedding gown Celia was carefully placing in a garment bag marked 'Re-new for You.' She was actually smiling for two reasons: one—she didn't lose her delicious breakfast, and two—the store seemed like a perfect metaphor for her current life. "I love the name of your store," she said to Celia.

"Thanks. It's fun to help people find new life for gorgeous clothing! And this is one of the few times a gown hasn't had to be altered," Celia said. "What a perfect fit! I hope you'll send me a picture of your big day."

"You can count on it," Kelly promised.

Molly's phone rang as they left the store. "My mom," she said to Kelly. "Hello."

Kelly could hear Babs' voice, even though Molly didn't put her on speaker.

"The Wendhams cannot come; they are already booked on one of those European river cruises at that time. They said to tell you they wish you could delay the date for them."

"Mom, I can't. It's the only week Peter has between semesters. Did I tell you I'm graduating with my master's degree this summer?"

"Well, I can't believe you won't make some kind of accommodation for my nearest and dearest friends."

Molly sighed. For a split second, she'd let herself hope her mom would acknowledge her huge accomplishment. She shouldn't have expected her to care whether she completed her master's degree. But it hurt. She paused, breathing deeply, remembering to let it go. "What about Harry? Can't he come with you?"

"Hairless Harry is ancient history!" Babs said, angry.

"You just went to Europe with him."

"Never, and I mean never mention that man again!" Babs yelled into the phone. "I'll come on my own. I'm a big girl," she huffed.

Molly never was quite sure why her mother was angry. She learned to either be quiet or change the subject. "I'm glad you can come, Mom. See you soon. Bye for now."

Babs had already hung up, even before Molly said goodbye.

Kelly waited a moment, then said, "I don't understand why your mom is like that, Molly. It isn't right that she isn't involved in your life. You know that, don't you?"

"I'm not sure that I do. She's never been involved. I can

never please her."

"I'm glad you're going to be part of our family soon. You'll have to tell us if we're *too* involved," Kelly laughed.

"I don't think that's possible," Molly sighed. "I'm really looking forward to being part of your family." She turned to look at the garment bag hanging in the back seat. "I can't believe we found the perfect wedding gown already. Thank you, Kelly! I'll always remember this time with you."

"Want to stop for coffee on the way home?"

They parked behind a charming coffee shop. From antique tables and chairs to an array of farming implements hanging from the ceiling, the decor visually transported them to America's heartland.. Molly spotted a burlap bag on the wall labeled "Illinois Seed Company."

Kelly noticed and said, "Close to our home state, huh? I miss Illinois sometimes. But I'll always be glad we moved to California to live near Brandon's parents, so our kids could know their grandparents."

"I wonder where Peter and I will be in ten years. I hope we don't move far away from you, ever."

"Thank you, Molly. We love spending time with you, too."

They placed their coffee orders and sat in comfy leather chairs to talk.

"Talking about moving far away reminded me about Oswald Chambers and his wife, Biddy. Want to hear a little bit of their story?"

She nodded. "The people you mentioned last night?"

"Yes. Their story is one of my favorite love stories. Oswald was born in Scotland, moved with his family to England and studied art in London, then in Scotland. He was an incredibly gifted artist, but felt God leading him to discontinue his art training and become a minister instead. His family told him he was making a huge mistake."

"So he didn't have his family's encouragement, either?"

"I never thought of that. You're right, Molly. Before Oswald met Gertrude, her own health problems and her family's financial problems caused her to give up her dreams of education. Her father died when she was a teenager, so she had to go to work to help her family survive. She'd been studying shorthand, with the goal of learning it so well that she could become secretary to England's Prime Minister, taking dictation at the incredible rate of two hundred fifty words per minute."

"Wow. That's fast."

Kelly smiled, remembering the story. "Gertrude and Oswald began to fall in love when they were both traveling to America from London aboard a ship—she was heading to a new job; he, to preach in America. After a lengthy correspondence, I think they married about two years later."

"Another marriage happened after two people traveled from London," Molly sighed, savoring sweet memories of how Peter came to London for her. A waiter brought their coffees to them. "This cappuccino smells delicious," Molly said. "Please tell me more."

Kelly paused to sip her caramel macchiato, thinking. "When he was getting to know Gertrude, Oswald nicknamed her 'Biddy,' since his sister was also named Gertrude. Years after she and Oswald were married; they went to Egypt, where he served as chaplain for the British troops during World War I. Biddy used her training to take meticulous shorthand of her husband's messages—capturing not only every word but his emotions, too."

Molly sighed. "All the pain of losing her father wasn't wasted, was it? God allowed her to develop skills she used to help people. Do you think He will use the pain of my childhood in some way?"

"Absolutely! The Lord never wastes pain when we yield our sorrows to Him. And Biddy experienced even more pain when her husband died in Egypt at age 43, after surgery to remove a ruptured appendix. Later, Biddy and their young daughter returned to London with boxes of notes from her husband's ministry. Over time, she published Oswald's messages in numerous books, with his name as author, not hers."

"I think I have one of them—'My Utmost for His Highest.' Peter gave it to me after we flew home from London. It's helping me understand the Christian life in profound new ways."

"I've been reading that daily study for thirty years—and I'm still learning from it."

"Thanks, Kelly." Molly sipped her coffee, pensive. "I want to be the kind of wife Biddy was—using my gifts to help people know God."

"You will be, Molly. You will."

CHAPTER THIRTY-FOUR

"Dan, will you get me the box on the top shelf of our closet? I need to start figuring out centerpieces for Peter and Molly's reception. Dan?"

He must be outside, Zoë concluded. She carried a six-foot step ladder to the master closet and reached for the box. Ten minutes later, Dan found her crumpled on the floor.

"What happened, Zoë?"

"I was getting my craft box off the top shelf. I guess I overreached," she sighed, then tried to stand up. She cried out in pain and fell back down on the closet floor.

Dan lifted her up and carried her out to the car. "Since it's Saturday, we'll go to the ER," he said, fastening her seat belt.

"Your X-rays revealed fractures at the lower end of the tibia and fibula," the ER doctor explained.

"How long before I'm up and running?"

"You've got a serious injury, Mrs. Johnson. We've made a referral for you to see an orthopedist early next week. Their office will give you a call. That visit will determine whether you need surgery..."

"Surgery? Zoë groaned. "But I have my nephew's wedding

to get ready for…"

The doctor continued, "I'm sorry, Mrs. Johnson, but you're probably going to need to delegate that one. You can't afford to put stress on your injury, or it might never heal properly. You don't want to risk arthritis or disability. For now, I'm going to apply a splint so swelling can safely occur. But, I think it's wise to expect a prolonged healing process— and a fair amount of time on crutches. Your orthopedist will be able to clarify the healing process, but it could easily take months for your leg to heal."

"Months? Crutches?" Zoë groaned again, her eyes brimming with tears.

The doctor touched her arm briefly, then turned to Dan. "Your wife cannot put *any* weight on her broken leg. Can you get someone to help care for her when you're at work?"

On their way home, Zoë began to cry in earnest.

"I know it hurts, Sweetie. We're going to stop and pick up the prescription the doctor gave you, OK?"

"Oh, pain isn't my main concern, Dan. It's the wedding! How are we going to prepare everything for Peter and Molly's reception?"

"I don't think we can, but I do know God will provide a way."

While Dan ran into the pharmacy, Zoë checked her phone. Three missed calls from Kate. She called her back. "What's up, honey? Everything OK with you?"

"Aunt Zoë, I can't believe you're so nonchalant! Uncle Dan called from the ER to tell us you broke your leg! What can I do to help?"

Zoë sighed. "At this point, I really don't know. All I know is that I have to stay off my feet—the doctor said I'm not to put any weight on my broken leg. How in the world can I get everything ready for Peter and Molly's wedding?"

"About that. We have an idea. Carlos' mom was here when we found out about your leg, and she wants to host the wedding at their home."

"I wouldn't dream of asking her to do that."

"You didn't ask. She offered. And she insists. She said, 'We're family. Families help each other.'"

"That's just too much to ask."

"Aunt Zoë, this is a *Latino* family we're talking about. She is already checking on florists."

"Then I accept. There really is no way I can host a wedding now. But have you talked with Peter and Molly?"

"That's my next call. Before Mamita starts decorating, I want to make sure it's OK with them." She laughed.

When Dan came to the car with her prescription, he was surprised to find his wife beaming with joy. "What happened?"

"You won't believe it! God really does more than we can ask or imagine!"

CHAPTER THIRTY-FIVE

Peter and Molly went to early church with his parents on Sunday morning, then had a quick lunch before leaving to make the two-hour drive back to campus. After they left, Kelly was quiet.

"Honey, what's wrong?" Brandon asked, clearly puzzled. The weekend with Peter and Molly had been wonderful.

"I'm really concerned about Molly. I didn't want to say anything when they were here, but she looks like she's dying."

"Dying? What are you talking about?"

"She had me help her put on her wedding gown. I almost cried when I saw her bones sticking out. I could count her ribs. She looks like she's starving to death."

"Hon, that's exactly why she's on a supervised medical diet. You heard Peter say her therapist told Molly she will hospitalize her if she doesn't follow the dietician's precise recommendations, right?"

"No, I didn't hear that," Kelly wiped her nose. "I've never seen anyone who is so thin."

"I just remembered. Peter told me about that while you and Molly were out shopping for the dress. Peter told me how thankful he is that she could drop two classes to focus on healing. Why don't we count our blessings? I've never seen those two so balanced and happy."

"You're right. But what about Zoë and her broken leg? Do we need to go help take care of her?"

"Dan told me he's taking her to see a superb orthopedist Monday, and he's going to have his teaching assistant fill in for him so he can stay home as long as Zoë needs help. He has plenty of family sick leave. Zoë's in great hands."

CHAPTER THIRTY-SIX

Zoë was a self-described "impatient patient." She hated having people wait on her. She hated not being able to get out of bed. She hated people coming to ask about her injury.

And Dan was starting to feel like his patience was being taxed to its limit. He was used to calmly teaching classes, engaging his students, and then coming home to a funny, pleasant wife. Though he taught psychology, the emotions of their current situation were unexpectedly challenging.

He was in the kitchen, intensely studying cupboards, trying to figure out where Zoë put the dishes he was unloading from the dishwasher. *I know I've helped her with this before. Why don't I know where anything goes?*

"I'll be right there, Sweetie," he responded when he heard her calling for him—again.

She was frowning at her cell phone. "I wish I hadn't answered this. Can you believe Gretchen is coming over? She didn't even *ask* if I wanted company. She told me she's coming to *help* me. And she's on her way here now!"

"Isn't that kind of her, to want to help?"

"You don't know Gretchen. She is definitely *not* coming to help. She's coming for meat." To Dan's confused look, she added. "Gossip. She loves to gossip. She wants all the dirt on my 'poor, unfortunate accident,' as she called it, so she can share it as a prayer request at all the groups she's in."

"Prayer is good, isn't it?" Dan sighed, afraid he knew her answer.

"Are you kidding? This isn't for prayer; it's all about gossip. Power and control. That's what she wants. Power and control."

"Why don't you take a nap, Zoë? You'll feel better when she comes."

"Why don't you answer the door? I think that's her now."

Zoë could hear Gretchen gushing to her husband in the kitchen. "When I heard about Zoë's accident, I felt horrible. I mean, just so, so sad. So I had to come and see what she needs. Is she this way?" Without waiting for a response, Gretchen rushed through the house, searching, until she found the master bedroom on her own.

"Oh, Zoë, you look horrible! I'm so sorry you were hurt!"

"Thanks, Gretchen."

"This is the first time I've been here. Your house is darling. Did you decorate it yourself?" She walked into Zoë's closet. "So this is where you fell? I heard you fell off a stool."

"A six-foot ladder."

"How in the world did you break your leg falling off a ladder? I mean, don't people usually break their legs in skiing accidents or doing something a bit more glamorous than falling off a little stool?" Gretchen guffawed at her attempt at humor.

"I guess I just fell on it exactly right," Zoë mumbled, feeling annoyed.

"Well, you know God never gives us more than we can bear."

"Really?" Zoë felt a surge of energy. Her volume increasing with each word, she said, "Gretchen, God often allows more than we can bear. Saying He doesn't 'give us more than we can bear,' is as untrue as someone saying, 'God helps those who help themselves.'"

"Well, doesn't he?" Gretchen looked perplexed.

"No, He helps us when we're helpless, powerless, destitute…"

"Um…" Gretchen tried to speak.

Zoë ignored her, adding, "And when something happens that truly is more than we can bear, God offers us strength and peace that passes understanding, if we'll only ask Him. Gretchen, some things really are beyond human understanding! Otherwise, how do you explain parents losing a baby—isn't that more than they can bear?" Zoë continued, her heart pounding. "Or a child who's bullied, or someone who's abused? I prefer to park on 'God is our refuge and strength, a very present help in trouble.'"

"Well, I don't want to overstay my welcome," Gretchen said, suddenly eager to leave.

In the kitchen, she patted Dan's arm patronizingly. "You really need to help your wife. She seems confused about some of the most comforting Bible verses there are."

"Like what?" Dan asked, beginning to grasp his wife's concerns about their uninvited guest.

"Well, like 'God helps those who help themselves.' Such a classic!"

He began to ask her, "And where is that in the Bible?" but Gretchen was already on her way out the back door.

From the kitchen, Dan could hear Zoë crying. Weak and in pain, she'd wept more in the past week than she had in the past decade. "Coming, Sweetie," he called.

"I blew it. I totally blew it with Gretchen!"

Careful not to bump her leg, he sat next to Zoë on their bed, reaching to gently pat her hand. "What do you mean?"

"I rudely corrected her statements about the Bible," Zoë said, her chest heaving with sobs. "I wasn't kind, patient, or loving. I said things she wasn't ready to hear, that didn't need to be said."

"Could you call her and apologize?"

"I could, but Gretchen will twist whatever I say."

"Hmm. You could pray," Dan offered. Softly, he added, "Churches often have two streams—one of Good News, the other of Gossip. People seem to love to drink from the Gossip Stream."

"You just reminded me I need to walk in the Good News and leave the results to God," Zoë said, dialing her phone, mouthing "thanks" to Dan as someone on the other end answered. Her voice gentle, Zoë began. "Hi, Gretchen, I want to apologize for speaking rudely to you today."

Fifteen minutes elapsed, with Zoë listening without saying a word. At last, she smiled into the phone, saying only, "Thanks again, Gretchen. Bye now."

"What did she say?" Dan asked, as soon as she set her phone on the bed.

"She told me I am arrogant and need to use this time of recuperation to learn how to be a truly humble person, like she is. She also told me to work harder on being a Christian."

"Whew," Dan responded, exhaling. "How did you stop yourself from reacting to her groundless criticism?"

"I didn't want to create new problems, so I kept telling myself to 'be still and know' God is God. And I thought about Jesus' humility each time I felt like defending myself." She sighed. "I hope she'll discover how to live by grace. But, I'll probably need you to remind me that God can protect me from her gossip. And I do want to be more humble."

"Does this mean you'll be spending more time with Gretchen?" Dan laughed.

"No, I don't think she's a safe person for me," said Zoë, pensive. "But there's one more apology I need to make today. To you. I've been a grouch, blaming my bad attitude on my broken leg. I forgot that God's grace is sufficient—even for this. Will you forgive me for being so demanding, so grumpy, so selfish?"

Dan quietly hugged her. "Of course. Welcome home, my love. It's good to have you back."

CHAPTER THIRTY-SEVEN

Instead of going to Carlos and Kate's cozy student apartment as originally planned, Peter and Molly were driving to Carlos' parents' home nearby, just outside Santa Barbara. Carlos and Kate were to join them there for dinner and wedding planning, since Dr. and Mrs. Cordoba had offered to host the wedding and reception when they learned of Zoë's broken leg. The wedding was only six weeks away.

Driving to the Cordoba home, Peter was quiet, thinking about Molly, wondering whether she was upset about the change in plans and wondering, in general, about their wedding.

Instead, she was worried about *him*. "Peter, are you OK with the change in location?" Molly asked, noticing that he seemed tense.

"I am. I've been at their house, and it's lovely. But..."

"What?" Molly felt a surge of concern. Her easygoing fiancé rarely expressed concerns—about anything.

"I keep having this image of you, walking down the aisle of the church where I work, the radiant bride coming to her groom. I know it's silly, especially since I remember you saying your mom wouldn't be comfortable coming to a church."

"Peter, it's not silly. And it's *our* wedding, not my mom's wedding. I didn't know being at the church mattered to you. I don't care where it is, as long as you're the groom!" Her smile filled the car. "Peter, if *you* want the ceremony there, let's do it!" She frowned, wondering. "But can we even get August 25th at this late date?"

"Here," he said, handing her his phone. "Could you text Pastor McIntosh?"

"Sure. I'll ask him what, if any, times are available, OK?"

When Peter's phone dinged ten minutes later, the answer was, "10a or 2p; we already have an evening ceremony."

"What time should we choose?" Molly asked.

"Let's talk with the Cordobas and see what time works for them."

"I'll text the pastor that we'll let him know later tonight."

"Please ask if he'll perform the wedding, too," Peter said, downshifting his car to second.

Peter's phone dinged again. "Hey, guys, remember? I already told Kate I'll do your wedding the 25th. Just waiting for time and location. LOL."

"I like him," Molly smiled.

"Me, too," Peter said, adding, "I'm sure Carlos' parents won't care if we just do the reception here and not the wedding ceremony. You'll like them, too, Mol. They're really laid back." He paused to listen to directions on his GPS, turning to Molly, "I've only been here once," he explained. "Do you really think your mom will be OK with the ceremony at church?"

"This time, I'm not going to *ask* her; I'll *inform* her when we decide." Molly beamed at her beloved. "I'd also like to start going to church with you, if that's OK."

Peter smiled. "Absolutely! I like going to church because it helps me fall more in love with the Lord. I know it's not perfect, but then, neither am I."

"Thanks for being patient with me all the past months I haven't gone with you."

"Molly, I love you. Your pace is my pace." He reached

across the car to hug her.

She sighed, hugging him back. "That you still love me, after everything, amazes me." Noticing the beautiful scenery, she changed the subject, exclaiming, "This is gorgeous! Where are we? Is this a resort?"

Peter pushed several buttons, keying in the code, then waited for huge wooden gates to swing open. "Um, no, it's the drive into Carlos' family home."

The long driveway wound through what seemed like a tunnel of trees, their arching branches shading the road from the California sun. They passed beautiful, landscaped grounds. "It's like a secret garden!" When they finally reached the house, Molly gasped. "I didn't know they lived in a mansion. Wow."

Peter laughed. "I didn't know you could be impressed by a house."

"I guess I *have* diligently resisted following my mom's footsteps. *This* is amazing!"

"Ready?"

"Can't wait!"

Before they could reach the massive front door, Dr. and Mrs. Cordoba were there to greet them. "Welcome! How glad we are to see you, Molly and Peter! Come on in. Carlos and Kate should be here any minute."

The two-story entryway was warm and inviting. Handmade tiles, of different colors and designs, covered the steps leading upstairs. Mrs. Cordoba saw Molly's upward gaze and said, "The second floor has six bedrooms and five baths." She laughed. "Lots of familia come visit us from Guatemala! We want everyone to be comfortable!"

Peter and Molly followed their hosts into a living room that was both massive and intimate. Elegant furniture provided comfortable seating for at least fifty people. An intricately carved Spanish balcony encircled the room. Mahogany floors were warm and inviting, with colorful rugs placed under white sofas and chairs at each end of the cavernous room.

Through a wall of windows, they could see the Pacific Ocean splashing below. Another wall featured a stone fireplace that looked like it had been shipped there from Spain. Triple French doors opened onto a courtyard where an incredible variety of palm trees and flowers proliferated. "This is truly beautiful," Molly said. "Thank you for inviting us."

Dr. Cordoba looked at his phone. "I'm so sorry. Carlos and Kate are going to be at least another half-hour. Carlos had to do something for his professor." Clearly proud of his son, he added, "You know he is a TA?" A gracious host, he directed Peter and Molly to comfortable chairs. "Why don't we have hors d'oeuvres while we wait?" he asked, nodding to a maid standing in the corner of the room.

Almost immediately a tray appeared, then another, with stuffed mushrooms, miniature quiches, chutney, cheeses, shrimp, crackers, fruits and vegetables.

"Please, help yourselves, enjoy!" Mrs. Cordoba smiled. "We have some important planning to do."

Peter spoke next. "You don't know how much we appreciate your offering to help us with our wedding."

"It will be our honor," Dr. Cordoba said.

"We wanted Carlos and Kate to have their wedding here, but Kate had always dreamed of having it at the campus arboretum, so who are we to take away our lovely daughter-in-law's dream?" Mrs. Cordoba smiled again. "But now we are blessed to have the pleasure of hosting you and your friends and family."

"Is it OK with you if we have our wedding ceremony at the church where I work and then come here for the reception?" Peter wondered, reaching for another stuffed mushroom.

"Of course! It is *your* wedding," Dr. and Mrs. Cordoba said together. "Now let's begin! How many people? What menu would you like? And what date and time?"

Peter and Molly were grateful they could answer most of the questions. "Not too many people. Maybe fifty. August

25th, we can have the church at either ten o'clock in the morning or two in the afternoon. Do you have a preference?"

"The afternoon would be lovely, because then we could welcome your guests here after the ceremony. As the guests arrive, we could have our butler pass trays of Veuve Clicquot Yellow Label Champagne with a strawberry garnish and sparkling water with a lime slice for those who prefer that. Either option is elegant and refreshing. Perhaps next, we could offer five or six hors d'oevres? Of course, we'll have an ice sculpture table. On that, would you like oysters, mussels and shrimp?"

Peter and Molly quietly nodded their assent as Mrs. Cordoba continued. "Our chef also prepares delicious dips— we could have two tables for those on the patio, if you like. Perhaps smoked Gouda dip, lump crab dip, and Formaggio Lagorai jalapeño dip?"

Dr. Cordoba said, "Please do not forget the white corn tortilla chips for those delectable dips!" Turning to Molly, he added, "We Guatemalans are known for our corn tortillas. They are the best in the world."

She forced a smile, feeling slightly overwhelmed by their enthusiasm.

Mrs. Cordoba noticed. "Molly, do you not like the menu? Perhaps other dips would be preferable?"

"Oh, no! Everything sounds delicious—but it is too much. You are being so kind. I don't know what to say."

"So you like these ideas?"

"Absolutely," Peter said.

"Good, good. Then the hors d'oeuvres will be followed by an early dinner, si? I think we should plan a meal for at least seventy-five, so you can invite the people who are important to you."

"Oh, we wouldn't dream of asking you to serve a meal, Dr. and Mrs. Cordoba. We were just thinking of cake," Molly said quickly. "You are already doing so much…"

"Please, our names are Miguel and Carmen Maria. No more 'Dr. and Mrs. Cordoba.' Too formal! Please call me

Carmen and him Miguel. And, my dear Molly, I wouldn't dream of hosting your party without serving a meal. You'll soon experience what a wonderful chef we have. Can you smell tonight's meal?" Her warm brown eyes lit in anticipation. "Roberto is preparing his fabulous Pan-Seared Filet Mignon served with Cabernet and Mushroom Sauce. It simply melts in your mouth!" Before they could respond, she continued. "Roberto is marvelous. But I think for your reception we'll need at least two, possibly three chefs."

"I, I don't know if I can afford that," Molly said hesitantly. "I don't think my mom is going to help pay for anything."

For a brief moment, Molly was afraid she'd offended Mrs. Cordoba, whose eyebrows arched as she loudly said, "Hrumph!" That was quickly followed by, "My dear, do you actually think we would allow you to pay for an event we *offered* to host for you?"

"I could probably pay you back for everything in a few months," Molly added.

"No, no, no! We wish to *give* you this fiesta as our wedding gift! Remember, Peter is already like a son to us, since his sister is our daughter-in-law. And you, Miss Molly, are our daughter-in-law's dearest and oldest friend. How could we do any less?"

"Thank you," Peter and Molly said together, hugging Carmen, then shaking Miguel's hand.

"What, no hug for me?" he asked, pretending to be indignant.

Molly blushed, then haltingly reached to hug him.

"I'm kidding, my dear!" His chocolate brown eyes crinkled with laughter. "Has no one told you I like to tease?"

"Well, stop teasing, Miguel! We need to get down to business!" Carmen ordered with a smile. "What entrees would you like, Molly?"

"Um, anything would be wonderful. What do you recommend?"

"Ah, you're my kind of girl! So agreeable."

Molly blushed again, remembering how she had initially

lambasted Kate for falling in love with Carlos. She thought, *Maybe I should request Humble Pie.* "Oh, please Mrs. Cor—I mean Carmen, could you choose the entrees? It sounds like you're an expert hostess. I don't have much experience."

She nodded, smiling. "Let's go to the kitchen. I asked Chef Roberto to prepare a few ideas."

Miguel and Carmen led them through a spacious dining room, where a wrought iron chandelier hung regally over a twenty-foot table.

"We can seat at least twenty-four people here. And here's the kitchen."

A massive island filled only a small part of the room. "This is Roberto. Ah, what a fragrant dinner you prepare!"

"Welcome to the kitchen," Roberto said. "And this is the lovely couple I've been hearing so much about," he said, reaching to shake Peter's hand. "I've prepared a tray of smoked Gouda dip, lump crab dip and warm corn tortillas for you to taste as you wait. Perhaps you will like these at your reception? I understand Carlos and Kate are running a bit late. I have adjusted our meal preparation accordingly."

Carmen nodded. "Thank you, Roberto."

"Perhaps we'll be ready for your delicious entrée in thirty or forty minutes, Roberto," Miguel said. "Kids, let's take these outside." Miguel picked up a tray. "This way, please."

"Here's the sample menu you requested," Roberto said, handing two pages to Carmen.

As soon as they were seated in wicker chairs on the adjacent patio, Carmen began to read Roberto's suggestions aloud. "Begin with a burrata salad with arugula, grenadine onions, an orange glaze or pomegranate vinaigrette." She nodded, pleased. "We'll serve that on chilled plates, verdad?"

Miguel laughed. "Of course, my dear! You know what's best."

"It is best," she said. "And you can quit teasing me about how I like to care for our guests. This is Peter and Molly's *wedding* we're talking about, the day they'll remember for the rest of their lives!"

"I agree, my dear." He turned to Peter, grinning. "Lesson Number One: agree with your wife."

Carmen, all business, ignored him. "Good. Let's see what Chef says. For dinner, he recommends entrées of Wagyu New York Strip Steak and Herb Seared Maple and Mustard Glazed Salmon. Very elegant," she said.

With the tantalizing smells of their dinner drifting to the patio from the kitchen and the conversation focused on food, Peter suddenly remembered he'd had nothing but appetizers since breakfast. "It all sounds great! OK if I sample these dips?"

"Dig in!" Miguel said, handing him a plate. "How about you, Molly?"

"No thank you," she smiled. "Since we've already enjoyed delicious hors d'oeuvres in the living room, I'm going to save room to enjoy Roberto's meal."

A table, set with six place settings of bright turquoise-patterned stoneware, was visible behind a trellis covered with tropical foliage. The compelling lyrical scent of jasmine danced into Molly's awareness. *I wonder if Heaven smells like this*, she thought. "Your garden reminds me of exquisite perfume. What flowers are so fragrant?" she asked their hosts.

Miguel responded. "Stephanotis floribunda is the botanical name; also known as 'Madagascar jasmine, Hawaiian wedding flower or bridal wreath.' A perfect flower for the bride-to be!" he said, picking one and giving it to Molly with a bow. "These are my favorites."

Carmen smiled at her husband, then at their guests. "That is where we'll eat tonight," she pointed to the table. It overlooked terraces resplendent with flowers of nearly every imaginable variety and color. The Madagascar jasmine bloomed near star and Chilean jasmine. A profusion of hibiscus flowered above orange, pink and yellow lantana; above those were begonias and passion vine and many other varieties of plants covering the remaining terraces. Molly's attention was drawn to the sound of a fountain bubbling nearby. Everything felt so soothing that she let herself simply relax in the scent of the flower she held.

"If the weather is good, we could seat forty or fifty people out here on the patio for your wedding reception," Miguel said. "We have tables and lanterns to make it very festive."

"If it's rainy, we can set up our party tent in the back yard. Bring your food with us, Peter, and come see," Carmen said, taking Molly's arm to lead them to lush grounds adjacent to an enormous Spanish-tiled swimming pool, Jacuzzi and outdoor kitchen. "There's also this area. It seats twenty." She paused, looking around as if pondering a large question. "Do you think this will be adequate?"

"More than adequate," Peter said, between bites. "I could never have imagined such a perfect place to have our reception!"

"I need to write down your address to put on the invitations, since we're creating and mailing them this weekend. We're cutting it a bit close, since it's only about six weeks until our wedding."

"That's plenty of time," Carmen said, thinking aloud. "Actually, rather than giving your guests our address, could we provide shuttles at the church to bring everyone here? People tend to lose their way on these roads. That would make it simpler for everyone. The invitation could say, 'Transportation to reception will be provided at the ceremony,' or something like that."

"That's a great idea," Molly said, writing down Carmen's idea, then showing it to her.

"Perfect, Molly!" Looking again at Roberto's menu, Carmen continued. "Do you like the idea of Parmesan Brussels Sprouts and Truffle Mashed Potatoes?"

"Yes, thank you!" Molly said.

Peter added, "Thanks so much, Miguel and Carmen. I know Zoë would thank you, too, if she were here."

"Oh, Peter, how is your aunt? We are so sorry she is hurt. We are praying for her every day."

"Thank you. She's not very comfortable. Apparently, she's

in a lot of pain and dreading the next month of recuperation."

"How can we help her?" Miguel asked.

"That's a good question. You could call her and ask. She might like some company," Molly said. "She enjoys just sitting and talking. She also would like to help with the reception in any way she can."

"And Uncle Dan might like some company, too, Miguel," Peter added.

"I have a question, Carmen," Molly said, surprising everyone. She didn't usually ask questions.

"You're a mom. Do you think I need my mother's permission to invite our friends Analese and Sam to the wedding?"

"Say more," Carmen said, puzzled.

"It's kind of a complicated story."

"Oh, I love stories!" Carmen enthused.

Molly described the wonderful reunion she'd had with Analese in London—and talked about Baby Molly, her namesake, and shared how much she wanted them to be at the wedding, then briefly described her concerns about the possibility of her mother being sarcastic or cruel to Analese and her family.

Carmen pondered her question for several moments. "You are asking this question about your mother, the person who isn't even interested enough to come to your important graduate recital next week? The mother who does not wish to help you with your wedding?"

"Um, yes."

"I think, my dear, that you and Peter should invite anyone you want to invite, without worrying what your mother will think or say. These friends, Sam and Analese, sound like delightful people. And Analese is aware of what your mother is like, si?"

Molly smiled. She really, really liked Carmen. "Yes."

"Miguel, shall we invite Sam and Analese and their babies to stay with us?"

"Of course!" he said. "We have plenty of room. And we love the sound of children in our home!"

Carmen continued, "There, it is settled! We will make sure your reception is a *wonderful* time! And let us not spend another second worrying what anyone might do or say! I rather like the idea of having your mother here for your reception. I might even plan something special for her myself."

CHAPTER THIRTY-EIGHT

Even though music was the realm of Molly's life where she felt most confident, preparing for her graduate recital produced unexpected stress. She brought that up during her session with her therapist the week of her recital.

"Brooke, I'm starting to wonder if I should cancel the wedding."

"The wedding? I thought you were talking about your recital."

"What if I'm one of those people who should never marry?"

"What makes you think that, Molly? Has something happened recently?"

"Yes, something has happened. One requirement my professor has for my recital is arranging music and performing it in a chamber group."

"Keep going."

"The violinist is someone I've known for several years—Julian and I have played in orchestra together, said 'hi' in the hallway between classes, things like that—but we've never been close. Now that we're rehearsing together several times a week, I'm starting to have feelings for him. He touched my arm the other day, and it felt like a charge of electricity."

"And this is a concern because?"

"Well, maybe I can't be with just one man. Perhaps I'm fickle. I mean, how can I feel attracted to someone else when I'm about to get married?"

"Because you're alive," Brooke smiled.

"That doesn't make sense at all!" Molly said, annoyed.

"Molly, the nature of men and women is to notice each other—even to feel things for each other. The people who remain successfully married are the ones who choose not to 'feed' those feelings of attractions for anyone other than their spouse."

"I don't get it."

"When you walk through an arboretum, do you notice the beautiful flowers and plants?"

"Of course. That's why you're walking through it."

"But do you pick them all to take home with you?"

"Obviously not. Anyone knows they are there to be looked at, not taken."

"What if you look at the human race in a similar way? You can notice interesting things in humans without 'taking' them for yourself."

"Hmm. Do you mean it's OK to notice a man is handsome and interesting, or that he smells good?"

Brooke laughed out loud. "So your violinist friend is handsome, interesting and smells good?"

Molly tried to smile but looked confused instead. "Well, yes, but what about my feelings?"

"OK, try this, Molly. Tell yourself this: 'It's OK for me to notice the beauty of God's creation, but not OK to take something—or someone—that belongs to someone else.'"

Molly paused. "You mean Julian belongs to someone else?"

"Every single person ultimately 'belongs to' the person he or she will marry. Not in the sense of being 'owned' by that person, of course, but in the sense of being 'one' with that person, as the Bible teaches."

"The two become one flesh?"

"Yes."

"That brings up a lot of other questions, then. I mean, you know about what my brother did. I was basically 'one flesh' with him, then, wasn't I—not at first, but later, every time he came into my room?"

"*Crimes* were committed against you by your brother. What he did was not about intimacy; it was all about power and control. He could have faced legal consequences for what he did. And the reason sexually offending behavior is considered *criminal* is because of the damage that abuse causes in victims. What we've been working on each week, though, is how you can move away from living your life as his victim to being a survivor—and ultimately, as a woman who thrives."

"But where does that leave me? How can I be a pure wife? I'm damaged goods."

"The shame of what happened is *not* yours, Molly. Even though your parents wouldn't listen to you or believe you were being hurt, you know you were. Now what is vital is that you realize you can be healed from that abuse—and that you are not 'damaged goods' but a lovely and beloved human being."

"There's more." Molly looked at the floor, her voice barely perceptible. "I was sexual in high school with the director of the modeling agency where I worked."

"Anson? You mentioned that your stepmother introduced you to him."

"Yes, and during the summer, I stayed alone at my dad and stepmother's apartment, and that's where it happened."

"Do you want to talk about what happened there?"

"I guess so. I've never really talked much about it. I told Zoë about the abortion, but not what led to it." She continued looking down, her voice a whisper, her hands trembling. "He treated me like a queen or something—taking me to Chicago's 'in' restaurants, hanging on every word I said, like it mattered to him—like *I* mattered. At first, it felt amazingly grown up to have this sophisticated guy wanting to spend time with me."

"At first?"

"Yes. At first, when he dropped me off at my dad and Mercedes' lobby. Then, when they left for a vacation in Spain, he came into the apartment with me, and I showed him around. When we got to my room, he started to undress me." Molly began to cry.

"What are you remembering?"

"I asked him to stop. And he told me, "Don't worry. I came prepared.""

"You asked him to stop?"

"But we were already making out."

"Molly, 'no' means 'no.' Anyone who continues after being told 'no' is abusing you."

"But, after that we were together over and over, all during the time Mercedes and my dad were gone. Whenever he brought me home from work, he came into the apartment— and into me. I didn't ask him to stop then. So wasn't I giving him consent?"

"Once a woman has been sexualized, there's a tendency for her to feel unlovable, unlovely, unwanted, if she doesn't continue being in a sexual relationship."

Molly felt herself falling back in time. Her voice choked as the words spilled from their hidden deep freeze. "I would try to call him, and he had excuses, oh, so many excuses, when I couldn't reach him. And when he found out I was pregnant, he suddenly disappeared," she said, wiping tears away as they tumbled down her face. "Mercedes insisted on an abortion when they returned. My dad and mom never knew. Mercedes said it was best to keep it to ourselves. The rest of that summer is a blur. My senior year is a blur."

"We can work on some practical things that will help you heal from that, too, if you want."

"Yes, please. Maybe later. Could we go back to my wedding? I still need to know if I should cancel everything, before it's too late."

"Sure, let's look at your specific concerns. Do you love

Peter?"

"Yes. He is the most incredible human being I've ever known!"

"And you have been engaged how long?

"More than a year."

"So you've had time to think about what you're doing, to be sure you know him?"

"I also know his family very well. Remember his sister Kate was my roommate throughout college?"

Brooke drew a vertical line on the center of a piece of paper. On the top of one column, she wrote the word "Pros;" on the other, "Cons."

"You want me to tell you the positives and negatives about marrying Peter?"

"Exactly."

"Positives are easy. He is kind, loving, we share the same beliefs."

"Which are?"

"You know—we believe in God, we believe marriage is a sacred trust, we believe family is more important than career or any kind of financial success."

"And your communication is improving." Brooke smiled. Molly and Peter had been meeting with her together, to build conflict resolution and communication skills. "That, by the way, is often challenging in marriages, in general." She studied the list. "What about 'Cons'?"

Molly sighed. "I'll be a bad wife."

"While I disagree with you on that, Molly, why would you being, as you say, 'a bad wife,' be a 'Con' specifically for *this* marriage? Wouldn't it deter you from any marriage?"

"That's what I've been trying to say! Maybe I'm just not marriage material! Haven't you been listening, Brooke?"

"Oh, I'm listening. But I'm hearing something different from what you're saying with words."

"Huh?"

"Your body language is saying you're afraid. Do you notice how you're clenching your teeth and hands?"

Molly looked at her fists, tightly balled. "Ouch," she said. "I'm even digging my nails into the palms of my hands. You're right. I *am* terrified. What if Peter finds out after our wedding that I'm not the woman he thinks I am? What if he finds out I'm damaged goods; I'm worthless?"

"Does he know about your brother, about Anson, about your other concerns?"

"Yes."

"And is he running away?"

"Quite the opposite. He keeps reminding me that 'the mercies of the Lord are new every morning,' and then he says, every time, that I'm not defined by my abuse, that He wants us to start our new life as absolutely, totally free from the past."

"Well, as a counseling intern, he surely knows that, although we're biblically 'free,' we still can be influenced by things that happened in the past."

"Of course. He just wants me to remember to 'walk by faith, not by sight,' and not be *controlled* by vacillating feelings."

"Molly, you just answered your own question," said Brooke. "What is it about the violinist you're concerned about?"

Molly looked down. When she spoke, her voice was a whisper. "Um, my feelings for him."

"Exactly! And do you have to be *controlled* by those?"

Molly hesitated, and then looked up, smiling. "I get it! Instead of trusting my feelings about *him*, I can make the choice to realize they're only feelings, not reality." She paused again, thinking. "This is like what you told me before. I can look at my feelings like I see the lights on my car's dashboard—they can inform me of things I need to pay attention to and help me see if I need to make changes or address concerns, right?

"Right. Love is not a feeling, by the way, though certainly wonderful feelings are produced *by* love. Instead, love grows as we make the choices to think loving thoughts and behave in loving ways."

"I get it!"

"Tell me what you 'get.'"

"My feelings for Julian are not my reality, so I can ID them as emotional reasoning, a cognitive distortion—and replace them with the truth. I can make choices every day to show that I do love Peter, and I can't wait to marry him!"

"Great!" Brooke nodded affirmatively, paused briefly, and then continued, "Do you think you're afraid of being sexual with Peter?"

"That's the weird thing. I am not. Quite the opposite, in fact. He makes sure we don't spend time alone right now, because both of us have incredibly intense desire for each other. He says, 'I want you to be free to be abandoned to lovemaking on our wedding night.' So we usually hang out at his aunt and uncle's house rather than either of our places."

"That's commendable," Brooke said, pausing to think, her expression serious. "I'm wondering, then, do you think you should call off the wedding now?"

"Ha, ha. You got me, Brooke. No way!" She pulled a tissue from the box beside her, placing it on her head like a veil. "Here comes the bride," she sang, laughing.

Even Brooke was surprised by Molly's uncharacteristic spontaneity. "I don't know, Molly, maybe you need to consider that violinist."

"Ha. Ha. Ha. No way! What you've helped me realize is that what I feel for Peter is in another stratosphere. They're the kind of feelings that will last."

"Well, feelings can change. You will have moments when you don't 'feel' great about Peter. Remember love is not just a feeling; it grows with choices."

"I do understand that. Like when I took off for London because I was so confused about—everything."

"Yes. In addition, life's daily demands can cause your feelings to go in different directions. Both of you can commit to making positive choices every day—choices to show love no matter how you feel, exhibiting God's love to each other rather than being controlled by changing human emotions."

"That seems like a contradiction. On the one hand, I shouldn't depend on feelings; on the other, I should?"

"That's not what I'm saying. I'm saying our feelings are often unreliable indicators of reality. God's love never fails."

CHAPTER THIRTY-NINE

Peter looked at the clock, realizing his first group of the day began in just five minutes. As the men walked in, it was obvious that some were ready to talk; others clearly were not. All seven men had just begun treatment the week prior. Two of them had just finished detox.

"I hate it here," one said, introducing himself to the group.

"You'll get over it," another man laughed.

It took ten minutes for everyone to get settled enough to begin their discussion. Peter's head hurt before the group began. It was pounding when it finished. He had just enough time to finish notes on everyone's progress before it was time for his second group to begin. He was looking forward to hearing how each of the men was progressing, especially since they had now been in treatment for six weeks.

Men filled their coffee cups or grabbed a soda, then sat in a circle. "Where's Simon?" Peter asked.

"I haven't seen him," Tyson said.

"I'll check," Peter said, texting his supervisor, Dr. Paul Nelson. When he didn't get a response, he began the group's discussion. "Last week, in AA's Step Four, we made a 'searching and fearless moral inventory of our character defects.' Now, working through Step Five, we've 'admitted to

God, to ourselves, and to another human being the exact nature of our wrongs.' How's that going, men?"

Tyson said, "I did it. I called my dad and told him about everything…" he stopped to dry his eyes with his T-shirt before he could continue. "And what we talked about is happening. I'm starting to feel things—like sadness, but you all have helped me be OK with feeling the feelings and not wanting to numb out with drugs."

"Good job," Abe called out. "Way to move out of the SBG," he laughed.

"I forgot. What is SBG?" Tyson asked, feigning ignorance.

The group said in unison, "Shame Blame Game."

Tyson laughed. "Just checking." He paused, suddenly serious. "Ever since I was a little kid, I blamed myself for other people's bad choices. Now I try to notice whenever I do that and live in the present instead. It's a huge relief."

Like popcorn, conversation continued, ideas bouncing from man to man. Some shared about conversations with family members, beginning to make amends; others about contacting friends or even former colleagues.

"We'll get into making amends in step eight and nine, so don't jump ahead of yourselves. But great work, everyone!" Peter said as the meeting drew to a close an hour after it began.

When everyone left, Peter stopped at Dr. Nelson's office. "Simon wasn't in group," he said.

"We found Simon in his room, just before group began. The ambulance got here just about the time your group was beginning. I didn't want to tell you while you were facilitating a group," Dr. Nelson said.

"What happened?" Peter didn't understand.

"He ODed sometime in the night. When he didn't show up for breakfast, I went to check on him and found him in his room on the floor, unresponsive. I was trying to reach his parents when I got your text during group."

"No, that can't be," Peter cried. "He was making great

progress! Last week, he told me he was going to call his brother and admit stealing from him. And he told the group that this is his third time in rehab and that he planned to succeed this time." Peter sighed.

"Well, he did call his brother, and his brother came to see him last night. That must be how Simon got the oxycodone, or whatever it was he ODed on. We are recommending an autopsy."

Peter's mind went numb. He couldn't think; he couldn't feel. His eyes stung with tears. "I should have seen this coming!"

"Peter, it wasn't your fault," Dr. Nelson said, emphatically. "Unfortunately, addictions can be deadly. This work is tough, and an overdose can happen to any addict, at any time, even with the best help in the world available." He nodded to his secretary, who was motioning him to take a call. "This is probably his family, calling back. Take care, Peter."

Peter went to the parking lot, as he did every day after his second group ended. It was time to drive to his second internship. But, instead of starting his car, he pounded the steering wheel. "What could I have done? I should have known!" The temperature in the car was sweltering. He turned the key in the ignition, waiting for the air conditioner to give him some relief. But he needed a different kind of relief. He called Molly.

"Hey, Peter! How's it going?"

"Molly? Oh, I'm so glad you're there. This is a nightmare."

"What's wrong?"

Her voice comforted him. "One of my clients died in the night. An apparent overdose."

"I'm so sorry, Dearest. What can I do?"

"Please pray. I don't really know anything else, and I couldn't talk about it if I did."

"I'm on it. Do you want to meet for a quick lunch before you see your afternoon clients?"

"Yes, that would help."

There was a café where they often met for lunch, and

Molly was already there when Peter arrived. He wasn't really hungry for food, but he was starved for a touch from his beloved. She hugged him, and he felt the tension melt away. "Let's pray now," she said. "You're going to make it. And it wasn't your fault, Peter."

"How did you know that's what I'm feeling?"

"I woke up this morning with a sense of concern for you, so I've been praying for you since then."

"You have?" Peter was incredulous. "I'm grateful for you."

"And I'm grateful for you."

"I'm starting to understand what Solomon meant when he said, 'Two are better than one.'"

Molly's smile was reassuring. "Do you think you need to take the rest of the day off, Peter? You could cancel your afternoon appointments."

"My first appointment drives an hour to get there; he's probably in the waiting room already, because he's always early. No, I'll go ahead. I feel a lot better just talking with you."

They ate quickly, hugging again when they reached the parking lot. "I'll keep my phone with me if you need to reach me at any time. And I'll make a picnic for us to take to the beach tonight, OK?"

As Peter drove the final minutes to church, he asked God to give him strength in his weakness. The client was there as he walked in. "Give me five minutes, Kent. I'll be right back."

He quickly turned on his office lights, then returned to find Kent standing, ready to walk back to the office with him. "I'm so glad we're meeting today," Kent said. "I didn't think I could wait to talk with you another day."

"What's up?"

"My best friend was in a car accident last night. He was pronounced dead at the scene. His family lives in Germany, so he'd given my name as the emergency contact. I had to go to the hospital at midnight to identify his body." He sobbed.

Peter couldn't suppress his own tears. "I lost someone last

night, too," he said, joining him. "I'm sorry," he added. "I shouldn't tell you that."

"No, it helps. I can tell you get it." Kent continued to process his grief, and the hour soon ended.

Peter's next client was waiting as Kent left. "Come on back."

She began talking as they walked to Peter's office. "My son is about to get expelled from his college. I don't know what to do." That hour, too, seemed to end before it began.

When his afternoon ended, Peter was surprised. *God's strength is made perfect in my weakness,* he realized. With a sense of joy, he also began to understand how much he valued each of his clients. *And now I get to be with the woman I love.* He walked to his car, smiling, then drove to Molly's apartment. She was ready with their picnic.

"I left a voice mail for you. Did you get it?" she asked.

"Oh, I forgot to check voice mail," he said, looking at his phone. "Here's one from work. Mind if I check?"

"Sounds important."

The morning hit him like a tsunami. The message was from Dr. Nelson. "We need to meet with you as soon as possible, Peter. Simon's family wants to talk with both of us tonight. Their plane lands at five, so can you be back by 7:30?"

"Molly, I'm sorry. This wrecks our picnic idea. I don't know what to say."

"Do you want me to ride with you for moral support? I can wait in the car."

"It's too hot to wait in the car. But, yeah, I need you with me. You could wait in the lobby, if that's OK."

"You still need to eat. Why don't we just stop at that little park down the street and eat, then go on to work?"

They ate in a quiet, comfortable silence.

"Let's pray for this family," Peter said. "I've been dreading this meeting but haven't even let myself imagine how his parents must feel. They've been suffering with their son's addiction; now they're suffering even more with losing him."

As they prayed, Peter asked God to help him know how to comfort the grieving family. He finished praying and turned to her. "Molly, I'm too young to know how to deal with this."

"I don't know if we're ever old enough to know how to help someone through grief like this. But isn't the Lord called the 'God of all comfort'? He can show you how to help them," she said, holding his hand.

They drove to the treatment center in a soothing sense of silence.

CHAPTER FORTY

Peter sat in the front row of the campus performance hall, excited to hear his fiancée, yet nervous for her. For the past few weeks, it had been difficult to find time to be together because she was practicing, arranging music or preparing in some other way for this night. He turned to look behind him, smiling when he saw his parents arrive. They sat in the front-row seats reserved next to him, Kate, Carlos, Carmen and Miguel. Dan and Zoë, her leg propped on a stool, sat at the far end of the row.

"You cut it close," he whispered. "Five minutes."

"Sorry, Peter, there was a ten-car pileup," his dad said. "We planned to be early."

"We were afraid we weren't going to get here at all," his mom added, sitting next to her son. She whispered, "Please pray for all the people in that accident. It was bad."

Peter nodded, giving his mom a hug.

They turned to watch as the solo violinist led fourteen musicians onto the stage. The concert hall was filled with the sounds of their instruments, tuning.

When Molly stepped onto the stage, the musicians and audience quieted. She looked around the auditorium, smiling, pleased that nearly half the seats in the large auditorium were filled. "Thank you for coming tonight." She motioned to the musicians seated behind her, who stood and bowed. "I appreciate each of you sharing your time and talent for my graduate recital." Beaming, she turned again to the audience. "I hope everyone has an enjoyable evening." Her smile was directed at Peter, and then she turned to sit with the musicians, who held their instruments up to begin.

The sounds of Telemann's Concerto for Two Flutes and Bassoon in B Minor filled the concert hall. A harpsichord and bassoon were featured next, playing Vivaldi. Though Molly was playing flute, she clearly let the other musicians take center stage. Then chairs were removed and others, rearranged, as twelve musicians left the stage.

Peter noticed a name he recognized on the program. Julian. Molly had been worried about feeling *something* for him. He smiled, grateful for the transparency in their relationship—and thankful that Molly was now confident that she wanted to be his, alone.

Preparing to perform the first movement of Mozart's Flute Quartet No. 1 in D Major, Julian entered first with his violin, followed by Evan on viola, then Rebecca, the cellist. Molly entered last, to enthusiastic applause. She was wearing a shimmery cobalt blue floor-length gown, her hair pulled back in an elegant twist.

Peter noticed that one lone strand of hair had slipped down onto her face sometime between Vivaldi and Mozart. *If only I could just put that back in place for her.* He had to force himself to concentrate on the music, not the musician.

Molly, Julian and Evan stood to play, while Rebecca sat next to her cello. The music was exquisite. "Beautiful," Kate whispered. Peter sat silently, transfixed by Molly, who left the stage again with the other musicians after they finished playing Mozart.

This time, Molly returned to the stage by herself, to play Bach's Partita in A Minor for Flute Alone.

As soon as the solo ended, Kate turned to Carlos, whispering. "Bach is Molly's favorite. Isn't she incredible?

And she has everything memorized!"

His mother said something to Peter as the audience continued applauding, but he was lost in thought. *This is my bride, my beloved. I can't wait to marry her!*

His mom said again, "Peter, do you want anything?"

"What?" he finally heard her.

"Can we get you a bottle of water or something? We didn't have time to eat, so we're going to the lobby to see if they have anything to tide us over. And we're all going out for dinner afterwards?"

"I'm fine, Mom. And, yes, we're planning on dinner." He didn't move during intermission. All he could do was think about his bride.

The second half of the recital was even more incredible, because a small ensemble of four musicians played several of Molly's original compositions. The last piece was a flute solo, with no other musicians on stage.

* * *

The day before her program was printed, she finally named her solo composition: *Sound of Light.* In elegant calligraphy under the title was John 8:12: *Jesus again spoke to them, saying, 'I am the Light of the world; he who follows Me will not walk in the darkness, but will have the Light of life.'* Following that, Molly added, *My life has changed—from darkness to light. 'Sound of Light' expresses my gratitude to the One who made the transformation possible—Jesus, my Healer and Restorer.*

* * *

Molly seemed transported to another place, her music transitioning from a minor to a major key, its tempo and intensity increasing. As Molly played, Peter wept, sensing her heart. Throughout the auditorium, the only sound was Molly's flute, the music of her soul.

After a standing ovation, the ensemble joined Molly for an

encore, which resulted in another standing ovation.

"How was it?" Molly asked Peter after the crowd left.

"I am speechless, my dearest. Speechless. This was the most wonderful concert I've ever attended. Your solo took me into light, joy, hope…I didn't know that music could capture emotions like that."

"You are slightly biased," she said, smiling. He was really the only one she wanted to please.

Dr. Thomson joined them. "Is this your family, Molly?"

"My family-to-be," Molly smiled, introducing Peter, his parents, Kate, Carlos and his parents.

"I imagine you are very proud of Molly's performance." Turning to Molly, she continued. "Not only was every piece flawless, you put your recital together in half the usual time."

"Thank you, Dr. Thomson. You just didn't notice the mistakes."

"Molly, that is because there weren't any! Congratulations, you have officially completed all of your graduate work! See you at graduation."

"Um, I'm not going to walk."

"Oh, that's right. I forgot. Well, now your wedding plans take precedence!"

With Carmen's enthusiastic urging, Peter and Molly had invited their advisors, as well as some additional faculty members and friends to the ceremony. The number of invited guests was getting closer to Carmen's seventy-five than Molly's original twenty.

"Some of the musicians from tonight are performing chamber music at our wedding," Molly told her.

"I know," Dr. Thomson responded, laughing. "They asked me if that could count for a music performance requirement. I told them it could, since I'll be there to observe them perform. Kudos again, Molly!" she said as she left them.

"We'll go ahead and get a table for our group," Peter's parents said. Everyone was still congratulating her as they left. Kate turned, clapping. "Phenomenal, Molly!"

Dan and Zoë waited to thank Molly.

"Truly superb," Dan said. "Thank you for sharing your magnificent gift with us."

"Yes," said Zoë, wiping tears from her eyes. "Beautiful! We're so proud of you."

"Thank you," Molly said quietly, somehow embarrassed by everyone's attention. Suddenly she felt weak. She had to sit down.

"Are you OK?" Peter asked, concerned.

"I think I'm finally feeling the effects of getting this recital together so rapidly."

"That's understandable," Dan said. "It was incredible."

Peter walked with Molly to his car, then they drove her to their favorite beach restaurant to celebrate. For the first time in months, Molly let herself relax, surrounded by the love of family and dear friends. Peter, Kate, Carlos, Brandon, Kelly, Dan, Zoë, Carmen and Miguel. She looked at the nine people gathered with her at the table and felt like she'd never experienced such joy.

"Thank you, everyone, for making this the best recital of my life," she said, meaning it.

When Peter was driving her home after dinner, she asked, "Can we talk awhile before you take me home?"

"Sure, at The Beanery?"

The coffee shop near Molly's apartment was open until midnight. It was one of their favorite places to talk.

"I've been thinking, Peter," she began.

"Should I be worried?" he asked, only half-joking.

"Very funny. I have no travel plans." She smiled. "I'm just wondering what to do next. I always thought I'd just keep going to school, get my doctorate and then either teach at the university level or perform in a symphony and teach private flute lessons. Now I'm not so sure. In fact, I feel so burned out on school, I don't know what to do."

"What if you simply take some time off?"

"Can you read my mind? That's exactly what I've been

wondering, but I haven't let myself even dream I could do it. Ever since I began playing the flute, I've practiced at least twice as much as anyone I knew. In college, I've studied…"

"*More* than twice as much as anyone I know," he finished for her.

"Right. But with the inheritance coming in October, it seems like anything could be possible for us. I'd like to have time to actually be with you—living life, having dinner together like your family does, or having time for us to go for a walk in the evening—not having the demands of grad school for awhile."

"My internship will be challenging for at least another year. Is that OK? I might not have as much free time as we'd like."

"That's exactly why I'd like to have some unscheduled time. Then I can have meals ready for you, or go out for lunch with you if you have to work at night."

He reached across their table to tuck her hair behind her ear. "I've been wanting to do this all evening," he said.

As he leaned toward her, she leaned forward and kissed him. "You wanted to kiss me?"

"Touch your hair was what I meant. But, yes, kissing you is even better!"

"We'd better change the subject. We don't have long to wait now," she sighed.

"It feels like too long sometimes," he sighed, leaning back in his chair.

"But we're going to make it. As everyone keeps telling us, it will be worth it for the rest of our lives."

CHAPTER FORTY-ONE

Molly had talked with Analese via Skype at least once a week since her return from London. This time, she couldn't wait to share her news. "Analese, guess what?"

"I can't guess. What?"

"Carlos' parents want you and your family to stay at their home when you come for the wedding! They have several guest rooms and no one else will be staying there. It's a beautiful estate, so you can play outdoors with the children, swim in their pool and have a bit of a vacation while you're here."

"Wonderful! We'd planned to stay with my aunt and uncle, but that's not going to work because they recently moved into a senior residential center. We'll stay at a hotel near them for a couple of days before we come to help you get ready for the wedding."

Molly heard Baby Molly crying in the background. "Do you need to get Molly?"

"I'm OK. The kids just finished dinner awhile ago, and Sam's getting Molly ready for bed. Andrew's already in bed."

"I'm trying to figure out if I should take a few months off after the wedding, and wait awhile before I get a job, but I feel like I won't be using my degree. What do you think, Analese?"

"I think it's a great idea. Molly, you've been pushing yourself, intensely, for years."

"Another concern is my trust fund. You're the only other person I know—besides my sister—who inherited money at a young age. I'm really confused about how to manage the money, learn how to be a wife—and, at the same time, not get lazy."

"Molly, you're the last person I can imagine becoming even remotely lazy!" Analese laughed. "But I'm happy to help you with ideas about managing your inheritance wisely."

"Great. Peter and I have talked about this. We actually want you to manage all of it, if you will. Neither of us has any idea what to do with millions of dollars."

"I'm glad you're thinking about what to do. Too many people who inherit money simply squander everything. Without proper planning, it's all too easy to spend millions in an incredibly short time."

"Another question, Analese," Molly sighed, trying to find words. "Do you think I'll be a good wife or that I can ever possibly be a good mother?"

"Oh, Molly! You'll be a wonderful wife. You have to stop listening to those old voices of condemnation. Think about the people who have criticized you in the past. Do you want to be like *any* of them?"

Molly paused. She hadn't thought of it that way. The critical voices in her head came from her dad, her mom, her brother, and her stepmother—all the people who had wounded her. She wondered why she was *still* letting them hurt her.

"You'll also be a great mom, Molly," Analese continued. "Just, please, whatever you do, don't wait as long as I did to have children!"

"What do you mean? You and Sam are great parents!"

"We do love being parents, Molly, but we are tired. We're older than you and Peter are—and we feel it every day. That's all I meant. I hope you'll have your children while you're young enough to keep up with them."

The two continued talking for another half hour, until Sam poked his head into the room. He smiled into the camera. "Hey, Molly Dolly! In a wee moment, I'm going to need to borrow my bride."

She laughed aloud at his teasing. "Will you two give a toast at the reception?"

"Us? Why, thank you! We'd be happy to," he said. "Do you want me to wear my Scottish kilt?"

It took Molly a second to realize he was kidding. She started to say, "Um, if you…"

He interrupted her response with a chuckle. Even his laughter was tinged with the heartening lilt of his Scottish brogue. "A kilt would be a bit warm in California, I do believe. But, now, my dear, we must go care for wee Molly Dolly!"

Molly smiled back. "Hug each other for me, and I'll talk with you soon! Analese can tell you about the wonderful place you'll be staying when you come for the wedding!"

Molly moved from her laptop to her cell phone to call her grandparents in Florida. As their phone rang, it occurred to her that she avoided them because they reminded her too much of her dad. "Nana?" she said when her dad's mother answered. "I'm sorry I haven't talked with you for awhile. Did you get my wedding invitation?"

"Of course we did! And we've already booked our flights! Is there anything you need us to do?"

"Just come and sit in the place of honor. I'm so happy you'll be there!" She paused. "Did you know Jennifer is my maid of honor?"

"Yes, she called to tell us! She's flying in to LAX the same day as we are! She said she'd rent a car and drive us to the hotel in Santa Barbara where everyone's staying."

"That's great. There will be a shuttle from the hotel to the wedding and then also to the reception site."

"Wonderful! Is your brother coming?"

Molly had anticipated that question. "No, he said he couldn't come to California right now. He recently relocated in Illinois and can't get time off his new job." She was thankful she could give her grandmother an honest answer. Peter had talked with Jeremy to see what his plans were. Molly was grateful her groom didn't want anything to happen on their wedding day to destroy her joy. Both she and Peter knew Babs would be pressuring her son to come, especially since her neighbors told her they'd already booked a European river cruise and couldn't come to the wedding with her. Suddenly Molly was afraid there would be fireworks between her mom and her paternal grandparents. "I should tell you that Mom will probably be staying at the same hotel. I hope that won't be uncomfortable..."

"We're grown-ups, honey. She'll just have to deal with it."

Nana had always been all business. Molly didn't need to worry about her grandparents at all. "Tell Grandpa I can't wait to see you two."

"He says to tell you he's happy for you, Sweetheart! We can't wait to see you, Molly Dolly."

She smiled, grateful to simply hear her Nana's dear voice.

"We're excited to meet your wonderful fiancé at the rehearsal dinner."

"Thank you, Nana. Peter's family is hosting that at our favorite beach restaurant in Santa Barbara. It's called The Fess Parker. It should be a lot of fun for everyone."

"And your wedding ceremony is in a church? Your mom is actually going to come for that?"

Nana's comment about her mom and church gave Molly the courage to risk asking a question. "Why doesn't Mom like church? Do you know?"

"Oh, yes, we know. She and her mom had a huge falling-out before your parents got married. Your dad told us it was during their final pre-marital counseling session, when the minister at her mother's church told them it was really important to integrate faith in their family life. Your mom got angry with the minister and told him what they did in their marriage was none of his business. She ended up storming out of his office and vowing to never step foot in church again."

"That's a bit extreme, isn't it?"

"Well, your dad thought it was. He said the minister was soft-spoken and kind and that he only meant to help them have a good marriage. In the end, they did get married at that church, because the invitations had been mailed and hundreds of people had already sent RSVPs. I think something else happened between your mom and her mother before the wedding, but I never really knew what it was."

"That explains some things, I guess. It's too bad my mom didn't listen to that pastor's advice. Maybe she and my dad could have had a different life."

"I know. Babs has always been confusing to us, too, Molly Dolly." She paused. "Now that you're almost a married woman, should I give you a more sophisticated name?" Nana chuckled.

Molly smiled. "I still like to hear you calling me 'Molly Dolly,' Nana."

"Good. When we see your mom, all we can do is try to love her, right?"

"Right. See you soon, Nana."

CHAPTER FORTY-TWO

"I'll be in LA this weekend. Are you and Kate free?"

"We'll make it happen, Jenn. If Kate needs her dress altered, this weekend is cutting it close."

"You're going to love the bridesmaid dresses I found for us in Paris! You did say you wanted me to find lime green dresses, right?"

"Wrong," Molly said, grateful she knew her sister was joking.

"Kate's dress is slightly different from mine. They are both teal blue, per your request. And they're a comfortably, luscious silk."

"Oh, I'm glad they're comfortable! And teal blue will be perfect with her red hair—and your blonde hair!"

"Mine has an open back, hers has a really cool strappy design. I know everyone says their bridesmaids' dresses can be worn later—and then they look so passé that they're relegated to get lost in someone's closet instead. I promise you, Mol, these can be worn again."

"Can't wait to see them! And you!" Molly added.

"I think I'll rent a car so you don't have to come to the airport. I know you're super busy. Plus it will be fun to see the area where you live."

"I have to move out next week, so my place is a mess, but it will be great to have you here. I have an extra bed for you. Next week, I'll start staying with Dan and Zoë until the wedding. You can see their place and Peter's, too—that's where we'll live when we're first married."

"Excellent!"

"So can you stay with me?"

"Just for one night. I have a flight out the next evening. I'm glad we can connect Friday about the dresses and finish any other plans you want to make."

"I actually don't have to do much. Carlos' parents are doing almost everything."

"This is the Carlos, married to Kate, whose family you were so critical of?"

"And I was wrong, Jennifer. I've never been so wrong about anyone or anything in my entire life! It has taught me a lesson I'll never forget."

"But why are *they* helping with your wedding?"

"Because they are a closely-knit family—and because Kate, Peter's sister, is married to their son. And Zoë, who was going to host the reception, broke her leg."

"Oh, now I get it. Well, it's really kind of them to help. I'm excited to meet them. Is our mom coming early to help you get ready?"

"Thankfully, she is not. In fact, she has made it crystal-clear that her only 'contribution,' as she put it, to our wedding is to show up. She says her presence will be our gift." Molly's laugh was hollow.

"Unbelievable. Simply unbelievable. You'd think she would want to do *something* to celebrate her daughter's wedding." Jenn's sigh was so loud that it felt like she was in the room with Molly. "Now I think you begin to understand why I'll never tell her about the trust fund."

"I guess. But I still don't understand why she didn't get those funds when she got her divorce settlement."

"She didn't get it because it was money our dad made after their divorce. He invested extensively—in Apple, among other stocks. And he had a prenup with Mercedes so she wouldn't be able to touch it. She also has no idea we're inheriting anything."

"That makes sense. We have enough complications with both of them to avoid a new one." The sisters laughed comfortably, appreciating how they now understood each other. "By the way, I've asked Analese to help me invest my trust fund."

"Good plan. She and Sam have given me great advice. Oh, I keep forgetting to tell you that there is a second payout of the trust fund five years after the first."

"What?"

"You'll get the same amount you get this fall again, in five years."

"That is more than I can even begin to comprehend right now."

"I get it." Jenn said, pausing. "Give it time. You'll know what to do when the time comes. Remember Proverbs 3:5 and 6?"

"Trust in the Lord with all your heart, and lean not on your own understanding..."

"In all your ways acknowledge Him, and He will make your paths straight."

"I have to keep remembering it's not my job to figure everything out. I can trust God to lead me." Molly paused, her mind drifting. "Hey, Jenn, I have a question."

"What?"

"Why are *you* still working? You could live off the interest of the money you have left, couldn't you?"

"I could, but I want to do something meaningful with my life. I doubt that I'll continue being a flight attendant, since the long hours and time zone changes are starting to get to me. I might consider working for some kind of relief organization instead. I've been doing some research into organizations that need help in the Greenwich area. I want the days or years I have left on earth to bring honor to God."

"How does that look, practically?"

"I'm still trying to figure that out. I hope it means that people will notice God in my life, in my words and actions—and that praise for anything good I do won't go to me but to the Lord, for all He has done."

CHAPTER FORTY-THREE

Jennifer's visit was a whirlwind. She came directly from the airport to Molly's little apartment, surprised to find almost everything Molly owned piled in boxes in the living room. "Peter and his uncle are coming to help me move tomorrow evening," Molly said. "But I have three glasses left that I didn't pack, if anyone wants lemonade or iced tea."

"Iced tea for me," Jenn said.

"Same here," said Kate.

It took an hour for Kate and Jennifer to catch up on the years since Kate's family left Illinois for California. "You were always the cool high school girl Molly and I looked up to," Kate said.

"I don't know if I were the right person for you to look up to," Jenn said, grimacing. "I was pretty confused about life—then and for the next decade."

"What changed?" Kate asked.

"I tried just about everything there was to try, traveled the world, and came up empty every time."

Molly's phone buzzed. "Sorry, I forgot to turn this off," she said, picking it up to do so. She groaned.

"What's wrong?" Jenn and Kate asked in unison.

"It's Mercedes. She has tried to call me at least five times *every* day for the last week."

"Maybe you should answer her and see if something is wrong."

"You haven't talked with her for a long time, have you, Jenn?" Molly turned to her sister, her face tense.

"No, to be honest, I haven't. It helps that I live outside the U.S. But she never really got her tentacles into me."

"Exactly," Molly responded. "I know she's only calling because she wants to get me back into her clutches. I just can't afford to let her influence me when I've made so much progress—and, especially right now, when I'm about to start my life with Peter."

"You're right. Absolutely right," Jenn said. "Sorry for the dumb idea."

Molly hugged her sister. "It wasn't a dumb idea. If she were anyone else, it would be good to reach out to her, to try to stay in touch. But, she has nearly destroyed my life twice now, and I'm not going to let it happen again."

"Good decision, Mol," Kate enthused. "Now, Jenn, let's try on these dresses for Molly! We're getting ready for your wonderful wedding day!"

* * *

The mood in Mercedes' spacious suburban Chicago penthouse was nothing like the one in Molly's California apartment. Mercedes threw her phone across the room, furious that her stepdaughter was patently ignoring her. "Something is going on," she said. "She must be planning something with those people. I hate them, every single one of them."

It was only four, but Mercedes angrily opened the chilled bottle of Santa Margherita Pinot Grigio. Instead of anticipating an evening with a man she'd invited to join her for drinks at the penthouse, after the intimate dinner she'd planned for them at The Capital Grille, she was alone—again. She grimaced, remembering his abrupt call an hour before.

"Mercedes. I can't make it for dinner after all. I had an emergency at work."

"On Friday night? And what is your emergency?"

"Um, the pipes in my office burst." His lie was laughable.

"Well, I certainly hope you don't drown," she said, hanging up on him. That was when she'd tried Molly. She needed relief.

She sipped the wine, savoring its sophisticated, clean scent and unwinding into the light flavor of apples and citrus. "Yes!" she said aloud. Mercedes smiled, loving her new idea. She googled a name, found the number and called, her smile broadening when the phone was actually answered.

"Babs Montgomery here. Chicago's Premier Realtors."

"Babs, I don't know if you remember me. This is Mercedes Mauritz, and I am calling because *you* are considered the best realtor in our area. I'm so happy you took my call on a Friday evening, because I urgently need your professional opinion about listing my penthouse."

Babs Montgomery rarely was at a loss for words. Could this be the woman who stole her husband's heart? Would she really dare call his ex-wife?

The polished voice continued to drone on, something about her interior decorator's numerous awards and wanting to be sure her penthouse delivered top market value. Babs had difficulty comprehending until she heard, "When is your first available appointment, Mrs. Montgomery?"

Too much of a saleswoman to turn down a hefty commission, Babs finally spoke, forcing artificial warmth into her words. "Ms. Mauritz, since you said it's urgent, I am available this evening at 8:00. Is that convenient for you?"

"That would be lovely," Mercedes said, somewhat surprised that her plan was working so easily. "Let me give you directions."

"Oh, I know how to get there," Babs said, swallowing the resentment filling her esophagus. Lately, every time she felt stressed, she experienced acid reflux. *This isn't so bad,* she told herself, silencing her pride. *I don't have anyone to be with tonight, anyway. And Jameson bailed on both of us. At least he didn't kill himself when he was married to me.*

* * *

Although the lobby seemed to have the same gleaming marble floors Babs remembered, the art was definitely new. It was like walking into a Chihuly collection, with a 30-foot vertical glass exhibit making the entire foyer pop with vibrancy. Contemporary art covered the walls. A doorman nodded. "Ms. Mauritz is expecting you," he said, pushing the button for the top floor.

Mercedes opened the door before Babs pressed her doorbell. "Thank you for coming. Wine?" she asked.

"No, thank you," Babs responded, needing to stay fully cognizant of her surroundings.

"Would you like a tour?"

"Yes, please."

Mercedes was thrilled to show off her home. "Let's begin in the Master. The entire penthouse is over 4,000 square feet. But the pièce de résistance is the master closet. I designed it myself!" Mercedes exclaimed.

Babs looked around the expansive closet, noticing shelf after shelf of designer shoes and purses. She listened as Mercedes pointed out built-in jewelry drawers, complete with locks; custom-designed hangers for haute couture evening gowns; and the dozens of built-in cedar drawers for her woolens. "Lovely," she murmured, wondering how anyone could be such a narcissist.

"Let's take a look at the other rooms," she said, suddenly feeling suffocated in this place her husband shared with another woman.

Mercedes, like an out-of-control fountain, continued gushing about her home. "Two guest rooms are down this hall. Both have en suites, of course. And this is where Molly stayed when she was here last Christmas." Remembering she was trying to win Babs over, not gloat over her, Mercedes added, "Wasn't it lovely we both got to see her?"

"Yes, yes, it was." Babs' voice was guarded. She felt a sudden urge to leave.

Mercedes nodded to a room on the left. "This was Jameson's study. And here is the den." She paused, carefully choosing each word. "Molly has a lot going on now, doesn't she?" Mercedes asked, fishing.

"Yes, mostly wedding plans."

Mercedes realized *her* plan was working. She seized the opportunity. "About that. My cleaning lady was here yesterday, and I'm furious, simply furious, with her. I had my invitation in a stack of mail on the counter, and Hannah threw it all away. I even checked recycling, but it was gone," Mercedes pouted.

Babs forced herself not to look shocked. She paused to find words she could say aloud. "Your invitation was lost?"

"Could you give me a copy of yours? It would help so much to be able to check dates. I hadn't even had a chance to look at my calendar to see if I can come. And I know how much Molly wants me to be there for her."

Babs felt a sudden, uncontrolled fury that her daughter would invite this woman to come to her wedding. She had to take three deep breaths before she trusted herself to speak. "Sure, I can bring it when I come back to go over details of other area listings that compare with yours, so you can choose your listing price."

"That would be perfect. When would you like to come back?"

"Let me look at my schedule and get back with you." Babs had her schedule on her phone, but she didn't want to divulge any more of her life. Not now. Not ever. "I do need to go now." She forced a smile, then walked briskly to the elevator, her thoughts sinking with each floor, wondering how Jameson could have ever married such a self-obsessed woman. As soon as she got into her car in the parking garage, she sobbed for the first time in years. *I didn't appreciate him when we were married. If only he were still alive, we could try again.* She knew it wasn't true, and she couldn't bear to think it. So, she pressed play, mouthing the words along with her current favorite motivational podcast. "Be the woman you know you can be. Be all you can be. Be more than you've ever been. You've got this."

CHAPTER FORTY-FOUR

Molly unzipped the oversized garment bag and gently removed her wedding gown. She gasped aloud, not because of anxiety but from pure, unadulterated joy. *I forgot how beautiful it is.* The lace was exquisite; the design of the gown was perfect. *I can't wait to be Peter's bride.*

Jenn, staying in the guest room next to Molly's temporary home at Dan and Zoë's house, stepped into the room as Molly was admiring her dress. "That is the most gorgeous wedding gown I've ever seen!"

Molly sighed. "I can't wait to wear it tomorrow. Can you believe it?"

"Absolutely. You're going to be gorgeous!"

Zoë limped into the room, clearly happy to be mobile again, even though she was sporting a walking cast. "Oh, Molly, your wedding day is tomorrow, at last!" The three women sat together on the edge of Molly's bed. "Is it OK if we pray?" Zoë asked.

"Of course. Please," Molly and Jenn said together.

Jenn began, "Lord, we love You! Thank You for bringing us here, for giving Molly these wonderful friends."

Zoë continued, "Please protect Peter and Molly. Bless their wedding day and each person who comes. Help everyone who's working together to make this a wonderful day. We want to honor You, God, since marriage was Your idea in the first place."

Tears streamed down Molly's face as she prayed. "I don't even know how to thank You, Father God, for protecting me and bringing me to this wonderful family. Bless Jenn and Kate as bridesmaids, and everyone else helping us, especially Carmen and Miguel—and help Zoë to be able to enjoy the day without a lot of pain, and especially bless Peter with rest." When she finished praying, Molly hugged her sister and Zoë, explaining, "Peter has had to work extra hours the last two weeks so he can take time off for our honeymoon. And he is still sad about one of his clients who died of a drug overdose."

"I understand," Zoë said. "I remember when Dan was an intern. Such long hours, and so many sad stories. You'll both learn to trust God with others' sorrows."

Jenn looked at her watch. "I've got to get to the airport to pick up Mom. Should I bring her here or to her hotel?"

"I guess you could ask her what she prefers," Molly said, looking at Zoë. "Is that OK with you and Dan?"

"If she wants to spend the afternoon here, that's fine. We can take her to the rehearsal."

"OK, I'll ask her. Are you sure that won't be too much for you, Mol?"

"It would probably be good to see her. At about three, though, Peter and I are going for a prayer walk—he wants to take me to the ocean and spend time praying for every aspect of the wedding and reviewing our vows. Then we'll go directly to the church for the rehearsal. So, you'd spend more time with her than I would. Are you OK with that?"

"Yes, I haven't seen her since I became a Christian. But I don't know if she'll want to hear anything about my life." Jenn sighed.

Zoë looked puzzled. "I just have to say it's difficult for me to imagine a mother not wanting to know about every detail of her two amazing daughters' lives—especially how discovering God's love has transformed both of them from the inside out."

"Please pray we can communicate that love to our mother," Jenn said, her eyes brimming with tears. "It's so difficult when she lashes out at us without even hearing what we're trying to say. I wish she'd let us truly know her—and try to get to know us."

Jenn came back from the airport alone. Her mother had her drop her off at her resort. "I'm much too tired from the flight to even think of being around people right now. I'll see you at the rehearsal dinner."

"Aren't you planning to go to the rehearsal?"

"Absolutely not. I hate churches, and it's going to take every ounce of energy I have to be in that church for the wedding tomorrow. The dinner is all I can handle tonight."

"Mom, why do you hate church so much?" Jenn asked softly.

"That, Jennifer, is absolutely none of your business," Babs snapped. She stared out the window during the rest of their drive, glancing repeatedly at her watch to be sure they'd be there in time for her scheduled appointments at the Biltmore Four Seasons' world-class spa. By opting out of what she called the 'run through' at the church, she'd have ample time before dinner for her *Four Seasons in One* signature spa package followed by a blow dry at their elegant salon. She tuned out Jennifer's voice. Staying at the Biltmore and treating herself at what was considered the most luxurious hotel spa in Santa Barbara was her compensation for having to travel alone. *I deserve it, after how hard I work all the time. Molly should have scheduled this wedding when my friends could come with me. I still can't believe she was so selfish that she couldn't wait until after the Wendhams returned from their trip.* Jennifer rudely interrupted her thoughts.

"Want to have a cup of coffee with me?" Jenn asked for the second time, hoping her mom would want to spend time with her. "I wish you were staying where everyone else is. I feel like I'm not even going to see you."

"I told you I'm tired. I have to brace myself for tomorrow."

"Brace yourself? Aren't you looking forward to Molly's wedding?"

"Not really. Especially since she invited Mercedes," Babs said, her face contorted with venom.

"Wait a minute, Mom. I know for a fact Molly did *not* invite our stepmother. She told me that specifically."

"Then why the heck did Mercedes tell me her maid threw out her invitation?" She paused, annoyed when she realized how she'd been played. "She had the audacity to ask me to bring her a copy of *my* wedding invitation. And she lured me to her apartment, pretending she wanted to list it. Which, of course, she never did," Babs hissed.

"You gave her a copy of the invitation?" Jenn groaned.

"I had no idea. She was quite convincing."

"Oh, I'm sure she was. This presents a huge problem. She will absolutely ruin the day if she shows up."

Babs didn't like being held responsible. "Look, I did nothing wrong. I'm sure she won't come. I mean, really. California is a long way from Chicago," she said, laughing mirthlessly. "OK, here we are. Just pop the trunk and I'll have the valet get my bag. See you at dinner. I'll cab to the Fess Parker." With a wave, Babs was gone.

Jenn forgot all about coffee in her impatience to let Molly know about this impending disaster. *On the other hand, I don't want to ruin Molly's day by giving her anything to dread.* Her mind racing, she thought of a possible solution. *I'm simply going to call Mercedes and pretend I want to know how she's doing.* She found a parking spot and pressed Mercedes' number. It went right to voice mail. *Just like it would if it's in airplane mode. She is en route here. I know it!* Her heart racing, Jenn called Carmen for advice.

"Hi, Carmen. Yes, I know. Tomorrow is almost here! Thank you so much for everything you're doing to make Molly and Peter's reception perfect. I have one more favor to ask of you, though. I just learned from my mom that she gave our stepmother a copy of the wedding invitation."

Carmen groaned. "I didn't think those two would even be in contact! How in the world did *that* happen?"

"My mom's a realtor, and Mercedes pretended she was selling her penthouse to get her to come over. Then Mercedes told our mom that her cleaning lady had thrown out her copy of the invitation. My mom believed her and actually gave her a copy of the wedding invitation."

"Do you have a picture of Mercedes?"

"She was a model, so I can find a picture online and text it to you."

"Excellent. Try to get one that's as current as possible." Jenn heard Carmen take a deep breath before she continued. "We'll get this figured out. We are not going to let anyone ruin Molly and Peter's day, are we?" As soon as they hung up, Carmen sprung into action, asking for favors to protect a bride she fiercely loved.

CHAPTER FORTY-FIVE

Molly beamed throughout their rehearsal dinner at The Fess Parker, excited for the surprise she planned for her beloved after the Santa Barbara Buffet.

Just as Peter thought the day couldn't get any better, Molly stood and began to speak enthusiastically to their guests. "You all know what an amazing man Peter is. There are few gifts I could give him that would even begin to show how much I love him. So, I tried to think of something he enjoys—something perhaps even some of you don't know about." She looked at Peter, grinning, then at the door.

In walked three musicians, all dressed in 70's attire. Spurts of laughter greeted their arrival. Molly continued speaking. "I asked Peter once how he defuses tension. He said he likes to listen to Keith Green on YouTube. Since Keith is already in Heaven, we have with us tonight, Keith's music—with Julian, Rebecca, and Evan, singing Peter's favorite songs."

The trio slipped into their retro role seamlessly. Clearly impersonating Keith, Julian sported a bushy brown wig, a floral print shirt and grey polyester bell-bottoms. Playing a guitar, he began to sing, his full beard somehow helping complete the transformation to 70's musician. With Rebecca and Evan singing back-up, the music was in three exquisitely-harmonized parts. "There is a redeemer, Jesus God's own Son. Precious Lamb of God, Messiah, Holy One. Jesus, my redeemer, Name above all names, precious Lamb of God, Messiah, oh, for sinners slain." By the time the song ended, most of the room was in tears, reminded that the upcoming wedding was a unique story of God's redemption.

The second the song ended, Peter was on his feet, shouting, "Encore! Encore!"

"Keith," pensive, began another song. "Make my life a prayer to you, I wanna do what you want me to. No empty words and no white lies. No token prayers, no compromise. I wanna shine the light you gave…"

Peter smiled at Molly, both of them nodding in agreement as the song continued.

"Well I wanna thank you now for being patient with me, oh, it's so hard to see when my eyes are on me…I want to tell the world out there, You're not some fable or fairy tale that I've made up inside my head, You're God the Son and you've risen from the dead…"

Observing everyone's responses, Molly felt happy, until she noticed her mother's angry scowl. Peter noticed, too, and leaned into Molly, whispering, so only she could hear. "That was incredible. I don't know how you pulled it off. But I'm so sorry I didn't plan anything for you. I thought you wanted to keep tonight simple."

"Tonight is perfect—but I wanted to do this just for you! You're always doing special things for me. Do you like your surprise?"

"Love it!" He noticed the musicians heading for the door. "Let's go thank them!"

"I think I recognize all of you from Molly's recital," he said, shaking their hands and laughing. "Well, I almost recognize you! What a transformation! It felt like we were really in the 70s tonight! Julian, you look like you could *be* Keith Green! Is he your favorite retro musician, too?"

"Thanks, Peter! Actually, I'd never heard of him before, but I spent a few hours getting to know his music on

YouTube." He grinned. "We had a blast preparing this for you. I hope you both know what an inspiration you are to us. You make us want to wait for God's best in our relationships."

Peter looked confused. "What do you mean?"

"We see how content Molly is, and she told us how you both want your marriage to honor God. Being here tonight, seeing how you love each other..." Julian, overcome by emotion, couldn't finish.

Rebecca, a flower pinned in her long blonde hair, nodded, continuing for him. "I agree with Julian. We've all settled for second best in relationships, many times. We've decided that, after seeing you and Molly, we're going to wait for marriage—and learn how to live in God's love for the rest of our lives, instead of the world's lust." She blushed, suddenly embarrassed. "I didn't mean to get so specific."

Evan, his dark eyes intense, picked up where she left off. "Thanks for letting us be part of this. We'll always remember what you've been showing us."

"We're grateful for how the Lord has led us. He will do that for you, too," Molly's eyes sparkled. "Thanks again! You helped make tonight perfect!" She noticed her mother rushing toward the door and turned away. "Sorry, everyone, I need to catch my mom before she leaves."

Babs didn't look back. "Mom, thanks for coming tonight," Molly called out as she ran toward her. She lightly touched her mother's arm. "Don't you need a ride back to your hotel?"

Babs squirmed away from her daughter's touch. "I'm going to cab back. I've got to get away from you religious nuts!"

Tears stung Molly's eyes.

Babs didn't notice. "I cannot believe you can turn a happy occasion like a wedding into something so boring and religious."

"Mom, we weren't being *religious* tonight. This was about Peter's and my *relationship* with each other, and with God. It's

God who brings us peace and joy. That's all we want for you, too…"

Babs held up her hand to cut her off just as Jennifer joined them. "Everything OK?" Jenn asked Molly.

"Not really. Mom was offended by our rehearsal dinner."

"What?" Jennifer caught her breath, momentarily speechless. "How in the world could such a beautiful evening offend you?"

"Great, you've joined the religious nutcakes." Babs grimaced. "You don't even see the problem, do you? This should have been a happy night. Instead, it was the Old Time Revival Hour."

Jenn found her voice, looking first at her mother, then her sister. "I don't know what an Old Time Revival Hour is, but I thought tonight was beautiful, and I'm happy for you and Peter, Molly." She turned back to her mom. "This is Molly's night. Try to support her for once."

Without looking at either of her daughters, Babs stormed to the curb and hailed a cab.

Jennifer reached Babs before she opened the cab door. "Why can't you stay here, with the rest of the guests? This is ridiculous, even for you, Mom. Come on, you need to apologize to your daughter so you don't ruin her wedding."

For once in her life, Babs paused to listen. "You tell her for me."

"I'm going to be staying at this hotel tonight, Mom, with the other wedding guests. I'll meet you in your hotel lobby and take you to the wedding. We have to be there early, especially since you didn't go to the rehearsal at the church." Jennifer wasn't letting her off the hook.

"Hey, at least I came to the dinner! Give me a break, Jennifer. I'll see you in the morning. I have a hair appointment at eight, so you can pick me up at ten."

"Mom, I need to pick you up at nine so we can get everything ready."

"All right, but not a minute before nine." Babs stepped into the cab, loudly directing the driver. "Get me to the

Biltmore Four Seasons ASAP."

Jenn walked slowly back to her sister, who was wiping a tear from her eye.

"She never changes, does she?"

"Nope. All we can do is lower our expectations. At least she's consistent!"

They laughed ruefully.

"Oh, she told me I could tell you she's sorry."

"You're kidding. She said that?"

"Sort of. I told her to apologize, and she told me to do it for her."

"I'm going to forgive her, right now, because I don't want to carry her negative baggage with me tonight, or tomorrow."

"Good for you."

Peter walked up to them. "Everything OK?"

"Mom was her predictably-negative self. But we're forgiving her and going forward," Jenn said.

"There are still a few guests inside. Want to join me to tell them good night?"

Molly, smiling, walked back into the restaurant, arm-in-arm between Peter and Jenn.

Kate and Carlos joined them as they thanked everyone for coming.

Jenn was the last to leave. "Jet lag is hitting, big time. I'll see you in the morning—and I'll bring Mom, OK?"

"You're the best! Thank you, Jenn. I love you," Molly said, hugging her sister.

"And now, my bride, I do have a surprise for you," Peter said, one hand lovingly on her back, guiding her toward the nearby beach, the other carrying a gift bag.

"A surprise?"

They sat down on a bench facing the ocean, the site of many of their late-night conversations. "For you, my love," he said, handing her the bag.

She pulled teal blue tissue out of the bag and handed it to him. "My favorite color."

"I know," he smiled.

Unwrapping a book, she read its title aloud, "My Utmost for His Highest." Then she noticed the names inscribed in gold letters under author Oswald Chambers' name. "It says Peter and Molly Johnson!" Molly jumped to hug Peter. "This is perfect! I love it! And I love you more!"

"I know I already gave this book to you, but it was paperback—and I thought we could share this leather edition for the rest of our lives."

She nodded, leaning against him as he read. "Could we read tomorrow's devotional?"

"August 25th," he began. "Our wedding day."

They sighed, amazed at that reality. Peter read aloud, his arm protectively around his bride. "John 15:15 says 'I have called you friends.'" Molly nodded as he read for several moments, ending with Chambers' statement, "It is a friendship based on the new life created in us which has no affinity with our old life, but only with the life of God. It is unutterably humble, unsulliedly pure, and absolutely devoted to God."

"That kind of friendship never ends," Molly said. "The one our Lord has given us to share."

* * *

Molly couldn't remember how she got to the church the next morning. She remembered carrying her wedding gown, careful not to crush it, excited to wear it. She didn't notice the two burly strangers stationed at the church doors. She only knew that this was the day that she would become Peter's wife.

Carmen didn't get to the church as early as she'd hoped to arrive. Last-minute reception details kept her home her longer than planned. Still, it was early enough. She sighed, grateful. It looked like the guests hadn't yet begun to arrive. She rushed to the two men stationed by the doors. "Any sign of her yet?"

"No, ma'am. We'll text if anything happens."

"Perfect. Thank you, Tony and Bud. And one of you will

be stationed at our gate immediately afterwards?"

"Absolutely," Bud answered, nodding vigorously. "I'm going to leave before the ceremony ends to go to Home Base, and Tony plans to stay on duty here, watching for Target One attempting to enter or leave the premises."

"We'll stay on High Alert," Tony added. "Don't you worry. We have this covered."

"You're the best!" Carmen smiled and went inside.

* * *

Kate and Jenn helped Molly into her gown in a cozy classroom set aside as the bride's dressing room. "This fits you perfectly, Molly," Kate breathed.

Jenn added, "It looks like someone custom-designed it for you."

"I think Someone did," said Kate.

Kate's three sisters popped into the room to cheer them on. "Oh, you are the most beautiful bride, Molly," Grace gushed. She turned to Kate. "And you were also the most beautiful bride on your wedding day, Sis."

Kate smiled as Jenn lifted Molly's elegant lace train. "It really does seem like this gown was custom-designed for you, Molly. I can't imagine you wearing any other gown."

"Your mom helped me find it."

Sarah said, "I wish we could stay with you all, but we need to go practice our vocals with the other musicians."

"And after that I'll begin your harp prelude," Grace added. "Hope you like it! Pachelbel's Canon in D is so beautiful. I'll begin on the harp, then the other musicians will join me."

"You all sounded fantastic last night at the rehearsal," Molly said. "Thank you for being part of today—and sisters for the rest of my life!"

Mary quietly asked Molly, "It is OK if I hug you? I don't want to mess up your gorgeous gown."

Molly answered by holding her arms out to her soon-to-be sister-in-law. "Hugs for everyone!"

Kelly, Zoë and Analese walked in at that moment. "You are the quintessential radiant bride," Analese said. "This is such a happy day—for all of us!"

"Thank you," Molly beamed, turning to display the back of her wedding gown. "I can't believe today is here. I can't believe it—yet I don't think I could have waited another day." She hugged Kate. "I love your brother! I love you!" She hugged her sister. "I love you, Jenn!" After hugging Kelly, Zoë and Analese, she added, "I'm so grateful for all of you! And, Kelly, did you notice my wedding gown still fits—even though I've gained seven pounds?"

"Congratulations!" Kelly and Zoë said in unison. They knew how diligently Molly had been working to gain weight, a goal few brides shared. "It fits perfectly," Kelly said. "It looks even better than it did the day you first tried it on." She hugged Molly again. "Want help with your veil?"

"Yes, please," Molly smiled, handing it to her. While Kelly was pinning it in place, Molly looked around the room, then at Analese, "Where are Baby Molly and Andrew?"

"Sam is trying to keep them calm until it's time for them to go down the aisle. Molly looks lovely in her flower girl dress, by the way. It's the one Jenn found in Paris at the same shop where she discovered the bridesmaid dresses. It's silk, with the most exquisite lace and tiny satin flowers, all in hues of teal blue, your wedding color." She held up her phone. "Here she is, a few minutes ago."

"Adorable," Molly said, studying the picture of her namesake. "Oh, look at the bows on her satin slippers! Precious! She doesn't look too happy, though."

"She doesn't love party dresses. It was quite a struggle to get it on her. And I don't know why. The silk is really soft, so it should be comfy." Analese sighed, then continued, smiling to reassure herself. "She'll be fine. And Andrew is beyond excited. He's wearing a little bow tie that matches Sam's. But I'm not sure he'll be able to calm down enough to focus on his ring-bearer responsibilities."

"I can't wait to see them!" Molly enthused.

Their comfortable conversation continued, then Kelly looked at her watch, startled. "It's time for us to be seated."

"Is your mom joining us?" Kate asked.

Jenn answered. "We asked her to come watch Molly get ready, but she's not feeling well."

"Where is she now?" Molly asked.

"In the day-care center at the other end of this hall. The pastor told her she could rest in there. Apparently they have cots for the little kids."

"Should I go get her?"

"Um, Molly, you're the bride. You can't let anyone see you in your wedding gown yet." Kate smiled. "I'll find her, OK? Your wedding begins in ten minutes!"

Just then Nana Montgomery popped into the bridal room. "Dearest Molly, you are a lovely bride! Just want you to know Grandpa and I are so happy for you, Honey."

"Thank you, Nana! It's good to see you. I'm sorry we didn't get to talk much at the rehearsal dinner last night, but we'll have time to talk at the reception, OK?"

"Of course, Molly Dolly! We love you!"

Kate walked briskly to the day care center, where Babs was sitting uncomfortably in a child-sized chair. For a split second, Kate glimpsed unspeakable sadness in her eyes. "Hi, Mrs. Montgomery. It's time for Molly's wedding to begin."

Babs stood, rapidly shifting emotional gears, intensely gazing at her watch. "Well, then, let's get this party started!" Without another word, Babs led the way back to the sanctuary door, where Peter was waiting to guide her to her seat.

Kate returned to the room where Molly and Jenn waited. The three women bowed, quietly entrusting the day to God.

Molly's smile seemed to light her entire face as she, her sister and Kate walked the short distance to the sanctuary, a walk taking her from one life to another. "I'm ready. I can't wait to be Peter's wife."

* * *

Peter stood with Carlos at the front of the church, his eyes riveted on the double doors, waiting for his bride to appear.

His dad stood by those doors, waiting to lead Molly to his son. "You are truly beautiful, from the inside out," he said as Molly stepped next to him. "Welcome to our family!"

"Thank you for being my honorary dad today."

"That, precious Molly, will be my great joy and honor for the rest of your life!"

She squeezed Brandon's hand, then stooped to give quick hugs to three-year-old Andrew and Baby Molly before they started down the aisle.

Sam fleetingly hugged the bride while remaining focused on his task of pulling Baby Molly, seated in a buggy brimming with rose petals. In his rich Scottish brogue, Sam turned to Molly, asking, "How do you like the wee bairn's wee bogie? Analese had quite the fun getting it decorated for today."

Brandon grinned. "I barely recognize that wagon." He turned to Molly. "All our kids rode in it. I can't believe Analese could make it look that good!"

Laughing, Molly and her soon-to-be father-in-law watched the antics of ring bearer Andrew and Baby Molly. Clearly annoyed by being confined to a wagon festooned with ribbons and roses, the flower girl repeatedly tried to escape. Every step or two, Andrew reached into the wagon to grab a handful of rose petals and enthusiastically throw them at random guests. Sam simultaneously attempted to lead Andrew forward and keep Molly safe, all the time whispering, "Your wee bogie will get there soon, dear wee bairn." Every few steps, he helped Baby Molly pick up fistfuls of flowers to drop in the aisle. When she noticed people watching her, she giggled, then picked up flowers with both hands, tossing them in the air with cheery abandon. They were definitely the live entertainment.

Peter looked past his sister Kate, then beyond Molly's sister Jenn, both beautiful in the gowns Jenn found in Paris.

But his eyes were locked on his bride. Everyone stood. It seemed as though Molly floated down the aisle to her beloved.

Peter's dad put Molly's hand in his son's hand, then stood next to Peter, transitioning from honorary father of the bride to the groom's best man.

Pastor McIntosh welcomed the bride and groom and their guests. He said, "It has been my honor to meet with Peter and Molly a number of times to prepare for this day. Rarely have I met a couple so thoroughly willing to live their lives in God's love, not only for each other but for everyone the Lord will bring into their lives. They want me to talk with you for a few moments about God's beautiful design for living in His peace and purpose. It is because Peter and Molly discovered that purpose that they are ready to enter life together as one. God's love is free for anyone who comes to Him," he explained, reading from Paul's letter to the Ephesians.

* * *

Outside the church, it was a different kind of day. Scanning the horizon from his watch at the front doors, Bud felt tense. "Looks clear. OK if I head to Home Base?"

Tony said, "Let's check the perimeter one more time before you leave."

"Good idea."

"All clear in the back parking lot."

"Still clear here. Yeah, you can go on to Home Base. I'll wait until everyone here leaves this area, then I'll join you. Unless, of course, we activate the RWC, in which case I'll remain with the target."

Tony heard music increasing in volume, then watched as smiling guests greeted the happy couple and their families in a receiving line that seemed to go on forever. For a few moments, he was distracted and missed the arrival of a sleek black Lincoln Town Car. His attention was fully engaged when the driver opened the passenger's door, and *she* stepped out, checking her hair in a mirror and smiling magnanimously at her reflection. Just before Tony noticed her walking toward the church, the bride and groom and their attendants had stepped into a waiting limo to be whisked to the reception site. All of the other guests were ready to leave, seated in the two trolleys rented for the occasion.

"Ma'am, one moment please. You look like you could use some directions," Tony said, briskly walking toward the new arrival.

"Why, yes, I could. I was going to follow the other guests' vehicles there," she said, pointing to the trolleys, sighing. "Traffic was terrible, and, unfortunately, it appears that I'm late for the festivities," she sighed, dramatically brushing a strand of platinum hair behind her ears. Her practiced smile revealed unnaturally white teeth.

"I would be happy to guide you to the reception. Those vehicles will be taking a circuitous route, which, unfortunately might be difficult for you to follow in weekend traffic." He nodded toward his vehicle. "By the way, I'm Tony, and I'm the reception site host."

"Tony, happy to meet you," she chortled. "I'm Mercedes, and the bride is *my* stepdaughter," she said possessively.

Tony tapped on her driver's window. "I'm on my way to the reception and will lead you right to it," he said happily.

"Whatever the lady wants," her driver muttered; ready to done with his demanding passenger.

"Why don't I just ride with you?" Mercedes turned to Tony. She paid the driver and waved him on, talking to Tony. "We already left my luggage at my hotel, so I'm all yours."

Momentarily startled, Tony said, "Sure, hop in." As she opened her door, he sent Bud a fast text: "pkg arrivd. RWC a go."

Bud looked at his phone just as Carmen and Miguel were arriving at their gate. "It's on!"

"Oh, I wish I could see this," Miguel laughed.

"Me, too," said Bud.

"Don't worry, Tony will give us a full report at the

Chamber meeting next week," Carmen said. They had hatched their ingenious plan during the Chamber of Commerce meeting just the day before. "This has to be one of our all-time most creative ideas," Carmen giggled.

Tony drove Mercedes to the country club ten miles away, where he walked her into the wedding reception—of his wife's cousin, Heidi. She, the family's practical joker, was in on the plan, and was excited to help pull off what Carmen dubbed "The Reverse Wedding Crasher." The timing of their arrival couldn't have been better, because Heidi's guests were already dancing, and the bride and groom were impossible to spot in the crowd of hundreds.

CHAPTER FORTY-SIX

Babs could not believe she was in such a palatial home. *Why hasn't Molly told me about her connection with these people? I thought her friends were a bunch of religious nuts. These are clearly important people.* She reached to feel the flowers displayed in an enormous antique Majolica vase on a table in the foyer. Trying to ascertain whether they were artificial or real, Babs frowned in concentration, unaware her host was standing next to her.

"Our florist prepares lovely arrangements, doesn't she? Santa Barbara's finest," Carmen smiled benignly. "Would you like a tour of the upstairs?"

"Oh, are you the maid?" Babs asked patronizingly. "If it's all right with your boss," she added.

Carmen laughed. "This is *my* home. I do believe it's 'all right,' as you say, since I offered a tour. And you are Molly's mother?"

Surprised, Babs blushed, momentarily mortified by her faux pas.

Carmen pretended not to notice, leading the way upstairs. "The banister was hand-made, as were all of the tiles, which are over a century old. They were once in a palace in Spain."

"Stunning. Very elegant," Babs murmured, forgetting her

embarrassment as she absorbed the house's impressive specifics, mentally calculating market value.

"This is the master suite." Babs' eyes were drawn first to the sitting area, its furniture obviously handmade, with matching sofa and chairs upholstered in silk.

"The rugs were made in Persia. About four hundred years old," Carmen said, reading the question in Babs' eyes. "And the bed is Spanish as well. About two hundred years old."

Babs noticed the hardwood floors. "Mahogany?" she asked.`

"Yes, all the floors throughout the house are either mahogany or hand-made tiles."

"The three upstairs fireplace mantels were also created in Spain," Carmen said, nodding toward the Spanish Beige marble mantel in the master bedroom. Babs stood transfixed, trying not to drool over the room's opulence, studying the mantel's intricate design of Acanthus leaf and square rosette carvings. Carmen led her forward. "Here is one of this room's two en suites." A large custom Jacuzzi tub, two sinks, red tile floors and massive wooden cupboards barely filled the expansive room. "My husband Miguel's en suite is on the opposite side of the room."

Carmen led Babs to the suite's adjoining balcony. They paused to look at the ocean. "Spectacular, simply stunning," Babs said, nearly speechless. "What does your husband do?"

"He is a cardiologist."

"Oh, where did he go to school?" Babs prodded.

"In Guatemala, first, at Universidad Francisco Marroquin, then he transferred to Johns Hopkins University School of Medicine, in Baltimore, Maryland, to finish his training in its exceptional cardiology program." Carmen slowly enunciated each word, her voice overflowing with pride in her husband's accomplishments.

Babs didn't notice. "Isn't it unusual for someone from Central America to even become a physician?"

"Not when he is from a family of cafetaleros."

"Cafetaleros? What does *that* mean? Cafeterias?" Babs'

voice held more than a trace of her usual contempt.

"It means his family has owned vast coffee plantations for *many* generations," Carmen said, trying not to be impatient with her boorish guest. Striding into the wide hallway, she changed the subject. "Would you like to see the guest rooms?"

Babs had no idea that her host had an ulterior motive in giving her a private tour. Her daughter-in-law Kate, though not a gossip, briefly answered Carmen's question about Molly's childhood several weeks prior. After the dinner she hosted for Peter and Molly, Carlos and Kate, Carmen had asked her, "I don't understand Molly's mother. Here the child has no father, and she said her mother isn't helping with the wedding. What kind of mother abandons her lovely daughter like this?"

Kate had explained, "Molly basically had to raise herself. Her mom's passion was her career in real estate. Her dad left her mom, first for a co-worker, then for a second wife who nearly ruined Molly's life during high school. Her stepmother, Mercedes, introduced Molly to the modeling world where she worked, then to the man running the agency." Kate wiped a tear from her cheek. "I don't want to say anything else except that Molly is still recovering from all the evil she experienced, not only then but in early childhood."

"I see," Carmen said then, beginning to understand why Molly seemed afraid to trust people. Now, with Molly's mother in *her* territory for the wedding reception, Carmen's plan was to influence her, using Bab's primary language— money—to prime her for Carmen's primary language—love.

"Your daughter is an exceptional person," Carmen said as she led Babs down the hallway to see the upstairs living room. "I imagine you love spending time with her."

"She rarely comes home."

"That can be remedied."

Babs thought she understood where Carmen was going— and felt annoyed. "Are you implying it is my fault my daughter doesn't come home?"

"Why would you think that?" Carmen said evenly, silently asking God for help.

Babs backed down. "Molly has been in a demanding grad school program."

"Oh, I imagine you've enjoyed attending her concerts," Carmen said, baiting her. "Her master's recital was outstanding. But, I didn't see you there."

"I am incredibly busy at work."

"Too busy to recognize your lovely daughter's accomplishments? She had two standing ovations. One for an original piece she wrote and performed, the other for the chamber ensemble she directed."

"Thank you for the tour. Your house is impressive," Babs said, backing out of the room to scurry downstairs to mingle with the other guests, away from anything that would touch her conscience. *I wish the Wendhams had come; they would be the perfect excuse to leave.* For the rest of the evening, she stayed as far as she could from her hostess, making small talk with anyone else who looked important.

She noticed an elegant couple seated on the patio. The woman exuded quiet confidence; the man was clearly a successful businessman. Their two children seemed well behaved—one a baby seated on the father's lap, the other a toddler playing with toys scattered nearby. *They look interesting,* Babs thought, wondering if they might someday wish to purchase property in the Chicago area.

"Hello, I'm Babs Montgomery," she said, reaching to shake the woman's hand. "And you are?"

"I'm Analese Craig, and this is my husband Samuel Craig, and our children."

The woman with piercing blue eyes seemed strangely familiar, but out of place. "Do I know you?" Babs asked.

"We met many years ago, in Illinois. I was Analese Harper then."

"But, but, you're just a housekeeper," Babs sputtered. "I guess you've made something of yourself. You look like you're somebody now."

Analese tried not to laugh out loud. She decided saying nothing was the only safe approach.

Sam, having heard of Babs' legendary put-downs, spoke in defense of his wife, an edge to his normally gentle Scottish brogue. "My wife has always been *somebody*, as you say. Even when she was cleaning your house, she was a Harvard graduate. She was also a stockbroker. She cleaned houses because she loves people."

"Then you were *impersonating* a housecleaner?" Babs said, indignant, her voice rising in volume.

"Was your house clean after I was there?" Analese quietly responded, genuinely sad to see Babs had not changed at all.

Babs tried to compose herself. "Your children are lovely," she said, using a word that stuck to her gums like day-old cotton candy.

"Andrew and Molly."

"Your baby is named Molly?"

"In honor of your wonderful daughter," Analese beamed.

Babs, for once, became quiet. It seemed Molly had a life she knew nothing about, if someone would even name a child for her.

She looked up, relieved to see Jennifer walking nearby. "There's my other daughter, Jennifer!" She stood to leave this second uncomfortable situation, but Jennifer had already reached them.

"Hi, Mom! Hi Sam and Analese and Andrew and Molly!" Andrew jumped up to hug Jenn.

"You know these people?" Babs asked, barely concealing her scorn.

"Mom, they live near me in Greenwich, London. Sam is the broker who helped me find the flat where I live." She stopped herself before she said, "the flat I purchased." One stipulation of the trust fund was that her mother never be told about it.

"I'm sure you rented a cute little place," Babs said, suddenly in a realm where she felt in charge. "Property values are so high in London. I bet you felt lucky to find *anyplace* to live."

"Yes, I am grateful." Jenn turned to Sam and Analese. "Molly wanted me to tell you it's time for the toasts. Can you come over to the bride and groom's table again? I'll bring the kiddos to you when you're ready."

Babs watched as Baby Molly happily reached for her daughter's arms and snuggled into her shoulder.

"You seem to know these people pretty well. Strange, isn't it?"

"Not at all, Mom. They're wonderful people. You seem to be judging them. Any particular reason?"

Babs didn't need a reason to 'judge' people. *What kind of group is this, anyway?* She gave her daughter a derisive glance before walking away to find somebody more appealing to talk with. Before she could find someone else, she heard an eloquent speaker and looked to see who it was. Her attention was riveted on Analese.

"Many years ago, I had the marvelous opportunity to meet this beautiful bride, when she was still in grade school. Though there were years when our paths went different directions, I must say it is one of the greatest privileges of my life to be here to celebrate this day. Peter and Molly, may God bless you. Sam and I commit to pray for you and Peter every day, celebrating the incredible love God has given you to share with a world that needs it." She raised her glass high. "To you, Peter and Molly! We love you!"

Sam spoke next, his rich Scottish brogue mesmerizing the crowd. "Though I only met Molly a short time ago, I feel as though I have known her for many years. My wife treasures her friendship, as do I. In fact, we cherish her so much, we named our baby girl after her." Jenn walked over to him with ten-month-old Baby Molly, as prearranged. Seeing her parents, she laughed. Sam held her, still smiling, for everyone to see, then turned to the bride and groom. "Molly and Peter, may your marriage hold the bright promise of new life, as you begin the marvelous adventure of being made one in Christ, going where He leads you, living daily in His light and love."

He clinked his champagne flute on his wife's water glass. "To the lovely bride and handsome groom. To life!"

The toasts continued with Kate and Carlos. As Kate began, she choked up, overcome by a sudden, unexpected confluence of emotions. Carlos stood, helping her. "My wife has been Molly's best friend since grade school. Together, they've weathered college—and life. And, I must say, no one is celebrating today more than my wife and I! To the wonderful bride and groom!" Kate poked him in the ribs, and he grinned sheepishly. "Well, *maybe* Peter and Molly are celebrating today more than we are!" The crowd laughed with him.

Molly's eyes shimmered with unshed tears as she listened to Carlos, speaking on behalf of a still-blubbering Kate. *This is a picture of God's grace—she loves me after everything I've done to her.* In her peripheral vision, Molly noticed another person—her mom. For the first time in her life, she saw her as the lonely, sad woman she really was. "Peter, come with me," she said, tugging at his arm.

Together they walked to Babs, standing at the fringe of the group, in a designer mother-of-the-bride gown that fit beautifully, flattering her still-elegant figure. Her hair and makeup, too, were flawless, but did nothing to conceal the hard lines of her face or the cynicism radiating from her eyes.

Carmen, watching the bride like a hawk, observed exactly what Molly was doing. She whispered something in Miguel's ear, and he sprung into action. Seamlessly, he moved chairs, Carmen nodding in approval.

"Mom, please come join us. We have a place for you at our table," Molly said.

Her mom, startled, followed them, relieved to have somewhere to go.

Carmen smiled. Mission accomplished. The bride's mom was being shown love, but was being seated in a safe place between Carlos and Peter, both who would zealously deflect Babs' barbs from the bride.

Waiting for Peter to pull out the chair for her mom,

Jennifer somehow remembered Molly had asked her to give a toast. She hugged Molly, then Peter, enthusing, "You two have a great life ahead of you! May the Lord bless you throughout your lives...just as He already has. And you'd better come visit me in London soon!"

CHAPTER FORTY-SEVEN

Molly awakened to the smell of coffee and remembered. *I'm Peter's wife! And we're on our honeymoon!* She tiptoed to the kitchen and put her arms around her husband. "Dearest Peter, this is the third day..."

He turned to encircle her with his arms. "...of the rest of our lives!"

For their first week of marriage, one of Peter's colleagues gave them the use of his family's cozy vacation cottage in Mill Valley. Situated on a hill, they had a perfect view of majestic redwoods and a mix of deciduous trees, where the antics of huge scampering squirrels made them laugh. But they didn't spend much time looking outside; they were thoroughly enjoying being inside, discovering their new life as one.

They spent only two days sightseeing. On one of those days, they began with an easy drive to the ferry in Sausalito. Molly continually looked for roadside signs to read aloud, establishing a new tradition. "We're open 365 Days Every Year," one sign stated. Beneath that, in crude black letters, it proclaimed, "Closed Today."

They were early, so spent time exploring downtown. "Ice cream!" Molly exclaimed, noticing the dozens of people walking past them carrying—and eating—cones and dishes filled with a treat she never allowed herself to enjoy.

"Want some?"

"Oh, it's still morning. And I shouldn't," Molly said, wishing she could.

"You absolutely can have ice cream on your honeymoon, Dearest!" He led her into Lappert's Ice Cream, where they ordered a sugar cone with two scoops of Caramel Coconut Macadamia Nut. They walked to the beautiful fountain across the street, where they watched people as they shared their treat.

"Thank you, Peter. You know me better than anyone in the world," she smiled, sighing with contentment.

"And since I do, I need to tell you this," he pointed to an imaginary spot on her shirt.

She looked down, and he grabbed her around the waist. "Gotcha!"

"I need to remember you never stop teasing," she said, not really laughing.

"I'm sorry," he said, meaning it, especially when he noticed that he'd accidentally smeared ice cream on her. "Here, I'll get that," he said, grabbing a wet wipe from his backpack, then dabbing at the spot.

"It's OK. I'm glad you're teaching me to be a little bit carefree," she said. "I'm trying to learn," she said, grabbing his hand and leading him toward the nearby harbor.

Live entertainment at the Sausalito waterfront included a man singing and playing guitar accompanied by his dachshund, barking on cue. "It sounds more like howling," Molly whispered to Peter, when the man bragged about his dog's musical abilities.

Peter walked to a kiosk to buy their ferry tickets while Molly turned to watch an incredible sight. Several feet from her was a young woman, dressed casually and wearing a top hat. She was creating enormous soap bubbles, using only an empty child's swimming pool and soapy bucket, into which she dipped an apparatus of ropes in various shapes attached to two poles, each at least six feet long. After she artfully dipped the ropes into the pail, she stretched the poles high, releasing colossal multi-colored bubbles that extended ten to twelve feet in length and sailed through the air over the crowd of people. Three enthusiastic small children ran underneath the bubbles, laughing, their arms splayed, jumping to catch the floating marvels. Peter, tickets in hand, came and stood next to Molly. They laughed with the children, fully enjoying the moment.

Next, they walked to the adjacent pier, waiting to board the ferry. Continuing their new tradition, Molly noticed a sign on the fence at the end of the dock. It began with the words, "Security Notice" and proclaimed, "Failure to consent or submit to screening and inspection will result in denial or recovaton of authorization to board..." Puzzled, she turned to Peter. "What is 'recovation'? I've never heard that word."

He stepped close to the sign and read it aloud. "It has to be a spelling error," he replied, grinning. "I think they meant 'revocation.' Apparently no one has taken time to really read it."

He laughed, until he noticed Molly's eyes filling with tears. "What's wrong, Dearest?"

"Give me a minute," she said, pinching her nose to distract herself from crying. She felt incredibly embarrassed, especially since dozens of people were lined up behind them, waiting to board. Once on the ferry, Peter gently guided Molly up two sets of stairs, thinking as they climbed to the top deck. He remembered his dad's advice on their wedding day. "Son, whatever you do, do not try to 'fix' your wife. When she's sad, just listen. Remember, God gave you two ears and one mouth—use them in that proportion." They found seats facing away from people.

"What's wrong?" he asked tenderly.

She stifled a sob. "That misspelled word reminded me of how easy it is to distort something—or someone. Just like on that sign, with one letter off, the real meaning of the word is gone."

He wasn't sure what she meant but kept his eyes alert, nodding, and hoping for clarity. "Say more."

She sighed. "It's like how I misrepresented who you are, like how I actually believed you were someone you aren't, and I forgot who you really are, and I said awful things about you...I almost ruined everything," she said, her shoulders slumped. "This—us—might never have happened."

He put his arm around her. "But we did happen, and we are married, my love. And we've already had this discussion, haven't we? The one where we agreed to live in the present, not the past?"

She reached into her purse for a tissue, and then blew her nose, loudly. "You mean we can have our own personal 'revocation'?"

He laughed. "Yeah. Great idea, my beautiful red-nosed bride. Let's revoke the right to go backwards in time, and stay right here, right now, loving each other for the rest of our lives." He grinned, "Yeah, let's call it our *recovation*."

They forgot anyone else was on the ferry during the rest of their exquisitely relaxing ride. Colorful boats of all shapes and sizes skimmed across the San Francisco Bay, sharing the sun-studded morning. Grey and black sailboats competed in a fast-paced regatta. The Golden Gate Bridge was clearly visible at first, then covered in dense fog. "This is a day I'll never forget," Molly breathed, leaning against her husband.

He held her hand. "Nor will I." The breeze tousled his hair, and his eyes crinkled in the sun. His smile, like his heart, overflowed. "I love you, Mrs. Johnson."

Her smile mirrored his. "And I love you—now and forever." She pinched herself, lightly.

He looked concerned.

She laughed. "I was just checking to make sure I'm alive. This is the best day of my life—being with you, being loved by you, being accepted as I am—even with my weird foibles."

"What weird foibles?" he asked, pinching himself, imitating her, laughing. "Yeah, it's real. We're alive, and we're both incredibly blessed to be able to share life with each other."

When Peter and Molly stepped off the ferry, they stepped around dozens of bicyclists that were ready to explore San Francisco on their "Blazing Saddles." Molly almost walked into one of them. "Sorry," she said to the rider, and then turned to Peter. "We could rent bikes and conquer the hills…"

"Or not," he said, recognizing her joke. She'd already told him she wanted a slow, leisurely day to walk around the pier.

The honeymooners stood watching sea lions for nearly an hour. As the loudly braying creatures competed for preferred napping spots along the waterfront, Peter and Molly laughed at the antics of two exceptionally stubborn sea lions. A wharf worker held a large blue piece of wood near them every time they tried to climb onto pricey dock spaces reserved for the boat owners who'd rented them. Seeing the blue board, or hearing it smack the wooden dock, the pair sulkily returned to the water, but only for a moment or two each time. The duo, apparently preferring the solitude of private docks to the huge areas covered with their peers, clambered back as soon as the man's back was turned. This was repeated over and over, until the man finally took a break—and the sea lions secured their naptime.

Peter and Molly sauntered through Pier 39, stopping for lunch of sustainable seafood at Pier Market, then for afternoon coffee at Boudin Bakery. Later, when people asked them what they liked best there, they both smiled and said, "I don't remember." They recalled their gratitude—for life, for each other—instead. But when Peter's dad asked if anything funny happened, their memories were crystal-clear.

Several times during their day on the Bay, people acted like they knew Peter. "Hey, I love your news reports," one said. Another called out, "Drew, see you tonight!" After the third time, Molly googled "Drew" and "news anchor." She handed her phone to Peter, "You do bear an uncanny resemblance."

He looked at the image on her screen. Their smiles were

similar. Both had sandy blonde hair. "I don't see it," he laughed. "No one has ever confused me with a TV personality before. Must be my present company."

Out of habit, she pulled her long blonde hair back in a ponytail, securing it with an elastic tie from her purse. As they walked, she turned into a souvenir shop. "Be right back," she called over her shoulder. Wondering what she was up to, he joined her. "Like this one?" she asked, holding up a nondescript blue ball cap. He tried it on; she tried on one to match and paid for both of them. "Now we're incognito," she laughed as she placed his on his head, covering his blonde hair.

They stepped out of the store, and someone called out, "Drew, have fun today! Glad you're getting a day off with your bestie!"

* * *

During the ferry ride back from San Francisco, they decided to prepare the rest of their meals in their romantic cottage. "What sounds good?" Peter asked Molly, holding her hand.

Molly looked across the bay, then at him, smiling. "You."

He laughed. "I meant for dinner."

"This is an adjustment. I'm not used to planning meals with anyone." Noticing his concern, she quickly added, "But it's a great adjustment. I love doing life with you—and it helps that I've already been learning how to eat regularly."

They stopped at the grocery store near the cottage, leisurely choosing food for dinner, breakfast and lunch. Peter held up a container of ice cream, "We have to try this! Look, it's actually called 'Blueberry Lavender *Honeymoon* Ice Cream,' and it's made in Tiburon."

That evening, Molly made a salad, then set the table with the cottage's Fiesta dishes, bright napkins and a candle while Peter grilled chicken and corn on the cob. "The table looks great," he said, serving the food with a flourish.

"And everything smells great," she responded.

Savoring each bite, they raved about how scrumptious their meal was—and dreamed about ways they could make their new home a haven, with simple touches like flowers and cloth napkins.

Peter cleared the table, then served their honeymoon dessert. "Looks delicious," he said, sampling it, grinning. "It *is* delicious!"

Molly lamented, "I haven't eaten ice cream in years. And now, twice in one week!"

"Just following your doctor's orders."

"I don't think *this* is the way I'm supposed to gain weight," she said, laughing. "But it's definitely a delicious way to do it."

The next morning, sipping coffee on the porch of their cottage, they both noticed three deer at the same time. "Shh," Molly motioned. For several minutes, they watched, amazed, as the deer ate a leisurely breakfast, one of them contentedly munching flowers, the others, feasting on ferns.

They found so much comfort in nature that they decided to spend the next day exploring nearby Muir Woods. Their anticipated relaxation was nearly destroyed by the tension of the drive down a steep, winding road to get there. It didn't help that the road was almost totally obscured by dense fog. But the moment they stepped into the ancient redwood forest, the stress disappeared, along with the clamor of school, work, recital and wedding preparations. All tension was replaced by an ethereal quiet that was both a holy hush and a resonating, exuberant song of creation.

Light played on the leaves of hundreds of trees, inviting Peter and Molly to slow down and enjoy its music. That sound of light gently overcame all other sounds, and the bride and groom were enveloped in peace.

ACKNOWLEDGMENTS

Kudos to Kay Tira and Erin Florian for their excellent editing and encouragement throughout the writing process. I also appreciate timely editorial input from Zach Davis, Robbie Fisher, Krystal Hearne, Val Moore, Amy Simion and Rosaura H. Zeghir.

The cover photo was taken by Alan Wibbels, and graphic artist Doug Sykes skillfully incorporated it into the book's cover design. Bentley C. Tate, M.D., M.Div., graciously injected medical support. Creative input from Daniel Diaz, Grace Eurglunes, Rachel Perkoski and Cheryl Seidel infused the story with joie de vivre. Josh and Lindsay Bruce helped bring Scotland to life, while international flight attendant Karen Knowles took *Sound of Light* to new heights. Many thanks, Chelsea Chadwick, Jacob Weeks, Corin McHargue, and Ron Noel for your superb tech support! To everyone (including those not listed here) who offered ideas during the writing process, my gratitude is beyond words!

I'm especially grateful for each person who faithfully prayed for the completion of this project. The prayer team includes people from around the world, including Criss Bertling, Clint and Amie Bokelman, Jean Bollon, Robbie Fisher, Erin Florian, Andre and Nadya Furmanov, Jessica Knapp, Karen Knowles, Melanie Levandusky, Ivana Meservey, Valerie Moore, Don Morgan, Rachel Perkoski, Tim and Sherri Peterson, Jorge Mario Reyes and Patricia de Reyes, Louann Saine, Suzan Sarris, Ernest Sauve, Jr., Amy and John Simion, Jeremy and Sarah Smith, Brenda Souto, Kimberly Stober, Linda Summers, Sandra Tate, Kay Tira, Karen Whitlatch, Linda Wibbels, Mel and Bev Wibbels, Rodger and Sarah Wittmann and Alex and Rosaura H. Zeghir. Many others prayed, and I'm sorry I don't know your names: please accept my profound thanks for your help. As Tennyson wrote, "More things are wrought by prayer than this world dreams of..."

OTHER BOOKS BY MARTI WIBBELS

Fiction

Secrets Behind the Door

Non-Fiction

Core Healing from Sexual Abuse: A Journey of Hope

Sanidad del Núcleo del Abuso Sexual:
Un Viaje de Esperanza
(translated to Spanish by Rosaura H. Zeghir)

Relationships Pure & Simple: A Biblical Perspective on
Relationships by Alan & Marti Wibbels

Pearl Girls: Encountering Grit, Experiencing Grace,
(contributor; compiled by Margaret McSweeney)

Books Available At

www.pbcounseling.com
and Amazon